SISTUHS IN THE STRUGGLE

SISTUHS IN THE STRUGGLE

An Oral History of Black Arts Movement Theater and Performance

La Donna L. Forsgren

NORTHWESTERN UNIVERSITY PRESS
EVANSTON, ILLINOIS

Northwestern University Press
www.nupress.northwestern.edu

Portions of the interview with J.e. Franklin previously appeared in an article by La Donna L. Forsgren, "The Black Arts Movement (1965–1976): An Interview with Playwright J.e. Franklin," *Callaloo* 37, no. 5 (2014): 1139–57.

Printed in the United States of America

10 9 8 7 6 5 4 3 2 1

Library of Congress Cataloging-in-Publication Data

Names: Forsgren, La Donna L., author.
Title: Sistuhs in the struggle : an oral history of Black Arts Movement theater and performance / La Donna L. Forsgren.
Description: Evanston, Illinois : Northwestern University Press, 2020. | Includes bibliographical references and index.
Identifiers: LCCN 2020014817 | ISBN 9780810142565 (paperback) | ISBN 9780810142572 (cloth) | ISBN 9780810142589 (ebook)
Subjects: LCSH: African American theater—History—20th century. | Black Arts movement—History. | Feminist theater—History—20th century. | American drama—African American authors—20th century—History and criticism. | American drama—Women authors—20th century—History and criticism. | African American women—Intellectual life—History—20th century. | African American women—Interviews.
Classification: LCC PN2270.A35 F67 2020 | DDC 792.08996073—dc23
LC record available at https://lccn.loc.gov/2020014817

For the sistuhs who struggled . . .

and for the sistuhs who continue the struggle

CONTENTS

BLACK THEATERS, CULTURAL INSTITUTIONS & EVENTS, AND ACTIVIST ORGANIZATIONS

Afro-American Studio for Acting and Speech: 1966–ca. 1982
Alvin Ailey American Dance Theater: 1958–present
AMAS Repertory Theatre (later Amas Musical Theatre): 1968–present
American Community Theatre (ACT; later ACT/Pro/Workshop): 1958–late 1980s
Atlanta Black Theatre Festival: 2012–present
Billie Holiday Theatre: 1972–present
Black Arts Repertory Theatre/School (BART/S): 1965
Black Ensemble Theater: 1976–present
Black Panther Party for Self-Defense: 1966–82
Black Student Union (BSU) at San Francisco State College (later San Francisco State University): 1966–present
Black Theatre Workshop: 1968–72
Child Development Group of Mississippi (CDGM): 1965–68
Congress of Racial Equality (CORE): 1942–present
DC Black Theatre and Arts Festival: 1986–present
Demi-Gods: 1970–74
Ebony Showcase Theatre: 1950–present
Free Southern Theater (FST): 1963–80
Harlem Children's Theatre Company: 1971–90
Harlem Writers Guild: 1950–present
Jomandi Productions: 1978–present
Junebug Productions: 1980–present
National Association for the Advancement of Colored People (NAACP): 1909–present
National Black Theatre (NBT): 1968–present
National Black Theatre Festival: 1989–present

National Theatre of Ghana: 1992–present
Nation of Islam: 1930–present
Negro Ensemble Company (NEC): 1967–present
New Federal Theatre: 1970–present
New Lafayette Theatre (NLT): 1967–72
Plowshares Theatre Company: 1989–present
Richard Allen Center for Culture and Art: 1976–present
Second World Black African Festival of Art and Culture (FESTAC): 1977
Smithsonian Folklife Festival: 1967–present
Student Nonviolent Coordinating Committee (SNCC): 1960–76
The Brewery Troupe: 1973–present
Urban Arts Corps (Corps): 1967–83
US Organization: 1965–present

ACKNOWLEDGMENTS

The seed for this project was planted during my dissertation defense wherein Dr. Harvey Young Jr. suggested that I publish my collection of interviews using Dr. E. Patrick Johnson's *Sweet Tea: Gay Black Men of the South* (2008) as a model. Of course, much more labor needed to be done before I could do this. The handful of interviews I had collected were New York–centered and focused on Black Arts Movement drama and ritual. If I wanted to provide a more national perspective of the work of black women intellectuals—playwrights, dancers, directors, designers, stage managers, theater founders, actors, producers, poets, painters, photographers, journalists, and teachers—I needed to conduct more extensive interviews.

Compiling this oral history took years to complete and would not have been possible without the support of those committed to the preservation and dissemination of black history and culture. The following individuals were extremely generous with their time: Dawn Alli, Aduke Aremu, Adrienne Charles, Nora Cole, Doris Derby, Cheryl Fabio, Nabii Faison, Shirley Faison, J.e. Franklin, P. J. Gibson, Micki Grant, `Fémi Sarah Heggie, Lee Hunkins, Judy Juanita, Woodie King Jr., Barbara "Sade" Lythcott, Haki Madhubuti, George Lee Miles, Barbara Molette, Carlton Molette, Halifu Osumare, Kathy A. Perkins, Shirley Prendergast, Ishmael Reed, Sonia Sanchez, Ntozake Shange, and Jackie Taylor. Thank you for your willingness to share your life experiences with me. Jim Peppler, thank you for your generousity.

A special thank-you to Dr. Harvey Young Jr., Dr. E. Patrick Johnson, and the late Dr. Paul K. Bryant Jackson. Harvey, you have supported me along the way as I have grown from a socially awkward doctoral student to a socially awkward (yet adept) scholar. Thank you, Patrick, for writing the award-winning book that inspired this project. I will be forever grateful for your willingness to share practical advice with me and for answering my countless questions about your methodology. Paul, I continue to miss your warmth, wisdom, and friendship.

The University of Notre Dame provided the intellectual community and financial support I needed to complete this project. A heartfelt thank-you to my writing crew Dr. Tarryn Chun and Dr. Anne García-Romero. Your friendship and encouragement continue to inspire me to be a better scholar and friend. I would also like to thank all my wonderful colleagues in the Department of Film, Television, and Theatre for their genuine interest and enthusiasm for my scholarship. This research was also made possible in part by generous support from the Institute for Scholarship in the Liberal Arts, College of Arts and Letters, University of Notre Dame. Receiving the Small Research Grant, Large Humanities Research Grant, Indexing Grant, and Publication Grant allowed me to purchase images and hire an indexer and small army to transcribe and edit interviews. Thank you, Steven Moore, Stephanie Perrin, Karin Arnold, and AAA Transcription.

Many talented individuals at Northwestern University Press have supported this project from its conception to publication. Gianna Mosser, Trevor Perri, Patrick Samuel, Jane Bunker, Liz Hamilton, Anne Gendler, and so many others have contributed to the completion of this book. I am equally indebted to Jo-Ann Morgan, James Smethurst, and Lundeana M. Thomas for their deeply critical and generous feedback.

Finally, I would like to thank my friends and family for their unconditional love and unwavering support. Thank you to all those who have offered everything from emotional support and play dates to a critical sounding board along the way. Mr. Fairbotham, my sincere thanks for being the best teacher my daughter has ever had. Layne, thank you for that one time you agreed to become the primary caregiver to our children so that I could pursue a career in academia. Thank you for the thousands of times you encouraged me when I felt like giving up. Jacoby, Piper, Cruser, and Emmett: thank you for the countless times you told me that I needed to stop typing midsentence and play Barbie and Legos with you. You are the greatest gift I have ever been given and the source of my strength. *I'll love you forever.*

INTRODUCTION

In Her Own Words

> For us, true speaking is not solely an expression of creative power; it is an act of resistance, a political gesture that challenges politics of domination that would render us nameless and voiceless. As such, it is a courageous act—as such, it represents a threat. To those who wield oppressive power, that which is threatening must necessarily be wiped out, annihilated, silenced.
>
> —bell hooks, *Talking Back*

I grew up among a circle of black women storytellers. My earliest memories involve listening to my mother and the women in my family discuss the circumstances that led to the economic devastation of their hometown. Before I could even read or write, I learned that Youngstown, Ohio, had once been a thriving city, boasting a healthy economy built on the production of steel. My mother remembers,

> We had black-owned businesses and there were jobs there. The main street had a drugstore, ice cream shop, and a lot of other businesses. Our ancestors had a bakery/candy shop on the north side. The economy was good and people had money to spend. Even people who didn't have a business could make a living wage. By 1972, things were starting to go downhill. The oil shortage happened across the U.S., but it really affected towns that made cars or the

> steel for cars. When the steel mills closed, that was the final nail. The whole town just collapsed.[1]

Indeed, the "final nail" happened on September 19, 1977, known colloquially as Black Monday, when debt led the Youngstown Sheet and Tube Company to abruptly fire five thousand of its workers. Within a decade, Youngstown lost an additional forty thousand jobs and the city's economy never recovered.[2] Those who could afford to move on relocated to better employment prospects. However, most of the black population—many of whom had traveled up north during the Great Migration (1916–70)—lacked the wherewithal to do so. With limited options, my mother and extended family stayed and witnessed a vibrant city transform into a severely economically depressed town, replete with drugs, crime, and poverty. As Youngstown crumbled around them, the women in my family worked collectively to ensure the survival of their children. These women used oral histories to transmit the past—including the importance of black-owned businesses, a living wage, and activism—to inspire their children to actively construct a brighter future. Their speech acts created not only a vital support system among everyday black women but also a narrative of resistance within black cultural memory.

I did not realize that the older generation of women in my family were, in fact, black women intellectuals until I encountered the writings of the black feminist and sociologist Patricia Hill Collins while in graduate school. Collins's *Black Feminist Thought: Knowledge, Consciousness, and the Politics of Empowerment* issues a call to reclaim black women's intellectual tradition. "African-American women not commonly certified as intellectuals by academic institutions have long functioned as intellectuals by representing the interests of black women as a group and fostering Black feminist thought," writes Collins.[3] Indeed, my own experiential knowledge confirms Collins's assessment that "in the comfort of daily conversations, through serious conversation and humor, African-American women as sisters and friends affirm one another's humanity, specialness, and right to exist."[4] While Collins does not further explicate the relationship between orality and black women's intellectual tradition, her call nonetheless situates black women's orality within both intellectual and activist traditions.

Nearly two decades later, the black feminist critic DoVeanna S. Fulton would bring greater clarity to the connection between black women's orality and intellectual tradition, defining this relationship as *black feminist orality*.[5] "Black feminist orality is a form of empowerment using vocal and oral means and is the foundation of a literary tradition of African American women's writing that is the progeny of a cultural tradition of verbally articulating the self and experience," writes Fulton.[6] Taken together, Collins's and Fulton's formulations suggest that empowerment, as well as the status of "intellectual," lies within black women's ability to articulate their unique awareness and perspective of the world. Their everyday conversations and actions, often hidden from the view of their oppressors, provide a safe space to express black feminist orality.

Black feminist orality, as both a tradition and method, has been purposefully and systematically maligned within dominant society and academic discourse. Marked both *black* and *female*, black women remain vulnerable to both gender subordination and racial oppression. These oppressive forces wreak havoc in their lives, provoking and sustaining their social, political, and economic disenfranchisement. Academia—a supposed haven for liberal thinking—contributes to this problem by maintaining ideologies that silence black women's voices. For example, while black women's intellectual and activist traditions have always existed, "women's history" did not develop as an academic discipline until the 1970s. "We didn't even know very much about how most women conducted and thought about their own lives because few researchers before us had thought to look beyond the handful of famous women," write the historians Sue Armitage, Patricia Hart, and Karen Weathermon.[7] These early researchers—many of whom were also engaged in the second wave feminist movement—relied on oral history interviews to recover women's history. Sherna Berger Gluck, Joan Jensen, and countless other pioneers of women's history situated their work as much more than a mere academic pursuit. "Documenting women's simultaneous agency and oppression empowered both us and the movement and contributed to a very critical re-visioning of women's history," writes Gluck.[8] Although constructing these early oral histories helped challenge patriarchy and empowered many activists and scholars, their focus on gender and *white women's* agency continued to silence women of color. Recognizing this problem, black women intellectuals of the 1980s and early 1990s developed a standpoint that privileged the process of black women investigators conducting oral narrative research with black women participants.[9]

Remembering the Sistuh(s)

Sistuhs in the Struggle: An Oral History of Black Arts Movement Theater and Performance embraces the spirit of our radical foremothers who used the method of oral history to reclaim black women's art, activist, and intellectual traditions. The title of this book celebrates the "sistuhs," or black women intellectuals who contributed to the creation and dissemination of Black Arts Movement (1965–late 1970s) theory, theater, and performance. The often-quoted Black Arts theorist Larry Neal describes this black cultural flowering as follows:

> Black Art is the aesthetic and spiritual *sister* of the Black Power concept. As such, it envisions an art that speaks directly to the needs and aspirations of Black America. In order to perform this task, the Black Arts Movement proposes a radical reordering of the western aesthetic . . . The Black Arts and Black Power concept both relate broadly to the Afro-American's desire for self-determination and nationhood. Both concepts are nationalistic. One is concerned with the relationship between art and politics; the other with the art of politics.[10]

Curiously, few scholars note that Neal describes the relationship between black art and politics in gendered terms. During this era, the colloquial "sister" or "sistuh" was used as a term of respect or endearment for black women. Yet "sistuh" also carried distinctively heteronormative connotations. Within the framework of the black liberation struggle, a "sistuh" was often expected to remain a submissive counterpart to her "brotha" or man. Neal's metaphor situates black womanhood not only as the embodiment of black art but also as the dependent helpmate of the masculine concept of Black Power. Rather than define the movements as "bedfellows," the historian Margo Natalie Crawford challenges us to reconsider the Black Arts Movement as the "artistic complication" of the Black Power Movement.[11] Indeed, interviews with nearly thirty sistuhs of the Black Arts Movement, their daughters, and colleagues reveal that while black women contributed to the dominant ethos of the Black Arts and Black Power movements, their theories of performance, theatrical endeavors, and activism also fostered critical departures.

Sistuhs of the Black Arts Movement conceptualized their own vision of the relationship between the black aesthetic, performance, and black empowerment, often while struggling to raise children and earn a living wage. These black women intellectuals served their communities as playwrights, dancers, directors, designers, stage managers, theater founders, actors, producers, poets, painters, photographers, journalists, and teachers. Despite experiencing sexism and institutional racism in U.S. society, as well as sexism in their own artistic communities, they negotiated a space to express their concerns as black women within the social activism of Black Power. They used their voice—through writing, visual text, and embodied performance—to galvanize their communities. For example, the multitalented Barbara Ann Teer wrote, directed, and produced ritualistic revivals at her National Black Theatre to empower her Harlem community. California-based choreographer Halifu Osumare conceptualized dance as a liberating force and performed at Black Panther Party rallies. Civil rights movement photographer, journalist, dancer, and teacher Doris Derby cofounded the Free Southern Theater as a vehicle to promote literacy and activism in rural Mississippi. J.e. Franklin, Martie Evans-Charles, P. J. Gibson, Barbara Molette, Sonia Sanchez, Ntozake Shange, and many others wrote plays that reflected the multiplicity of black women's lives. Finally, Shirley Prendergast became the first African American woman to earn a United Scenic Artists of America union card in lighting design in 1969. After breaking racial and gender barriers—albeit briefly—on both Black Arts and Broadway stages, she then used her agency to mentor countless black designers, including award-winning lighting designer Kathy A. Perkins. These artists offer diverse perspectives on the black aesthetic, the role of artists, and black activism. Collectively, their narratives challenge politics of domination that would relegate black women's labor and intellectual tradition to the margins of history. Furthermore, their efforts to express black America's humanity, disseminate black art and intellectual thought, and demystify black women's oppression laid the groundwork for an emerging black feminist theater.

While recent studies have begun to explore women's poetry of the Black Arts Movement, few book-length projects critically examine the relationship between their embodied performance, written/visual works, and activism.[12] Lundeana Thomas's *Barbara Ann Teer and the National Black Theatre: Transformational Forces in Harlem* (1998) provided the first book-length project to critically examine a black woman intellectual's conceptualization and dissemination of the black aesthetic as it relates to embodied performance. Unfortunately, decades have passed without in-depth studies of black women theater artists of the movement.

Thomas's pioneering research on Barbara Ann Teer's art and activism provided the foundation for my first book, *In Search of Our Warrior Mothers: Women Dramatists of the Black Arts Movement* (2018). The most comprehensive examination of black women's contributions to Black Arts Movement theater, *In Search of Our Warrior Mothers* utilizes historicized close readings of unpublished plays, video recordings, original interviews with playwrights, and black feminist theories to clarify how the works of Martie Evans-Charles, J.e. Franklin, Sonia Sanchez, and Barbara Ann Teer relate to the subsequent emergence of black feminist drama. I argue that the rise of black feminist drama was a development within the Black Arts Movement, not a sharp break from it. In so doing, the study dispels mythology of a homogeneous Black Arts ideology by revealing the nuanced tensions within and among the Black Arts, feminist, and Black Power movements. Ultimately, *In Search of Our Warrior Mothers* recovers a significant moment wherein the recuperation of black women's culture became an integral element of black empowerment.

Sistuhs in the Struggle marks both a continuation and departure from this first book. Both studies celebrate black women's contributions to Black Arts Movement theater and advocate for black women's intellectual history. *In Search of Our Warrior Mothers* details how black women used dramatic works to illuminate their concerns as black women. Their works addressed the black family's survival in and through white supremacist structures, the Great Migration's influence on black culture, and the failing public school system, to name a few.

However, rather than privilege dramatic works, text-based criticism, and the Black Arts Movement's impact on the Harlem community, *Sistuhs in the Struggle* provides a more national perspective of black women's accomplishments and creates space for black women intellectuals to vocalize their standpoint and perform their own visions of the past. *Sistuhs in the Struggle* therefore builds on the efforts of Loften Mitchell, whose *Black Drama: The Story of the American Negro in the Theatre* (1967) and *Voices of the Black Theatre* (1975) use oral histories to offer a rare glimpse into the largely untold stories of twentieth-century black theater. *Sistuhs in the Struggle* also breaks new ground by focusing on black women intellectuals and thus provides much-needed chapters in the history of Black Arts Movement theater and performance and black intellectual thought.

Orality and Performance

In keeping with the spirit of the Black Arts Movement, *Sistuhs in the Struggle* uses orality and performance as a productive means to communicate, interrogate, and celebrate black history and culture. The theater historian Mike Sell notes that the movement "founded its politics on the valorization and exploitation of performative modes of culture," believing that theater and performance could "answer specific sociopolitical needs, particularly to a community that is economically depressed and politically advanced."[13] To this end, Black Arts Movement proponents created bold new works drawn from sources ranging from black diasporic folklore (including pretextual West African cultures) to contemporary jazz music.[14] Their collective efforts, as Sell argues, demonstrate an early knowledge of what would become performance studies.[15] The significance of orality and performance in Black Arts Movement discourse, however persuasive, remains highly contested among scholars of the movement. For example, while the historian James Smethurst agrees that the movement "elevated the oral over the written, and public collective performance over individual modes of cultural production and reception," he also offers a word of caution against minimizing the significance of printed text and textuality in disseminating the black aesthetic.[16] "Rather than being a mere adjunct, the written/visual Black Arts text frequently existed in symbiotic relation to performance," writes Smethurst.[17] While *Sistuhs in the Struggle* does not purport the *primacy* of orality and performance for advancing the black aesthetic, the study does use critical performance ethnography to further explicate these early endeavors.

Whereas oral history provides a means for recovering the experiential knowledge of black women intellectuals, critical performance ethnography allows me to attend to the *process* of such an endeavor. Critical performance ethnography empowers narrators by validating their speech, gesture, and dialogue as cultural performance. The performance studies scholar Dwight Conquergood discusses how cultural performance functions as a liberating force for poor or marginalized people. "Denied access to middle-class 'public' forums, cultural performance becomes the venue for 'public discussion' of vital issues central to their communities, as well as an arena for gaining visibility and staging their identity," writes Conquergood.[18] As such, cultural performance provides black women intellectuals the ontological space to attend to the intersections of identity, as well as validation of their lived experience through *witnessing*. As a witness to their performances, I took on the vital role of demonstrating the value of their narratives. In so doing, I became a coperformer, adding dialogue and nonverbal expression to encourage the performer to continue their narrative. The performance studies scholar E. Patrick Johnson identifies this complex exchange as a key aspect of critical performance ethnography. Johnson writes,

> Critical performance ethnography alters the traditional relationship between researcher and subject, demanding an ethical response from the researcher in witnessing and validating the narrative of the interviewee. Their relationship becomes reciprocal, and the importance of dialogue cannot be overestimated.[19]

As black women intellectuals generously offered a glimpse into their lives, I responded in kind, verifying their narratives with my own experiential knowledge or information gleaned from secondary literature. During our time together, we conjured their lived experiences, producing a host of emotions such as laughter, tears, and even righteous anger. Yet always present was a keen awareness that *we* were enacting and recovering a chapter of history.

Critical performance ethnography, with its focus on ethical responsibility, encourages researchers to recognize their own positionality. The performance studies scholar D. Soyini Madison argues that "positionality is vital because it forces us to acknowledge our own power, privilege, and biases just as we are denouncing the power structures that surround our subjects."[20] My positionality as a black woman, scholar, and artist put me in a unique position to initiate, participate in, and witness critical conversations among black women intellectuals in a mode more recognizable to the academic community. Oral history allows me to bridge these two (seemingly disparate) modes of knowledge and in so doing attest to the black feminist scholar Barbara Christian's assessment that "people of color have always theorized—but in forms quite different from the Western form of abstract logic . . . often in narrative forms, in the stories we create, in riddles and proverbs, in the play with language."[21] As I compile these oral histories for an academic audience, I also recognize my position of authority. With a keen understanding that a chapter in black women's history is at stake, I feel great responsibility to accurately interpret and represent the narrators in this study.

My interviews with black women intellectuals—both insiders and outliers to tightly knit Black Arts Movement circles—reveal a wealth of information about how black women artists navigated the black freedom struggle. For example, as the playwright, poet, and former editor of the *Black Panther* newspaper Judy Juanita reflects on her past, she reminds activists of today to situate writing as a form of activism. She also forewarns that the problems that impact black communities—including the infiltration of drugs, the HIV/AIDS epidemic, police brutality, school shootings, and a host of other social ills—serve as an early warning system for the greater U.S. society. The playwright, poet, and teacher Sonia Sanchez admonishes us to remember the importance of socializing black children to safely navigate a world that does not value their humanity. Three years before the formation of the Black Lives Matter movement, Sanchez expresses the concern that when black Americans travel—regardless of their appearance, economic class, or perceived "innocence"—they run the risk of encountering harassment or even death at the hands of police. The playwright and poet P. J. Gibson uses her voice to share personal experiences of rape and abuse so that the greater black community might break their silence about these issues. She explains how the personal is political and how her experiential knowledge impacts her woman-centered plays. Doris Derby situates theater as a powerful tool to educate the most vulnerable in our society. Having witnessed the devastation that Jim Crow laws wrought in the lives of black Americans in the South, she expresses the importance of documenting such atrocities, as well as archiving black cultural achievements. These and many other narratives demonstrate a diverse system of negotiation, one that was informed by the intersections of their identity; their interest and knowledge of black history, culture, and religious practices; the eras, geographical location, and field in which they worked; the level of support they received from artistic and activist groups; and the quality of mentorship they received. While the multiplicity of voices (at times) contradict one another and most assuredly cross disciplinary boundaries, these variations demonstrate the complexity of black women's lives.

Narrative Slippage

While there are clear advantages in gathering oral histories (especially when researching marginalized subjects), there are also limitations. First, obviously I could not interview every black woman intellectual who made profound contributions to Black Arts Movement theater and performance. In addition, lack of contact information, poor health, or an untimely death precluded many interviews. Unfortunately, there is no centralized record that includes the names of women who participated in theater and performance during the Black Arts Movement. Records from Black Arts theaters, many of which were short-lived, were sometimes unintentionally destroyed or remain in private collections. To compound this problem, it was commonplace for artists to abandon their "slave name" (i.e., legal name) and adopt a new name that represented their religious affiliations or political views of the time. Locating these individuals proved even more difficult. Left with only traces of the past, I used performance reviews, previously published interviews, magazines of the era such as *Negro Digest/Black World* and *Black Theatre*, and word of mouth to locate the names of black women intellectuals of the era, many of whom appear in this study. I then relied on an online subscription to the Whitepages telephone directory, helpful informants, and (only as a last resort) Facebook to contact potential narrators. Fortunately, some of the children and colleagues of those who had either died or were unable to complete an interview were willing to discuss their mother's legacy with me. In sum, it took years to collect these interviews.

The reliability of narratives also varied: lapses in memory, self-censoring, and personal agendas occasionally led to vague, inaccurate, or even rehearsed answers. I essentially asked nearly thirty interviewees—ranging from age forty-one to eighty-eight years old—to remember events that occurred upward of fifty years ago. While I provided interview questions at least twenty-four hours in advance of each interview, there were moments during several interviews when a narrator could not recall a name, title, or date of when an event had occurred. A few narrators relied on their handwritten notes to assist them in their recollections. For example, one narrator read some of her responses to me while another seemed to be reciting a response to an often-asked question. I also encountered two narrators who remembered the significance of their work at opposite ends of the spectrum: one situated their work at the center of everything (and I mean *everything*), while another minimized both their accomplishments and the systemic racism and sexism within the theater industry, to the point of unreliability. Others initially appeared hesitant to share less-than-flattering information about cultural heroes, major events, and their peers. Encouraging credible and unadulterated responses from narrators proved challenging as the significance of this project remained ever present.

To further complicate matters, an artist's current interpretation of their work sometimes contradicted their original conception. For example, when we discussed her play *Uh, Uh; But How Do It Free Us?* (1974), Sonia Sanchez remembered her black female protagonist breaking up with her emotionally abusive boyfriend at the end of the play. By speaking the dialogue that she imagined her fictional character would have said, Sanchez performed an alternative ending that reaffirmed the strength of black womanhood. After thanking her for performing such an impassioned speech, I asked follow-up questions and tactfully read her original stage directions, which clearly indicate that the protagonist remains in her toxic relationship. Sanchez simply giggled and, with a twinkle in her eye, stated, "I might be rewriting my play right now." Moments of narrative "slippage" and subsequent reflexivity should encourage us to consider not only how an artist's ideology shifts through the years but also the critical tension between memory, orality, and cultural performance.[22]

For these reasons, I do not rely exclusively upon narrative accounts, nor do I claim that this collection of narratives serves as a "definitive" oral history of Black Arts Movement theater and performance. Yet it is the only book-length oral history project dedicated to the voices of black women intellectuals of the Black Arts Movement. While I cautiously use the experiential knowledge of narrators as the foundation for this study, I also include primary- and secondary-source material to critically engage with the gaps and silences in their accounts. I use production reviews, performance recordings, unpublished playscripts, program notes, and previously published interviews to help me discern the reliability of narrators and, if possible, verify their accounts.

From Margin to Center

Sistuhs in the Struggle includes four chapters and a conclusion, all of which examine the lives, struggles, and triumphs of black women intellectuals who contributed to the creation and dissemination of Black Arts Movement theory, theater, and performance. Inspired by the structure of E. Patrick Johnson's *Sweet Tea: Black Gay Men in the South*, I organize multiple narratives thematically to find moments of commonality and difference among narrators. Each chapter begins with a brief introduction that offers historical contextualization, analysis of narratives, and my personal reflection of the theme presented. However, the majority of each chapter consists of the actual historical narratives as told by black women intellectuals. A brief biographical sketch and notation about where and when the interview took place occurs the first time a narrator speaks. While I have added dates and edited the transcribed interviews for clarity and thematic purposes, I try to maintain the narrator's regional dialect and speech pattern unless expressly told not to do so. I also share details about the physical presence of informants to offer readers a glimpse into the world of black cultural performance.

Chapter 1, "Spiritual Sister: The Black Aesthetic, Feminism, and Black Power," explores black women intellectuals' thoughts on the relationship between black art, feminism, and Black Power politics. Narrators discuss their motivation for participating in the Black Arts and Black Power movements; theorize their own conceptualization of the black aesthetic; share their thoughts on the legacy of Malcolm X, the Black Panther Party, and the long civil rights struggle; and remember their standpoint on the feminist movement.

Chapter 2, "Black Theaters Matter: The Art of Institution Building," allows black women intellectuals—including theater founders, managers, administrators, designers, and actresses—to share their thoughts on women's contributions to the institutional development of the Black Arts Movement. The discussion includes experiences working at the National

Black Theatre, Urban Arts Corps, Negro Ensemble Company, Free Southern Theater, New Lafayette Theatre, Black Ensemble Theater, AMAS Repertory Theatre, Harlem Children's Theatre Company, New Federal Theatre, and Billie Holiday Theatre. In so doing, narrators detail both the accomplishments and unique struggles black women artists encountered while leading and participating in Black Arts and Off-Broadway theaters.

Chapter 3, "'Traveling with Ears to the Ground': Black Arts Movement Drama, Ritual, Teleplays, and Musicals," recognizes that black women intellectuals did not limit their writing to the bounds of Black Arts stages. The chapter includes interviews with writers Sonia Sanchez, Ntozake Shange, Halifu Osumare, J.e. Franklin, Micki Grant, Jackie Taylor, Judy Juanita, Aduke Aremu, Barbara and Carlton Molette, P. J. Gibson, and Lee Hunkins. These narrators share their approaches to playwriting (including the art of writing womanist drama); their challenges and triumphs writing plays for television, as well as for Black Arts, Off-Broadway, and Broadway stages; and their collaborative endeavors into musical theater.

Chapter 4, "Performative Embodiment on Black Arts and Alternative Stages," offers an interdisciplinary glimpse into black women's performative endeavors. The chapter investigates their contributions as dancers, actors, directors, lighting designers, and managers both onstage and behind the scenes of Black Arts, Off-Broadway, Broadway, and concert stages. In this way, I hope to recover the outliers of the Black Arts Movement who voiced their opposition to some aspects of the Black Arts ethos yet demonstrate that they were nonetheless committed to the liberation of black men, women, and children. Including their narratives within a discussion of the Black Arts Movement theater and performance provides a more dynamic view of not only the competing modes of artistic inquiry of the time but also the importance of artistic agency.

"Legacy," the book's conclusion, allows black women intellectuals to consider the long-term impact of their art and activism, as well as future directions of black theater and performance in the United States. Appendix A offers my reflections from the process of compiling this oral history, and Appendix B provides brief biographies of key narrators for further reference. Collectively, these narratives offer a glimpse into one of the greatest periods of black cultural flowering of the twentieth century.

CHAPTER 1

Spiritual Sister: The Black Aesthetic, Feminism, and Black Power

> Stories are important. They keep us alive. In the ships, in the camps, in the quarters, fields, prisons, on the road, on the run, underground, under siege, in the throes, on the verge—the storyteller snatches us back from the edge to hear the next chapter. In which we are the subjects. We, the hero of the tales. Our lives preserved. How it was; how it be. Passing it along the relay. That is what I work to do—to produce stories that save our lives.
>
> —Toni Cade Bambara, "Salvation Is the Issue"

When I consider the most iconic images of the sixties, I instantly recall Blair Stapp's 1967 photograph of Huey Newton, cofounder of the Black Panther Party, sitting in a wicker fan-back chair with piercing eyes staring defiantly at the camera while clenching a spear in his left hand and shotgun in his right. The party's minister of information, Eldridge Cleaver, credited for the composition of the photograph, frames Newton with a zebra hide on the floor and African artifacts arranged at his sides. The carefully constructed image presents Newton as a powerful black leader determined to reclaim his kingdom. His weapons of choice, coupled with

Huey Newton seated in a wicker chair, 1967. Photo attributed to Blair Stapp; composition by Eldridge Cleaver. Courtesy of Merrill C. Berman Collection.

the prominent display of African art, suggest he will use both armed force and African diasporic culture as weapons against his enemies. While aware that the *Black Panther* newspaper purposefully constructed images such as this to galvanize black America into action, I did not fully appreciate the role that black women played in shaping its circulation before conducting these interviews. For example, I learned that after Cleaver fled to Cuba to avoid charges of attempted murder in 1968, the journalist and activist Judy Juanita assumed his role as the newspaper's editor in chief.

Despite the popular belief that the Black Panther Party was dominated by men, Juanita remembers using her voice to promote the party's Ten-Point Platform while also espousing her own feminist beliefs. Juanita's account attests to the importance of black women's activism within the

Black Panther Party, a narrative that has been corroborated in the more recent scholarship of black women historians such as Angela D. LeBlanc-Ernest, Tracye A. Matthews, Mary Phillips, Jane Rhodes, Robyn C. Spencer, and Rhonda Y. Williams.[1] Of course, not all black women intellectuals felt that black nationalist organizations were providing a means for black female empowerment. Rather than flatten this dynamic debate into a monolithic narrative, I present these competing perspectives side by side to demonstrate the nuanced tensions in black nationalist discourse.

While none of the black women intellectuals I interviewed joined feminist organizations during the seventies, some joined black sororities and many voiced black feminist attitudes from within the black freedom struggle. However, this does not mean that black women did not take part in or found feminist organizations. Rather, many of the black women intellectuals I interviewed chose to work within the confines of black nationalist groups because they felt that the feminist movement did not address the intersections of their identity. Moreover, some believed that joining a feminist organization would alienate them from their black male comrades or cause division between black men and women. In other words, the essence of the adage "What happens to one of us, happens to all of us" greatly impacted their worldview. Finally, nearly all the narrators expressed a knowledge of how sexism and racism impeded their daily struggles to survive and provide for their children. What little time they had available was spent creating art and advocating for the betterment of their entire community.

Although narrators provide testimony of the collective strength of black nationalist organizations, they are mostly silent about the later contributions of black feminist organizations within the liberation struggle. From the black women's club movement of the turn of the twentieth century to today's Black Lives Matter movement, black women have a tradition of working collectively—whether or not they assume the label of "feminist"—to ensure the survival of their entire communities. If anything, organizations such as the Combahee River Collective (1974–80) have taught us that it is possible for black women to espouse feminist beliefs without in any way mitigating their concern for the welfare of the entire black community. With the benefit of hindsight, black women intellectuals such as Juanita now situate their early activism as a form of de facto feminism.

Juanita's account also alludes to occasional strife among organizations that espoused the ethos of the Black Arts and Black Power movements. As a poet, San Francisco State College student activist, Black Panther Party member, and participant in the Black Student Union's Black Arts Cultural Troupe, Juanita felt pulled in multiple directions. Joining the Black Panther Party allowed her entrée into events at Cleaver's Black House, a political and cultural center in San Francisco. Her experiences at Black House made her keenly aware of the critical tensions among black nationalist organizations. While her narrative does not provide detailed descriptions about these internal disputes, she does reveal that as the "factions separated," they were "antagonistic towards each other." As a result, she felt compelled to make a choice between her art and activism and ultimately chose to devote her energies toward activism within the Black Panther Party. Her perception was that the Black Panther Party afforded black women personal autonomy, whereas black cultural nationalist organizations confined black women to the margins in the limited role of child bearer. Juanita's account, coupled with the narratives of other black women intellectuals, reveals critical tensions between and among black cultural and black nationalist organizations.

When discussing opportunities for black women artists during the Black Arts Movement, narrators offered a range of responses from strong disavowals of sexism to personal anecdotes about navigating sexist practices within black artistic circles. At two contrasting ends of this spectrum are the accounts of Negro Ensemble Company stage manager `Fémi Sarah Heggie and the poet and playwright Sonia Sanchez. Heggie remembers that "they did not allow women into that inner place. You may have thought you were. But you just weren't." However, Sanchez recalls that sexism did not exist in the early days of the Black Arts Movement. Rather, sexism was more intimately connected to black nationalist organizations that emerged later and espoused certain roles for women. *How can both women have lived and worked in New York and yet have such different recollections?* To begin with, black women never have and never will have a single monolithic experience. Numerous factors influenced Heggie's, Sanchez's, and other black women's perspectives of the movement. Indeed, circumstances such as the time and geographic location in which they worked; their age, disposition, and personal biases; the ability (or inability) to identify mentors and assert their authority; and the type of work they performed influence each narrative. However, what is undeniably clear is that black women intellectuals carefully negotiated a space to express their thoughts on the black aesthetic, black womanhood, and the struggle for black liberation.

While sexism did exist within the movement and greater society, it is also important to note that most of the black women intellectuals in this study were supported by male colleagues who mentored them, produced their works, and published their writing. For example, the Obie Award–winning playwright Ed Bullins published several of Sanchez's plays and cultivated the talents of Martie Evans-Charles at his Black Theatre Workshop.[2] The producer, director, and Rites and Reasons Theatre founder George Houston Bass taught playwright J.e. Franklin the fundamentals of playwriting and crafted techniques to help her and P. J. Gibson find their voices as playwrights. In addition, many black women intellectuals—Aduke Aremu, Evans-Charles, Franklin, Gibson, Micki Grant, Heggie, Kathy A. Perkins, Shauneille Perry, Shirley Prendergast, Ntozake Shange—worked with New Federal Theatre founder and producer Woodie King Jr. and credit him for cultivating or sustaining their theater careers. When asked about his efforts to create a more inclusive artistic community, King remembers,

> My mission in my life and in the organization I ran was always to integrate minorities and women into the mainstream of American theatre. That meant someone could come with these plays that everybody would think would be great and if it didn't fit into those objectives, it didn't work for me. That was the mission and it still is.[3]

Guided by this mission, King consistently produced plays written by black women and that privileged black women's subjectivity. In other words, King made the concerted effort so works such as Franklin's *Black Girl* (1971) and Shange's *for colored girls who have considered suicide/when the rainbow is enuf* (1975) could find a place in American theater.[4]

In addition to naming the male comrades who supported their work, some of the black women intellectuals in the study critiqued the historiography of the Black Arts Movement. Among their concerns were the erasure of black women theater artists, the marginalization of theaters that operated outside New York, the disconnect between Black Arts theater makers and earlier predecessors in current historical narratives, and the periodization of the movement. For example, Sanchez questioned why Black Arts Movement playwrights—especially women dramatists—have not received recognition for influencing Shange's development of *for colored girls*. When asked about her relationship to the Black Arts Movement, Shange confirmed that Sanchez and Barbara Ann Teer's National Black Theatre played important roles in shaping her black feminist drama. Inspired by the ethos of the Black Arts Movement, Shange considers her work the embodiment of the black aesthetic. Cheryl Fabio, a documentary filmmaker and daughter of the late Sarah Webster Fabio, also questioned why art created on the West Coast often receives little critical attention in Black Arts narratives. Similarly concerned with the New York–focused accounts, the playwrights Barbara and Carlton Molette credit arts departments at historically black colleges and universities in the southern United States as a major catalyst for training black artists and advancing the Black Arts Movement. More specifically, the Molettes note that conferences held at the Center for African and African American Studies at Atlanta University (later consolidated with Clark College as Clark Atlanta University) were among "the most influential gathering places in the sixties and seventies." In addition, when asked who mentored them, the Molettes recognized that their early mentors predate 1965, seen as the origin date of the Black Arts Movement with LeRoi Jones/Amiri Baraka's founding of the Black Arts Repertory Theatre/School (BART/S). Artists such as Abram Hill, Paul Robeson, Loften Mitchell, William Branch, and Alice Childress influenced many black artists of the sixties and seventies and yet their names are often omitted from narratives of the movement. Furthermore, Doris Derby, John O' Neal, and Gilbert Moses's cofounding of the Free Southern Theater predates BART/S. While scholars continue to designate BART/S as the institutional origins of the Black Arts Movement, these narratives demonstrate that we must also attend to the early theoretical writings and artistry that inspired the cultural workers of the sixties and seventies.[5]

Finally, black women intellectuals expressed concern that scholars mark 1975 or 1976 as the demise of the Black Arts Movement. For example, the lighting designer and black diaspora scholar Kathy A. Perkins notes that while scholars posit the midseventies as the demise of the

Black Arts Movement, Black Arts theaters were still opening in 1976. The institutional development of the Black Arts Movement, according to Perkins, continued into the late seventies. She further explains that it wasn't until the 1980s, when historically white theaters received major grants to produce black plays, that historically black theaters lost funding and began closing. Furthermore, the actress, playwright, and Black Ensemble Theater founder Jackie Taylor maintains that the Black Arts Movement "wasn't born in the sixties." In other words, Taylor conceptualizes the movement as the manifestation of all black culture: its past, present, and future.

Disparate opinions about the periodization of the movement demonstrate the importance of distinguishing the *institutional* and *theoretical* development of the Black Arts Movement. In considering the legacy of the Black Arts Movement, the scholar Mike Sell writes,

> Black Arts as *theory* survived the death of the Black Arts as *movement* . . . The Black Arts as theater transformed abstract aesthetic into movement, concept into politics. But once the theaters and the momentary communities that they represent were destroyed, the Black Arts Movement crossed the horizon beyond which European traditions of politics, aesthetics, historiography—and property—could not clearly see.[6]

While institutional development waned in the late seventies, the theoretical underpinnings of the Black Arts Movement—including its celebration of the black aesthetic—continue to inspire black artists today.

Sonia Sanchez

Sonia Sanchez (b. 1934) remains one of the most prominent figures of the Black Arts Movement, and her performance of poetry has been credited as a foundation for hip-hop.[7] Her performance of her poetry, coupled with her revolutionary drama, inspired a generation of artists to use art as a vehicle for social change. We met at her home in Philadelphia, Pennsylvania, on June 30, 2010. Her graciousness and gift for storytelling quickly put me at ease as our scheduled two-hour interview transformed into the most memorable daylong conversation of my life. As we talked in her home and ran errands in her neighborhood, I grew inspired by her narrative of survival.

I was talking to Haki Madhubuti this morning before you came. What women writers have done is that they have taught men writers and men period about their sexism. So, some people want to say that black men were really sexist.

During the sixties and seventies?

Yes! I say, "Why are you talking about black men?! America was sexist!" You have got to understand that it wasn't just black men. They were doing what everybody else was doing. What the white church was doing, the black church was doing. What white professionals were doing, black professionals were doing. What the university was doing . . . that was the reality. You just can't say, "Oh, the Black Arts Movement was sexist." Oh, shut up. Every organization in America was sexist during that time. At the inception of the Black Arts there was no sexism. I'm telling you it didn't come until afterwards in the seventies. It wasn't the Black Arts, per se. It was those organizations that began to come out with ideologies as to the role of the black woman. The Black Arts never said at the beginning there is a role for black women. I got onstage with Askia Touré, Ed Bullins, Bob Hamilton, Baraka, and Marvin X. They didn't say, "Sonia, you're a woman. Go first." I usually went someplace down the line right before Baraka. Sarah Webster Fabio would organize something like that. But what happened was that at some point, organizations came about. They acknowledged that they had positions for women.

Like the US Organization?

The US Organization. Baraka also became a member of US Organization.

Some members of the US Organization went on to say, "I don't agree with this anymore."

Yes, they changed. Baraka left it, you know. The Nation of Islam did it. There was a role for women in the Nation. A lot of the organizations

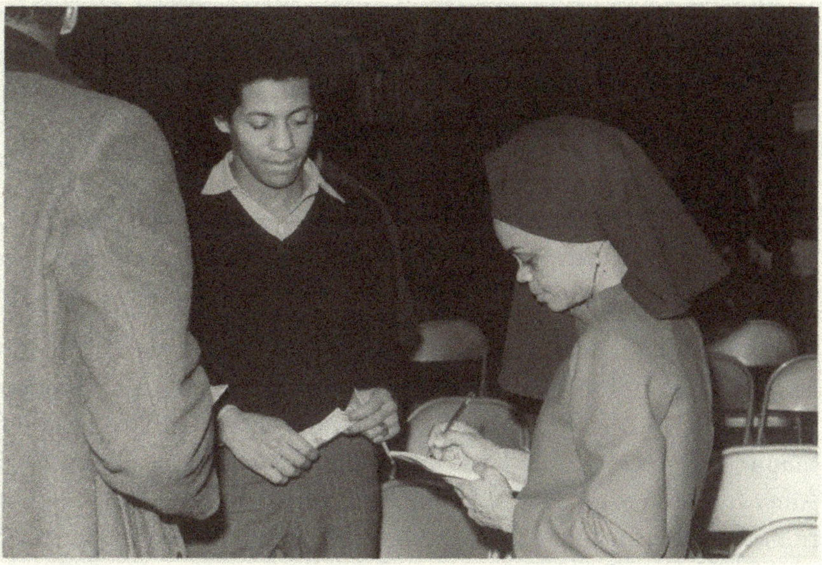

Sonia Sanchez, 1972. Courtesy of The New York Public Library, New York Public Library Digital Collections. http://digitalcollections.nypl.org/items/6c8df720-49fc-5281-e040-e00a18062f9d.

that were even supposedly, as you say "revolutionary." Leftists: they had a role for women also too. So, that's why I'm saying to you: everybody looked at women as . . . One of the things that would happen in organizations is they would say, "Okay Sonia, would you be secretary?" I'd say, "No" [*chuckles*]. "That's not my role. I'm not going to be secretary. Get a man to be secretary." I'm very serious about that. You can understand sometimes why I had trouble. Which is an understatement.

Do you think that your position as a well-known poet helped you navigate these waters?

Well, my sister, at the beginning I wasn't a "well-known poet." Like everybody else, we were all going out there beginning at the same fashion. The difference that happened between some of us is that we started out all writing and talking about changing everything, but we also stayed activists at the same time. Therefore, as a consequence, we also got a broader audience. In other words, we didn't just stay home and write and then say, "I'm publishing this book." We wrote, published books, but went out there also. Some of us taught. I had generation after generation after generation after generation of students, literally. I taught for close to forty years, and that's a long time to teach, my dear sister.

I've read in several different pieces that you were considered an integrationist before becoming involved with the Black Arts Movement. Could you discuss your early political activism?

I'm always so amazed by terminology. How we move towards terminology and say, "This person is integrationist, this person is separatist." How I dealt in America is that I was educated by America. What I did simply in America is that I was struggling as a young black woman in America trying to do things. My information, in terms of politics, came from the people who taught me, this country, and the books that I read at the same time. I had not encountered a number of people who would at some point begin to change me and the way I looked at the world. So, I don't know if that term is too easy for people. Anyone who says, "I'm an integrationist" always understands that he or she is living in a place called America and that as a consequence you are oppressed. I don't care where you live, whether you know that that's the case. It's not anything that's not going to be known. So anyway, I just have great difficulty with terminology because the next question would be, "When did you become a separatist?" The point is that I was militant. I had been a person talking about change—I like that better—all my life. One of the things I did in New York City was I ran with people who were going to run as a Freedom Democrat under the Kennedys. That was pretty progressive in New York City. I ran with people who were considered leftists. In New York City, you run with people who are doing all sorts of things. So that's what I did: I ran with people who were teachers, who were leftists, who belonged to civil rights organizations. I belonged to New York Congress of Racial Equality. Those are the organizations that I belonged to and I dealt with.

Let's talk about the occasion when you were first introduced to Black Arts philosophy. Where were you, who spoke to you, and what did you think of it?

Well, there was no formal introduction to the Black Arts Movement for me. My introduction to things that were important and about being black in America happened from people like Brother Martin Luther King and Brother Malcolm X. Also, being involved, listening to people beginning to talk about their work. I was at some program and some young woman stood up and recited Margaret Walker's poem "For My People" [1942]. I could not believe that poem existed and I had not known that it existed. It was an amazing poem and I remember going around saying, "What's the name of that poem again? Who wrote that?" They said, "It's on your program: 'For My People.'" I said, "But it doesn't have a name here." And someone told me, "Margaret Walker." I went to the Schomburg Center for Research in Black Culture and I found that poem, wrote that poem out (there's no such thing as Xeroxing something), read that poem out loud, and cried.

We had been exposed to black writers in Birmingham, Alabama, at our assemblies. You would hear a Langston Hughes poem or a Countee Cullen poem. You would hear all these black folks who had written poems. So, it was not an alien thing for me to know black folks wrote poetry. Of course, when my sister and I came to a place called New York City, we were asked to sing the national anthem [at a school assembly]. We stood up and began to sing "Lift Every Voice and Sing" [1919]. We realized other people were singing, "Oh say can you see"! Me and my sister looked at each other: "Oh, it's the other one" [*laughs*].

Black culture has always been an important part of your life?

Yes. The Black Arts formalized what some of us already had experienced and what we already knew. The Black Arts formalized many of the ideas that we had read about and had seen at some point. The Black Arts made us begin to put into action those ideas that we did not have the organizational way of putting into action before.

How did you first meet Amiri Baraka?

Well, I studied with Louise Bogan and in the Village on Charles Street. One night, we went to the Five Spot in the Village and Baraka was sitting at the back listening to music and writing. I realized at that time that he was doing reviews on jazz for *DownBeat* [est. 1934]. When I passed by with my group from our workshop—that had evolved from out of Louise Bogan's workshop at New York University—he looked up and said, "Sanchez! Why don't you send me a poem for an anthology I'm doing coming out of France?" I said, "Okay." [The group of students from Bogan's workshop said,] "That's LeRoi Jones, the Beat poet! The great playwright!" I said, "I know." They said, "He wants you to send a poem!" I said, "Oh, he doesn't want a poem of mine. I mean, how does he know about my poem?"

Well, girl, I forgot about it and about three weeks later we finished our workshop and someone else was playing at the Five Spot and we went in to hear it. Baraka was sitting there and I saw him and I thought I'd pass by him, but he looked up and said, "So you don't want to be in the anthology, huh?" I turned around and said, "Oh, my goodness! Were you serious?!" He said, "Sure, I was serious. I asked you, didn't I?" So, I told everybody goodbye. I went and got in my Volkswagen, zoomed up the West Side Highway, went into my apartment, pulled down my typewriter, pulled out some poems, typed up some poems, came back out that night, and took the poems down to the main post office. About two weeks later, I got a letter from him that said, "Dear Sonia Sanchez . . ." [*laughs*]. He had accepted it. I still have the journal.

Did he then invite you to come and read your poetry at the Black Arts Repertory Theatre/School?

No. He was still in the Village at that time. I got to know him through some of the plays that he did down in the Village. I was there when either *The Toilet* [1964] or *Dutchman* [1964] opened, I'm not sure which one. I went to a reception that someone gave for him on Park Avenue with a lot of people. It was quite a reception. This man who gave the reception had the most exquisite African art in his apartment. It was the first time I had seen a lot of African art. Anyway, after Malcolm died, Baraka (who at that time was LeRoi Jones) sent out letters to all the artists that he knew saying, "Come and be a part of this great Black Arts Movement where we're going to, in a sense, change the world." He sent that to musicians and painters and poets and playwrights. We all gathered there and listened to the idea that we could be these transformative people in this building on 130th Street. Using art as change for community. We were going to the community, being in the community, and beginning to talk about art that would transform a community.

You were a part of the Black Arts Repertory Theatre/School.

Yes. That's where the Black Arts Movement formally began—when Baraka came up from the Village and bought a brownstone at 130th Street and said simply, "We're going to do this work for the people. Not art for art's sake, but art for the people." We involved ourselves with the neighborhood. We would have theater and workshops for the children. We would have people come in and read their poetry. It was at the Black Arts Repertory Theatre/School that I saw Abbey Lincoln come in and do a talk on "Who Will Revere the Black Woman?" She had the most beautiful natural on her head. It was later published in *Negro Digest* [September 1966]. So, it was those kinds of things I began to see: black plays, black musicians, and black artists moving in and out of the Black Arts Repertory Theatre/School. [I was] a part of something that was trying to put into place an ideology that people were developing and thinking at this point.

After the demise of the Black Arts Repertory Theatre/School [in 1965], we began the San Francisco Black Arts Movement out in California. At the same time, we were involved with black studies. Baraka came out there and did work in conjunction with the black studies program at San Francisco State College. He was basically doing the Black Arts over again. Ed Bullins, Marvin X, Baraka, and Eldridge Cleaver. It was like transferring BART/S to a place called Black House that Cleaver stayed. We did plays. We did all the things that we had done in the place called New York City.

What did the black aesthetic mean to you?

I was a person who never tried to put definitions on things because there will always be somebody who will come and say, "That's not true." The black aesthetic meant to me that you had black people beginning to formulate ideas about a way to live in this country, a way to think in this country, a way to teach in this country, and a way to write in this country that would benefit, first of all, black people and eventually would benefit the world. That was my idea, always. That was what propelled me. This whole idea that people began to add to it saying that there's a black way of looking at the world. There is a black way of seeing the world. I always thought that at some point I had to see the world from eyes in this country that had been exposed to everything that the South (discrimination), the North (discrimination), my education (discrimination), the church (discrimination), the government (discrimination), the country (discrimination). My whole point simplified was to put the African back on the world stage. That's what that was about for me. First you had to recognize that you were not on the world stage. Many people did not recognize that, but when I began to move in this world, I realized that they had taken the African—meaning us—off the world stage, period. As if we had not been a participant on this world stage. Our job was to put the African back on a world stage and to answer the most important question that needed to be answered: what does it mean to be human?

What was your experience like working with other women dramatists such as Martie Evans-Charles, of the New Lafayette Theatre?

Yes, I remember Martie. I remember seeing some of her plays done. We didn't work together at all. I think she's a good playwright. I think that all the women playwrights were working at a disadvantage because most of the playwrights were males. Aishah Rahman, who teaches at Brown University, wrote *Lady Day: A Musical Tragedy* [1972] about Billie Holiday. It is an amazing play. No one ever writes about how we influenced Ntozake Shange. She never told me, but when I came home to New York she and Thulani Davis came to see me. Shange told me she was writing, and I read a couple of things and encouraged to her write. The language, you knew. She was in school with Thulani at Barnard College, which is the female branch of Columbia University. So, therefore they had seen us: all the females writing and the male writers also too. All their plays were very much inspired by how we were writing and what we were talking about. I think that as a playwright Shange was very much influenced by Baraka and by the women playwrights also too.

You mentioned that most of the playwrights at this time were men. Who were the other major women playwrights of the Black Arts Movement?

The first book that Ed Bullins edited, *New Plays from the Black Theatre* [1969]: Salimu was in there. Aishah Rahman . . .

What about Sarah Webster Fabio?

Sarah? I never saw her plays, but I saw her poetry all the time. She did a lot of performance work like Barbara Ann Teer. If I remember correctly, it was this kind of music with reading words. I remember her doing that, but I'm not too sure about her plays. Of course, Martie Evans-Charles, Barbara Ann Teer, and J.e. Franklin.

Because there was such a small group of women writers, did you all have the opportunity to ever interact?

No. Because we were so busy trying to stay alive [*laughs*]. It was not a thing like: let us show up together and sit down and talk about how we as women playwrights survive. I taught school, I came home, and fed my children. My dear sister, if the Black Arts Movement did anything, it showed that you can be brilliant, a playwright, and a poet but go through the same thing like everybody else: get a babysitter, feed your children, bathe your children, cook. I would get standing ovations but I would come home and my children would say, "What do I have for dinner tonight, Mom?" What that does is that it centers you. There's no place for ego there.

Family keeps you grounded?

It keeps you more than grounded. It keeps you very much in keeping with what is really going on in the world. What is really going on in the world is that you get off that stage, you autograph some books, and you come home. You then feed people, go down to the basement and wash clothes, and you get the kids up and give them oatmeal (which they hate) in the morning. You drive them to school, go do your class, and then you write. Remember I was a professor, so I had to grade my papers. You could tell the students just so many times, "Oh, yeah, I'll bring it in next week" [*laughs*]. So, I would grade papers but then I would write from 12:30 until 3:30 in the morning, put it down on my desk, stretch out sometimes on the couch, and get up at 6:00 a.m. to turn the heat up. Then go downstairs, take a shower, get dressed, wake the kids up to get dressed, have food on the table, and then get ready to go. That was a hell of a start of a day, my sister. By the time I got in my class sometimes—the class met at 8:40 a.m.—I was tired already, but you couldn't say to the class, "You know, a funny thing happened to me on my way to teach you this morning." That's reality.

Ntozake Shange

Inspired by the poetry of Sonia Sanchez, Ntozake Shange (1948–2018) became renowned for her choreopoem, *for colored girls who have considered suicide/when the rainbow is enuf.* The 1976 production of *for colored girls* garnered an Obie Award, Outer Critics Circle Award, and an Audience Development Committee Award and marks the second straight play written by a black woman to appear on Broadway. This groundbreaking production utilized poetry, dance, song, and music to express the intersectional concerns of black women in the United States.

My interview with Shange took place in South Bend, Indiana, on April 27, 2018, just six months prior to her death. Although I was meeting a legend, it came to feel more like I was having an everyday conversation with one of my aunties as she transported us back in time to the revolution fervor of the seventies.

Who mentored you?

I'd say it was my peers for the most part. I learned a lot from Thulani Davis, who was my classmate at Barnard and first editor. We had a magazine called *Phat Mamma* that was a collection of poetry, hand-notated music, short stories, and photography by black women at Barnard College.

We printed it ourselves. We got a grant from the college to pay for it. I think we made five hundred copies, and there are maybe ten left of them besides the ones that people have in the world. That was our first publication in 1969 or 1970 and we continued writing from that point on. I'd say from a distance—because I didn't know them at the time—I was inspired by LeRoi Jones (before he became Amiri Baraka), Ishmael Reed, Sonia Sanchez, and Carolyn Rodgers from Chicago.

Had you read Sonia Sanchez's plays as well?

No, only the poetry. I didn't read Zora Neale Hurston until 1970 because her work was not republished until 1970, so it wasn't available to me. Then I read *Their Eyes Were Watching God* [1937], and that influenced me a great deal. I think you can see that in *Sassafrass, Cypress, and Indigo* [1982] that Zora Neale Hurston had influenced me a lot.

What about her work influenced you?

To take daily elements of our lives and find the remarkable and beautiful in the ordinary.

What about Sonia Sanchez?

I was inspired by her attention to femaleness, struggle, and rhythm.

You're very precise in what you have to say about your influences.

Well, I've thought about it.

What about Carolyn Rodgers? She was a wonderful human being. I was able to meet her in Chicago before she passed.

Oh, I never met her. I loved her feistiness and her lack of fear for making her poems look the way she wanted because they didn't necessarily look like poems. They could have been prose pieces. And she didn't care. She wanted them to look that way because that is the way they said it to her, and so that is the way she wrote them. I also liked her use of colloquial

English or Black English. I loved her sense of humor and her daring. She challenged people to prove her wrong or to say she was wrong.

Amiri Baraka?

The delicacy of his imagery. The veracity of his passion and his clarity about race and class. He had a keen sense of what it meant to be black and constricted in the North.

Are you thinking of works like Dutchman [1964]*?*

Well, *Dutchman*, *The Toilet* [1964], *Slave Ship* [1970], *Preface to a Twenty-Volume Suicide Note* [1961], and there's another early volume of poetry . . . it has escaped me now. I am much more familiar with his early work than I am with the later things. I like the early work better because it's not so rigid and lacking in lyricism.

What about Ishmael Reed?

Ishmael's dedication to the exploration of African American and non-European culture and his infusion of those realities with contemporary life of people of color is really important to me. The end of *Mumbo Jumbo* [1972] was very important. He had a glossary and bibliography so you could go and discover for yourself where all this information came from. So, I was able to give myself a whole other history major by studying Ishmael Reed's scholarship. I still find his work to be very helpful in that sense because I believe—and I think he proves in a way—that the work cannot come out of nothing. The work comes out of a history of a people. Ishmael has dedicated himself to studying our history. That's why his work on Haiti and his work on Oakland are so important because it allows us to be grounded in who we are as opposed to going off on flights of fancy or something that we believe is Africanesque and it might be based on nothingness or on a stereotype that we heard somewhere.

You mentioned that when you saw a production at the National Black Theatre it was the first time you got to see African American and African history from a folkloric perspective. It sounds like your formal education did not teach you about black history and culture.

No, it didn't.

It seems like the Black Arts Movement really changed your perspective.

Absolutely.

What role, if any, did the teachings of Malcolm X play in your life and career?

When I was in high school and Malcolm X was assassinated, I essentially wrote a eulogy for him. My Italian American teacher wrote on the back of my paper, "Don't you think you're beating a dead horse?"

How did you respond to that?

I got furious and I showed my mother and she said, "He's just a jackass guinea."

"Guinea"? I've never heard that before.

That's another word for Italian. [His comment] made me very angry. I had taken to heart what Malcolm X's teachings were as a high school student. I believed that we should be doing for ourselves, that we didn't need to integrate because I was integrating places. I had integrated as a child and I had found it to be an abysmal, humiliating experience. I didn't see any reason to go to school with white children. Everything that Malcolm X said seemed to reinforce my own experience as a child in the white world. I believed in Malcolm X and I was really devastated when he died. I tried to make my work depend on black history and black lives for its validity. So, I didn't write about integrating white schools because why give white people that much attention? I didn't write about my feelings about white people as a subject matter of my work because why give them that much attention? Why make them the center of the world when my house is filled with black people? No white people lived in my house so why would I spend that kind of time talking about them?

Sounds like you were hearkening back to W. E. B. Du Bois by creating art that was for black audiences and about black people's lives.[8]

Yes, yes.

In an interview with Kellie Jones, you state, "I'm a daughter of the Black Arts Movement even though they didn't know they were going to have a girl."[9] *Could please elaborate on that idea?*

Well, I'm associated with the Black Arts Movement, but I'm actually younger than most of them. In the early sixties and midsixties, I was in high school and college, and that was the height of the Black Arts Movement because *Black Fire* came out in 1968 and that was the culmination of the big literary phenomenon of the Black Arts Movement. I didn't start writing until *Black Fire* came out. I was very influenced by all of the writers and painters I could find who were members of the Black Arts Movement, even though I didn't know that's what they were until later. But they were all guys. The only woman I knew about was Sonia Sanchez. Nikki Giovanni I didn't associate with the Black Arts Movement because she didn't seem terribly political to me. I associated Sonia Sanchez, Carolyn Rodgers, and Jayne Cortez with the Black Arts Movement. But then all the rest of them—David Henderson, Ishmael Reed, Amiri Baraka, Joe Overstreet, Al Loving, and Ed Bullins—there's a whole plethora of guys.

Ben Caldwell.

Ben Caldwell. All those guys. Ron Milner, Woodie King Jr., Larry Neal, and Owen Dodson. That's enough of them. Anyway, I was surrounded by guys. Even when I became a black woman writer-poet, there were mostly guys at the readings. There were very few women reading. I would be the only girl at the open readings. It would be all men. That is what I meant by that quote.

What did the black aesthetic mean to you at this time?

It meant a rejection of rigidity of European form and subject matter so that ideas of beauty and structure related more to African and Afro-American-centered ideas so that beauty was not necessarily being lily white with blond hair. Beauty could be black with thick lips and form could mean not a sonnet but an improvised solo in a jazz situation, or it could be a salsa rhythm as opposed to a four-rhythm or a three-four cross beat. It meant a change from all of the things that I had been introduced to as "art" as a child and growing adult.

Do you feel your work reflects the black aesthetic?

I hope so.

Jackie Taylor

Similar to Shange, Jackie Taylor (b. 1951) also encountered the Black Arts Movement as an adolescent. A talented actress, director, playwright, singer-songwriter, producer, and artistic director in her own right, Taylor founded the Black Ensemble Theater in Chicago, Illinois, as an outgrowth of the Black Arts Movement. In so doing, Taylor created the space and support she needed to define "revolution" on her own terms. I met Taylor in her office at the Black Ensemble Theater on January 19, 2017. I was impressed by not only the grandeur of the Black Ensemble Theater building but also the high level of respect the staff members afforded Taylor. A wall of bookshelves lined her office wall, housing her original playscripts, numerous awards, and an impressive collection of Elvis Presley knickknacks. I found Taylor's candor and no-nonsense approach to art, business, and life quite refreshing.

Did you read the writings of Amiri Baraka and if you did, what did you think of them?

Of course. I was exposed to African American writers, directors, and producers. I grew up in that era, so of course. Some things I agreed with and some things I didn't.

What did you agree with and what didn't you?

I do not feel that we can be successful as a human race if we focus on isolation. We are only going to survive as a human race together. It will not be all white people. It will not be all black people. It will not be all brown people. To continually think and operate in that fashion is destructive. It was necessary in the sixties in terms of revolution because we had to think about survival, period. So, I agreed with a lot of what was being written.

The mechanism of how to achieve African American equity is what was different for me. To simplify it: Malcolm perpetuated "An eye for an eye and a tooth for a tooth," but he also perpetuated "If you're not part of the solution, you're part of the problem." Now I wholeheartedly embrace "If you're not part of the solution, you're part of the problem." I do not embrace "An eye for an eye and a tooth for a tooth." I don't embrace that at all. Dr. King talked about assimilation and turn the other cheek and nonviolence. I don't believe in assimilation and I don't believe in turning the other cheek, either, but I do believe in nonviolence. But I don't think the way to achieve equity is through assimilation. I think you lose yourself. You lose your identity. You lose your culture. And what are you assimilating to? That doesn't make sense to me. If you hit me, I'll be damned if I'm going to turn the other cheek for you to hit the other one. That's not going to happen. I'm not going to go pick up a gun to shoot you because that's not going to help me at all. But we're going to have some kind of conversation. We're going to have to talk. Something's going to have to happen. I am going to respond. I am going to react, but I think I can do it with action, words, and exposing your ignorance. The only thing you can think to do to me—because of who I am—is to be violent against me? That's pretty stupid.

I have asked others if they feel that their work supports, contradicts, or critiques Black Arts rhetoric of the time. It sounds like your work supports some of the rhetoric that was being espoused and critiques other elements.

Absolutely.

What did the Black Arts Movement mean to you?

Well, first of all: it's not over. There's a history of black theater in this area dating back to the 1800s, a black Shakespearean theater company. The Black Arts Movement is the leader in transitioning culture and has been as far back as when we were slaves. We would do our dances and dominant culture would take our dances and name them something and say they did it. Like the cakewalk or the waltz. It's still true today. We create something as artists and the dominant culture takes it and turns it into theirs. So, we've always been the leader. The Black Arts Movement is not something that comes and goes and it wasn't born in the sixties. It's been going on. It means that as a people, we have to embrace this movement much more than we do. We have to understand that our culture all around the world is highly respected and prolific.

The movement continues because we, as a cultural mass, need to understand and embrace our greatness on a much larger level. So, I don't think the Black Arts Movement is for the rest of the world. First of all, in this country they tried to change our history, not teach our history, or push it down, like in *Hidden Figures* [2016]. That's a prime example. Who knew this stuff? But they do it all the time. It's part of this racist systematic culture in this country, period. If you want to research people like Muddy Waters and Howlin' Wolf and artists way before that, go to Europe. Even though there is a racism over there, it's different than over here. You're going to get that kind of thing in all cultures because human beings are basically stupid. Yes, we're stupid. We divide ourselves according to our color. What the hell does that have to do with anything? We're just stupid.

The Black Arts Movement, it never stops and it should never stop. We shouldn't look at it as, "Oh, okay, that started in so-and-so because President Franklin Delano Roosevelt gave this money and it started the such and such movement." No, that movement was already there; it just didn't have money. Then he gave us some money and it became recognized. We've always been prolific. We've always been so strong in getting our art form out, even in a country that tried to destroy it and tried to wipe it away. We have such great artists; they just can't do that. So, the Black Arts Movement wasn't in the sixties and ended in the seventies. The Black Arts Movement is now.

Were you ever at any point a member of a black feminist organization?

No. I didn't believe in all that stuff.

Tell me about that. What were your thoughts about feminism or black feminism?

I didn't put it in any category. It's like: I'm a woman and I'm equal, period. You're going to treat me as an equal. If you don't, I'm going to scream and holler and I'm going to go off. You want a fight? Come on. Match for match. I just didn't feel the need to. I think those organizations are great because they promulgate and they tell who we are, but don't lump me in a category because I'm a woman. Of course, I'm equal. I'm not going to prove to you that I'm equal. So yes, in order for us to get the rights that we deserve, we have to make our voices heard and those organizations do that. But did I feel the need to be part of those organizations? No.

Did you ever join any black nationalist organizations like the Black Panther Party?

No! Because they didn't know how to treat women. If you were a Black Panther, you were secondary. They treated their women terribly. They were there to serve the man so that he can go out and do what he does. When I listen to men today—black men in different positions—women are so secondary and such objects. It's a damn shame. So, no. I wasn't part of that because I didn't believe in serving you. Who the hell are you?

Judy Juanita

Much like Taylor and many of the other black woman intellectuals in this study, Judy Juanita (b. 1946) was inspired by the activism of Malcolm X. As a college student at San Francisco State College during this era, she specifically remembers Sanchez's poems as her entrée into Black Arts Movement writings. Juanita's work redefines the meaning of "activist" to include her labor as a journalist, student, and creative writer. As a journalist, she served as editor in chief of the *Black Panther* newspaper. As a San Francisco State College student, she helped found the first black studies program on U.S. soil. As a poet, she performed her works as part of the Black Student Union's Black Arts Cultural Troupe productions. After taking part in a four-hour interview with Juanita, I can attest that she is an incredible storyteller and has lived a life that most people can only dream about. Our interview took place at an Oakland café on August 14, 2018.

Malcolm X's autobiography, written with Alex Haley, was like a bible in the sixties. We studied it. We read it over and over again. It was a wake-up call. It was black history, black politics, black revolution, black protest, and black literature all in one book. In spite of Alex Haley [being] very middle-class and maybe even being a member of the CIA or the FBI, it didn't matter. The message came through. What impressed me about that book and about Malcolm X—because I have taught him several times in different speeches and so forth—is his astonishing humility. Humility is a mark of greatness. I don't care if you are learned or not.

Why did you join the Black Panther Party?

I signed up and joined the Black Panther Party because the party's indignation and cry for self-determination matched my own. I became a member and went through basic training, like an army. You took "Political Education," or "PE," classes; many of them I hosted at my own apartment. We'd be studying Marxism, black history, Leninism, Marxist Leninism. Frantz Fanon's *The Wretched of the Earth* [1963] was almost like the Bible. In weapon-handling classes, we learned how to handle weapons, clean them, and so forth. Part of being a member meant setting up rallies at different colleges and schools and disseminating important position papers and quotes to the media outlets (that was a specialized skill, of course).

Who mentored you? How were you mentored?

All the radical brothers at Merritt College, which was then called Oakland City College. They were mentors and that was that accidental radicalism where I just went out on the lawns and listened. We listened partly just because we thought they were comic. We were sixteen and seventeen—what did we know? So, the radicals throughout the Bay Area were mentoring us. I read their newspapers and so forth. Later, we had

PE classes; those were very important. We would see movies like *The Battle of Algiers* [1966], so that put Frantz Fanon into visual perspective. I always need a visual. So, that was mentoring, and I just read and devoured black history. I just loved it.

Which past artists or writers influenced your work?

Frank O'Connor, Emily Dickinson, Marianne Moore, and Langston Hughes. In my teens, I had *huge* responses to novels by Philip Roth, Bernard Malamud, and James Baldwin. Then I liked the works of Gwendolyn Brooks and Margaret Walker. I would like to talk about Frank O'Connor, an Irish writer, best known for his short stories. He has a story called "Guests of the Nation" that had a profound impact of my writing *Virgin Soul* [2013]. That story is the basis for a whole book of short stories called *Guests of the Nation* [1931]. It is a story about a prisoner of war who becomes friendly with his captors but then has to be killed by his captors. The whole book of stories is about the Irish rebellions, but it is also about daily life during that period. It is about the small people. I love that book. I love the Irish. My dad's grandfather was an Irishman. They are a beleaguered people who have been chased out of different countries; I identify with them. I love Emily Dickinson. I hope it is not egotistical, but I call myself the Black Emily Dickinson. I don't have that recognition, and I know that I am writing for the ages.

When you were introduced to Black Arts Movement writings, what did you think of them?

I was shocked by them. Reading Sonia Sanchez's poems and manuscript was really my first introduction. First of all the simplicity, meaning she used people's language. She adopted as a mentor E. E. Cummings and his lowercase letters. I would try to figure out what that meant, but I was kind of getting that it meant the little person. The "i" was everywoman, the everyman. I love E. E. Cummings, and I related to his work, so I can see that immediately. So, I was shocked by it, but they were like a *drug*. They still are. I can just sit down and lose myself in them. The vigor. The sense of history, which I love. The self-righteousness. Whether I agreed with it or not, seeing these people who were so full of themselves just cracked me up. And it still cracks me up.

You were only twenty-three when you started teaching at San Francisco State College.

Twenty-three years and two months. I had a baby just five days prior to getting the job.

How did you get that job?

We were the students who led the San Francisco State strike in 1968–69. We *owned* the campus. We had the power to negotiate our demands at the end of that strike. We brought the school to its *knees*! We created the nation's first black studies program. When it came time to choose the faculty, we chose Dr. Nathan Hare to come out and head the faculty, and we chose all the other people on the faculty. By that time, I was pretty much off campus because I was having a baby. However, the person who was initially selected to teach black journalism is named Vernon "Vern" Smith. He is a noted journalist and wrote an important biography on Hank Aaron when he was making his home-run record.

They came to me. I had a lot of experience teaching but not at the college level. I had been a teaching assistant in the psychology department, but I had a lot of experience in journalism. I had been the editor of the *Black Panther* newspaper. I had been the editor of the strike journal. That's how I got it. I was a student the first couple of years of black studies throughout the country. Students ran it, and we kept black studies community oriented because that was the purpose of black studies. The purpose of black studies was, of course, to expose everyone to all this knowledge that they had been deprived of and have education serve the community and not just serve the corporate interest. However, it got co-opted. The administrators brought in all of the new Ph.D.s and people who had already gotten their Ph.D.s who did not have consciousness.

Why did the students invite Amiri Baraka, Sonia Sanchez, and other artists to campus?

They all came way before the black studies department was in operation. They came in the spring of 1966, when I first went to San Francisco State. The Negro Student Association was in operation, and that represented black students on campus before 1966. One of the great revolutionary acts was that we changed the Negro Student Association to the Black Student Union. Ours was the first black student union in the country. So people started naming their unions after San Francisco State's Black Student Union. Also, what changed was, of course, our directive. We were very much influenced by the radicalism of Malcolm X; by the Afro-American Association led by Donald Warden, which was very prominent in the Bay Area and centered in Oakland; and by the civil rights activities here. We had sit-ins here at the Sheraton Hotel and Auto Row, where there was a great deal of discrimination.

As kids, it was just the thing to get on the bus and streetcar and go over and watch the protests here in Berkeley or in San Francisco. It was fun. It wasn't being political. It was hanging out. So that is why I became an accidental radical. I just absorbed it by osmosis. When I got to San Francisco State, that's when I turned into a thinking radical. I saw that this is where I wanted to be. The Black Student Union then brought Amiri Baraka—he was LeRoi Jones at the time—and Sanchez to campus.

What did the black aesthetic mean to you?

At first, I understood it as protest literature, and this is just from reading it as it came out. I had many of the initial publications of Third World Press by Don Lee (before he was Haki Madhubuti) and yes, Carolyn Rodgers. As I got more into it I could see it as historical documentation. When I began to write it myself, I did not want us to be limited by it being protest literature. It wasn't just going to be historical documentation because I had *lived* through much of this. It was going to be pure distillation of an unseen, undervalued life.

Do your early writings contradict, complicate, or critique the Black Arts ethos?

No. That is why I did not publish much then. I had a critical view of what I had seen which I could talk about and explain to friends. "Oh, yeah, let me tell you how it really was." But that wasn't popular. That wasn't permitted. I'll give you an anecdote. This is around 1979. I went to a black conference in New York City and Jayne Cortez spoke. She was ferocious on the podium. I had jewels out to there. I was dressed sharp. I finally got to ask my question, and I said, "What about when you want to write something that is critical of the black experience or of the black political viewpoint?" She shot me down. She said, "First of all, I'm tired of all these Ntozake Shange wannabes. And the second thing is you're probably not going to get published anyway." Then she just dismissed me and went on. But that didn't stop me. I'm *black*. I've grown up in a black environment. I've grown up in the black church. I've grown up in huge clans. I'm used to sharp-tongue people. I'm used to sarcasm. I'm used to satire within my whole family. Everything that I hear from black comedians whom I *love to death*, I've heard some variations of it from my family members. So, this was a family member saying, "Shut up, girl. Get grown first." So, I kept going about my business of getting grown. Yes, I was shocked, but I think that subconsciously I made a decision. First of all, I *am* going to get published. Second of all, I am not a Shange wannabe. Third of all, when I get into a position, I'm not going to knock somebody like you just knocked me just because I'm cute.

You mentioned that you saw contradictions in the church and then you saw it in the movement and you wanted to be critical of those contradictions. What were some of those contradictions?

That the women do the bulk of the heavy lifting. That women do the behind-the-scenes work. The women are the worker bees and the men preen. And the men often are sexual predators. I saw that with the preachers often and I've exposed that in almost all of my work. I saw the women who the preachers had affairs with come to my mother, Marguerite, who was a Miss Prissy. After all of this gossip, they would come into the house, and she would just be typing like this [*imitates her mother typing*]. And they would say, "Marguerite! The preacher, he just . . ." Of course, I'd be the little girl with the pigtails washing the dishes or eating that scrumptious food that they'd bring. Good food was a payment that women gave to one another. So, I saw those bonds between women. I saw that sexual predatory conduct and I didn't like it at all. I felt sorry for the preachers' wives, but I also felt sorry for those women because as they got older I saw that they were discarded. Sometimes the preacher would prey on childless women. So, I began to see that children can be a protective factor for a woman because you can just absorb yourself into their lives and set up a barrier between you and predatory men.

Now, of course, fifty years later, many people are noting, "Oh, the Black Panther Party was not about the guns and so forth." The women contributed. We ran those programs. We were two-thirds of the party. We innovated, ran, and serviced many of the programs, including free breakfast for children, free health clinics, food giveaways, and shoe giveaways. There were seventy-some-odd programs created, including getting families to the prisons to visit. These are innovative programs that the government has now duplicated. If the party was two-thirds women, all you could see were those guys holding the bayonets and rifles, but behind the scenes: there we were. Just working away. Worker bees!

Let's talk about Eldridge Cleaver's idea of "pussy power." What did you think of it when you first heard it?

I believed it and I still believe in pussy power. It's in *Lysistrata* [411 B.C.E.]. The women stop the Peloponnesian War. This is an idea as old as history. It came up in Spike Lee's *Chi-Raq* [2015], because these men somehow have these penile desires to destroy people. We spent four hundred years developing the airplane only to use it in World War I to drop tear gas on people. I have a character say that in one of my plays. This is terrible. So, *no*. He was right at that time. You have to remember the Panthers and the Nation of Islam at that strata of the long movement—we're the only ones who reached out and put hands on the dispossessed or what Karl Marx calls the *Lumpenproletariat*. I say it in the play *Life Is a Carousel* [2017]. The play is all about Baraka and the movement. Marx said that when the lumpen come into politics, they bring those qualities with them: stealing, prostituting, all the things you have to do when you are on the bottom of society to survive. They have to be trained through political education not to do that. I state in *Virgin Soul* that there are always going to be some who are just renegades. So, Eldridge was saying, "Women, don't just give it up liberally. Use it, in a sense, to control the men." We call it "pillow talk." You don't want to go out there without your car registered, without your license, without your insurance. For a while there, they were using up the defense fund on people getting arrested for petty traffic offenses. At that point, Huey Newton said, "We're not putting out any more money for this petty stuff. Everybody get your cars registered." So, pussy politics I totally understand.

I think some people take issue with the idea of pussy power because it implies that the only source of power black women have is in their vaginas. It sounds like you didn't interpret this idea that way.

He is saying, "Be wise about it; don't just spread your legs." Because remember, this was right at the time of the sexual revolution. So, for the first time in human history, women had control of their sexuality. A woman could have sex and didn't have to be stuck with a baby. A woman could have sex and didn't have to marry the dude even if she didn't like him. Eldridge, to me at that point, was saying, "You need to be a little bit more savvy about this." That was how I interpreted it and that's irrespective of the fact he talks about rape in *Soul on Ice* [1968] and that he beat Kathleen Cleaver, which I acknowledge in several writings. I only acknowledge it because it's public knowledge and has already been documented by somebody else.

What was college life like prior to the formation of the Black Student Union?

There were very few black students. Out of maybe eighteen thousand, black students were in the hundreds. People had their own communities. It was very cliquish. The black Greeks—the Alpha Kappa Alpha and Delta Sigma Theta sororities—really ran the social spectrum, and I was not in any way interested in that. My mother had told the classic story of the paper bag skin test to get into the black colleges in the South. My mother and father went to Langston University in Oklahoma, and that's where they met. My mother told me a comparable story about a black Greek male group tying a boy to the train tracks as an initiation ritual, and he didn't get out of it and the train ran over him. I say comparable because I don't know if it's true or not. My mom told some stories. My mom could be a fabulous storyteller.

How did black students go from having their own cliques and Greek life to forming the Black Student Union?

James "Jimmy" Garrett is responsible for that. He came back from the 1964 Freedom Summer. He had been active in the Student Nonviolent Coordinating Committee, so he and others purposely chose San Francisco State as an organizing mechanism [after] realizing that San Francisco State attracted more working-class students than University of California, Berkeley. They came to San Francisco State to organize that summer of 1966. After the Black Student Union had organized, far more students from all different races went down to help organize with the Freedom Rides and voter registration. When they came back to San Francisco State that fall and were running the tutorial centers—they were out. They radicalized the whole campus. The whole area was extremely radicalized by organizations like Students for a Democratic Society [1960–74], W. E. B. Du Bois Clubs of America [1964–70], which was noted by J. Edgar Hoover as a communist front organization, and the Communist Party of the United States of America [1919], all these left-wing organizations and also free-love organizations. So, to go to San Francisco State was exciting every single day. Police were there. The news was there. My parents used to say, "The only way we are going to catch Judy is to turn on the six o'clock news." It was a joke in the family, but it attested to the fact that I wanted to be *there*.

The LaBrie brothers—Gerald LaBrie, also known as "Abdul Karim," and Aubrey LaBrie—brought in a lot of interesting courses in what was called the Experimental College. The Experimental College was already extremely active in 1966–1967, so you could get all these courses. Not only black history courses taught by the LaBrie brothers but also courses on the Maharishi Yogi. Transcendental Meditation was very big. I took tons of classes.

Halifu Osumare was there at that time.

She was Janis Miller then. She and I were students together. I knew her. She's super great! But do you see what I'm saying about the cliques diminishing? This was exclusive: "Oh, you have to be light-skinned to be an AKA [Alpha Kappa Alpha]. You can be a Delta [Sigma Theta] if you are brown-skinned." It didn't disappear, but there was so much that was far more interesting to me and to many others. All this stuff wasn't exclusive. Anybody could be a part of any of this.

In your article "Meeting LeRoi Jones" [2017], you write that "as a black activist, I advocated for change in the black community in Oakland and San Francisco. Two factions split—the artists and the activists—and I had to choose."[10] *Could you tell me more about the "change" you wanted to see happen and why you felt that you had to choose between art and activism?*

I chose activism because I had seen and heard about police oppressions in Oakland. My earliest memories of the police and their interaction with black people were very traumatic scenes of big, white men being menacing figures in blue uniforms to black people. I have seen more than enough of spread-eagled young black men on the ground next to police cars. So, I knew that what the Panthers were talking about was true. I didn't at all like the role I saw women play in the cultural nationalist movement. It looked to me like the women had to be subservient and got stuck having babies rapidly. One after the other. I had come from a very religious household. I was busting out, okay? Being locked back down was not on my agenda. I wasn't even interested when any of those brothers approached me. Before jeans were frayed, I used to wear my jeans frayed, and of course that means a lot of your skin is showing. There would be considerable amount of thigh showing, and I was told in several instances that was not kosher. Why didn't I wear a wrap? I'm a great Buddhist, but you can't force me to do anything. I do what I want to do. So, the cultural nationalist movement: I saw right through it.

Why did you feel you had to make a choice between art and activism?

Well, you made a choice because the factions are separated. They weren't violent towards one another, but they were very antagonistic towards one another.

This is happening at Black House, or just overall?

Yes. It is happening in Black House. Interestingly enough, now that four to five decades have gone by, everybody is acting like we were all together at that point. We really were together because we were all in the long movement, but there was internecine. Brother to brother. Internecine, meaning inside the family. Inside the family there was boom-boom-boom, head-to-head. It was bad conflict. It was like, "You better not show your face up here." So, you did have to choose and you signified. Women: you signified by the way you dressed. If you wore the long African wraps which impeded movement and the headpieces then you could do one kind of thing. To me, you were more ornamental. Whereas if you were going to protests where the police were about the "vamp," as we used to call it: you better be able to run fast. I was in several riots where I had to run. You're not going to be running in that African wrap.

What kind of change did you want to see happen?

At that time, we wanted all of society to change. We wanted the destruction of the "American way," of the American system. We wanted a complete and utter revolution. All those requests? They weren't requests, they were *demands* on the Panthers' Ten-Point Platform. We want all political prisoners released. Full employment: yes! You can employ everybody somewhere, some kind of way.

One of the things you mentioned is that now when people look back at the past, at places like Black House, they remember, "Oh, we were comrades." This wasn't your experience. Why do you think that folks want to remember the past this way? Why would we want to create a vision of unity when that just wasn't the case?

For one thing right now, the political atmosphere is requiring everyone to be a Black Panther. Whether you believe in taking up arms or not. At this point, the beast that those of us who were militant were pointing to has now uncovered himself and *everybody* knows who the beast is. In the sixties, we used to say—it was a Marxist idea—exposing the contradictions or *heightening* the contradictions. Here's a contradiction. The Statue of Liberty says, "We welcome your poor, your huddled masses." The contradiction is: no, not everybody is welcome. Only people from certain countries are welcome or only with certain skill sets are welcome. That's a contradiction. Well, now the contradictions are heightened because we are seeing all this fighting over the borders and immigrants. This is showing what American immigration is really about. We want people who are able-bodied. We want people who are going to fit in and not stand out. So, that's a contradiction. When the athletes kneel—whether they understood it or not that "The Star-Spangled Banner" was very racist in its third quatrain or third stanza—they're doing the same thing the Panthers did. They were standing up in the capital of Sacramento. They're just doing it on the football field. That raised arm and that kneeling stand is just as confrontational as the Panthers standing on the same ground, the same day, the same time that Governor Ronald Reagan was standing there. It is the same. People are now taking the same step people took then.

Some people are just using ego to say, "I was there back then." When actually, we know there were about—at the height of the card-carrying Panthers—five thousand and two-thirds of those were women. Of course, that doesn't account for the many fellow travelers. So, I don't get an attitude because you want to call yourself a Panther. You notice I put in *Virgin Soul* the ones who were there when the police came. That's the difference between those of us who participated in the Panthers and our parents who supported us: their names are in the Counter Intelligence Program [Cointelpro; 1956–71] book. Their addresses were in there. Their phones were tapped as well as ours. We put our parents' lives at risk. My mother still gets checked [at the airport].

In your essay "Five Comrades in the Black Panther Party, 1967–1970" [2016] you write that "our gang of five affected policy and high-level decisions by virtue of our intense participation, outspokenness, our spacious Potomac St. flat which became a safe house, our connections to our families and communities."[11] *Could you tell me more about your intense participation during the early years of the Black Panther Party?*

The five of us were the first students to become members of the Black Panther Party. Of course, I have noted that Huey Newton and Bobby Seale came to San Francisco State recruiting just like Clorox or IBM. We went to the meeting, and they had a sign-up sheet in the back. So, we joined and immediately we became known. They called us the "sisters with skills" because each of us fell into doing something that was needed right away. I worked with the newspaper with Eldridge and Kathleen Cleaver in their apartment. JoAnn Mitchell, who was the toughest one of us all and from the Hunters Point community, was often the Officer of the Day because she could handle men and women. She could handle the lumpen, the middle class, she could handle anybody. One friend was from a very middle-class family and had natural accounting skills, so she became the treasurer of the party, and another friend became Bobby Seale's scheduler and secretary. Another one became the office manager, so she managed the office from day to day. We went in there and worked full-time. We left school and joined the Black Panther Party and immediately began that administrative, behind-the-scenes kind of work in secondary leadership positions.

The Black Panther *begins as a community-minded newspaper but then becomes this international force that connects large groups of people. Could you tell me more about your work with the* Black Panther *newspaper?*

This is how we put out the *Black Panther* newspaper, or the *Intercommunal News Service*, as it came to be called. We got documents, position papers, and editorials from Huey Newton, Bobby Seale, Eldridge Cleaver (who was the minister of information), and George Murray (the minister of education). Remember George is my friend? George, who was my fellow student at San Francisco State, had handwriting that drove me absolutely nuts. Pages and pages of it, because, of course, he was a genius, but it looked like chicken scratching and it took me *hours* to transcribe. Nobody thinks of that as revolutionary work—transcribing the chicken scratching of an intellectual. But that is what I did. I am doing this because I want future generations to understand that we [women] did a whole lot of stuff. We were active. We were fully committed and fully engaged. There were endorsements, poems, and then reports of police brutality and repression started coming in from all over the Bay Area, then from all over the United States, even the world. Some of these needed to be retyped and spell-checked, which I did. We were able to reproduce many directly. Emory Douglas, the artist, did the entire layout and the editorial cartoons. Huey's picture almost always front and center, those eyes above the fold, always glistening with black defiance. Once we were through, we hand carried it across the Bay Area (or wherever it was) to the printer. When we got it back, we sold it alongside the rank and file. It was a lot of fun.

Your experience really redefines what it means to do revolutionary work.

Behind. The. Scenes! I loved behind-the-scene work because behind-the-scene work ensures that the upfront work is right. It gets it together.

You were a powerful voice of the Black Panther *newspaper. Your essay "Black Womanhood #1" [1967] demonstrates how you were shaping the paper.*[12] *You discuss relationships, black womanhood, hair politics, and black masculinity. I don't think people fully appreciate what that means to have that kind of a voice.*

Well, at that time, my sisters in the safe house that was at 47 Potomac Street and I were often called "difficult." It means we questioned everything. "You think so? Oh, really. Why do I have to do that? What, you're going to give me ten dollars to do this? No, I need twenty dollars." We were practical. We all came from middle-class, working middle-class, two-income families. All five of us came from homeowners, so that meant that we knew what it took to run a household. Three of us were the oldest daughters in our household, and we all knew how to cook. If you are an oldest daughter in a black family you have to know how to cook. So, we were out there. We were loving it but we were practical.

How did you negotiate your interests as a black woman within the Black Panther Party?

We looked out for one another. You asked about the safe house. Here is an instance on how we looked out for one another. This was an actual incident that I fictionalized in *Virgin Soul.* The guy's actual name was Terry and I changed it to Barry. Terry had an interest in me and I didn't have an interest in him. Terry was the first fugitive to come to the house. We had a nine-room flat in San Francisco. It was huge because there were five of us.

Then the Panthers started coming over because we had a beautiful park right outside our window. We were on the bottom floor. So, the Panthers could come and we would fix food for them and they would do their military drills right outside the window and so forth. One day, they came and when they left Terry was still there. The fictional Geniece [who represents me] says, "I love me some revolutionary brothers but they need to get into Ivory soap." So, I am pointing out the class distinction there. That here are these middle-class young women encountering the lumpen. So, the voice comes back from another room because this is a spacious house, "Ain't nobody gonna have to do nothing except fight for this funky system to be overthrown." Geniece shouts back, "Now who left you here?" This is realistic; this is what happened. "Chairman Bob, that's who and if you don't like it, talk to him." I was very upset and I was criticized often for my bourgeois tendencies, which I didn't think I had because I was so down-to-earth. But I did. Geniece says, "Chairman Bob, my foot." She goes to the kitchen where Li-an (who really represents JoAnn) is picking up. JoAnn could kick anybody's ass, man or woman. So, Li-an says, "He's staying with us. He needs a place to lay low. He's hot." Geniece says, "Well, wait a minute! We need a house meeting for something like that!" We had house meetings as roommates every Saturday where we ironed out any problems and so forth. Li-an says, "Couldn't wait. Bobby needed a place for him today." In the book and in life, JoAnn was going with Bobby Seale. So, this is that pillow talk that goes on. Then Geniece says, "What happens if he hadn't found a place to stay?" Li-an says, "Look, this is the deal. Can you dig it?" That was a common phrase: can you dig it? Meaning, "Just get ready for this." So, the discussion was over.

But listen, this is the protectiveness that I say that sisters did for each other. We protected one another. That was my protection. That is why I say "de facto feminists." Nobody had to tell us; nobody had to read us a memorandum on feminism. No, that is feminism in action. If he tries to mess with you, tell him I will personally kick his ass.

Tell me more about de facto feminism.

I am what is called an independent scholar. During the book tour for *Virgin Soul*, people kept asking me about the role of women in the Black Panther Party, the role of women in the movement, and the relationship of the movement to feminism. Black women—come on! We've been feminist before time because in the United States we had to take control of households. We had to take control of our own love life without any men around. We either had to sell pleasure, unite with other women, or go to other races. We had to do it. Like your great-grandma [who worked in a Catholic school kitchen to afford an education for your mother]. We had to get out and work. We weren't going to let those children starve.

One of the primary gaps that is going on between feminism and black women right now, particularly in this entertainment and workplace, is #MeToo-ism and sexism. I feel that the white actresses who are protesting are protesting because they lost an opportunity at careers. But this was an opportunity that black women were never given in the first place.

Why did you decide to leave the Black Panther Party in 1973?

I never officially left the party. I never officially dropped out of school. I always kept my status at San Francisco State active. Around 1968, my boyfriend, Clarence Thomas (who became my husband), and I went back to campus and organized. He became the campus coordinator for the Black Panther Party. So, all of us went back to campus armed politically and literally. Guns. We went back to organize for the Black Panther Party on campus. The brothers then used the money from the student body fund—that's public fact now and the FBI knows it—to buy guns for the Panthers. That was on one front. Remember: the Panthers were active on a number of fronts. Aboveground and belowground. The safe house is a belowground activity. Selling the paper on the street: that is aboveground. Then we came back to the campus and used all the organizing principles that we learned in the Black Panther Party to organize the strike, which, at four and a half months, was the longest student strike in history and changed the face of higher education in America and, therefore, the world. That is the reason why you're sitting there in your position.

Then you get the emergence of other fields.

Yes. Feminist studies is because we kicked ass. We sacrificed.

That leads to one of the things you write about in De Facto Feminism. *You write that black people often serve as an early warning system for the American populace.*[13]

Flint, Michigan. Brown waters are going to be anywhere! "Oh, it can't happen to us!" The children have been disappearing in the foster system in Florida like flies. Oh, no. Florida is everywhere. These children in foster systems are disappearing all over the place. Listen. Charlie Parker, the bop musicians, and Billie Holiday on drugs in the thirties, forties, and fifties were an early warning system for drug-heroin usage. The hippies who rebelled against the Mad Men society in the sixties found out drugs. Then you have Art Linkletter's daughter jumping out of the building because she's high on LSD. We were the early warning system for that. Thank you so much for reading me carefully. I'm grateful.

I really appreciate that you celebrate the poet and playwright Carolyn Rodgers in De Facto Feminism. *I met her and was scheduled to speak with her about her dramas, but she passed away before we could complete the interview. I love that you include her because she contributed profoundly to the Black Arts Movement. You list her as one of the cofounders of the Third World Press. During my interview with Haki Madhubuti, he told me that neither she nor Johari Amini were cofounders but that later black women scholars positioned them that way. He states, "There are no documents with their names on them. None. They put no money in the press. Carolyn Rodgers stayed there six months in my apartment in Englewood and we only had one or two meetings; that's it. I care for Carolyn and Johari. I published two of Carolyn's books and about two or three of Johari's books. Now that's not to say that Carolyn did not contribute to the Black Arts Movement and didn't do beautiful work; she did. But she left the Third World Press and there's no ill feelings."*[14]

I think that is an interesting point to be explored. It seems like I remember *her* saying it to me that she was in this little basement apartment with him and Johari Amini, and they put it together themselves on a mimeo machine. That is what I remember.

She was incredibly talented and generous. On one occasion when I asked about her poetry she told me, "My dear sister, I write plays too."

She was a real poet. Just incredible. She had chops as a poet period. Hands down. This is what a real poet is like. It doesn't matter if a person who has that real talent—meaning something that is innate and that they then developed—changes religions or politics. They still have it. Baraka had the innate gift and he developed it whether it was towards black politics, in the Beat Generation movement, or trying to be an imam with the Islamic faith. It didn't matter. He's a writer. Writers write. She taught me that.

I love that you were supported by other women. I do wonder what happened to Panther women who did not have the kind of community that you had.

They became disillusioned. Some became broken people. Then they went on to hopefully heal themselves through other movements, organizations, or trends in society. My heart aches for a couple of Panther women who I know did fall by the wayside, but for the most part women were able to thrive and everybody got collateral benefit. For instance, after the strike, many people were able to graduate. Instructors, partly as a revolutionary tax, were signing our graduation papers, letting us turn in papers on the strike or papers on oppression. I graduated the semester of the strike. This is what I have learned: everybody doesn't have to participate in everything, but there always has to be a core, a conjuring, a unit of people who are passionate and willing to do anything. Usually that is young people, not when you're old.

Halifu Osumare

Halifu Osumare (b. 1946), a brilliant dancer, choreographer, and scholar, attended San Francisco State College alongside Juanita during the tumultuous sixties. Similar to Juanita, she remembers women playing important roles behind the scenes of Black Power organizations. However, rather than remain in the shadows, she "assumed" her power by conceptualizing dance as a liberatory force and performing at Black Panther rallies.

I first crossed paths with Osumare's name when I read Ntozake Shange's author's note in a publication of *for colored girls who have considered suicide/ when the rainbow is enuf.* "Halifu Osumare's The Spirit of Dance, a troupe of five or six black women . . . depicted the history of Black dance from its origins in Western Africa thru the popular dances seen in our streets. Without a premeditated or conscious desire to create a female piece, that's what, in fact, Halifu did. [I] absorbed some of Halifu's confidence in her work, the legitimacy of our visions," writes Shange.[15] Clearly, Osumare played a vital role in shaping Shange's development as an intellectual and performer. Osumare, in turn, received the name Halifu—Swahili for "the independent, rebellious one in the family," from Shange.[16] I wanted to know the full scope of Osumare's contributions, and she graciously agreed to take part in a phone interview on July 20, 2018.

You mention in Dancing in Blackness: A Memoir *[2018] that the Black Panther Party was "not my personal approach to black liberation."*[17] *What did Black Power mean to you at that time?*

I was not the type that was going to go put on the black leather jacket and parade and pick up a rifle. I just felt that was not my personal approach to take that kind of public militant stand, but I was definitely waking up during that period to how much we had been miseducated about our history. I was definitely aware of the injustices that were going on within the black community. I felt that I had to do something—even though I wasn't going to go join the Black Panther Party and do the public marching—and be a part of the various specific community programs that were happening in East Oakland where they were located. I had to do something to express this newfound militancy. I did have a sense of militancy, but I needed to find *my* way of expressing that, and it was through my dance. It was telling a story and showing the decency of black culture and the way in which we were such a strong people to have survived such devastating history. I felt like my way of using dance and theater was the way that I needed to show my militancy. I found a way to position my approach within the overall program that they were doing.

Dancing in Blackness *discusses your experiences at San Francisco State. You write that the Black Student Union (BSU) president, Jimmy Garrett, told you to drop white students from your dance class. You write, "I certainly was for the good cause. I had stopped straightening my hair, gotten a short Afro, paid my BSU dues and had read Frantz Fanon's* The Wretched of the Earth, *but I would be damned if I was going to be dictated to about who could and couldn't take my dance classes."*[18] *How did you gain that sense of confidence to be able to take that stance?*

That's a hard question for me to answer. I think it just comes from who I am as an individual and a person. The very first line of my book is "Halifu in Swahili means the independent, rebellious one in the family."[19] The second line is "My mother tells me I was a headstrong child from the beginning."[20] My sense was: no one was going to tell me what to do. I was going to define myself. My actions: I was going to be accountable for them. I was not going to be a follower. I was going to be a leader. I was going to be a rebellious person following my own inner direction. When I got the name, I realized, "Wow, this is who I've always been." It was not difficult for me to do that. It would have been difficult for me to say, "Okay. I'll tell the white people not to take my class." *That* would have been difficult.

It didn't take me anything to stand up for myself as a woman. Here was the head of the BSU: Jimmy was in the newspapers and he was on the television. He was a very powerful figure in the growing defiance that became the major 1968 San Francisco State strike. For me to just stand up to him and say, "You are not going to tell me what to do" really showed that not only was I a self-defined black person but a self-defined woman. All I can say is that is just me and it has always been me. I could not see someone telling me what I needed to do. I wanted to put that story in there because it really defined me as an individual. It defined how I saw my growing black consciousness that was not about exclusion of other people but was about really promoting my culture and putting it into the larger mix and educating *everybody* about my culture. That is how I saw my part within this growing Black Arts Movement. We obviously were at the basis of American culture in terms of our dance, our music, our popular culture, our influence, and I wanted *everybody* to recognize that.

You mentioned that you were defining things on your own terms. There was an ongoing conversation about what the black aesthetic meant. What did it mean to you?

I felt that the black aesthetic was something that was growing and we were all becoming more and more aware of it. What the Black Arts Movement did was make us all more aware of the great contributions of black culture—the kinds of ways in which we have expressed through the arts who we are as a people. The big key that the Black Arts Movement did was link the art to politics. I began to see again that I could make my political statement about my growing black consciousness through dance, especially in collaborating with other artists. I was known as a dance improviser. I could get up and interpret any piece of music—especially if I was inspired by it—without any hesitation. It was like the spirit was calling me and I would jump up; I would make the music visible. I was also very much into collaborating with poets and writers, and so my whole relationship with Ntozake Shange grew out of that kind of collaboration of her poetry and my dance. So, the black aesthetic meant that I could commission my growing black consciousness, because it was definitely developing. I was just waking up to who I was as a black person at that time. I could use that awakening in collaboration with other artists and we could make strong political statements together through the arts.

You describe yourself during the seventies as being "naturally a feminist without publically proclaiming it, focused on the sociocultural state of black America through dance."[21] *In what ways were you naturally a feminist?*

I see personal identity as not something that is just put on but something that is very deep within. As I mentioned before, my sense of rebelliousness is very much deeply ingrained in me as a part of my personality that spilled over into every aspect of my being: my sense of gender, my sense of my culture. Like many black women who were beginning to also express themselves as women, I didn't really even call myself a feminist. The feminist movement coming out of the Black Power Movement and the civil rights movement—I just felt that I was naturally a woman. Katherine Dunham was famous for saying (in terms of her dance company which she put onstage), "We did not say black is beautiful; we just showed it." That is the way I felt as a woman. I didn't have to go around saying, "I'm a woman." It was obvious. I didn't have to proclaim it. When I was challenged, I stood up for myself. To me, that was being a feminist without necessarily proclaiming it. I didn't let men tell me that I couldn't be a leader or be within certain social settings. I just asserted myself as a natural course of things and to me that was being a natural feminist without necessarily proclaiming it. I knew who I was and I *assumed* my power.

Did the feminist movement appeal to you in any way?

Yes. I felt the same way as the Black Power Movement. I felt women were definitely not considered people. I saw that in the civil rights movement. We had men who were out front being men and the women being support networks in the offices behind the scene. I saw all of that. I knew that whatever I got involved in I was going to be a leader. That is just my natural stance. I am not necessarily a support person. I know that if I have a skill and it is needed by the group, I am going to step forward. So, because I am like that I really did not feel that many of my male counterparts objected to how I was situating myself. It was just accepted. I didn't feel that I was really being pushed to the background during a lot of the concerts, performances, meetings, et cetera. I felt like I could say what I wanted to say and I did.

How did you navigate moments of friction?

This is a certain kind of inner courage, that's all I can say. I have always had it and I feel blessed. I definitely know it is not something that everybody has. I have never been willing to take a back seat. I would always stand up for myself and I feel blessed to have had that without having to go through a lot of challenges in order to find it.

Shirley Prendergast

Shirley Prendergast (1929–2019) also entered the world of black art through dance. The Obie Award–winning lighting designer continued to work across the realms of theater and dance as well as Broadway and Black Arts stages throughout her illustrious fifty-year career. She is remembered not only as the first African American woman to garner a Broadway lighting design credit but also as an incredible mentor who supported a generation of artists. Her mentee, Kathy A. Perkins, hosted our phone interview in her North Carolina home on May 21, 2018. Although Prendergast's brief narrative does not offer much personal disclosure, I sensed that doing so may have been a protective measure. This seems understandable considering the struggles she must have endured as a trailblazer for African American women designers.

I didn't know anything about the Black Arts Movement. What I knew is that I could get a job doing work with the black dancers. I knew that I could talk to the choreographer, and I got to talk to other black designers like Marshall Williams and whatnot. He was the designer for a theater in some place upstate, and I used to go up on Friday after work and help him with whatever he was doing. I learned a lot.

Did you conceptualize what the black aesthetic meant to you?

No. I know what dance meant to me. It meant you could sculpt the dancers onstage and people would understand what they were doing.

Were you influenced by Malcolm X or other black nationalist leaders at the time?

No, not really.

It sounds like you are aware of them but just not necessarily influenced by them.

Precisely. I was influenced by what I felt should happen. Let me put it that way.

Micki Grant

Just as Prendergast created space for African American women designers on Broadway and Black Arts stages, Micki Grant (b. 1941) achieved a similar feat in the realm of musical theater. The Obie Award–winning actress, lyricist, and composer collaborated with many talented black artists of the day, including producer, playwright, director, and Urban Arts Corps founder, Vinnette Carroll; producer and director Woodie King Jr.; playwright J.e. Franklin; and director Shauneille Perry. *Don't Bother Me, I Can't Cope* (1973), perhaps her greatest collaboration with Carroll, garnered a Grammy Award for best musical theater album and Tony Award nominations for best musical, best book of a musical, and best original score. The production also broke ground, with Carroll becoming the first African American woman to direct a musical on Broadway. Grant and I discussed these achievements, as well as the barriers that prevented more opportunities for black women artists, during our two-hour interview in her tastefully decorated New York City apartment on August 16, 2018.

I really love the songs in Don't Bother Me, I Can't Cope. *Some of the lyrics also include commentary about women's liberation. Do you consider yourself a feminist?*

I just never thought about it or gave it a title. I was just who I was: being competitive and worthwhile and on a par with other people who wrote, who may happen to have been male!

Do you know if Vinnette Carroll considered herself a feminist?

I don't think she thought in that way either because both of us were firsts in many ways. She was the first [black] woman to direct [a musical] on Broadway. She won an Emmy from television. She had firsts and I had firsts. I don't think we did it because we were showing off. At that point in time, I think we were women doing what we wanted and had to do. I'm sure I was being treated in certain ways if I look back on it, but I never saw it because, for some reason, I was never really dismissed.

Why do you think that's the case? Is it your brilliance? You're very talented.

Maybe it had to do with the work. Also, I was a performer as well. I wrote and starred in *Don't Bother Me, I Can't Cope*, so it may have been the combination.

Nora Cole

Grant's artistic achievements created more opportunities for African American actresses such as Nora Cole (b. 1953), who admits that she would have been otherwise confined to more stereotypical roles. Cole received actor training from the Goodman School of Drama in Chicago and Vinnette Carroll's Urban Arts Corps, known colloquially as the Corps. Among her many productions at the Corps, Cole performed as Obiah Woman in Carroll's *The Ups and Downs of Theophilus Maitland* (1976) and Singing Mary in the 1982 revival of Grant's *Your Arms Too Short to Box with God.* Our interview took place in the living room of her spacious vintage New York City apartment on August 16, 2018.

What did the black aesthetic mean to you? Was that something that you were thinking about, or were you more focused on making a living?

I was just thinking about work. At the same time, I don't think you thought about it so much because that's what you were going to be hired in anyway. I wasn't going to be auditioning for . . . I can't think of a white show. There were a lot of black shows on Broadway and there were black shows going to Broadway. They didn't always last. I did my share of Broadway shows that opened on Thursday and closed on Sunday. You weren't going to be able to be in a Broadway show that ran for a year or two years or three years. You weren't going to be able to skip from one show to another like a white gypsy dancer could. But [you could find work] between the Rosettas and NECs [i.e., black producers such as Rosetta LeNoire and black theaters such as the Negro Ensemble Company]. I didn't do productions with Woodie King Jr. until the late eighties. I worked with Vinnette up through 1986, at least.

So, there were opportunities there.

Right. Rosetta LeNoire used to have a summer program. It was about six, seven, or maybe eight people. You did this combination of music and poetry and you traveled around to senior centers during the week. That was a good little summer gig to have. I think I replaced Loretta Devine. That was work and it was in the daytime. You traveled to Queens, Brooklyn, the Bronx. You have to put together a lot of different jobs to make your nut for the month.

Are you familiar with the writings of, say, Amiri Baraka? At that time, he was talking about what it means to produce revolutionary theater. Do you believe that the work done at the Urban Arts Corps supports or contradicts those ideas?

To be a black theater artist is revolutionary in and of itself. Even today, if I tell somebody I'm an actor they don't really know what it means. Usually people say, "Oh, I did a play when I was in high school." People don't know what it means to live your life as an artist. It is full of insecurity [*laughs*]. It is not for the faint of heart. I have always been conscious about the things I perform and the things that I choose to do. How I am represented. I can read a script now with black characters in it and go, "A white person wrote this." I go look up the playwright and see where they're coming from. What is their angle? Now people want diverse material, so they throw in a black character. Okay, deconstruct this character. What is the background of this character? It doesn't make sense. This is a white person's point of view, and they don't know. Usually you get misrepresented whether it's intentional or not. So, I'm very conscious about that now, but part of my spiritual ethic and my black consciousness ethic has always been a part of my choice about material that I'm going to do or not do. There's just some things I'm not going to do. Even today, as liberal as our culture is, there are roles that are not for me.

There was this big poem at the end of *When Hell Freezes Over I'll Skate* [1979] which Vinnette quoted very often herself. It became a signature coin. It's a signature coin for me now and it's a poem by a woman named Jackie Earley. It's called "The Gospel Truth" [1972] [*recites entire poem*]. I used it in one of my solo shows because I got permission from Jackie Earley. Last I knew, she was in Florida somewhere. I don't think it's ever been published. Jackie Earley is a Nikki Giovanni contemporary. Vinnette put "The Gospel Truth" in several pieces. It's a great ode to black men and black women. The whole first section is, "The gospel truth is that / The blackman cannot be destroyed / . . . He has a force, a Spirit honey / That cannot be killed."[22] There was a whole section about the black man and a whole section about the black woman.

When you talk about Amiri Baraka and black consciousness—that's the kind of poetry that Vinnette liked. That's the kind of stuff that she would have Micki write. When we did *When Hell Freezes Over I'll Skate*, which was one of her recycled pieces, the entire first act was all Paul Laurence Dunbar poetry. Then the second act was poetry mainly by a woman named Linda Michelle Baron. She started out using a lot of different poetry, but I think because of copyrights, she just went with most of Linda Michelle Baron's poetry. There was also some Langston Hughes in there, a little Nikki Giovanni in there, but the whole show was all black poetry put to music and dance. The poetry was arranged so that it created scenes and relationships between people. In the vein of the choreopoem. It was about the drama, poetry, music, and dance and using all of those mediums to express black love, black relationships, black class, and black poverty. It was about us. At that time, our black audiences—say, my parents' generation—were familiar with all those Paul Laurence Dunbar poems and they loved it. Vinnette's productions were always about celebrating and uplifting. She was going to bring that show to Broadway.

All of the theater companies and artistic directors—Vinnette, Rosetta, Woodie, Douglas Turner Ward, Ernie McClintock, Barbara Ann Teer, and all the other people that I didn't work with—were all about creating theater that reflected our community. The black community. A lot of the plays that came out of NEC got labeled as "kitchen dramas." We're artists; we don't know how odd we are. What we do is so normal to us, it's like breathing. And you're just driven. Theater is a performing art. It's not a novel. Plays are meant to be performed. Plays are meant to reflect the community. Let the community look at it, see themselves, and take from it that they can be better, do better, and just provoke thought. This is why art is so important in a culture. It's not all about entertainment. It's really about looking at ourselves, seeing ourselves, and taking little microcosms of ourselves and dissecting who we are and why we are in relation to each other.

It's an extraordinary thing to be a black artist in a culture, to be the minority in a culture when you know being an artist is not a popular or not even necessarily a position of admiration unless you have achieved fame or fortune. To take the chance as an artist, a performing artist, a visual artist, and within a minority community and being misunderstood. That is something that you have to do. That it's a normal thing for you to live a life of insecurity. That you are chosen or it has chosen you to be this member of the community and do this. Whoever the storyteller was in a tribe or whoever was the vocalist: everybody can't do that. Talk about stepping out on faith takes on a whole new meaning.

J.e. Franklin

While Cole believes in the importance of black actors stepping out on faith, J.e. Franklin (b. 1937) conceptualizes playwriting as an important tool in supporting this endeavor. Indeed, Franklin considers playwriting an important means of supporting young students and performers to take their first step toward freedom. Franklin has received numerous awards and honors for her work, including a Drama Desk Award for *Black Girl* (1969). Initially a teleplay, *Black Girl* was later revised into a feature-length film and Off-Broadway play directed by Shauneille Perry and produced by Woodie King Jr. at the New Federal Theatre. My interview with Franklin took place July 12, 2010, following the production of *Coming to the Mercy Seat: J.e Franklin's Ten-Minute Folk Dramas* (2003) at the National Black Theatre Legros Cultural Arts in New York. We sat together on a park bench facing the Hudson River for several hours as Franklin discussed her art and activism.

When I went down to Mississippi in 1964 to work with the Freedom Democratic Party, which was really the beginnings of the party, I started working in voter registration at the Freedom School in Harmony, Mississippi, and wrote my first play, *A First Step to Freedom*. It was not a full-length play, by the way. It was a play that was drawn from the students' words and their understanding of what was going on in their lives. I was very good at listening to dialogue and then recording what the children had said. And based upon the stories that they had told about their conflict in the community: white riders—night riders coming in and shooting them up—and the conflicts that their parents had with the white people in the community. I wrote a play based upon the words and the language and the images that they had used. I did it because the children had no books and the children could not read. The children were in their seventh, eighth, and ninth grade [and] still struggling to read the *Fun with Dick and Jane* [1940] book. [These were] students who were just totally turned off, students who had been taken out of school, and sent to pick some white man's cotton, and who were marked "present" and just passed on from one grade to the next.

I was heartbroken by what I saw and I didn't know how to fix it. We didn't have any books. We were chased out of every place we tried to set up a school in, and so we ended up just trying to conduct classes under the trees. Someone had sent an old rickety typewriter and a mimeo machine. You had to ink the drum and then you had to hook the paper on the drum and you had to crank it up with your hand and print the plays up. So, I wrote this play, *A First Step to Freedom*, on legal-sized paper and read the play out loud to the children whose words I had used to write the play. Based upon their memory of what they had said, they were able to match up the lines on the paper, in the script, with what they had said, and they learned how to read that way. And it was indeed their first step to freedom. And in many ways, it was my first step to freedom, too, because I hadn't written a play and I wrote a play.

Why did you become involved in this thing called black art?

Well, to be honest, I'm not sure that that's what it was called back then. It was just black people making art. I think that term probably came later on, but at the time we wanted to see change, and we thought our art could make a difference, and maybe it did. But at the time we weren't really thinking about Black Arts. We were just thinking about something we could use to get children to respond. I was just very interested in education. I wanted to do something about the fact that here the children who had been left out, held back, and weren't doing anything. Nobody was trying to reach them or reach out to them. [I wanted to do] something that could connect with them and I just kept doing it. Just the success of that first play. They performed it in the [Sharon Waite Community] Center that we built with our own hands. We had to start from scratch: we had to find the lumber and get the measurements, get the hammers, get the nails. We built that little center with our own hands.

What did the black aesthetic mean to you? I'm sure you heard that phrase spoken of many times during the midsixties, midseventies.

I heard the term used. I didn't think at the time that it meant that black people had an aesthetic. I think that it meant that as opposed to the white value system, the white way of looking at things, the white viewpoint, and the white lifestyle. I think they meant that we were not involved in the day-to-day energy. Now there's a type of energy and a mode of being and a mode of understanding the world, human beings, nature, and what life is all about. I felt that at that time black people understood it differently. We understood racism differently. I don't think white people had the same understanding of racism that we did. Even today I don't think they do. Some of us don't have the same definition.

Kind of like a section of your world around you?

Yes. A view of the world, a perception of the world, an experience of the world. The way we have experienced it. The way we experience our self and other people. It is radically different than the way white people experience themselves and other people. It's radically different. It's designed that way. I think that when people say, "The Black Aesthetic" or "The Black Arts Movement," what they mean is it's a way of saying "The Human Aesthetic" [or] the "Human Arts Movement." Simply that energy that gets left in a place where it was born, where it came into being. That human energy, as opposed to that energy that is a part of white society and white culture, that they deliberately designed to be antithetical to the human energy. They deliberately designed it to be nonsensory, disembodied, dissociated from human life. People who are caught up in that get shaped and fashioned in a way that's radically different from the way people live and work within the human world and experience the human world in a natural universally human sense.

When people say, "Black Arts," they're simply talking human arts. I think that the ten-minute play series [*Coming to the Mercy Seat: J.e. Franklin's Ten-Minute Folk Dramas*, directed by Chantal M. Legros and

Charles Murray] that you saw last night kind of bears that. There were white actors on the stage, there were Latino actors up there, and they were performing in plays written by me from drawing on human energy. I don't think that they were very comfortable with it at first because they were telling the director the energy was different, but they were finally able to connect with the stories and characters. It was something that they recognized on some kind of subconscious level that they were finally able to go into. That's what it was that they had missed, that they had been denied access to was human energy. It wasn't black energy.

Would you describe your drama as womanist or black feminist?

No. I don't get involved in that because black people's struggle involves black men and black women and we're in this together. When we're pulled over in a car we're pulled over because we're black. Because we're not white. I've never seen any instances where something impacts on black women that doesn't impact on black men. It impacts on us as a family. If I'm angry, I take that anger with me into my community and the men in my community feel it the same as the women in my community.

So at one time there was this attempt to get black women to join the feminist movement. But that hasn't been our problem. Black women have always been involved in all aspects of community life. White women were fighting to get their liberty from white men, the kind of world they live in. They were the ones who were marginalized and denied equality. They weren't fighting for us. They were fighting for themselves. They were telling us about themselves. About what was going on in the white families, as if we didn't know. We knew [because] we worked in those homes. They don't know what goes on in our homes, but we worked inside white homes as domestics. I was a domestic worker, so I know what goes on.

You were a domestic worker?

Sure. I worked with my mother. My mother went to work, I'd go to work. She had to make a bed, I had to make that bed. She had to cook, I had to help peel the potatoes or do something.

So you saw firsthand.

Being in a white home ironing and cleaning, you see how white people relate to each other. You see the children coming in, disrespecting their mother, their father. Talking to their mother, calling her the "B" word and the "S" word and any other word you can think of. I was young and I'd never seen anything like that before. So yes, white women needed to be liberated, but from those white men who won't even call them by their names sometimes. Yes, they needed a feminist movement, but black women didn't need that. We didn't need that and they were trying to make it seem as if it was, "Their problem was our problem." No, their problem was not our problem. They had a separate set of problems that did not involve us. Primarily their problem was they were the targets as we saw it. They were targets of an attempt to . . . crush their own humanity. Yes, to crush their own humanity.

How so? Explain.

Well, I think it has to do with the definition of what white racism is. The Kerner Commission [i.e., *Report of the National Advisory Commission on Civil Disorders* (1968)] put the term out there, but they didn't assign it. What black people needed to know was . . . the procedural tool, the unhooking white people's souls from their flesh to protect the soul from the interior corruption and assault of the flesh. Which means that they've got to intrude in their whole ontological structure, they've got to intrude in their human unfolding. They have to wall off the soul from the flesh. They have to block that humanity from unfolding. When one does that, one has to have their cooperation, their participation in that. When one involves them in that, they're not going to be free people. So the feminist movement really was an attempt to get free of the stuff that goes on in white society.

All that was not going on in black society. We can look at our music and our dance forms and everything else that we do to know that we don't have that in our community. White people try to bring it over into our community, and for some reason they acquiesce to it in their community. They allow themselves to be disembodied and dissociated. They knew that was happening just as a man knows he's been circumcised. He misses something. They knew part of themselves was missing.

Having this different history and this different way of thinking . . . you didn't feel there was any way to build alliances with white feminists?

Now, how can you build alliances? By the laws of gravity. We know that we're human and are tied to the earth. They're trying to be governed by the laws of inertia, which means that they have to disembody, they have to dissociate themselves from the ground and unhook their whole identity from the whole seminal human substance. They have to unhook that and you can't. They're not born that way. They're systematized. That's the code that it signaled and by the time they realize, it's too late.

Were you ever a member of any black nationalist organizations? For example, the Black Panther Party, Nation of Islam . . .

I worked with the Panthers in Washington. I never joined their organization formally, but I worked in the soup kitchen they had.

In 1965 Amiri Baraka founds the Black Arts Repertory Theatre/School. This idea of revolutionary black theater is in the air. How did you define your own work? For example, did you consider yourself a black revolutionary playwright?

I'm not sure I even understand what the term means: black revolutionary. What does that mean? I really don't know what it means. I certainly want to see some change and I think that we can do that through the arts. If there is change, the word "revolution" simply means "turning around again." That's all it means in the strictest sense of the word. If we get a dictionary definition of the word "revolution." Revolve. Turning back. Turning around and turning back. I would like to turn some things around. Everybody thinks that revolution [means] violence. You can have a spiritual revolution. I think that there does need to be a spiritual revolution. There needs to be a revolution, for example, in the way we define the word "human." Sometimes people say "human" and their reference is "superhuman." That's what they're talking about.

Could you talk a bit more about your conceptualization of "freedom"?

Well, it's an interior spiritual power. Yes, a quality of the personhood. We're free. We're not feeling guilty about nothing. We haven't done nothing to nobody. We're free. That shows in our art. Our art is free. Now as for the liberation thing, yes, we wanted to be liberated from white people's stopping us on the street for walking around black. Of course, you want to be liberated from that, but that doesn't have anything to do with our society. We don't have any laws in the black world. We have rituals. We only have the one institution and that's the black church. It's always been a liberated institution. We don't have jail. We didn't set these jails up.

Can you talk to me about how the black church functions as a liberating institution?

It's very liberating and if it weren't, we'd all be dead. The black church keeps us alive, because it talks about the liberators in the Bible. Jesus was a liberator. He was a revolutionary. Some people even said he was a radical. When he preached in the marketplace he used his parables to get people to think about the relationship between themselves and others, and themselves and God. This was liberating. All of our lives, ever since we were brought here on the slave ships, we were talking about liberation. We haven't been talking about freedom, necessarily. We've been talking about being liberated. Liberation is an external thing. Your oppression is outside yourself. And so, liberation really is . . . well, look at the word: "liberty." We want some liberties. Oppression doesn't give you liberty. We want our chains broken. That's what we want. That's what liberation is: being able to physically move about this planet. Because it's our right. We're entitled to it.

Doris Derby

Franklin and Doris Derby (b. 1939) share a passion of using theater as a tool to educate and liberate the minds of black children and other vulnerable communities. When I arrived at Derby's Atlanta, Georgia, home on April 20, 2018, she had a series of photographs, books, and memorabilia displayed on her dining room table. Notes from her early students were artfully arranged alongside her original photographs taken of Muhammad Ali, Martin Luther King, Nina Simone, Alice Walker, and other prominent civil rights workers. A series of white binders lined every bookshelf. I later discovered that these binders contained her photography: prints, negatives, and contact sheets. A treasure trove of the civil rights movement.

As Derby sifted through the traces of her past, it became clear to me that she had a story to tell. But she would do so in her own time and in her own unique way. At one point, she reminded me, "Like I told you: I wouldn't do it over the phone. Given the intent of what you want, my life and the work I've done can't be parked into an hour or two." As she welcomed me along her journey, I developed an even deeper appreciation of her talent as a photographer, dancer, teacher, activist, painter, and archivist. While I was aware of her contributions as cofounder of the Free Southern Theater (FST), I was saddened to learn that her labors had at one point been forgotten by FST's heir apparent, Junebug Productions. Perhaps more important, I learned that theater was simply one "vehicle" used to achieve her life's mission of archiving the past.

My life has many phases. Two of them are my civil rights phase and my phase at Georgia State University. I became director of the Office of African American Student Services of Programs at Georgia State and an adjunct associate professor in the anthropology department.

Oh, my goodness. Alice Walker [indicating photo on the dining room table].

Yes, that's a photograph I took of Alice.[23] We worked in Mississippi together. She was a volunteer with the National Association for the Advancement of Colored People's Legal Defense Fund in the sixties and early seventies. That's where she met her husband, Melvyn R. Leventhal. One year, Alice asked me to come and take photographs for her for a book cover that never materialized. Later on—probably 1999 or 2000—she gave Emory University her personal collection of letters, art, and literature. So, when they had the opening in 2010 and my husband, Bob Banks, and I go and I see this picture on the wall—it is an enlarged print of her—I said, "It says photographer unknown. What?! I can't believe this." I was saying something about that, talking to my husband. There's a white lady standing nearby. She overheard and she said, "Did I hear you say something about the photo?" I said, "Yes, that's my photograph." She

Alice Walker, volunteer with the National Association for the Advancement of Colored People Legal Defense Fund, poet, writer, and teacher in Mississippi, 1972. Photo by Doris Derby. Courtesy of Doris Derby.

says, "I am working with the exhibit. I'm going to see about getting that changed right now." So she did. She changed the label and put my name on it. So that's that.

So, the different phases in my civil rights movement work in Mississippi. One was my first year when I went to work in the Adult Literacy Program. That was a SNCC [Student Nonviolent Coordinating Committee] initiative, and I also was a SNCC field secretary [from 1963 to 1972]. John O'Neal, Gilbert Moses, and I founded the Free Southern Theater in 1963. For various reasons, in 1964 I left for New York as a component of continuing the literacy project. Then I came back to Mississippi the spring of 1965 when the first Head Start program in the country was being started. Polly Greenberg was the center director of the first Head Start program, which was called Child Development Group of Mississippi.[24] They asked me to be a head resource teacher. Polly Greenberg wrote in this book, *The Devil Has Slippery Shoes: A Biased Biography of the Child Development Group of Mississippi (CDGM), a Story of Maximum Feasible Poor Parent Participation* [1969], about different things I did as a teacher. Because of my record of achievement there, they asked me to go to another center to teach teachers, to work with parents, and to be the model teacher in the documentary film *A Chance for Change* [1965].

I did not know the history of the Head Start program.

Well, it is complex, but it basically grew out of the movement. *Today* is the book that I created for my Head Start center in Newall Chapel, which was later published by CDGM. But when it was published, it didn't have my name on it. Katharine Capshaw had been doing research on children's literature and discovered this book but didn't know who did it. The day that she tracked me down she had talked to Polly Greenberg to find out who did the book. She said, "Well, I'm not sure but you might . . ." It had the name of a photographer named Matt Herron, but he was a photographer for Head Start overall. They changed some things about the book after I submitted it to the headquarters to be published. They got somebody else's pictures and added them to the book. But basically, the idea and what I did [remained]. My idea was to take pictures of the children in my center in their activities and include their reactions and words matching the photographs.

Now remember: we didn't have many books and supplies, because I was in one of the first Head Start centers. Since I am a creative person, I had to create materials for the children. Outside in the yard, I had the men in the community gather scraps—tires and different pieces of wood—and had them all painted and sanded down into different things to make play equipment for the kids. I did the same thing inside. With this *Today* book, I took pictures and had them printed. I showed the kids the pictures and asked some questions about them. They responded. I wrote the children's' responses down and put them together with the pictures. When the book was published by the Head Start center—which had its headquarters in Mount Beulah, Mississippi—it didn't have my name on it. When Katharine Capshaw saw this book, she said, "Oh my God, this book is completely different than other children's books."

Do you realize that in the few minutes we've been chatting that there have already been two instances where your name has been removed from your work?

What was the other instance?

The Alice Walker photograph that you took.

Oh yes, that was later. Where it was just omitted.

You wouldn't consider this an ongoing trend of your work not being credited?

I don't know, because you don't find out about these things until much later. If I hadn't been at the exhibit, I never would have known. But I straightened it out. And in this case, because I'm out there in the universe, things come to me. At any rate, Katharine Capshaw's *Civil Rights Childhood: Picturing Liberation in African American Photobooks* [2014] talks about this whole concept of the children in the pictures, doing different things, and being substantiated in their own element. Not working around the white man or just posing, standing.[25] Play was the cornerstone of psychological transformation encouraged by the CDGM.

So, all these books and images you are showing me provide a bird's-eye view of what you have done throughout the years?

Yes. I come from a multidimension of the arts, black culture, creativity, and self-discovery that had a bigger mission. It wasn't just theater. Theater was one thing. Theater was a vehicle. It is a part of the mission. I keep all documents.

Why do you document everything?

Because I'm an archivist. My overarching mission was to preserve the history and culture of black people through oral [history], written [documents], artifacts, and artwork, because when I was in elementary school

Painting by Doris Derby of two grieving children during the civil rights movement, 1965. Photo by Doris Derby. Courtesy of Doris Derby.

we didn't have anything related to black history. We didn't see ourselves in books, movies, positive images, and so on and so forth. But I knew that through our creativity, achievement, and survival that this was not the case. Through my own relatives I saw what they were saying and doing for our people. I saw achievement. I set out to do something different: to be able to gather our history and have it. Maybe establish a museum or work in a museum and be a teacher [to] be able to educate and do what I felt I didn't get from the teachers. I did teach the third grade for a couple of years, and then I went to work in the civil rights movement. So I have boxes of papers, pamphlets, photos, and books. I have all the letters my grandparents wrote. Since elementary school, I realized we did not have historically what we should have to document our presence in America. We did not have acknowledgment of our contribution as black people, but I had it in oral history through my grandparents and other relatives.

These are my paintings [*indicates paintings displayed on basement walls*]. I was also a painter. I've had those since the fifties and sixties. They're not supposed to be anybody specifically. Those were painted when I was in the South and some in New York.

[Reading date on painting] *1965. Oh! Is that blood depicted there?*

Yes. That was related to the murder of civil rights people and what happens to the children. I don't remember specifics, but there were children left without fathers or mothers.

I didn't notice the blood when I first looked at the painting. All I saw was the sadness in the children's' eyes.

Of course, there were a lot of assassinations and murders of civil rights people.

Your photographs from the late sixties truly captured what life was like for blacks in Mississippi. Did you take courses in photography, or are you self-taught?

Well, I started out being self-taught, and then I worked with these professional photographers and I learned from them. [*Recalling the names of her comrades as she flips through photo albums*] Margaret Walker Alexander: a poet, writer, novelist, and faculty member at Jackson State College. [She was also the] founding director of the Institute for the Study of Black Life History and Culture. I actually worked with her as a consultant on some of her projects at Jackson State. Joyce Ladner: she worked with SNCC. She was a student when I was working in the Adult Education Literacy Project at Tougaloo College. She has gone on and accomplished so many things, including becoming a faculty member and interim president at Howard University. Julian Bond. Queen Mother Moore. Carolyn Travis. Carolyn's father, Mr. Travis, was involved in the civil rights movement, too. When different SNCC folks would come from out of town, he would let them stay at his house temporarily. Jimmy Travis worked with SNCC. He was shot when he was doing civil rights [activism]. One or two of the bullets were still lodged somewhere in his back or his neck. When I first came to Jackson in August 1963, I stayed at their house.

What kind of work did you do with Fannie Lou Hamer?

I was around working with the Freedom Democratic Party she was working with. At different activities throughout the state, our paths crossed. One time, we even spoke on the same platform in Ohio. It might have been even in Youngstown. I took photos of the Bolivar County Vegetable Cooperative she started in Mississippi.

Did you ever get to hear Malcolm X speak?

Yes. My uncle had a store, and I started working in his record shop on 116th Street when I was in fifth or sixth grade. The mosque was right next door to our record shop. I worked there on the weekends. Around the corner from that was the Muslim restaurant, and Malcolm was in there a lot—meeting and eating. I didn't necessarily try to know him individually, but he was around and I'd hear him talking in the late 1950s and early sixties. He came to our campus at Hunter College in the Bronx, so it was over a period of time that I knew that environment and I heard him speak. I thought he was saying some definitely important things.

Did he inspire your work at all?

Not necessarily. I was already inner driven. I didn't need to have other people out there to inspire me to do it. I already was doing it. I might want to be around other people who were doing it to learn from them and their experiences, I guess you could say. I was inspired already from inside and from my upbringing, my family, and from my exposure to the arts. I didn't have to be up close and personal, although I was at various times. I spent a lot of time at the Schomburg Center for Research in Black Culture in Harlem.

During the sixties and seventies, there is a lot of conversation about the black aesthetic. Amiri Baraka publishes his manifesto "The Revolutionary Theatre." What was your response to these types of manifestos?

I was aware of it and I was around with them. So, it may have been an influence somewhat, but I was doing my own thing, listening to my own inner voice. I belonged to the Harlem Writer's Guild when I was in high school, and that was in the fifties. I was around with writers like John O. Killens, Rosa Guy, John Henrik Clarke, et cetera. When I was part of the civil rights movement, I had my own things going on. I would want to hear them and I was excited to hear them, but I wasn't trying to quote them. I was just seeing how they were expressing themselves and I was expressing myself.

What did the black aesthetic mean to you?

It was self-expression regarding myself and my people and what was happening to us. The beauty of us and our environment and our family. What was happening to all of us. How we were tied in to the culture of Africa and each other. How racism was affecting us, affected our grandparents and my parents, and what we could do to combat it. I was certainly glad that other people were doing all this, but my self-expression was evolving through the arts, especially visual art and dance.

Did you face any particular challenges as a young woman coming of age in the sixties and seventies? For example, did you feel that you were at a disadvantage?

Not really. I was so inner driven that I found ways around those things. One thing that I found was when I had certain things I wanted to do I would find [others]. I was out talking to people and seeing what they were doing. I would be around people who were pursuing something that was important to them and it matched what was important to me. Then that connection would [allow us to] work together in achieving a certain something. That was the key thing: we were on the same pursuit, learning from each other, and supporting each other. I wasn't relying on one person. I was always able to approach different people at different age levels, get information, gather what I wanted, and create something new.

Were you ever a formal or informal member of a black feminist or feminist organization?

Not that I can think of, but I don't know how you would define it. I've been a member of black women's organizations that do things for women but not what you would call a "black feminist organization." I am a member of Zeta Phi Beta sorority; The Links, Inc. [est. 1946], Atlanta chapter; and the Justice, Unity, Generosity, Service, International [est. 1953]. I was a member of the National Women of Achievement [est. 1975] and the National Coalition of 100 Black Women, Inc. [est. 1981] in Atlanta.

Has feminism ever interested you in terms of your work as an activist?

Not really because I believe I am more a womanist as Alice Walker defines womanism. To me, the family is important. Whereas I see that there are inequities with men and women, I work with it through traditional black women's organizations. I think these groups that I have worked with are within the old frame of the black family. For me, the black family is the core. I don't see trying to save women versus men. I showed you my article "My Involvement in an Era of Change—the Civil Rights Movement" in *The Nation's Longest Struggle: Looking Back on the Modern Civil Rights Movement* [2013]. Family is what that article is about. I start out with my family. Regardless of the first questions that the person asks in an oral interview, that is what I brought in. I said, "I will not say that me in the movement just started with civil rights. It started because of my family." I told you my grandmother and my uncle (my mother's brother) were charter members of the NAACP in the 1920s. I didn't know that until Maureen Lee's *Black Bangor: African Americans in a Maine Community, 1880–1950* [2005] was written, but the spirit of the way that my mother and her siblings were raised came to me. And what my grandfather did as a black businessman and family man. It's as if I was here to continue their work in community leadership, social justice, black family activism, and the arts.

My grandmother was a part of the national women's club movement in Bangor, Maine. She was a member of the Mother's Club, and they helped black women in the community. I see these clubs that I belong to now as a part of that earlier movement. To me, history is important; continuity. By being in those clubs, the family unit is important. I don't *have* to be in the feminist movement. There are some things that they are doing that is important, but that's not part of my journey. Most of those white women didn't stand up for us when we were in slavery or Jim Crow. It's black women coming together that is the most important thing. The feminist movement's okay for people who want to do that. I can collaborate with any group, but my core is first black family (men, women, and children), the black community, the diaspora, and our country—the place where we were born and raised in.

Aduke Aremu

Working along the same lines, Aduke Aremu also founded her own theater as a means to educate black communities about their history and culture. As a self-identified "revolutionary," Aremu used her intelligence, business savvy, and talent to establish the Harlem Children's Theatre Company while in her early twenties. I met this award-winning producer, director, playwright, poet, composer, and lyricist in her Atlanta, Georgia, home on October 13, 2017. Cloaked in an elegant African-print floor-length dress, she greeted me warmly and encouraged me to abandon my "professional" persona and have a more natural conversation as she lounged on a settee. As I toured the home, I noted that nearly every room contained her personal collection of African art and artifacts that she began collecting during her first trip to Nigeria in the late sixties.

Aremu demonstrated her keen intelligence and passion for the arts and education throughout our three-hour interview. She is a natural storyteller, and her husky voice and Brooklyn accent (peppered with the occasional Yiddish phrasing) quickly drew me in to her experiences during the sixties and seventies. The only major change in her demeanor occurred when she recounted her lost opportunity to have her most popular musical, *The Liberation of Mother Goose* (1973), produced on Broadway. She remembers that this exposure could have made her play a household name, but instead the opportunity was given to a white playwright.

What do I do in college? I'm an English major for one year. I was feature editor on the Hunter College newspaper; that's how I was able to do interviews with black people like Stokely Carmichael. Remember: I've already heard of all this from John O. Killens. I have all these people in my head. What is this Black Arts Movement? What is Stokely Carmichael talking about? Who is Miriam Makeba? So, I invited Stokely Carmichael to Hunter College. He came, spoke, and then he gave me a private interview. I published the interview in the Hunter College newspaper. He told me to be myself. He said I was very gifted. He said, "You're very talented. Keep doing what you're doing." At the time, I was just regular. I was a journalist and poet writing for the newspaper. So, after Stokely Carmichael spoke, we closed Hunter College down.

All the city universities went on strike. The handful of black Americans who were at these schools—like City College, Brooklyn College—were doing this at the same time, not being aware that, later on, all of us would meet up. For example, Dr. Askia Davis became superintendent of New York City schools. He is a good friend of mine. He was closing down Brooklyn College. We were simultaneously, as young people, exploding and not knowing who the other people were. We were closing down Hunter. We chained the doors. Nobody got in and we were singing freedom songs in the hallway. Hunter College was a very prestigious school, so we're upper middle-class. They didn't bother us because we're the only black kids. There were only twenty-five of us. So, what are they going to do to us? Are they going to arrest all of us? The whole black class is there together. We ate lunch together every day in the cafeteria. All of us pledged to sorority or fraternities. That was our way of socializing because Hunter was all Anglo-Saxon. We were the only blacks in a lot of our departments. I was the only black in theater. What happened is that we formed a comradery. Most of us are still friends to this day.

What was the purpose of shutting Hunter College down? What did you want?

We felt there was nothing about African American studies. There was nothing about black history. We didn't have any black speakers come in to talk to the school. I think Stokely Carmichael was one of the first. We just felt, as African Americans, we wanted our people represented on the faculty and we got our wish. They formed the SEEK Department, which is the way of bringing blacks in. A lot of fabulous people came to the school and became professors: the anthropologist Dr. Pearl Primus and historian Dr. John Henry Clark. We were able to open up the university to understand that African Americans had intelligentsia who were already scholars and they needed to be at our school. This all took place my freshman year.

How did you negotiate a space for your vision within the New York theater scene? Were there times where you came up against men who—

Of course. I would just smile and be feminine and sweet. I said to Woodie King Jr., "Okay, I love you. I got to go. I'm gone." In other words, I don't get in an argument. This is Aduke. I'm not working for you like that. I'm not your slave girl. I'm not here to do your legacy. If we're not in a collaborative relationship then I might as well do my legacy. I'm not trying to be your side piece or your stepping-stone. Why? It's just not favorable for my spirit or for who I'm supposed to be. God gave Aduke a certain talent; a legacy. Why wouldn't I do what I was given? Sometimes there are conflicts; that's why I don't say anything. I just get real quiet and drink a cocktail and go about my business because I'm not doing that. You got to live your destiny. You got to have people who understand you're a visionary and that you were given that fortunate role by God.

Did you ever join any feminist organization?

I joined a sorority. It was fun. I have sorority sisters, but I'm a guy girl. I like talking to guys. I like to find out what they're doing and what their secrets are so that I can emulate it from a female point of view. In other words, how are they navigating this? I do it from a feminine perspective. And I get along very well with men. I have lots of male friends who have known me from the time I was twenty. They're still my friends.

Dawn Alli was my administrator. She was in college and she was really broke because remember she had broken up with her husband. They were divorced and she was raising her daughter, who became a doctor. Her daughter was in my theater, too. Dawn needed a coat, so I went to Macy's department store and bought her a rabbit-fur coat for Christmas. Her boyfriend said, "What woman gives another woman a rabbit coat? Is she a lesbian?" Dawn was really pissed. She said, "Aduke? Hardly! That ain't how she rolls." He said, "Well, why would she give you a coat?" She said, "Because that's what Aduke does." You need a coat, but not just any old coat [will do]. You're working with me and I have money, so let's go get you a fur coat, girl. You have to have a fur because we're roaming around collecting money from Chase Bank. Please, come in your fur. That's how I always have been. If you're with me, then all of us need to be on the same level. If you're on a higher level than me, then bring me to your level. Help me get to what that is, as opposed to wanting me to look lesser than or to have less than. I don't like that.

Were some people intimidated by you? Perhaps some women?

Of course. I don't deal with women. You heard what I just said. I don't have a lot of female girlfriends.

What did the Black Arts Movement mean to you?

The Black Arts Movement meant that first of all, we as creative people—writers, directors, producers—needed to know who we were and where we came from. Basically, our voices were literally speaking for our people, even if we didn't claim it. In other words, every time an African American writer or producer or director in theater says something, they're literally speaking for their race. Some of them claim that, "Well, I'm not really writing for my people." But you represent them; whether you want to or not. So, everything you do—good or bad—you're representative. That was one of the responsibilities I took. Every time Aduke ventures out and does anything, I'm representative of my people. That's really what it did for me. It also changed the stereotypes of how we were viewed in literature or plays or poetry. Also, it indicated that all black writers are not the same. That was the stereotype. Aduke writes totally different than Tyler Perry. I write different from J.e. Franklin. We're different! We can't be hung up on the fact that we are different. So, I have a problem with people who give festivals and every single play has the same voices. There are a lot of different ways of formulating literature or theater or poetry. We have to respect that. Diversity is what makes us rich.

Dawn Alli

After the departure of costume designer and administrator Myrna Belgrave Simmons (later Omodele Folayani), Aduke turned to Dawn Alli to oversee administrative responsibilities at the Harlem Children's Theatre Company. Alli served the company for ten years before stepping down to join the theater faculty at the

University of Ibadan (Nigeria). I met Alli at Aremu's business office in Atlanta, Georgia, on October 14, 2017. By the conclusion of our interview, I recognized that Alli's soft-spoken and shy demeanor belie her high level of self-confidence and internal strength.

How did you discover black history?

I got married young at nineteen and I moved to Newark, New Jersey. When I moved to Newark, that changed my life. I moved from a basically white environment to an all-black environment. When I moved to Newark, that was the height of the real civil rights movement. I lived on South Tenth Street between Avon and Clinton Avenue, and Amiri Baraka lived across the street from me. I went to rallies. People were all out in the street in Newark. I went to the mosque because Malcolm X went to the mosque in Newark.

Did you ever join the Nation of Islam?

No. I went. I was there during the riots. You could hear the gunshots. My husband was a cop, and while they were rioting he would come home and say, "How are you? All right?" His friends were out in the street. So that was the beginning. Then I went to Kean University, but at the time it was Newark State College. I was with the first group of African American students at Newark State under the Exceptional Educational Opportunities program [EEO]. I majored in English, speech, and theater. The first semester I had the head of the English department as my instructor. I will never forget this: I used "natural" as a noun. I was writing an essay and I said, "So-and-so had a natural." He told me "natural" was not a noun and I couldn't use it. He gave me a C on the paper. I went to see him and said, "What do you mean, 'natural' is not a noun?" He said, "Well, it is not a noun. It is an adjective." I said, "Well, in my culture 'natural' is a noun. It is the name of a hairstyle." Then he said, "Well, if you're not prepared to be here, you shouldn't be here." I was a member of the EEO program—I don't even know if they have that program anymore—but it allowed young minorities to go to university without having to take entrance exams. At that time, the data showed (and it still shows) that we do not always do well on standardized tests. They weren't designed for us and still aren't. However, we did well when we got into school with just a little bit of help and a mentor. Eight hundred of us were [admitted and] only two hundred and some graduated. I was the only one who graduated with honors.

When he told me that I basically didn't belong there because I wasn't prepared—some people dropped out and some people went into other majors—it just made me stubborn. I went home, I cried, and I got really mean stubborn. I went to the handbook and I went back to the head of the EEO program and told him what [the professor] said. He said, "These are all your rights. You have a right to this tutoring. He has to see you for so many hours every week. These are the questions he has to answer about every single paper." I did that for the entire semester. He looked at my face for so many hours every week. Everyone from his department looked at my face for every week. When you do that to someone, they stop harassing you. You make a name for yourself that if they give you below a B, this is what you are going to do to every single professor. What you do is you level the playing field so you are marked like every other person. They realize that for the whole semester they are going to have to look at your face and answer every question. You are going to say, "I don't understand. Please explain it to me again." You are making them become a remedial English instructor because most instructors cannot teach; they lecture. So if you are not bright, you are not successful. Children from all backgrounds in New York could learn theater. They could learn advanced lines, read advanced scripts, and sing advanced language because we were all teachers as well as artists.

You mentioned that you experienced the same kind of discrimination at NYU.

You always experience it. You experience it then and today. You have to keep a sense of humor. You have to be calm. You have to realize that everything that you do is basically for your survival, your happiness, and your family's happiness. You have to float above feelings of angst and rage and have a sense of gratitude for where you are. Gratitude grounds you and you enjoy your life, your family, your hobbies, and you rise above all of that.

What happens to the people who don't rise above the angst and rage?

It makes you ill. You die young. You're bitter. You hurt yourself and you hurt the people that you should love. If we are not loving to the people that we should love and be kind to, oftentimes we destroy ourselves. I am not saying everyone does that. But many times, we are not kind to ourselves because we can't rise above our pain. It is like we are in a perpetual state of post-traumatic stress syndrome. We are battling ourselves because we don't have control over our lives. We go into our homes, into our churches, back to our families and try to control that arena, but what we are really doing is we are destroying that arena. We have to be able to realize we have to have gratitude that we have survived and make the arenas that we want to control. We can't control the job. We can't control that we haven't gotten tenure. We can't control that someone said something nasty to us at work. We've got to realize we cannot control that and have gratitude for our children, family, church, loved ones, and community and rise above that.

Where does the trauma come from? Are we talking enslavement or more recent events?

I'm talking we are enslaved right now. You can make three hundred thousand a year and still have post-traumatic stress because you make the money but you are still stressed because we are not equal. We want to be. We want to feel that we are. This is why so many African Americans hated President Barack Obama. He didn't do anything wrong. What he did was make us face the fact that we are not seen as equal and it scared us. It made us feel sad. It made us feel angry.

For many, having a black president has represented the obtainment of racial equality.

But there is no equality in this country. The truth of the matter is: there is no equality with any minority, and that is the hardest thing for us to face. When I lived in Africa, I was a minority and there was no equality. I was, "Ou boi white with some peppa." When you are a minority, you are never equal. That's why there's Pakistan. Because there was no equality when Pakistan was part of India. That is why there was a war in Nigeria between Biafra and Yorubaland. When you are a minority, there is no equality. Mankind is just not that enlightened yet. So you have to get to a point where you are grateful for what you have. That doesn't mean that you don't demand human rights, work for it, strive for it, write for it, or march for it. But it means you have to realize you're going to have post-traumatic stress and that you have to work on being kind and gracious to your family, to friends. It just means that you have to be self-aware. If you can't be self-aware then it means you have to get help. One of the interesting things about theater or drama or music is it is a vehicle where you can get help.

Aduke mentioned building a tribe. Is that what you're getting at?

Yes! It builds a community. While it is a release of stress and allows you to commune with something deeper than yourself, it also molds and builds minds. It is the most powerful tool on the planet. Drama and music are as powerful as a religion.

When did you discover the power of drama and music?

We studied Martin Luther King's writings in college. We took apart "Letter from Birmingham Jail" [1963] and several other of his writings line by line, sentence by sentence, paragraph by paragraph, and you understood the *power* of writing. The *power* of words. How he constructed that letter to attack America's seven core values. I realized that that is what caucasians have done since the writing of the Constitution of the United States of America. That is what they are doing today in advertising. They attack our seven core values, and African Americans believe in those seven core values. That is why we die for this country disproportionately. That is why we have stress because we die for this country. Then we go to jail for this country. We get victimized for this country. We don't know because we don't become educated on a higher level enough to know that we are being manipulated by something as simple as core values. Because the core values are in drama and theater and television shows and movies. When the majority of our theater, film, and music is constructed by another culture, then we are entrapped. That is why I worked with the Harlem Children's Theatre Company.

What did the Black Arts Movement mean to you?

I found it exciting. I realized that it was important for young people. I believe that it was part and parcel of the civil rights movement and that it was absolutely necessary for people to be aware. I believe that is the reason people the same age today are not aware and don't know their culture and history. It is almost like when the Black Arts Movement stopped; the awareness of their culture stopped. You could ask someone little questions about their culture and their history, and they don't know.

In your opinion, which black women artists were making profound contributions to theater during the 1960s and 1970s?

Barbara Ann Teer's National Black Theatre was a grassroots A+ theater company. Barbara Ann Teer had class. She gave a sense of dignity and pride to the community. She had a sense of culture. She made the community feel proud and she gave people back a sense of culture. I think that's important. She made people aware of who they were, where they came from, and she made them thirsty to know more. It was a ripple-down effect. I think that is one of the things the Harlem Children's Theatre Company did. It was a ripple-down effect that started with the children and rippled down to parents.

`Fémi Sarah Heggie

`Fémi Sarah Heggie (b. 1948) likewise took on administrative responsibilities and made profound contributions to the growth of black art and activism during the sixties and seventies. While Heggie initially performed unskilled tasks such as washing costumes, she eventually acquired the skills to hold the position of stage manager at the Negro Ensemble Company (NEC) and Woodie King Jr.'s New Federal Theatre. Our interview took place in her vintage New York City apartment on June 7, 2018.

What was your experience like attending Sarah Lawrence College?

They were terrible to black students. We held rallies and took over buildings.

How many black students attended?

Twelve girls. It was an all-girls college. One girl killed herself. Yes, it was not a good scene. I envied those girls who were able to manage. I wasn't able to manage because I had all that anger from being molested and bringing that with me. I'm just eighteen, nineteen years old. You don't know. You're going to a university or college that's pulling you towards the knowledge of *their* lives. There were no black studies courses at all.

So, you escaped an abusive home environment only to encounter another one that didn't really recognize—

—You at all. Nikki Giovanni started becoming popular around that time, and she was cursing in her poetry and stuff. I started doing that in my writing class. I started to say, "Fuck this, fuck that." They're talking about iambic pentameter, John Keats, Percy Bysshe Shelley, Lord Byron. I'm like, "Nikki Giovanni." To them it's like, "What?!"

Did you have an awakening after that?

Well, yes. After that I went to the dean and told her, "I feel odd. I do not feel like I fit in." I'll never forget that the dean said, "Ms. Heggie, I'm sorry; I can't help you." After she said that, that's when everything started. We had little meetings. We took over one of the buildings.

What inspired you all to occupy the building?

Well, you don't want to kill anybody. You just want to be noticed and heard. You ever hear of Students for a Democratic Society [1960–74]? They were mainly white students and they were existing on the campus at the same time. They took over the administration building at the same time. Those girls were very racist, biased, privileged. So it wasn't like it was a unified anything. I hit one of those girls one time because we were coming out of the freshman dorm and she said something about "nigger." I remember she had red hair. They told me her father was the governor of Colorado or something. But I hit that girl and knocked her down. Remember: I got a lot of anger coming with me and I don't know it! I said, "If you ever say nigger and if I even hear that somebody says that you called them a nigger, I want you to remember what just happened and it will happen again." I never heard anything again and no one arrested me.

What did you all demand from the college and what did you achieve?

Well, now Sarah Lawrence College has black studies. They got more black teachers and they also admitted men in. There is nothing like a horny white girl when there's a black man around. Especially in the late sixties. It was so discouraging because we had done all that work and protested and you walk around campus and all you smell is reefer and see these white girls with these black men. Those were not good days for who I was. I remember one day I walked off campus and I just kept walking. Ironically, my partner teaches there now and I have taken classes there.

This is me, Jodi Braxton, Connie Van Brunt, Beth Bragg, and Linda Coratus or something like that [*indicating photograph of the 1969 Sarah Lawrence College protest, counterclockwise*]. This is Lynd House, the building we took over. Jodi, believe it or not, is now a minister. Beth was seeing one of those Black Panthers. I would say, "Beth, you shouldn't be with this guy; they're targets. You don't want them to know who you are." The FBI, in those days, tried to break up those kinds of groups. So, Beth married the Panther. I just found out that Beth died last year. She was my friend. She would do things like take over the freshman lounge for her room and make them give her a key. Yes, that was Beth.

Did you join any black nationalist or feminist organizations?

No. I knew Stokely Carmichael. Well, I'm getting ahead of myself. After working for the *Southern Courier* [1965–68] in Alabama, I would go down South in the summers from Sarah Lawrence and write stories. They were still picking cotton in 1967 and 1968. I met this man who was picking cotton. He had seven kids and he had to keep going home every day and

`Fémi Sarah Heggie at the *Southern Courier* office, Montgomery, Alabama, ca. 1967–68. Photo by Jim Peppler. Courtesy of Alabama Department of Archives and History.

let the others go to pick enough cotton. He asked me for a cigarette and I just started crying. I gave him all my cigarettes, I gave him some money, and I thought, "Wow, this guy smokes. That's another expense." That's the way I'm thinking. That's not how they're thinking. George Wallace was the governor at that time. I would go to the courthouse sometime and just sit in the courtroom to see what kind of cases were coming up and write about what I was seeing. I had a white photographer, Jim Peppler, who would write with me. He had to drive me because they would not allow black folks to sit in the front seat. I used to always tease him because in the North, rich people sit in the back seat of a limousine or whatever you are driving. But no, you couldn't sit in the front seat. So, I would always say, "Ahead, James!" And mess with him all the time. We had big fun and we would drive down to Mobile, Alabama, or different places to get stories. Oh, there's some backward people down there, even today.

What was it like meeting Stokely Carmichael?

I wasn't impressed, if that's what you mean, because I had met so many people. He was okay. But you see, in the movement black women didn't count. I knew his secretary. Her name was Coco. I remember once I left Alabama [in 1968] to go cover a story: the Resurrection City protest. Resurrection City was fenced in on some lawn in Washington, D.C.[26] This is before the Negro Ensemble theater. I remember I came back from Resurrection City and went to Hattie Winston's house because I was so discouraged because they shot *me* with tear gas. I'm like, "I'm a reporter." So, I realized I was black then. I had no idea because my grandmother never told us to discriminate against anybody—and there weren't even white people around in Kansas City. I went to a predominately black school in California, and I was just trying to survive and then I end up in this white school in Upstate New York. It was really a shock being tear gassed. Tear gas burns. I left there with mud on my pants. I even remember what I had on. It was summertime and I wore shorts and a sweatshirt and I got on the plane like that. I went to Hattie's house and just sat there. I was in shock. I never went back to the *Southern Courier*. While I was in D.C., before getting shot with tear gas, I was staying at Coco's house and they were having a meeting—Stokely, H. Rap Brown, all those people were at her house. I was catching a plane to go somewhere. Coco told me fifteen minutes after I left, they got raided and they were all thinking I was a spy. But see, for me, spirit has always gotten me out. Always.

How would you position yourself within this idea of the Black Arts Movement?

I think I might have been one of those by default. I was there and I did my best.

We talked earlier about Amiri Baraka and the idea of revolutionary theater. There were also discussions about the black aesthetic. What did the black aesthetic mean to you?

Oh, sure. I knew his sister. I knew him. He was LeRoi Jones. His sister was Sandy Lane and changed it to Kimako. They did not allow women into that inner place. You may have thought you were but you just weren't. Have you talked to anybody that has told you that they were a woman who was a part of it?

It is one of the most heated questions, and I am getting a variety of answers. Some women say, "I just went about doing what I wanted to do, and if I was included in that, great. If not, it didn't bother me." Others said, "No. I carved out my own space and this is how I did it. I didn't allow people to make me a secretary. I refused to do that."

That's what I'm saying.

Others still say, "Oh, no. The Black Arts Movement wasn't like that at all."

Women?

Yes. I'm getting a spectrum, but most women say, "I had to carve out a space."

Yes, exactly. Those were women who I think were conscious of who we are and what our places were in the day. There are always going to be women who follow guys to whatever. That's why Donald Trump is president today. Those white women knew they weren't supposed to do that, but they followed their husband. I guess my childhood was so wrought with pain and just getting out of there was like, "Whew." I never felt that I had to either separate myself or gravitate toward that. I was just so glad to be free. I didn't know when I was living there, going through that hell, about Martin Luther King because I was trying to survive. When you're trying to survive, you know the world is there but you don't see it. When I came home from school I wasn't allowed to watch television. I would sit in the living room. My aunt had plastic on everything—the furniture was white—and you couldn't sit there. It was like prison.

This is the aunt that you lived with as a child?

Yes. The "demon seed" I called her. It really hurt me more what she did than what her husband did because she was my blood. You want your mother, your sister, your aunt to love, protect, and care about you. She was my father's sister and she did not protect me. She acted like, if you're doing anything with my husband, when I get back here, I'm going to send you to the reform school. I'm twelve. I'm thirteen. I used to think, "Why does she hate me so much?" I used to look at the picture of my father that she had. She would not give it to me because I wanted it in my room.

Did you eventually get the photo of your father?

Yes. I remember it was outside the room on a little desklike thing. I used to think as a little girl, if I could have that picture in my room . . . I thought if he was in there maybe he would protect me. My aunt said, "If you weren't my brother's child, you wouldn't even be here."

That is the most heartbreaking story anybody has ever told me.

Really? I assure you, it gets a lot worse. But that's what my life was about coming up. So, I didn't know who Dr. King was. I didn't know Malcolm. I never met him.

Why didn't you join a feminist organization?

I think they are all the same. You need to know who *you* are. I think the reason why so many people hate Oprah Winfrey is because she knows who she is, she has known for a long time, and she has made it work for her. She didn't come back to get your hand and say, "Come on, let's do this and this." She didn't hire fifty thousand black people. She decided: in this country, the way to do this—and who I am—is to make sure I got these white folks.

That sounds like your advice to stage managers: get a mentor working on Broadway.

Yes, go straight there. Don't stop. Because the world is not changing like that. It just isn't. We are in a new time now where I do not even think these young people care. I'm speaking generally. There's a disconnect. When we were much younger in our teens and twenties, I think we were all on the same path in terms of who we were. What we thought about in terms of black people—that's why I mentioned rapping. Because it was the first time men and women *talked* and shared ideas, as opposed to being looked at like a piece of meat, and it was great.

You see, I just love black people. I always have. I loved Malcolm. I loved Dr. King. I don't have a problem with any of these guys. I never did. I loved Martin more because my grandmother was a church person and my father was a minister. I actually forgot to tell you that for a year after high school Preston L. Holmes and I went to a program at Yale University called Transitional Year Program. They don't have these things anymore. Preston is my friend Tricia's brother. He's the producer of *Girls Trip* [2017] with Queen Latifah and Tiffany Haddish. He coproduced *New Jack City* [1991]. We were all in the program. I don't know what they thought they were transitioning, but that is what we learned at Yale. That is where I was in 1968 when Dr. King passed and I remember that it affected me profoundly. All the black kids wanted to go to Harlem, but they wouldn't let us out of New Haven, Connecticut.

Were they fearful of riots?

There were going to be riots, yes. So, we all threw rocks and broke the windows in the bookstore at Yale. We did what we could do, but it wasn't so much anything except angry. It wasn't like, "The establishment . . ." It was just anger. I was deeply affected by his death. Malcolm's death: I was like, "Wow!" It was more like that. I wasn't a part of that.

Barbara and Carlton Molette

Much like Heggie, Barbara Molette (1940–2017) explains that she was also on the fringes of black nationalist and feminist organizations of the time. Early in her career Barbara worked as a costume designer, model, artist, and actress while her husband, Carlton Molette (b. 1939), refined his craft as a scenic designer. As they continued along their educational paths, the couple found time to raise a family, publish their academic findings, and write more than twenty plays together.

I first met the Molettes at the 2013 Black Theatre Network conference in Winston-Salem, North Carolina. Having previously read their plays and critical writings, I was excited to meet them in person. They were the epitome of grace as we discussed their latest academic book, *Afrocentric Theatre* (2013). As with every aspect of their lives, the husband-and-wife team preferred to be interviewed together, so I sat in my office while the Molettes spoke on two phones in their Atlanta, Georgia, home. Our phone interview took place on January 18, 2017, just weeks before Barbara's passing.

BARBARA: I was first introduced to Malcolm X as a teenager. I would say I was about fourteen years old. Some of the black girls in my high school were converts to the Nation of Islam, so I went to some of the meetings. They usually took place Sunday afternoons and they were in various houses that had been turned into temples.

CARLTON: When we were teenagers and young adults, he had not really emerged as the national force. It was the Honorable Elijah Muhammad who was the national force.

BARBARA: Right. I remember hearing some of the lessons that were being taught and thinking, "I wonder what is going to happen to these people eventually?" Because some of the lessons were very vitriolic, very anti-U.S.A. basically. They seemed to go against what we had been taught in school, at home, and even further. At the time, what I thought was, "This is not what I know in my community. What is going on?" I was more curious as to what was going on because they knew something I didn't know. I didn't know how to take it. Now I would know how to take it.

Did you join a black nationalist or black feminist organization during the sixties and seventies?

BARBARA: I did not.

CARLTON: As a matter of fact, you were kind of negative about all the feminist organizations that you came in contact with.

BARBARA: Yes.

Could you share some of your experiences interacting with feminist organizations?

BARBARA: Well, all the feminist organizations that I came into contact with were white. The Black Arts organizations did not seem to be organized as "organizations."

CARLTON: It was more of a movement than an organization.

BARBARA: We were married by the time the Black Panthers came along and living in Florida. So, I really didn't feel I had time for them. We were doing our thing and they were doing their thing. We took in kids when Carlton was teaching at Florida A&M. Our house was open and kids came. Some stayed with us and so I never felt the need for a formal organization to participate in.

What did the Black Arts Movement look like in the South?

CARLTON: I think that by and large, you can go down the list of places like Atlanta, Greensboro, Tallahassee, Houston, Nashville, and there are lots of others that I'm not as intimately familiar with [and understand that] the Black Arts Movement basically grew out of the arts departments on historically black college campuses. There've been a couple of books about how essentially the school of visual art is an outgrowth of the Texas Southern University art department. I'm deliberately taking it away from theater to make it more inclusive.

I appreciate that, because the Black Arts Movement encompassed all the arts.

CARLTON: The Black Arts Movement in Houston? I think the most significant figure in the Black Arts Movement in Houston is John Biggers,

Barbara and Carlton Molette, School of Communications at Texas Southern University, 1976. Courtesy of Carlton Molette.

who was head of the art department at Texas Southern University in the sixties and seventies.

BARBARA: Yes, I would say that.

CARLTON: Anyway, historically black college campuses. Certainly, the Center for African and African American Studies at Atlanta University. We mentioned when we first moved back to Atlanta in 1969 there was the Black Image Theatre. Both of the founders were [alumni of historically black college campuses]: one a graduate of Morehouse, one a graduate of Spelman. I think you can go around the country [and see this].

BARBARA: Yes. But if you will notice, most of the innovative arts movements have been in the South, rather than elsewhere. Well, I would say New York but . . .

CARLTON: Yes, it gets recognized when it goes to New York and is commercially successful. I don't think it was an organized movement. It was just people that we have known since the mid- to late sixties starting to do things in Greensboro, Nashville, Memphis, Houston, and New Orleans. We sort of knew about each other and supported each other's work and would occasionally do a play. "Oh, we read in the paper about the play and that you did such and such. Can we get ahold of that script?" It was that kind of connection. We would end up at conferences, but they were not usually arts conferences. They were black studies conferences. They were more based in the politics of the movement. Again, probably one of the most influential gathering places in the sixties and seventies was the Center for African and African American Studies at Atlanta University. It was a major international conference for many years. People would show up from places that would come as a surprise to me. Folks would show up in Atlanta from West Africa. The conference dealt with politics and academics, and so the arts was a section of it. The person who was over the black arts part of the conference was Baraka. But it involved lots of other aspects of the movement, other than simply, "What does our art look like?"

What did you think of Baraka in terms of his art and politics?

BARBARA: Well, we wrote a paper.

CARLTON: There's a British woman who got permission to republish *Four Black Revolutionary Plays*, and she wanted a new introduction. I know she promised to pay us for writing the introduction, and we wrote the introduction and then we never got paid. As far as I know it never got published. If it did get published, it didn't get published in the U.S. I don't think she was really happy with the essay that we wrote, either.

What did you say in your introduction?

CARLTON: There are a couple of things about Baraka. I would say, as the Eurocentric tendency trains you to do, you skip over the ninety-nine percent of the positive and move to the things that you disagreed with him about. To a very large extent, his worldview was based in socialism. Not that I think capitalism is the solution to the world's ills, but I don't think socialism is either.

BARBARA: Any "ism" cannot possibly be a solution.

CARLTON: The last time I actually sat down face-to-face and had a conversation with him was around 2008. I was surprised and taken aback by the extent to which he still seemed to want to believe that socialism was the solution. Now, I don't think that impacted significantly on his art and I think that's a good thing. I had problems with his politics because I think socialism is just another Eurocentric Band-Aid. But his art gets at some fundamental truths about America.

BARBARA: I think the most significant truth is revealed in *The Toilet* [1964], strangely enough.

What fundamental truths do you feel are revealed in The Toilet*?*

BARBARA: That people tend to be mean towards each other and there's no reason for this meanness to go on. People don't know how to cope with each other. They don't know how to cope with each other when they disagree or when somebody is different from them.

CARLTON: Yes. One of the things that I'm constantly drawn to with Baraka is the original work that attracted white critical attention. I think most Americans still can't accept the reality of *Dutchman* [1964]. I can remember once I did a seminar at the University of Iowa and Baraka was one of the guests that came in as part of the seminar. A young black male graduate student during the question-and-answer portion said, "Well, it's been *x* number of years since you wrote *Dutchman.*" Essentially the question was, "Don't you think we're past all that now?" Baraka's response essentially was, "Well, there are a lot of people who still haven't gotten *there* yet." How long ago was that?

BARBARA: That was in 1985.

CARLTON: Our most recent foray into presidential politics in this country is proof that we still haven't gotten there. There are still at least a couple hundred million people in the United States who are willing—for whatever reason—to cheer when somebody says, "We should build a wall along the Mexican border."

BARBARA: And are still willing to throw 90 percent of the people in the United States under the bus.

CARLTON: Yes. Well, it's not 90 percent, but it's clearly way more than the majority, including a whole lot of white people. One of the issues of the Black Arts Movement and what we have come to deal with in a lot of our recent work is that the problem is whiteness, not white people. Whiteness. Because there is no such thing as whiteness.

BARBARA: Or white people.

CARLTON: If we can ever get to the point where we are willing to admit that there is no such thing as white people, then we can start to try. But the fundamental American truth is that we still can't really even talk about this. We can talk about it in certain circles, but in some kind of a national forum? You can't really address. If we admit that there's no such thing as a white person, what do we do? How do we learn to identify ourselves and move forward? The whole thing about "I am a white person" is a myth. Historically, there is no such thing. You can go back in time to a point where there is no such thing as a white person.

BARBARA: You know what, Carlton? I think Ta-Nehisi Coates's book *Between the World and Me* addresses that.[27] I'm more than halfway through it now. If you try to identify people by the color of their skin or by saying, "You are white, I am black, you are red, he is yellow," you miss the fundamental essence of the person.

CARLTON: Well, it's something that Martin Luther King tried to get across and clearly even the people who now want to celebrate his birthday don't get the fundamental thing of what he was talking about. He phrased it in a traditional Baptist-minister terminology: that it's the content of your character. But he essentially is saying the same thing. I didn't really start to come to grips with this until we moved to Connecticut; that was in 1992. All of a sudden most of my students were white. That had never been the case before for me.

BARBARA: Well, me neither.

CARLTON: The issue that I had to confront at the University of Connecticut is that there was a white female faculty member who was trying to create a movement to protest the fact that the university had hired this white guy to teach black theater [*Barbara laughs*]. Her black students said, "No, he's not a white guy." That was me. Her response was, "Yes, he is."

BARBARA: Well, I'll say that I had a colleague at Florida A&M that said, "You are the blackest man that she has ever known." She meant that sincerely.

Who mentored you?

CARLTON: Many of our early mentors' work predates the Black Arts Movement. So, one of the problems that we constantly have with the definition of the Black Arts Movement is folks that get left out of it. For example, Abram Hill wrote *On Strivers' Row* [1938] the year before I was born. When you talk about the Black Arts Movement in New York, to not go back to Abram Hill and Paul Robeson?

BARBARA: And Loften Mitchell.

CARLTON: Loften Mitchell, William Branch, and Alice Childress. It's like, "Well, wait a minute." What is the basis for leaving their work out? Because it occurred before a certain date?

I think we like to categorize and place people, concepts, and such into neat little boxes. So, what you're basically saying is that these concepts and ideas began long before they were formalized in institutions such as the Black Arts Repertory Theatre/School.

BARBARA: Right.

CARLTON: Yes. Obviously, there was some new rhetoric that came along out of the Black Arts Repertory Theatre/School. This is in no way intended to demean the accomplishment of that, but it had a foundation. We have to acknowledge the foundation. Particularly since, for us, we're of an age where when we start talking about mentors, we're talking about people who predated the Black Arts Movement for the most part.

BARBARA: Right.

CARLTON: Another thing that we often talk about as mentors—not only as theater artists but also as being a couple—is Ossie Davis and Ruby Dee. So, you have all these people when you talk about the Black Arts Movement. Bill Blanch is another person. Where do they fit into it? Those who were all important to us in terms of mentoring and welcoming us into the club at an important time in our careers. I think their contribution to the Black Arts Movement is extremely important. One other thing is that journalists like to create dichotomies when dichotomies don't exist. It helps sell newspapers, and I get the fact that it helps sell newspapers. But one of the dichotomies that journalists created is the Negro Ensemble Company versus . . .

BARBARA: The New Lafayette Theatre.

CARLTON: But you can take this all the way back to Booker T. Washington versus W. E. B. Du Bois. This is a journalist-created argument. It's like, "Where does the New Lafayette Theatre and the Negro Ensemble Company and the Black Arts Repertory Theatre/School and Barbara Ann Teer's National Black Theatre [fit]?" These groups were all different.

BARBARA: And they served different constituencies.

CARLTON: But they were all important to the movement. George Napper, a sociologist whom we worked with at Spelman, wrote a book called *Blacker Than Thou: The Struggle for Campus Unity.*[28] There was this whole rhetorical argument of, "What I'm doing is blacker than what you're doing." There was a lot of that going on. When *Rosalee Pritchett* opened at Negro Ensemble Company [in 1971], two former students of mine used to come to our house and eat. They were working at the New Lafayette Theatre and came to see *Rosalee Pritchett* and they brought in Ed Bullins. So, this thing about a feud? Yes, they had differences of opinion, but they were all trying to achieve the same goal.

What was that goal?

CARLTON: To empower black people. In some way, shape, form, or fashion. To make black people feel like their culture and their heritage was valuable.

P. J. GIBSON

P. J. Gibson (b. 1951) also believes in using her talent as an activist and playwright to educate and empower black people. When we met at a New York City café on June 8, 2018, I discovered that despite the abuse and heartache she has experienced in life, she has not lost her natural warmth and kindness. Her loyal rescue dog, Cookie, sat at her feet during our four-hour interview.

How do you situate yourself within the Black Arts Movement?

Well, I was part of the Black Power Movement. I was an activist. I'll give you an example. When I was in Trenton, New Jersey, we made the news in Vietnam because the fights in our high school were incredible. I mean knock-down, drag-out fights in the halls. People thrown over balconies. My graduating high school class was a thousand thirty-one, so if you were caught on the Italian side of the high school, you would get your behind tore up. If they got caught on the black side, you could get tore up. The only way you were safe was if you were a member of a club or an athlete. Depending on wherever you were when things got crazy you were protected.

I was a member of the Mayor's Youth Council in the city. I remember standing up there in an open forum saying, "Don't burn down your own neighborhoods. If you have to burn something, go to their neighborhoods and burn them down." Well, that is how I was. There was an area down at the Miller Homes which needed a red light. If it had been a white neighborhood, they would have had a red light. They did not have a red light, so this truck kills a child. That was during the movement and the riots. It was just blowing up. The police threw a pregnant woman in their van and slammed the doors on her legs. It was craziness. I was working daytime at the post office after school. I knew enough about private property and city public property to tell this growing mass of folks who approached us, "Stay on the grass. We have permission to be on the grass. You can protest on the grass. Do not go on the sidewalk. Definitely don't go in the streets, because if you go out there, the police will beat the hell out of you." And they did have permission, because the people's houses were private property. Then I left there, went to work, and all hell broke loose because people went over across the line.

Scholars mark the time period of the Black Arts Movement from 1965 to about 1975 or 1976. Some interviewees believe the movement went later into the seventies.

I think it continued way up into the seventies. I lived in it. I was *in it.* These are just my thoughts, but unless you are a part of the originating founders, you are like different kinds of foot soldiers. There are people who are out front. Take Alice Childress. She and I were friends. The late Kathleen Collins and I were friends. When Kathleen Collins died, I got the word when I was in a Puerto Rican museum. I just sat there and cried because at that time, Kathleen and I were the only ones writing for black middle-class people. People came after us, but we were the only two then. When Kathleen died, I was left on my own. All of the writers: none of them were writing about black educated people and the dilemmas and craziness of their world.

There was a lot of writing going on. A lot of the people had already been recognized as writers prior to Kathleen's death. The guys were writing the "guys plays." Those are the things that are of interest to them and you write about what you know. I didn't need to see another black man slap another black woman. I just wasn't going to do it. I just couldn't do that. I will not denigrate. My ancestors didn't give me this gift for me to do that. I'm not saying that should not be seen and not done; but not by me.

Do you feel that you faced any particular challenges as a black woman playwright?

If you look at it that way, the commercial people with money don't see that as something of interest to them. I understand it. I can't expect any other to really care about what is happening in the lives of the people I know. Why should they care?

That's true, but then we run into a problem because none of those people who look like you are making those important decisions.

They could, but they don't. There were people who had money. There have always been people who had money.

Did you ever think about founding your own theater?

I had to pay the rent. I never thought about being a struggling artist. Absolutely not! I've been poor. When I say "poor," I mean three pounds of chicken wings for a dollar was good. My mother made her own salad dressing from ketchup and Miracle Whip.

Did you ever join any feminist organizations?

I'm not a joiner.

You're a leader?

No. I don't know that I'm a leader. I am an observer who investigates, interprets, and regurgitates it as art. I *think*. There are certain kinds of organizations you have to join, but I spend most of my life alone. Unfortunately, there is a lot of betrayal in my life. If the people you love say they love you and do those things, what are strangers going to do?

You write in Destiny's Daughters: Nine Voices of P. J. Gibson *[2003] that, "On the heels of the Black Power Movement, times were difficult for students of color on my campus."*[29] *Could you tell me more about how "times were difficult" at Keuka College?*

Oh, they would come by and do like that [*rubs her arm*] to see if your color came off. I had an afro; they would go down into the afro.

They would touch your hair? Daily microaggressions.

Oh, yes! The John Birch Society [est. 1958] was there. They're the cousins of the Ku Klux Klan [est. 1865]. We were in a small town. The only way you can get to Keuka is to go around the lake. The only black people that were in that area were migrant workers or on the military bases. There were no black people there. In my freshman year, it was ironic that we had twenty-five black and Puerto Ricans in our freshman class. It was an all-women's college at the time. There were a couple Asian students. There were a couple blacks who were upperclassmen. One of them was Jackie. We had a family system in college where you had a "big sister." Jackie was my "big sister" and my friend. She was very fair-skinned. I always think it's weird, because in our family we have from vanilla to the color of your hair in one family, and nobody is slipping out on anyone. Hobart College was an all-guys' school and had twenty-five black and Puerto Ricans, but their guys didn't like us. They only liked the white girls, so we dated the Cornell University, Colgate University, Hamilton College, and

Syracuse University guys. These guys would come down, pick us up, and take us back. This is 1969; this is the Black Power Movement. We're in there partying with the brothers and somebody took a needle across the turntable. The music stops. Everybody's like, "What?" We're partying to James Brown. One of the guys said, "This party's not continuing until that white honky she-devil gets out!" We're all looking around the room for the white honky she-devil. Jackie. We lit into him. Because her mother and her father look like you.

Her parents are my complexion?

[*Nodding agreement*] So, Jackie had to deal with that. There were so many things that happened that first year that seventeen of the original twenty-five left the college. Out of that original, I think there were just five of us that graduated.

Lee Hunkins

Gibson's good friend and former colleague Lee Hunkins (b. 1930) is a talented writer in her own right. While she has written many plays, she is perhaps best known for her work on the PBS series *Reading Rainbow* and for her two-hour teleplay *Hollow Image*, winner of the 1978 ABC Theater Award. Hunkins has received numerous awards and honors for her writing, including two Emmy nominations. Our interview took place at a New York City restaurant on August 17, 2018.

You're writing during the Black Arts Movement. A time where many black artists and theorists are talking about revolutionary theater, the black aesthetic, and so forth. Were you engaged in these conversations?

No, I wasn't.

Why not?

Well, I don't know. For some reason, I was more concentrating on my work and my plays. Maybe it is because in coming up the way I did in that little [radius of] 110th Street to 155th Street, I was wearing blinders. I never seemed to take time to go and find out about what was happening in Harlem. It was like I put a world around myself and that is where I stayed in.

What kind of art did you want to create?

I came up in a time when movies did not show many heroes. I came up with Mantan Moreland, Willie Best, Hattie McDaniel, Butterfly McQueen, Louise Beavers, Rex Ingram, and Paul Robeson. When we saw Mantan Moreland in murder mysteries, we'd say, "Oh boy!" We didn't have anybody else. Sidney Poitier wasn't up there at that point. I wanted to show people that could be middle-class or poor. I was trying to just show mainly black people who were very proud and loving. I guess just taking a thing from my own family. I wanted to have plays that people would enjoy but they could identify with. They could see themselves on the stage. A lot of these plays, movies, and whatnot that are out there are still not us. Television definitely is not. We are all over the TV but not with what should be. That's fine. I think there is room for everything. But there is also room for drama. *Where are our dramas?* I mean ordinary people like me where I could see myself up there. We aren't there. I have had opportunities come along where, say, CBS broadcasting company was having a diversity meeting and I sent them a script or something. They paid me and then they said, "No." They weren't going to do it and that ended that. It was a comedy that I called *Country Cousin*. So, that went down the tubes. I didn't write a lot for television or anything. I mainly wrote for the stage, and all the plays have a theme that is trying to say either, "Be who you are" or "Don't give up," or "Together we can do this." I try to give strength to characters to make an audience be able to relate and say, "Yes, that is my stuff." That was my main objective in my plays and still is.

I was also curious about your political leanings. Were you at all influenced by Malcolm X or black nationalism of the sixties and seventies?

Not to a great extent. I know I went to hear Malcolm talk once or twice. I went to wherever he was going to speak. There were people that I looked up to like Martin Luther King.

Were you ever involved in the feminist movement?

No. Never directly involved.

Kathy A. Perkins

While Hunkins did not discover her passion for theater until a decade into her career as a Social Security administrator, Kathy A. Perkins (b. 1954) had a much earlier awakening. Originally intending to become an actress, Perkins enrolled at Howard University in 1973. However, she quickly realized that there were more opportunities afforded black women offstage and began studying lighting design. Her award-winning designs have appeared on Broadway, Off-Broadway, on regional and international stages, and at the Smithsonian's National Museum of African American History and Culture. Our interview took place in her North Carolina home on May 21, 2018. Before we began our interview, we discussed how her seemingly intimidating presence belies her warmth and generous spirit. She welcomed me into her home, offering a delicious soul-food dinner and guest bedroom to help defray my costs for travel.

You mentioned, "I just knew what I wanted to do." What kind of art did you want to create?

I knew I wanted to be a lighting designer. At the time, I really enjoyed concert lighting, but I was still doing plays. I had to do plays in the department, but I was really gravitating towards anything that was music. When I left graduate school, I worked with a lot of dance companies in New York. I worked with Dianne McIntyre's Sounds in Motion. That was my very first job out of graduate school. She was based on 122nd Street and Lenox Avenue. It's a choice place right now in Harlem.

Were you introduced to Black Arts Movement writers while in college?

Those people used to come on campus. Either Baraka came to the department or he was on campus because he was going to Howard University. He did *Dutchman* at Howard before my time. That was the other great thing about Howard: they were constantly bringing people to campus for us to meet. I remember that's how I first met Woodie King Jr.

All of these conversations about what it means to create black art are happening. What did the Black Arts Movement mean to you?

I guess I'm like other people: I didn't even think about it. I'm just doing black theater, dance, and concerts.

What did the black aesthetic mean to you?

I didn't really think about that then. That was something much later when I started teaching. I knew there was a difference in working on a black show versus a white show. I remember when I got to the University of Michigan in 1978, I worked on a Henrik Ibsen play or maybe it was Tennessee Williams. I noticed there was a whole difference in the rehearsal process. I just felt the work appeared so technical. I don't think I've ever worked on a black show that we didn't start off with a prayer. Whether you were religious or not. It's like we're going to all get together and honor the ancestors or somebody. So, that was something that was new for me.

I remember talking to someone about some of the differences in black theater, and one of them was that you don't necessarily sit around and do a table read. It's like, "Well, you've got your script. Get onstage." Was that something that you saw?

Glenda Dickerson was the type of person who did that. She liked people on their feet right away.

It wasn't until later when you began teaching that you realized there was a black aesthetic?

I realized there was a black aesthetic when I began to teach in white institutions. I went to Switzerland and said, "Oh, I need these colors." The guy looked at me like, "We don't use this kind of color in Switzerland." Everything was pale: pale pink and pale, pale blue. I came from a concert background and enjoyed using saturated colors. I still do. The six months I was over there I was using all these pale colors. When I came back, I did this annual event booked in the Academy of Music called DanceAfrica [est. 1977]. It's one of the biggest African dance festivals in the country. It was started by the outstanding Chuck Davis, who died last year. So, I remember when I was hired to do DanceAfrica, I was lighting one of the grooves, and the guy who is over that particular dance company looked at me and said, "You must have been trained by white people." It's like: is this a compliment or is this an insult? I said, "Why do you say that?" He says, "Why are you using all these pale colors? We black folk; we want some color up here." When I started to think about it, I guess there is a black aesthetic. I guess I just lost it being in Europe those six months.

You mentioned earlier that situating 1975 as the demise of the Black Arts Movement seemed a little abrupt because there were all these Black Arts theaters still around and many more opening. How do you conceptualize the movement's periodization?

I wouldn't say it ended in 1975.

I wrote 1976 in my first book. Are we talking into the early eighties?

No, I wouldn't go that far. That's when theaters started closing. I put down in *The Routledge Companion to African American Theatre and Performance* [2018] time line three theaters that opened [around 1975], and there were probably more. In the eighties, you had all these black shows opening. That would be interesting to explore. It depends on how you define the Black Arts Movement. I know in the eighties a lot of theaters started losing funding when the Lila Wallace grant came out, because white theaters started saying, "Oh we do black plays too, so why do we need black theaters?"

CHAPTER 2

Black Theaters Matter: The Art of Institution Building

> We must begin building cultural centers where we can enjoy being free, open and black, where we can find out how talented we really are, where we can be what we were born to be, and not what we were brainwashed to be, where we can literally "blow our minds" with blackness.
>
> —Barbara Ann Teer, "We Can Be What We Were Born to Be"

Why do we need black theaters? Many black artists of the era grappled with this question but perhaps none so eloquently or as passionately as the Black Arts Movement theorist Barbara Ann Teer. In her manifesto "We Can Be What We Were Born to Be" (1968), Teer disavows the need for black artists to integrate into U.S. theater, identifying and critiquing the ways in which mainstream theaters perpetuate racism and harm the psyche of black actors and audiences. Rather than continue to participate in the circulation of inauthentic and stereotypical images of blacks, Teer issued a call for black artists to build new black cultural centers and for black audiences to support these efforts. "When we begin thinking and using our energies in this direction, we will be on the right road toward rehabilitation of black America and our ultimate survival as a people, that is where our real contribution lies," writes Teer.[1] Following her own counsel, Teer turned her talents inward toward the black community and established the National Black Theatre (NBT) in Harlem, a theater that continues to thrive under the direction of her daughter and namesake, Barbara Ann "Sade" Lythcott.

Teer's call to establish black cultural centers was met with harsh criticism from black artists who desired entrée into mainstream commercial theaters. Lythcott remembers,

> What she was saying was so radical. When you write something and you put it out in the public, you have to be open for criticism. But the criticism really destroyed her. As a result, she didn't feel safe in public anymore. When you open yourself up to be vulnerable and you get bashed, you never want to do it again. My mom from that point on became fiercely private, which is why she's never written a book. She wrote massive amounts of writing but was afraid to publish anything because it hurt so bad.

Despite criticism, Teer continued to create art that reflected her artistic aims, garnering many awards for her efforts, including a 1973 first annual Audience Development Committee Recognition Award for Excellence in Theatre. Ultimately, founding the NBT provided the space, talent, and community support Teer needed to conceive and implement her theories of acting and ritualistic performances. Having complete artistic control—something black women artists rarely received—was essential to Teer's success. In fact, interviews with black women intellectuals of the era reveal that founding one's own theater afforded the greatest artistic autonomy.

With the advantage of hindsight, we now understand that Teer's concern for the sustainability of black theater was not unfounded. Her provocative manifesto engages many of the questions contemporary theater artists, critics, and historians have yet to fully explore. *What is the current state of black theater institutions in the United States? What are their strengths? What are their challenges? What obstacles impede their growth?* To begin answering these questions, I turn to Plowshares Theatre Company (est. 1989) artistic director and cofounder Gary Anderson's "Black Theatre Survey 2016–2017: A Report on the Health of Black Theatre in America."[2] Anderson's study—which includes data gathered from seventy historically black theaters (both Equity and non-Equity), ensemble companies, and play festivals across the United States—concludes that the current practices of black theater lack long-term sustainability. "Regardless of where the theatre resides or its pedagogy, the challenges to sustainability were remarkably consistent from region to region . . . The threats impacting this sector of the American Theatre have progressed over more than 30 years and cannot be neglected any longer," warns Anderson.[3] Funding remains a vital concern for both predominately white theaters and historically black theaters across the country. However, a major difference is that historically black theaters rely on African American patrons and donors.[4] Anderson suggests that if the survival of black theater is intimately linked with the health of the black economy, we must do more to increase our support of black-owned businesses and earnestly engage in grassroots fundraising efforts.[5] It is my hope that by examining the grassroots efforts of black women theater and company founders of the Black Arts Movement, we might draw inspiration from their stories and increase our efforts to sustain historically black theaters.

Interviews with black women theater artists of the sixties and seventies reveal that they dealt with many of the same threats that black theaters of today encounter. Anderson writes that in order for contemporary black theaters to flourish, they must expand funding options, cultivate the talents of black actors and playwrights, educate and increase audiences, and generate greater media presence.[6] While this may seem a tall order, the following narratives attest that black women theater founders, cofounders, and administrators were able to accomplish these feats without white or male privilege. These pioneers did so by constructing a clear mission for themselves, using their business savvy to network and create media attention, and maintaining an unfailing belief in their abilities in the face of adversity.

As I listened to their trials and triumphs of navigating Black Arts and commercial theaters of the sixties and seventies, black women intellectuals taught me additional elements needed to sustain black theaters. First and foremost, it takes a tribe or community of talented artists and networkers to build long-lasting institutions. Aduke Aremu relied on a board of directors made up of artists, politicians, and local influencers to mentor and assist her in locating funding for her Harlem Children's Theatre Company. She also understood the worth of black audiences and designers, producing entertaining works that spoke to the black community's needs and aesthetic values. Second, many black theaters did not survive because they lacked diversified funding. As more than one narrator attests, black theaters need multiple sources of income, ranging from ticket sales and patronage to federal grants and private foundations. Third, black theaters need to purchase real estate to ensure longevity. While it was difficult for Barbara Ann Teer and Black Ensemble Theater founder Jackie Taylor to find banks willing to offer them loans to purchase their buildings, they ultimately proved successful and developed cultural institutions that remain visible today in Harlem and Chicago, respectively. In contrast, the decision to lease a space rather than raise funds to purchase a theater building remains one of the Harlem Children's Theatre Company administrator Dawn Alli's major regrets.

Finally, black women theater founders were successful when they were able to identify the next generation of talented black artists and give them opportunities to refine their craft. At times, this meant taking a risk on untested artists. Yet the theater, television, and film industries have all benefited from their efforts. For example, Vinnette Carroll's Urban Arts Corps helped launch the careers of performers Phylicia Rashad, Debbie Allen, Richard "Dickie" Evans, Adrian Bailey, Reggie VelJohnson, Nora Cole, and many others. Black women theater founders and administrators also fostered the careers of award-winning black women designers, some of whom appear in this study. The following narratives explore the challenges and triumphs of black women's institution building and demonstrate why black theaters continue to matter.

Jackie Taylor

After establishing a reputation as an accomplished film actress, Jackie Taylor used her celebrity status to promote her burgeoning Black Ensemble Theater.

You mentioned the film Cooley High *had a great message. What was that message?*

Violence is about as stupid as you can possibly get. Go after your dreams.

Jackie Taylor as Jonny Mae in *Cooley High*, 1975. Still image. Courtesy of the author.

Performing in Cooley High *was a great experience, but I also know you had some negative experiences working in the film industry.*

I had negative experiences with scripts that I had to read. The film industry at that time was black exploitation. I thought, "Okay, we're getting ready to make *quality* films." However, that was not the case. *Cooley High* was a great exception to the rule. The scripts that they asked me to consider were just *degrading*. To me, it was just anti everything: black, woman, human. They glorified drugs and violence, and the women were simply reduced to nothingness. It was very upsetting. At that time, I was a public school teacher. I had taught many children to be positive and believe in themselves: "Don't believe the hype about the projects and that you can't make it. Learn how to solve a problem without reverting to negativity and violence." I had taught thousands of kids by that time and I knew that those kids would not be able to decipher "Miss Taylor the actress" from "Miss Taylor the teacher." As soon as they saw those movies they would say, "Oh man, she's full of it. Look at that?!" Everything that I've taught, trained, and built in them would go out the door. I wasn't going to sacrifice my kids for that nonsense. It was stupid. It was racist. It was ignorant. I didn't want to perpetuate it.

What did you do instead?

I started a theater company because I wanted to do something. It was just not enough to say, "Oh, this is horrible!" I created a theater that would tell the truth about African American people, perpetuate the greatness of who we are, supply jobs within the community, deliver positive messages, and serve thousands of children and help them understand that they are somebody. They deserve the positive of life rather than the things that they were going through.

At the age of twenty-four you took out a five-thousand-dollar loan to start Black Ensemble Theater in 1976. Were you inspired by anybody at the time?

No, I wasn't inspired about anything. I wanted to start a theater company that would contribute to the community the way that I wanted to contribute to the community.

Many theaters don't make it, and you're celebrating your fortieth anniversary. What did you learn during those early years of operation?

I learned that theater was a business. That's the first thing that I learned. It's a business and in order to have a successful business, you have to have more money coming in than you have going out. That's the bottom line. The second thing was I needed to market it. I needed to promote it. Nobody's going to come if they don't know that it's there. I needed to be innovative in *how* I was going to market it, so I created stories. I created interest. I called the press. I let them know what I was doing and why I was doing it. I starred in the productions because at that time I had a very strong following as an actress. I had created a name and a buzz, so I used it. I remained visible and in the press for all kinds of stuff. I knew I needed people to support what I was doing or it wouldn't survive. I started building a board of directors at that time, and those were the first things that I actually learned.

How did the concept of theater as business influence the types of works produced at Black Ensemble Theater?

Well, at first, I thought, "What should I do?" The mission of the Black Ensemble is to eradicate racism. In order to do that, you cannot do that in a vacuum. You have to do that with audiences of all colors and kinds or you're talking to the choir. You're not going to get to a solution to the problem that way. So, I had to attract a diverse audience. At first, I started doing different kinds of theater like *A Raisin in the Sun*, and the actor Harry Lennix performed in *Julius Caesar*. Different things that we thought would attract a diverse audience. We did not. We did attract an audience. Our productions were very good and audiences loved it, but we weren't doing what the mission was. I kept trying to hit on what would attract a diverse audience, because before you can educate people, you have to get them in the room. So, I said, "Okay, what is diverse already?" Music crosses cultural boundaries, it brings people together, it does something to people, and it doesn't matter what color you are. Every person—no matter what language they're singing in—connects and relates to beautiful music. I said, "Okay, maybe we need to be doing music." We started with *The Other Cinderella* in 1976 and I played Cinderella. We still produce that every couple of years and it's always a big sellout.

After that, I went into traditional theater. I had a friend who came to me about an idea of *Muddy Waters: The Hoochie-Coochie Man*. He had written the script for his high school. I took the script, rewrote it, and said, "You know, the blues has cross-cultural boundaries. It is embraced by both black and white." *Muddy Waters* would be a good idea. So, I produced *Muddy Waters: The Hoochie-Coochie Man*, and that was 1984. The theater totally sold out to a mixed audience. It was like, "Where did they come from? Okay, we've hit on something here." Then I said, "Let me try this again." I produced *The Otis Redding Story* and *again*, I found [success]. Black people: we're wonderful. Everybody wants to know and experience our history. We don't embrace ourselves, our greatness, and our history the way we should, but other people do. Which is a shame, but it's true. That's when I said, "Okay, we're going to continue to produce musicals. We're going to deliver in our musicals messages that will show the humanity of who we are and will demonstrate the commonalities of who we are and help us to respect each other." That was our genre. People loved our musicals. People always comment that they feel so good when they leave Black Ensemble Theater. They feel inspired. They feel uplifted.

You noticed in those early days how people communicated with each other. Usually when people go into the theater, they communicate with whoever they're with. They sit there and they're in their comfort [zone], but our productions: people started to connect to each other. They started to look at each other. They started to talk to each other. They became a community, because it was the same people coming over and over. Then you noticed that after the production, people stopped in the lobby and started talking about something they saw in the play. "I didn't know that black people went through that." "Oh girl, that wasn't even the half of it!" This is good. We're on the right track. That's how we started producing musicals that would facilitate transformation.

Now, today we have not only me as a playwright. I have a group of twenty playwrights called Black Playwrights Initiative who write specifically for the Black Ensemble Theater so that all the plays can help us to achieve our mission and to give people what they come to expect at the Black Ensemble Theater. There's a wealth of product. There's a wealth of talent. We're building a second theater so that we'll keep our basic product of the musical, but there's all kinds of ways to explore how to do this now. We want to experiment. I liken Black Ensemble Theater to a business like a McDonald's hamburger. McDonald's has a franchise, and no matter what's going to happen you're always going to get a McDonald's hamburger. They're never going to take that off their menu. But they've learned to add a McFlurry shake during Irish time and add McRibs during special times and put some salad on there because the parents need something. They've learned how to diversify their product and that has helped them to strengthen. I want Black Ensemble Theater to diversify because that's going to help not only attract a new audience but also strengthen the kind of product that we have to offer.

Do you believe that you faced particular challenges as a black woman navigating theater of the 1970s?

As a black woman, I'm navigating right now [*laughs*]. I learned very quickly that I was considered a second-class citizen by the country and a third-class citizen by my people, as a woman. I learned that very quickly.

But I wasn't second-class to nobody and neither was I third-class. I was first-class all the way and if you didn't see it, that's your damn problem! I made no excuses. I played no games. I shot from the hips and if you thought I was an angry black woman, that's your damn problem! Because just like you have a reason to feel how you feel, I have a reason to feel how I feel. I'm not going to allow you to use your ignorance and your prejudices to subdue or stop me from doing what I need to do. So yes, I had to *navigate*, but I wasn't playing no games. I wasn't acting like, "Oh, I'm this kind of woman" or "Oh, I'm not that smart" or "Oh, please help me." You know, stupid shit. No. Anybody that you ask: they will tell you I have always been quite upfront, honest, and I don't hold no punches. I call it the way I see it and if you don't like it: fuck you.

How did people respond to that?

Some people were offended: "How dare you?!" Some people were very racist and thought, "Who the hell do you think you are?" Then some people embraced it.

I would have been one of those that embraced it. I love it.

Shirley Faison

Shirley Faison notes that Barbara Ann Teer also encountered challenges as a black woman artist and theater founder. Yet Faison ultimately remembers Teer as a visionary who would not allow others to marginalize her.

Do you feel that Barbara Ann Teer faced particular challenges as a black woman artist working in Harlem during this time?

She did face particular challenges, but what she did was she legitimatized Harlem as the cultural capital of the world. What she talked about was the opulence of Fifth Avenue. That's one of the main reasons why she built NBT and then put African artwork in front of it: to make a statement. Not everyone in Harlem was as committed as she was to making

Harlem a particular way. Some people sold out a little bit . . . or a lot. One of the council members—I think it was Congressman Rangel—called her a samurai at her memorial service. He talked about how she told him, "You go out there and do that and let me make the noise." So, she would make noise for them. She would say what needed to be said so that she would show up like the kook. But it needed to be said.

Was she influenced by other theaters?

No. She knew all of them, but she was doing something different. She wasn't doing the same thing everybody else was doing. Now people talk about touching the audience and stuff like that, but back then that was like . . . "Okay?" She was innovative. She was different. She did it before Diana Ross said, "Reach out and touch somebody's hand" in Central Park.[7] She touched people there, but this is before all of that.

She was ahead of her time.

Very much so.

It sounds like some people misconstrued what she was doing. Some even attempted to marginalize her, but she resisted.

She wouldn't allow anyone to marginalize her. She was a force.

Sonia Sanchez mentioned that she watched productions at NBT. Do you recall any other black cultural leaders and artists visiting the theater?

Harry Belafonte, Patti LaBelle, Gil Scott-Heron, and I remember Stokely Carmichael came. Sometimes you didn't know who was there. The other thing we used to do back then were symposiums every Sunday. Anybody who was doing something in the world was there on a Sunday. We presented them to the Harlem community, and they would get to sit, talk, and sing.

NBT also offered performance classes. Could you explain what those were like?

I was from Massachusetts and a little bit uptight. I remember that the classes allowed me to loosen up, to actually move this part of my body. They dealt with a lot of things at the workshops regarding relationships and the Five Cycles of Evolution. There was Teer Technology of Soul, where you were able to be bold and fearless in your presentation. It was life changing, the ability to be bold and fearless. The ability to actually communicate with people and not worry about what they think about me.

Ntozake Shange

The creative work done at Teer's NBT also influenced the development of Ntozake Shange.

I went to Barnard College, which is at 116th Street and Broadway, and the National Black Theatre was on 125th Street, so I could walk to it. It was close to the Apollo Theater [opened 1914]. I used to go to the Apollo every Saturday morning for the children's shows because they were half price, and I used to go on Wednesday night because it was amateur night, so I'd be up in the neighborhood. I would go up there to the National Black Theatre because they were involved in ritual and unmasking the mystery of African movement and storytelling. So, as opposed to having us hear Uncle Remus stories, you would hear stories about the achievement of Hussain or the elder and his daughter or the mother of the clan and her daughters or the wives of so-and-so. We would hear stories from them as characters as opposed from animals who were supposed to be people. It was one of the first times I had an opportunity to hear history from a folkloric point of view that was not condescending or paternalistic.

Micki Grant

Micki Grant lived and worked in New York City at the same time as Teer. Although the two never collaborated together, Grant did cultivate a longtime working relationship with another important black woman institution builder: Vinnette Carroll.

The person with whom I accomplished the most was, of course, Vinnette Carroll. We did at least six productions or more together. We brought each other to Broadway.

How did you two meet?

Glory Van Scott, who was a singer, was doing some of my work in her solo shows and she was also doing a piece for Vinnette Carroll. Vinnette had an Off-Broadway theater called the Urban Arts Corps. When Glory mentioned me, she said, "Micki Grant is an actress, but you should hear what she's writing. She writes songs as well." So, Vinnette asked me to come down and I came down. I took my guitar and played two or three songs and that's it.

Can you tell me what kind of director she was, in terms of her process?

Vinnette was a wonderful actress who didn't want to act. You've probably seen her if you've watched some of these old movies. She would amuse me. She would say something in a rhythm that she wanted you to do. She was very expressive, and I guess that came from the acting part that was in her that she always claimed she didn't want to do for herself. But whenever she got the opportunity, she did a couple of great movies.

Vinnette Carroll passed not too long ago, so I can't ask her questions about her life. What do you think people should know and remember about her work as a director, actress, or theater founder?

Well, she was an actress, so she brought that to her directing. If you're an actress, you know what emotions are and what you're looking for more so than a person who hasn't. So, she could see things in people that they maybe couldn't even see in themselves. I can't remember her name, but she was a buxom actress. Vinnette gave the buxom actress in one of the shows the love song. You would think that she's going to give it to the person who was light and slender, but she gave it to a woman who had curves instead. Actually, she went on to get her own TV show later.

So, Carroll worked against type and in so doing gave people opportunities that they otherwise would not have had.

Yes. Several people who came out of the Corps became very successful: Phylicia Rashad, Debbie Allen, Reggie VelJohnson, and Richard "Dickie" Evans. I call them the "babies" because they started at the Corps and you didn't know where they were going.

Nora Cole

Nora Cole also remembers Carroll as a significant force in her life. The training she received at the Corps continues to inform her work as an actress and director.

They brought Vinnette Carroll in as a guest artist during my second year at the Goodman School of Drama. Of the three years I was enrolled as a student, they had about six or seven black students. That was the most black students they had ever had, so they thought, "We need to do something for them." They brought Vinnette in to do a workshop in 1975, but the workshop was not just with us; it was also with second-year students and grad students. We worked on *The Crucible* [1953]. Vinnette liked big dramas and *The Crucible* is a big drama. So, within this workshop, I was Elizabeth Proctor and my husband was white, so it was all mixed up. We barely got to finish it because she had to leave for another project, but that is how I met Vinnette. That is how Charlayne Woodard met Vinnette. Charlayne was a year behind me, and she ended up doing *Don't Bother Me, I Can't Cope* [1971]. Vinnette said, "Well, when you graduate, come to New York. Come to the Corps."

I moved to New York on my birthday the fall of 1976. I knew Vinnette, a musician that used to play with George Vincent, and my friend Joseph Bigelow. Joseph had been a costume-design student at the Goodman, but he got kicked out because he did a project outside of school. He had a loft down in SoHo right at Canal and Sixth Avenue. I stayed there for six months, and within two weeks I was working on *The Ups and Downs of Theophilus Maitland* with Vinnette. After being taught a cockney and an Irish and a standard British dialect I had to do a West Indian dialect. I had no concept of that.

You've worked with incredible black women directors and theater founders. Glenda Dickerson, Rosetta LeNoire at AMAS Repertory Theatre, and Vinnette Carroll at the Urban Arts Corps. Could you share some of your memorable experiences working with these women?

I spent fifteen years with Vinnette. I was twenty-three when I moved to New York, and you are still a baby in their eyes. You grow from the relationship of parent-child to director to collaborator to artist. And what do you know? Because I would say, "I'm not making any money." And my dad was like, "Well, but you know it's Vinnette Carroll, so you better stick with her." Vinnette was a taskmaster. She could be brutal. I mean *brutal* in the rehearsal space. We would rehearse for hours and hours. One time the stage manager tried to remind her about a break, because you're supposed to have a five-minute break. She lit into him and hollered and screamed, and he was about this tall by the time [she finished]. So, Vinnette always had stage managers that knew her temperament. We're on a showcase code, so you get paid car fare.[8] We rehearse and rehearse and rehearse and not always with a performance date in sight because she's developing a piece. One of the showcase codes is you can rehearse for four weeks and you can do Thursday through Sunday for four weeks. But when Vinnette was ready to let the public in, it was packed [*slaps hands*]. People would be lined up. The Corps was housed in a tiny space, but people would be lined up and she could create the most amazing material. She could put together a company. What Vinnette would do is she would audition people. If she wanted to hear you sing she would say, "Well, just sing 'Happy Birthday.'" I don't really sing that well. Vinnette loved really good singers. She loved really good actors. During the rehearsal period, she would weed people out. So, you show up to rehearsal one day and say, "Where's Jonathan?" He didn't get a call. Jonathan's not here anymore. It would just crush actors because it's not like you would get excused in any kind of formal way. You just never heard from them.

Why did she do that? That's not the traditional way of making theater.

As much of a taskmaster and as hard as she could be, she didn't like confrontation. She left that to somebody else and she didn't want to deal with that.

She left that task to, say, the stage manager maybe?

Stage manager or her head administrator. She never had more than two people working in her office. Vinnette could've just lived in a rehearsal room directing for the rest of her life. That's what she loved to do: just be in a rehearsal room and develop.

So, for her it was about the process even more than the finished product?

Ultimately, yes.

Let's talk more about the process of working with her. You sing "Happy Birthday," you get cast, and you may or may not maintain that role. What was she looking for at that point in her performers?

She would shift people around. At one point, she said to me, "Just learn the whole script." And I learned the whole script. In *Theophilus* I was the Obeah Woman. I had to learn this African chant in a dialect [*chants*]. Then it would go into this dance, and we're in this tiny theater. We've got musicians. There's a choreographer. She would just painstakingly, scene by scene, work through things. At one point, we were like, "We're gonna get Vinnette a chessboard with little figures on it so that she can go home and play with them." Because we would be on our feet for hours and hours. "Move over here. No, move over there." But by the time we finished, everybody knew the whole show so well, which is why Vinnette could make changes during intermission of shows.

When you're performing in front of a live audience?!

Yes, she would. *Your Arms Too Short to Box with God* was a big show that opened on Broadway in 1976. Vinnette was good at developing raw talent. That show had real gospel singers in it who weren't used to doing the discipline of theater and eight shows a week, but Vinnette whipped them into shape and it was amazing. Delores Hall . . .

She won a Tony Award for best featured actress.

I just [loved] everything about it: the choreography. That show went to Broadway three times. Jennifer Holliday did *Your Arms Too Short to Box with God* in 1980 before she did *Dreamgirls* in 1981.

So, she could spot talent a mile away.

Oh, yes.

It sounds like you also had that raw talent when you came to New York and Vinnette Carroll really cultivated that.

Yes. I was not planning to sing at all. I thought, "Oh, that's something I'll do in my thirties. I'll do a club act or something." I was not trained for that, but with Vinnette, with youth, and just as an actor you're taught to never say, "I can't," you learn how to do it and you come back. If you want to do a Vinnette show you've got to sing. She would ask dancers to sing "Happy Birthday" or actors that really couldn't sing. Most of her pieces had dance and a music component. Almost anything I did with Vinnette she had done earlier versions of before. So, I didn't do *Box* until the eighties.

I have you down as doing at least three shows with her: The Ups and Downs of Theophilus Maitland *[1976],* Your Arms Too Short to Box with God *[1977], and* Alice *[also titled* But Never Jam Today *(1979)]. What other shows did you work on together?*

Vinnette—and other writers do this too—recycled shows. Like *Theophilus.* When I did it years later in Florida it was called *I'm Laughing but I Ain't Tickled* [1976]. Now, *I'm Laughing But I Ain't Tickled* was another show that was poetry and song.

You write in your article, "She influenced me as a director before I ever knew I could direct."[9] *Could you tell me more about that?*

Vinnette could make ten people onstage look like fifty. She loved the old Busby Berkeley movies. She would make a third act out of her curtain calls. Just having people coming and going and doing and entering. She was an amazing stager. I learned a lot about staging from her. As harsh as she could be—you could go onstage an emotional wreck from the rehearsing and just spent—I always trusted her eye. I never doubted her direction. As an actor, it taught me how to direct myself when I did other projects with directors that weren't as talented. If I was going to do the project I knew how to get the best out of my performance and save what I presented even if it wasn't a very well-directed piece.

How did her previous experiences as an actress shape her directing methods?

By the time I met Vinnette she had established her career, had almost gotten a Ph.D. in psychology, and had people in her first companies a good twenty, thirty years my senior. She had been through it with actors and developing pieces and dealing with personalities. So, I was in the last group of Corps Kids. There were many more before me.

Alice was a show that we did. We would also rehearse and rehearse to do presentations for producers. We'd put on a really good show and then we'd go home and think, "Do you think they're gonna pick it up?" We did that for a couple of years with *Alice*. Then we got called down to the theater one day. We did a presentation but didn't know that we were auditioning for our roles. The Actors' Equity Association rules have changed since then because of situations like that. The producers Mike Nichols and Lou Allen wanted the show but they wanted Debbie Allen, Paula Kelly, Jane White, and Alice Ghostley in it. Most of us either ended up understudying the roles that we had created or just weren't in it. You didn't get a contract for it. That's not legal today. Now, there are really no more showcases. They do workshops, but now there are these different tiers and you have to sign off on things. Actors started getting part of a percentage of the profits once [collaborative productions like] *A Chorus Line* [1975] made money. That whole development process for *Chorus Line* was people telling their stories. Dancers telling their stories in the rehearsal and then them taking it and adapting or rewriting or tweaking it.

Do you know how Vinnette Carroll felt about that?

She knew that if she was going to get *Alice* produced that's what she was going to have to do. And she wasn't thrilled. Jane White was thirty years my senior, and she performed the role that I had been building. I was an emotional mess because I didn't get it. How could this happen? But I got my union card with that show. There are white contracts and there are pink contracts. White contracts are principal roles. Pink contracts are chorus roles. What Vinnette did—which I did not understand for many years—was get me a white contract for a role I'd never heard of: the Red Queen. There hadn't been a Red Queen before. Vinnette had a Black and a White Queen in the show. There was a Red Queen in the novel *Alice's Adventures in Wonderland* [1865]. The first day of the rehearsal, after the table read, it was like, "Oh, that role is cut." But I was still on a white contract and I still got white contract money.

She engineered that for you.

[*Nods*] But I was crying in rehearsal every day. I had to go to the rehearsals with Jane White and watch her rehearse. And I didn't understand. I was so green. But that was a huge emotional experience for everybody.

She needed the show to get produced, but it also sounds like she was looking out for you.

Yes. Vinnette could just be comfortable in a rehearsal room and rehearse. She didn't want anybody to see her productions until she's ready. Well, she wouldn't even let the producers see. I'll never know what happened between Vinnette and producers, but I know she never had a great relationship with them. When the hammer came down it was like: the show is closing. It was never pretty.

For her? Or for you?

For everybody because everybody loses a job. By the time we do *Alice* you've made an investment of about two years. When I did *When Hell Freezes Over I'll Skate* at the John F. Kennedy Center for the Performing Arts, we were less than two weeks out of going to Broadway. The producer was Michael Stevens, and he was running the Kennedy Center. That really blindsided us when we went in to go do the show and the company manager says, "Here's your paycheck. Here's your train ticket home Sunday. Show's closing."

Is this partially due to a lack of communication between Carroll and her producers?

That's something either Micki Grant or Anita McShane could answer because I don't know. I'm sure there were times when there were changes that Vinnette did not want to make but the producers probably wanted her to make. I know that to be a fact. And the people who are putting money up for your show; you can't keep them out. Vinnette was like, "They can't come to the theater. Don't let them in." Part of it I'm sure was Vinnette's personality and part of it I'm sure was that she was playing with the big boys.

In your 2012 article "Vinnette Carroll: The First Black Woman Broadway Director," you write, "I could never lose sight of the fact the she was a Black woman in a very elite, White circle. She played with the big boys. She had few properties and they had everything else, namely money and theaters."[10] *How did she negotiate her interests as a black woman director and theater founder within these elite white circles?*

Well, ultimately she didn't. Vinnette burned a lot of bridges other than Frankie Hewitt. I don't know if that ever went sour or not. Frankie Hewitt is the one that first produced *Your Arms Too Short to Box with God* at the Ford's Theatre in Washington, D.C., in 1975. Her relationship with producers never ended well, and that meant shows closed. When I did *Your Arms Too Short to Box with God* in Paris [during the mideighties], the producers that had produced the tour that I had done before and produced it on Broadway the third time were going to sue her for taking the show to Europe because they had planned to take the show to Europe. I remember hearing that.

So, legalities were not her strong point.

Yes. Well, I think she might have . . . that's where you get into real legal stuff. We only did it in Paris; that's not all of Europe.

I don't know if you can answer this, but why did she choose to play with the big boys? Why not go the route of someone like Barbara Ann Teer?

Barbara Ann Teer never took a show to Broadway. Barbara Ann Teer never did a national tour.[11]

Did she ever discuss with you the possibility of performing in Harlem, rather than Broadway? Was that ever a possibility?

I was not familiar with Barbara Ann Teer. When the National Black Theatre came along and I started hearing her name, I took a friend of mine. I was like, "You know we need to go up there and see a show. We need to support them." So, there was this show that ran for a long time. We went up to see the show. It was terrible.

Why was it "terrible"?

It was community theater. And it was not good community theater. Aesthetically it was not . . . and I'm a little biased because I know Barbara Ann Teer has gotten all this attention in later years when people have died out and everything. Barbara Ann Teer was not competitive at all with what Vinnette was doing or Douglas Turner Ward or Rosetta LeNoire or Ellen Stewart or even Ernie McClintock, who was further uptown in Harlem than even Barbara Ann Teer was. Also, her theater company was based around a kind of cult. And it was about that and the theater that came out of it as opposed to the kind of theater that the other black theaters were doing. If something happening was really good, it would draw producers in.

Even at black theaters?

Not "even at." Surely at black theaters. That's how *for colored girls who have considered suicide/when the rainbow is enuf* developed.

Was it important to Carroll to have black audiences at the Corps?

Yes. She was connected to AUDELCO [Audience Development Committee]. When AUDELCO first started out in 1973, these were black theater buffs. They went to see everything. There weren't a lot of them. They would call Vivian Robinson, and she would get a whole lot of black people there. You're not dealing with computers or even radio announcements. It's word-of-mouth and flyers if you have them. I still don't worry about audience development. I don't care if there are three people in the audience. I'm rehearsing. I'm doing what I'm supposed to do. That's somebody else's job. People in Vinnette's office got on the phone and there were always audiences there. I was always amazed that the theater was always packed.

Aduke Aremu

While Carroll's lack of communication may have led to tumultuous working relationships with her producers, Aduke Aremu used her strong interpersonal skills, charm, and business savvy to build a strong network of support as she navigated her interests as a black woman theater company founder.

The first musical director of the Harlem Children's Theatre Company was Robert Williams. He's a very old-school jazz musician and he was hanging out with Marcus Miller, who was very young. All of these guys began to work with me musically, so I was able to create musical sounds in my theater that were professional. So, the Harlem Children's Theatre Company was not a kiddy company; it was a real sophisticated musical-driven colorful collection of young people. They never wanted to be called kids, because that was not who they were. They were young performers. Some of them were as young as seven and went up to thirty-five. A lot of them never left. They just came back doing different things.

You graduate from Hunter College, travel to Africa, return to New York, and found the Harlem Children's Theatre Company. Tell me about your experiences founding the Harlem Children's Theatre Company.

We got back from Africa and formed the Harlem Children's Theatre Company. I became the artistic director and the writer. Myrna Belgrave Simmons was the costume designer and the arts person, and the two of us went to it. We went to a gentleman by the name of Mical Whitaker, who is a director-playwright. Harlem was controlled by Mical Whitaker, Ernie McClintock, Woodie King Jr., Barbara Ann Teer, and Roger Furman. These were the companies. We were the young kids on the block.

Would you also include someone like Robert Macbeth in that list?

They were all there. The Weusi Artist Collective building was up. That's the artists: Ademola Olugebefola, Otto Neals, and Abdul Rahman. We were the young setters. We were twenty-one. We were very politely aggressive. We went to their theaters and introduced ourselves. We went to their meetings. We talked to Ed Bullins. Roger Furman fell in love with me. Roger Furman and Ed Bullins were like, "Who is this kid? My God, who are these people?" Our flyers were phenomenal looking. Myrna's brother was a graphic artist and professional who worked on Wall Street. He did all of our flyers, so they were state of the art and on colored paper. Myrna and I would take a glue gun, go throughout Harlem, and put our stuff on every door.

So, people started looking for us. "What is the Harlem Children's Theatre Company?" We were working out of a school in Harlem. We had hundreds of kids because we're not charging any money. Tamlyn Bey was in my original group of kids because I taught him in East Harlem. Tamlyn Bey has now become a famous artist. So, a lot of my kids—there were hundreds of them—came out of East Harlem and were making names for themselves. One of my kids, James Bond III, got picked up on my stage and went straight to Hollywood. My kids were getting picked up because I was training them. We were just relentless, training during the week, on Friday night, all day Saturday (sometimes until midnight), and Sunday after church. We were training in every art form.

What did your training look like?

We believed in all of them: music, dance, drama, and art. All the kids had to do all of it and that was our motto. We were working out of a school. This principal, Mrs. Lipton, thought we were deep and she gave us her school. We didn't have any money. We were doing shows at the school and anywhere else that we got invited. We had costumes. They were like, "How are these people getting costumes? They don't have any money."

How did you acquire costumes?

Myrna was a costume designer. She would go out and beg up stuff and we would sew. We had fabulous costuming. We had music people that we were working with. The whole Spanish community supported us. There was a settlement house in East Harlem that took us over. We did shows there. Mical Whitaker was very supportive of us. He was the one who formed my first board of directors. Him and Roger Furman said, "Girls, you all got to get organized. Now, come on. You have to have a board of directors." So, we got a board. Our board of directors had thirty people on it. Everybody in New York was on my board. I had Roger Furman, Mical Whitaker, politicians, all my church ministers, Mary Pinkett. Mical Whitaker went out and got famous black radio hosts. Everybody: Vaughn Harper, Mel Wolford, and all the nightclub owners were on my board. These are my big brothers. I'm this skinny little black girl running around doing theater for young people, which they thought was just fabulous. They didn't realize it was going to become serious. They were like, "Oh, this is so cute!" So, whenever we needed to do a fundraiser, I would get Leviticus for free. You remember Leviticus? This big nightclub owned by these powerful black people. You see, I had just studied in Africa. So how do you do it? You create a tribe! It's not about one woman—even though I did emerge as a playwright and became very renowned—it's about a tribe. The tribe protects you. The tribe gives you money. The tribe brings in the dowry.

Is Barbara Ann Teer a part of your tribe?

Yes, she was with me. We did the peace meeting at her house in Harlem. Barbara said, "I would like for you to join National Black Theatre and become . . ." I said, "I don't want to become part of National Black Theatre. I want to call it the Harlem Children's Theatre Company. We're going to have our own company, but we love you. We're friends. We're just all going to be together, Barbara, but we're not joining anybody. We have our own vision. We know what we want to do here." They all offered me space and partnership. We said, "No, we're good." They're like, "How could you be good? You got one hundred kids and you're running around . . . What kind of foolishness is this? Aduke has tribes of kids onstage!" I had one hundred kids on stage at a time in groups. First group, first song; fifty of them. There were tribes of them. Every kid who ever did anything was on my stage. They knew they were going to sing, dance, act, and they loved it. What happened? I made a decision because we used to do think tanks. We would sit around just like we're doing now.

Who's "we"?

Me, Myrna, Mical Whitaker, and all of us. We'd sit around and say, "What's the next level?" Remember: we're very disciplined. I was always the one saying, "Meeting! What's next? We can't stay in this school forever. We need a space. And guess where we're moving? We're going to Forty-Second Street." Everybody said, "What are you doing? You're going out of Harlem?" I said, "The Harlem Children's Theatre Company is our name and it's our spirit, but we don't have to be in Harlem. We're universal. We're world performers. Harlem Children's Theatre Company is where *we are*. It is not the location!" It was controversial. I had a meeting with Roger Furman, and he said, "Where are you all going?" I said, "We're going to Forty-Second Street." Why? We've just been offered this phenomenal space for what? A hundred dollars a month in this big office building. Now, the Anglo-Saxons are looking at us because of all my board of directors. I have Dr. Kevin Cahill, who was one of the richest doctors in New York—he was Governor Mario Cuomo's doctor and the doctor for the pope—on my board. Kevin Cahill loved me. When I went to Africa the first time, I got sick. I picked up parasites, and I looked in a book and Dr. Kevin Cahill came up as the top tropical disease specialist in New York. I went to his office to be cured—which took only a month—and convinced him to be on my board. He became one of my mentors and put a lot of money in my company. He was deep. He was

Irish American. It's all God and the spirits. It has nothing to do with Aduke. Dr. Kevin Cahill and I had the meetings in his office, which is on Fifth Avenue. He is giving me advice and he brings Governor Mario Cuomo on my board. Cuomo then hires me to be a commissioner in New York. While I'm teaching, I'm a commissioner too. All of my political people are now coming together. I have the Anglo-Saxons, the African Americans, and the Caribbeans (Brooklyn is a Caribbean stronghold). I'm very close to Myrna, who is Barbadian.

So, we go to Forty-Second Street! Myrna decides she's going back to Africa; I lose her. Myrna goes back to live in Nigeria. She is really a cultural nationalist. She became head of the Education Division in Barbados. I was the talker. I was the one that went out and talked to the people. She didn't do that; but she could. She's powerful. She had powerful contacts in the Caribbean community and the government. I was the one who went out bold and daring. After I had lassoed the cow, Myrna would come. Together we made a phenomenal team. Then she left, and I accidently picked up my administrator (who is now my best friend), Dawn Alli. I said it's all God-driven, because I'm living in Brooklyn running this theater by myself now. I met Dawn because she was the wife of my boyfriend's best friend. My boyfriend's a very wealthy guy out of Newark, and that's how I meet Imamu Baraka [Amiri Baraka]. Now I'm connected with Imamu Baraka and all of them because my boyfriend was part of the Jersey Black Arts Movement. So, they're coming to visit me and I'm looking at this young woman. She was very bright. I'm always minding other people's business. I said, "First of all: two things. You need to go back to school and get a degree. How old are you? You're what, twenty? You're going to work for me and I'm going to give you a salary." The theater went a whole different direction. A fabulous direction, but it changed.

People don't understand that success—especially for us in the black diaspora—comes from our interpersonal power. I believe that as a people, we're very powerful spiritually and intellectually. But that's the power that you can't give away. When you lose your connectiveness as a group of people, you lose your power. You have to stay connected, because each of us has such tremendous gifts and these gifts multiply when we come together. The Harlem Children's Theatre Company was always run as an ensemble company, even though I was like the Pied Piper. It was run in an ensemble concept. Totally.

What was the mission of the Harlem Children's Theatre Company?

The mission was to change the world. To convince the world that children's theater—especially black children's theater—is intricate in every black child's life. That they have to be exposed to the arts at a high level because the arts develops their creative intuitiveness. Howard Gardner talks about this and he came out of Harvard University. He talked about the multiple intelligences. Black people have multiple intelligences and sometimes they're not recognizable. Some of my most gifted kids started out with academic difficulties. Teachers would call me up and say, "Aduke, can you do something with this child?" They were gifted beyond belief and they needed—just like I had needed for my little interesting personality—an outlet. When I was ten or eleven, my mother had the wisdom to allow me to blossom. I had a hundred things I was doing. I had all my clubs. She allowed me to be free intellectually and culturally and I developed into who I am. That's what my mission was in life and still is. I believe in busting the door open. I'm a revolutionary. That's what that training was. If they say no, you keep going until they say yes.

You mentioned that you knew J.e. Franklin and were familiar with her work.

I read her play *Black Girl*. I see J.e. Franklin a lot. When you're in this business of the arts, you run across people. We have had conversations. In fact, we've been on panels together, but we're not budding friends. In this world, some people you're very close with, others you have a casual relationship with. I try not to make enemies. I try to basically be the "every child." In other words, relationships are really important to me. I believe in lots of dialogue, lots of food. When I went to Africa, I saw how these empires were built. It's a conglomeration of teams of people with specialties, and everybody stays in their area of specialty but they work as a collective. So, when I went to meetings with my team, a lot of times I didn't even talk. I let them talk. "What are we going to do next? What do you think?"

So, we're doing productions all over the city. Anybody invites us, we go. I wrote the play *The Liberation of Mother Goose* [1973], which became my signature piece in my career. It caught on. I began to get funded because of Ellis Haizlip, who became my godfather. I went to his Channel 13 office and sat with him. I put on my best clothes—you know me. I had on this brown coat. I'll never forget because I love costuming clothes and I was good at it. I went in and he said, "Only twenty-two and you come in here looking like you're related to Jackie Onassis. Sit down. I'm going to get you funded. What I'm going to do for the next five years is I'm going to mentor your company." I said, "You've got to be kidding." I didn't know him from Adam. Meanwhile, I had Roger Furman mentoring me. So, they all joined forces.

You go to the tribal elders to get clearance; they gave me clearance. I met with the kingpins Ernie McClintock, Roger Furman, Voza Rivers, and Woodie King Jr. As a black woman, I had enough common sense to meet with the men. I was a lady. I said, "Listen, things I'm not interested in: sex, drugs, or crazy stuff." That's Aduke. I don't take drugs and I'm not perverted. I said, "So, if those fit then we're cool." I was real fresh. "I can do all of it but those three things are off-limits. I don't care who you are. I don't care what you do. I don't care what your religion is. I don't care what your sexual preference is. I don't care if you're a drug addict. I don't care. Just, I'm not one." I really blessed them—Woodie and Roger and Voza—because they gave me the green light to be a phenomenal producer-writer. You got to have people who pat you on the back and say, "Go for it, girl." I would run things by them, and I followed their advice.

Then something happened. Theatre Row, which was up the block [in what] is now a famous area between Ninth and Eleventh Avenue, was looking for theater companies to move in there. The whole area was full of prostitutes and whatnot. They were going to renovate a theater district on Forty-Second Street. They asked me if I wanted to be one of the companies. So, what happened when we went to Forty-Second Street? A lot of powerful people starting backing us. I went to D.C. and met with Vantile Whitfield and told him, "I know I'm doing young people theater and I know you're all funding theater. I need to be funded." He said, "How much?" I said, "If you could give me around twenty thousand dollars, I'd appreciate it." And he gave it to me. You know Peter Bailey? Peter Bailey was the "Prince of Journalism." Every time I opened a show, Peter Bailey put me on the cover of the *New York Amsterdam News*. Once the *Amsterdam* picked it up, all the other newspapers followed suit. Then Ellis Haizlip got us money and contacts.

Aduke Aremu with the Harlem Children's Theatre Company at the Second World Black African Festival of Art and Culture (FESTAC), Nigeria, 1977. Courtesy of Aduke Aremu.

We went to Nigeria to do the Second World [Black] African Festival of Art and Culture [FESTAC] in 1977. [*Pointing to framed poster on wall*] That's us up there. We led the parade and Barbara Ann Teer was on that plane. All the other companies went to FESTAC. Robert Williams was still with us. He led the parade playing the trumpet and all my fifty kids marched in. That's the photo. The Nigerians have it in their embassy. They said they had never seen anything like it. I had fifty kids marching, singing. We placed at the National Stadium. Reggie Life directed it. He was a fabulous director. John Parks was the choreographer, and he was with Alvin Ailey. I always took the best people.

Which show did you bring to Nigeria?

The Liberation of Mother Goose. It was touring everywhere. I'd say, "I've written four more plays." [They'd say,] "We want *Mother Goose.*" Nigeria was the turning point for us in terms of color. I got to see hundreds of dance companies from all over the world. I met Ademola Olugebefola on the plane. I sat in the front with all my kids, and everybody else was in the plane in the back. Nigeria was a phenomenal experience.

We went from Forty-Second Street to the Apollo Theater. We did performances every Saturday for three months at the Apollo. All my plays that were written were done: *JuJu Man* [ca. 1973], *Babylon* [ca. 1973], and *The Liberation of Mother Goose*. That's when I won the AUDELCO for *Babylon*. I hired everybody. Pat Cummings did my graphics. Myrna Colley-Lee, who married Morgan Freeman, was my set designer. I had The Brewery Troupe [est. 1973] doing puppets in some of my productions. I believed in collective. I had tremendous artistic people on my team. When we left the Apollo, we went into Douglas Turner Ward's Negro Ensemble Company [NEC]. I sat with Douglas, told him what I needed, and he gave me the theater for free. Yes, he did.

Why?

I don't know! He liked me. He said, "You're very bright! You're working fifteen hours every Saturday." Every Saturday from seven in the morning until midnight I was in a theater. I never saw the sun on Saturday. This went on for years. They knew how hard I was working. So, Douglas said, "What do you need?" I said, "I need your theater. I don't perform anywhere that's not fabulous for my people." I was very fresh. "I want to be at NEC." He said, "Why?" I said, "Because you're fabulous and I want to be here, too." He gave me the theater. Fred Garrett was the point man. Fred said, "How much money do you have?" I said, "Well, I think our entire budget is gone by now." Fred said, "Aduke . . ." But you got to be cute, too. Now, this is the female thing. I had on red platform shoes, bell-bottom hip-hugging jeans, a halter, and a straw hat because I had just got back from the Virgin Islands. That's how I went in to see them. I was always like that. I said, "I just got back from the Virgin Islands. I'm sorry I didn't have time to really change. I hope I'm okay." That was my interview and outfit with Douglas Turner Ward. I think we talked for three hours.

Now, could you have gone home and changed?

Yes, I could have. I was a femme fatale. I believed that, as a woman, we have certain abilities that you need to utilize. It's kind of like those European divas or African women. They know who they are. So, you use that. Not for sexual favors, which is what I called low-level feminine ability, but you use your charm and your femininity, and a man could never say no to a lady. Be honest. How is a real man going to say no to a woman? It doesn't work like that in the norm of human being. All of them knew what I knew, and I would say, "I know you're going to really . . ." Douglas said, "You got it." We used to talk a lot after that. We became friends. I said, "I love your work. I'm teaching your work and I'm producing your work onstage." I did *Day of Absence* [1965] so much. I love that play. I was teaching at Essex County College in Jersey. I had a lot of college adjunct positions, and I always directed his play. I liked the whole symbolic thing he did. Fred Garrett orchestrated [my productions at NEC]. My plays came in: sold out. I never had an unsold-out audience in my life. People just loved what they saw.

Edgar White. That's who I loved! He was this strange esoteric playwright, so I used a lot of his work. Edgar White's plays were deep. They were not like the regular mama drama: "Oh, I saw your mama. Where was she?" None of that. Edgar White was experimenting with art forms, and that's what I did: illusion, metaphors, language. White was my kind of playwright.

The Billie Holiday Theatre needs a lot of credit. Every play I wrote was opened at the Billie Holiday Theatre. There was a woman there by the name of Toni Brabham. Marjorie Moon replaced her, but Toni Brabham was the one who brought all of my plays into the Billie. Her thing was, "When you write a new play, I'm the first theater that gets it." That was our contract with her.

Did you ever work with Marjorie Moon?

Yes, I did. On and off. Then I go see *The River Niger* [1972] by Joseph Walker at Demi-Gods and lost my natural artistic mind. I said, "Joseph Walker is bad." I went backstage and said, "Listen, you don't know me. I'm with the Harlem Children's Theatre Company." He said, "I know who you are." I said, "I want everything you got. I want your choreographers. I'm getting ready to go into the Public Theater." Ellis Haizlip had orchestrated me going into the Public Theater with Novella Nelson. Ellis Haizlip is mentoring me and he is selecting my venues. Mical Whitaker is no longer with me. We're changing artistic teams. We're moving into a different direction. So, the person who comes on board musically is

Jimmy Justice. He used to work with Harold Wheeler on Broadway and was one of the most famous and incredible composers in New York City. I wanted Jimmy Justice as my musical director because we're moving out of jazz music and into commercial-sounding musicals like a real Broadway musical. Plus, Robert Williams wanted to take some time off because he had seven children and he was an on-the-road artist. I asked him, "It is okay if I bring in Jimmy Justice?" He said, "Sure, Aduke. I've had a long run with you. I made a lot of money. I'm good." So, I brought in Jimmy Justice. My whole life changed. Jimmy Justice was the baddest musical composer known to man. His songs are still in my show.

Joseph sat me in his kitchen and stripped *Mother Goose* apart. He was a fabulous dramaturg. He said, "You're not taking this piece anywhere." I was so insulted, I said, "Are you serious?" He said, "I know you're famous and it's been done a million times and everybody in the world loves you, but you're going to have to rewrite the script." We talked for hours over it. He said, "Aduke, there's no such thing as a final script. Let me get real with you, dear. You're writing because God told you to write it. I love that. That's beautiful. But now God wants you to rewrite it and do it again" [*both laugh*]. Wait a second. "God gave you the vision to write it. Now, use your technical ability and work on the script. You know theater. You graduated with a degree. You have a master's now. You're working on your Ph.D. in theater. Rewrite the script. Make it a masterpiece." I said, "It is." He said, "No, dear. It's not. It's a phenomenal *production* piece because you're a badass producer. You can produce anything, Aduke. You can take toilet paper and make it look fabulous because you know how to do this. You're an artist with words and color and costuming and dance and music. You know how to put this together." Up to that point I had directed all my own plays. He said, "You need to bring in a director." I was like, "Oh, Joseph. I don't know." He said, "You got to step back now. I need you to release this to some directors because you're a really good writer. Release it." I'm breathing hard like, "Oh my God." I said, "Who. You?" He said, "Me? I'm one of them, but there are a lot of us. Release it." We stayed in the kitchen all night long. I was sweating. I left the next day and rewrote the whole play.

How did you go about rewriting The Liberation of Mother Goose*?*

I sat at my kitchen table—which is what I do—and I rewrote the whole play by hand because now we're going into the Public Theater. Ellis changed my director. Ellis said, "I need you to go after Gilbert Moses. So, go backstage. Tell Gilbert I sent you." Now Gilbert Moses is on Broadway directing *The Wiz*. Gilbert and Geoffrey Holder. Geoffrey Holder was also the costume designer for *The Wiz*. So, I went backstage, Gilbert walks out, and I said, "I'm Aduke Aremu—Ellis Haizlip sent me—I want you to direct my next play at the Public Theater." It was one sentence. He said, "Who are you?" I said, "I'm Aduke Aremu, I have a youth project, and we're going to Public Theater. Ellis Haizlip told me to get you as my director." He said, "I can't do it." I said, "Yes, you can. Can I come meet you? When can I come to see you?" He was living in Tribeca. He said, "Come by my house." I said, "Okay. When? Tomorrow? I'm free." He set a time. He didn't think I was going to show up. I got there, ring the bell, and guess who's sitting there? Dee Dee Bridgewater is with him because they were married. I said, "I need you to direct my piece at the Public Theater." He said, "I cannot do it, Aduke. I can't." I said, "Yes, you can." All day. I come out of there and said, "Ellis, he said no." Ellis said, "Don't worry about it. Something's getting ready to come down. Keep your eyes to the ground. He got fired from *The Wiz*." Remember he got fired? He got fired and the next day he called me, "I'm free." I said, "You're the director." I was in heaven. Gilbert directed it. I had Lillias White, who had worked for Joseph Walker. Joseph Walker built the set along with Myrna Colley-Lee. I had Gwen Jackson as a choreographer. Joseph Walker brought his whole team in and said, "When you open, it's going to blow people off the river." It went into Public. It was supposed to go to Broadway but something happened.

What happened?

I don't know. Oh God, Joseph Papp and I had a long conversation. He took that Elizabeth Swados piece [*Runaways* (1978)]. I was so over it. He was mentoring this white hippie writer. She became very famous for a long time. Elizabeth Swados—whoever she was. She had a lot of plays running at the same time. She went to Broadway. Yes, she did. That's how it works in black theater. He took her to Broadway. My mentor Ellis Haizlip said, "Don't worry about this, Aduke." Okay, so next step. Ellis calls me up and says, "You need to go to the Kennedy Center." Now, when Jackie Onassis has given you a ten-thousand-dollar check: they come to you. They wanted a command performance of *The Liberation of Mother Goose* at the Terrace Theater with all the Kennedy family in the audience. It was an invitation-only audience and you couldn't get into the show. Black tie. I thought, "I'm game."

I met Jackie Onassis on Forty-Second Street. She was at one of those meetings with the corporation, and I walked over to her and said, "I'm upstairs. This is the Harlem Children's Theatre Company." We were running our big banner outside. She said, "What do you do?" I told her and said, "We need money bad and my godfather is Mario Cuomo." The Cuomos and the Kennedys are very close. "I'm his commissioner. I need help with my little black kids up here. You've got to help me." She called the Ford Foundation and I had her check the next week. That's how I put down my dance floors and my mirrors. So, the Kennedy Center wanted a command performance, and I said, "Are you not going to let the black people of Washington see this show?" They said, "What are you talking about?" I said, "You have got to have another performance on Saturday and it's got to be free." I got what I wanted and the University of Maryland and Howard University produced the Saturday performance. It was big. The orchestra pit looked like who's who in America in terms of music.

Jim Henson did the mask in one of my sets. I kept that mask for years. It was a juju man. It was as big as this wall [in my house]. Jim Henson also did the heads for my tap dancer rabbits and Mother Goose. You have got some history to talk about! The Saturday show was sold out, and some of my kids' parents never got in to see their kids. People were lined up all down the block. To them, this is like Broadway. All of the performers were young kids. Noreen Crayton played the lead. She became a famous singer. Dedra Tate, who became vice president of Motown, was in it. My kids all did well. We tore the Kennedy Center off the rocks.

How many performers did you have in this production?

There were about fifty or sixty. They were fabulous. After we performed at the Kennedy Center we did a European tour. Brian Way's Theatre Centre, an English children's theater company, invited us over to London. I took fifty kids to Spain, England, Germany, and France. We met with Brian Way, did workshops for our kids, and the kids performed in London at the Theatre Centre. They believed in improvisational theater and wanted to know what we were doing. We were also being advised by Dr. Mort Clark, who was teaching at the University of Westchester County. He was a big-time children's theater advocate and he had me on a lot of panels about youth theater. Mort Clark—I called him my Jewish godfather—was the one who got us into England. He wanted us to go meet with Brian Way, who had also written a lot of stuff about children's theater. Nellie McCaslin—who was my professor at NYU when I had started working on my doctorate—put me in her book somewhere.[12] So, people started writing about my technique. They want to understand my technique. How do I get fifty black kids onstage? How do I write my plays? What is the structure? So, I began to read every children's play, and none of the plays were like my plays because all my plays were musicals.

You mentioned that Novella Nelson mentored you. How did she mentor you?

She worked at the Public Theater with Joe Papp. She was one of his administrative members, and he sent me to her to be mentored because I was getting ready to go into a production of *The Liberation of Mother Goose* at the Public Theater. He wanted me to grow as a producer. He sent me to her, and she gave me a lot of good advice. She said, "You will be very successful, Aduke. Handle it like a business." And I did. It's a business. A nice business, but don't not have checking accounts. Don't not know who you pay. Don't have any of that kind of stuff going on. That was even before theater administration was big. They started giving degrees in it because so many companies would get in trouble. She told me, even before that, "You've got to have that done."

Dawn Alli

Dawn Alli's administrative skills contributed to the growth and ultimate success of Aremu's Harlem Children's Theatre Company.

I was involved with the Harlem Children's Theatre Company before we moved to Forty-Second Street. I'm a founding member. I was involved before Myrna Belgrave Simmons left. I started out ironing costumes. I carted costumes from Mrs. Jones's house in Newark to wherever we were doing a show. While I was in college getting my undergraduate degree, I was working with the theater company for four years. I finished my undergraduate degree and went to graduate school at NYU and still worked with the theater. I worked with the Harlem Children's Theatre Company nine or ten years before I went to West Africa. When I moved to West Africa, I worked for about a year at the embassy in Ibadan. I did event planning and administrative work. I was in charge of budgeting, petty cash, library, some testing, and then we did one of the first watch-night programs for the elections. The head of the theater department came to the watch-night program, and he liked how it was planned out and designed. He asked me if I wanted a job at the University of Ibadan. He told me to apply, and I got that job. For the rest of my years in Nigeria I worked at the University of Ibadan.

So, you started off ironing costumes and ended up staying with the Harlem Children's Theatre Company for nine or ten years. How did you become more and more involved?

I originally took some science classes. I wasn't sure what I was going to do. Since I started to work with the theater, I got more involved. I began to do backstage work with the set and costumes. I did some mentoring work with students who were working their lines. I eventually became an English, speech, and theater major, and then it was a natural progression. I became the Harlem Children's Theatre Company administrative director. The business end: going to meetings, filling out paperwork, paying bills, and answering telephone calls. I was also theater production manager, and I taught the drama classes: articulation and movement. The nine or ten years were over before I knew it. Had I not moved, I think we would have done some other things. In retrospect, we should have bought a building. That would have been the next logical step because I am business minded. I would have said, "We need to do fundraising for buying a building." If we kept Forty-Second Street for eight years, with that amount of rent, we could have paid a mortgage. Even if we got something with a hundred, seventy-five, or fifty-year lease, that would have made more sense than Forty-Second Street.

But at the time, your space was inexpensive. Aduke mentioned that she secured your building at Forty-Second Street for only a hundred dollars a month.

When we first got the space. In the beginning the space was inexpensive and the space paid for itself because it gave you more funding.

Tell me more about what it was like being a black woman involved in the business end of theater during this time. Did you encounter other black women administrators?

Yes. Barbara Ann Teer. Hazel Bryant was part of the group we worked with when we were going into the Forty-Second Street Theatre Row. She died about that time. She was on the production end; she was not on the theater end. Vy Higginsen, the producer [and coauthor] of *Mama, I Want to Sing!* [1983] was on the production end. That musical went on to make her a millionaire. That is one of the first "black-based" musicals. It started the rage of black musical theater.

Did any of these women mentor you in any way?

No. Aduke and I worked together and we did not have female mentors per se. I would say the female mentors we had would be Vivian Bright. She was a businesswoman and she was Aduke's sorority sister. The other people who mentored us were men: Ellis Haizlip, Woodie King Jr., and a couple of others. Tony Brown helped us.

How did you navigate New York theaters as a black woman?

We just worked. We filled out the applications for funding. Aduke wrote the plays. We decided where we wanted to produce them. We made appointments and we worked. My two oldest children came to the theater with me. They were in theater productions. When we went to tour Europe, my oldest daughter and Aduke's son toured with us. When I went to Nigeria, England, and other countries, my children came with me. They saw the world.

What did the Harlem Children's Theatre Company teach?

The Harlem Children's Theatre Company instilled a sense of pride, dignity, accomplishment, and a gut-level knowledge that you can be and do anything. It's the quality of your soul and the integrity of your person—not what anyone thinks of you—that determines who you're going to be and what you're going to be. For example, my daughter is a doctor. Originally before I was married and moved to West Africa, I raised my daughter by myself. What the theater did for her was make her realize that you could do anything. You can stand on this stage. You can read your lines in front of hundreds of people. You're relaxed. You're composed. You can speak. If you can do that just one time: you can do anything. For a large number of young people that are not going to be jocks, that are not going to play an instrument, this is a powerful tool. You don't need a piano. You don't necessarily need to read music. You just need a stage, a piece of paper with a script on it, and someone willing to teach you. You can take students, put them on a stage, give them a play, and put some lights up, and change who they are, who they *think* they are, and who they *can be*. That is why I stayed for ten years.

When I look at music and I look at all these people who have all this money and I see someone with five, ten, twenty cars and they have thousands of dollars' worth of jewelry on their back—it's just so sad. If I had that kind of money I would start a school. If half of us who have money started a school in a state or a city that we lived in, do you realize what we could do? We could change the history of our people.

Doris Derby

As with Alli, Aremu, and many others in this study, Doris Derby was deeply committed to using theater as a tool to educate and empower black communities. Nearly two years before Baraka would found the Black Arts Repertory Theatre/School, Derby turned thought to action, joining forces with Gilbert Moses and John O'Neal to cofound the Free Southern Theater in Tougaloo, Mississippi.

The Free Southern Theater, beginning in the year of 1963–64, had workshops on Tougaloo College campus while I was there for the literacy project. By the summer of 1964, the repertory company of the Free Southern Theater started and began taking plays around the state. It became a matter of where do you perform these plays? We performed them at Freedom Schools, Head Start centers, churches, colleges, and on porches and outside on the farmland owned by independent black farmers. We performed in communities where civil rights organizations were active.

What was your purpose for creating art?

I wanted to develop a body of work through my own Afrocentric creation as well as acknowledge other creations within the African diaspora by collecting them. I wanted to add to collections in libraries and museums with the things that I felt were important; needed to be uncovered, researched, expressed; and that would validate and acknowledge all of our contributions for ourselves and our connections with black people from all over the world. I saw that we had people in the Caribbean, Africa, South America, North America, Europe, and all over. We're making these connections and these contributions and white people are taking credit for that. They're using our contributions and they're not acknowledging what we're giving to America. They are not acknowledging what we're giving to Europe or how our culture is a part of their culture and making the culture look good and be outstanding.

Day of Absence [1965] was one of the plays that we did with the Free Southern Theater. I love that play. That was one of the best plays I felt that we had done. I was not with the Free Southern Theater the whole time that it was in existence.

Only the first year, right?

Yes, the first year. When I came back to Mississippi, I did go to some of the other plays, but I was not active in the theater as an organization official. I was doing other things at the time. I had decided that I was not going to move to New Orleans, Louisiana, when the Free Southern Theater moved. My attention was with working the Freedom Democratic Party, the Head Start centers, and the co-ops. I was still in contact if they performed in Jackson, Mississippi, or somewhere where I was, but I was doing other things. I had my own mission and dedication to what I was doing at that time, so I wasn't going to go back to the Free Southern Theater. It had been established and it was going on. I was part of getting it going, but there were so many other things that needed to be done. Economics. Helping people to have a way to earn a living through handcraft, vegetable, and housing co-ops, through acquiring skills. People were getting thrown off the land and they needed to earn a living. We were trying to see to the voting. Some people say, "Well, the civil rights movement was over in 1968." No. Some movement people left, but I stayed, as did others. The people who were living there had to continue on with civil rights. All the activities had been established and we weren't going to just leave people to fend for themselves. The Student Nonviolent Coordinating Committee [SNCC] went through some political changes, but I continued working with the Poor People's Cooperative [1965–1970s], the Liberty House Handcrafts Marketing Cooperative [1965–72], and Southern Media, Inc. Again, my own commitment to black social justice was my mantra: black achievement, history, et cetera. I continued even after I came to Atlanta, Georgia, through my work at Georgia State University. You see, the core never changed.

Scholars Errol Hill and James V. Hatch write that in "October 1963, Gilbert Moses, Doris Derby, and John O'Neal at Tougaloo College Drama Workshop in Jackson, Mississippi, christened themselves the Free Southern Theater (FST) (1964–1980) and set forth goals, which were as original as they were brave."[13] *I'm interested in hearing, from your own words, what you considered to be the goals of the Free Southern Theater? Do you consider them "brave"?*

The goals started out in one way and evolved further to provide a vehicle of expression for all persons involved. First of all, the Free Southern

Theater was the cultural arm of SNCC. A cultural arm to take black theater around black communities; to use theater to present issues to reflect our past, present, and future goals.

The shows were originally free of charge and later there was only a small fee, making theater accessible to everyday people.

Yes. Accessibility is an important issue in the movement. Theater was one vehicle to bring black history and culture to the community. Talkbacks after performances was a way to learn about things that were important to them and to the movement. The Free Southern Theater was a vehicle to encourage people to write and be involved in theater. We started having story circles, where after the play you have people talk to each other and tell their story.

And so as far as being brave? Yes. Everybody that was involved in the theater was brave, especially for those people who come to the play, because there was also antagonism and hostility with anything that black and whites were involved in the name of the movement, in the name of progress, and in the name of integration and education. There were very few outlets for upgrading education, economic development, the arts, and so on. You had some of the black colleges that were supportive of the movement, you had Freedom Schools, and you had churches, but you needed to have something that was consistent with the same message that went to all different areas rather than just each individual area doing whatever was available to them. You had something that had a core, and it could go around in different places: in the state as well as in other states. So, there was lots of bravery because everybody faced possible hostility, beatings, guns, bombs, and jail. When I worked for the Head Start program and when I traveled I was in positions where there were threats. When you were staying somewhere there could be violence against the people who were hosting the civil rights workers. If you were ever riding in a vehicle with blacks and whites together, that was a possible threat to the establishment. You could get shot, beaten, jailed. Violence was something that could happen at any time, for any reason, by racists who wanted to maintain segregation, political and economic exploitation of black people and other people of color.

You worked on public relations with John O'Neal at the Free Southern Theater. I was curious to know what your day-to-day duties looked like?

Well, we weren't doing the Free Southern Theater as a full-time job. The Free Southern Theater was something that was a side thing. John O'Neal and I worked in the literacy project together and Gil Moses was with the *Mississippi Free Press* [1961–64]. So, John and I talked up the Free Southern Theater to students, faculty, and SNCC contacts coming through Tougaloo College. We were based on the campus of Tougaloo College. So, public relations wasn't a day-to-day or nine-to-five job. We did it when we could, depending on who we were with and what activities. Public relations meant that as you meet people and as you are doing things, you're talking about it. How can we plan? What can we do to take the theater around? We worked with the theater department at Tougaloo College under Bill Hutchinson, who was the head of the drama department. Tougaloo was a hub for the civil rights movement, so when people were visiting we were talking to them about the Free Southern Theater. Sometimes we were working with SNCC in the evenings or on the weekends and would talk to people about the Free Southern Theater and how we could utilize churches or Freedom Schools which were going to be set up the summer of 1964. Such questions like, where were they going to have Freedom Schools? How could we have performances? What type of facility was a Freedom School? How did places and purposes overlap? All of that is public relations. How do we help you and help us facilitate what we were doing? Do we have the same target audience?

Speaking of audience, scholars Errol Hill and James V. Hatch note that "FST soon learned that the urban scripts of Baraka and Caldwell were inappropriate for their churchgoing audiences, in whose buildings they frequently performed."[14] *Could you describe typical audiences at Free Southern Theater?*

Well, again, you have different audiences. When we had the Free Southern Theater workshop on Tougaloo campus, there were students. You had civil rights movement people. You had northern volunteers and Mississippi audiences. You had people outside of the civil rights movement people. You had people who were aware of the civil rights movement goals and you had people who were new to the movement and who were afraid even to be involved. You had volunteers coming from all over the country, and they were part of the audience. You had the people in rural areas and in small towns as audience members. So, that was a target audience. And some people—they listened. Some plays that were performed—people didn't understand what you were talking about.

You had a spectrum of audiences and you were performing plays like Day of Absence, *which you said was one of your favorites.*

Well, yes. That one was a good one. But something like *Waiting for Godot* [1953]? Gil Moses wanted to experiment with that, but it wasn't good.

But you said Day of Absence *was "good." Why was it good?*

I saw it with the college students. I think it was good because the makeup of the actors was mixed as far as older people; people who were just living there; people who had gone off to enlist, attend school, or work elsewhere and come back; military people; farmers; workers; and women who had gone out to work for white families as housekeepers et cetera.

The Hill and Hatch quote makes it sound like audiences were shocked watching productions of Baraka's plays. Yet some of his plays were meant to shock audiences.

Well, maybe they were, but I don't know how many performances of Baraka's plays that they did anyway. And don't forget, the Free Southern Theater started performing in 1964, but it went for a long period of time. I'm not sure if Baraka's plays were necessarily out in the 1960s.

Free Southern Theater performed Slave Ship *in 1969.*

Yes. So, by 1969 things had progressed. I have pictures of *Slave Ship*. I actually saw that. I don't really remember [the production]. I think it was good, but I couldn't give you an opinion about it because I only saw it just that one time.

I know you helped establish the Free Southern Theater and then you parted ways to do other things, but were there any productions that you found particularly memorable?

Well, they did *Purlie Victorious* [1970] and *Roots* [1958].

The 1966 production of Roots *seems like it was a big hit based on what I've read.*

Later on, it wasn't a priority. I went to see a play and it was good, but there were so many other things I was involved in. I wasn't in tune with criticizing [theater]. All "it was this and it was that." I wasn't doing that. I just hoped people learned from the play's content.

It also doesn't sound like critics would come and review these early productions?

Well, critics weren't relevant. Now, plays that were performed in New York: there were critics up there. But I wasn't there doing that. John and Gil. The thing is that they were interested in being theater professionals. I wasn't. I was interested in having a theater there for the purposes that we stated. "We need a theater for this, that, and the other thing." I was not interested in being a producer or director or playwright or an actor. I was interested as an organizer, just as I am with film. I am active within the film industry. I've been executive producer and coproducer for three documentary films. I want to see more black documentary films out. I want to give input. I don't have to be the editor. I don't have to be the director to see that it's *there*. That's what I wanted with the Free Southern Theater. I wanted theater to be a vehicle that we could use as a communication mechanism and as a means of expression. One mechanism that young people could be involved in because they wanted to tell their stories. I wanted to see our theater as a black cultural institution in Mississippi. That's [my purpose] with the theater. When I was living in New York and I went to Off-Broadway plays, I saw the importance of presenting our stories to live people where you could have interaction, inspiration, and appreciation. I wanted to see different, realistic, human relationships happen. I didn't have to be doing anything but witnessing and learning.

Not the actual artistic work.

If it had stayed, I would have, because I was going to be in charge of the dance element in theater.

Why did the Free Southern Theater leave Mississippi?

It left because . . . it's in the book [*The Free Southern Theater, by the Free Southern Theater: A Documentary of the South's Radical Black Theater, with Journals, Letters, Poetry, Essays, and a Play Written by Those Who Built It*, ed. Thomas C. Dent, Richard Schechner, and Gilbert Moses (1969)]. If I had stayed with the company I would have produced dance theater. I probably would have done something with stage props, scenery, or something like that. I would have sat back and said, "This, that, add it." Give ideas to it. Also, I would have been an executive producer and raised money and do public relations. I left because when we were doing publicity and fundraising, Richard Schechner, head of the drama department at Tulane University in New Orleans, invited us to come to talk about how he could be supportive. Then he later said, "Why don't we move the base of the Free Southern Theater to Tulane University?" He said he could provide a lot of resources and that the theater could also still go back to Mississippi and to different places. We had in mind to branch out from Mississippi to maybe Georgia and Alabama and so on. John and Gil had goals of being in the theater and so they thought that his offer would benefit themselves as well as the theater because of what Richard was providing.

Did his offer benefit John O'Neal, Gilbert Moses, and the Free Southern Theater?

Well, it did. What with the kind of influences he did have, so on and so forth, it ended up that Free Southern Theater did survive from there, and different things blossomed out of that and it was good. It birthed another theatrical group, Junebug Productions. So it all worked out. But a career in theater wasn't what I wanted. I was committed to it being in Mississippi working as an arm of SNCC and staying there. I didn't want to move to go with the theater, because that was not my primary goal. And so they went and I stayed. But at the time, I wanted to continue on with the literacy project and work with SNCC and other projects. Both John and I were SNCC field secretaries, so we were doing other things out of the Council of Federated Organizations [1962–65] office. That was the hub. I didn't want to move the base. So, they wanted to move the base and it was two against one.

Was the decision to move the Free Southern Theater to New Orleans based on a vote between you three cofounders?

Well, it's like, "Okay. That's what they want." That was one place where the male-female thing came in. But I wasn't looking for a career in the theater, so that was another thing. I think that they thought like males at that time, but obviously I didn't and I had other things that I was doing.

You said, "They thought like males at the time." How so?

Well, yes. Being very superficial they thought, "Oh, yes. Doris could be the secretary, make the coffee, or do whatever we want to do with her." But, no. It wasn't like [I was going to be the] girl taking notes. I always continued to do what I wanted to do. Yet they knew that I was a creative, independent thinker and doer and could not be manipulated.

So, others can try to put you in a box but you're not staying in that box.

No, I'm not getting *in* the box.

What was it like working with John O'Neal and Gilbert Moses?

Fun, intellectually stimulating, productive thinking. Well, we would all argue (friendly and intellectually) and discuss things all the time. Deliberate back and forth. John and Gil would have long discussions; I didn't. I'm like, "I don't have much time for those circular discussions without action." See, they became roommates, so they loved to have discourse late at night, and I'm a doer. You can go to the website of Junebug Productions, and there is a video that you should listen to.[15] I think John describes how the three of us were there at the apartment and they were smoking. I didn't smoke. And their legs were going, feet tapping up and down like that, and they were talking so excitedly. They were always beating around the bush and extending conversations, laughing and all that. John talks about how they were pontificating about this and that and the Free Southern Theater. "Oh yeah, it would be great if we had this and that and the other thing." I said, "Well, okay. If we've been talking about having a theater in Mississippi, that's what we need to do. Let's do it." In other words, "shit or get off the pot." That's how we decided to take the action from just talking to actually taking steps to start the Free Southern Theater.

`Fémi Sarah Heggie

Similar to Derby, `Fémi Sarah Heggie worked behind the scenes and used her stage management skills to support Woodie King Jr.'s New Federal Theatre and Douglas Turner Ward, Robert Hooks, and Gerald S. Krone's Negro Ensemble Company (NEC).

When I came into the city one time, I went to the Negro Ensemble Company. It was about 1967 or 1968, and they were doing a play called *Song of the Lusitanian Bogey*. This is the first play I ever saw in my life, and don't ask me how I ended up there to see this play. It turns out it was their first play. I didn't even know that. So, it is very interesting how spirit moves you around your world and gets you to places you are supposed to be. I sat there and cried because David Downing played this innocent person coming from the bush area into Johannesburg and he was saying, "What's that? What's that? Well, what is that?!" Someone said, "It's a bank." He said, "What is a bank?" They said, "It is where they keep the money." He said, "Money? I could use some money." And he goes walking up to the bank and gets thrown out. So, all these things that happened to these black South Africans were portrayed in that play and I said, "I've got to be a part of *this*." At the same time, the New Lafayette Theatre existed uptown in Harlem, and the second play I saw was *Clara's Ole Man* [1968], written by Ed Bullins.

What did you think of that production?

I loved it. There was something in me that just loved this whole mode of communication.

But wasn't Clara's Ole Man *considered controversial?*

Well, of course. You see, I like Rod Serling because you never know what the end is going to be. With *Clara's Ole Man*, I was like, "Whoa!" I like to feel that in my body. Like I haven't figured everything out. I always try to figure out what's going on. Try to surprise me, okay? And he did it. I did some of Ed Bullins's plays in my day.

You performed in them?

No, I never performed. I was always the stage manager. I tried to act once. I was taking some classes with Dick Anthony Williams, God rest his soul, and I had written this poem about a woman talking about what she felt in this dime that she was putting in the telephone to call. So I got up and recited the poem and sat down. Dick said, "No, get back up." He made me go to the point of actually being that person. Then I said, "I could never give this—myself—to the world every night for a show." I really admire people who can do that. I can't do that. But my partner, Hilda Harris—she's in the other room—was an opera singer at the Metropolitan Opera for about twenty years and the first woman of color to do trouser roles.

So, you saw the Song of the Lusitanian Bogey *at the Negro Ensemble Company. Later, you see* Clara's Ole Man *at the New Lafayette Theatre. The play blows your mind. When I interviewed Sonia Sanchez, she said that plays about queer black couples were often presented as the butt of a joke. This production was the first time she saw their humanity and it made her pause.*

She's right. I remember she and Nikki Giovanni and there was a third one. They used to come to NEC and do talks. I don't remember who the third person was.

So, you go from reading Nikki Giovanni's poems to meeting her.

Oh, yes. In those days, we all met each other. We just did. Especially if you were in the arts, because we were all together. Today you would be hard-set to try to meet anybody.

How did you go from seeing a play at NEC to working with them?

When I was in Alabama, I came back up to interview Douglas Turner Ward, Hattie Wilson, Leontyne Price, and Rosalind Cash. Just to show people in the South what black people in the North were accomplishing. That was my mission at that time. When I met Doug and the people at NEC I asked about work there, but I didn't get any answers or anything. I met this woman named Carolyn Jones, and out of college I went and stayed with her. I don't know if I met her in a club or what, but you could do that in those days. Carolyn hired me because she was the manager at the Negro Ensemble Company. I was there forever. I worked box office, I did costumes, I worked backstage, I worked everywhere. You did everything in those days.

Someone was willing to teach you those skills?

Yes. On the third floor, we had Lloyd Richards, and he had a class up there for actors. The first Negro Ensemble Company was a group of people; they did all the plays as actors. Adolf Cesar, Robert Hooks, Douglas Turner Ward, Ros Cash, Frances Foster, Art French, Will Jay, Judyann Elder (whose husband wrote *First Breeze of Summer* [1975]), and Tony Blue. That was the core of the first Negro Ensemble Company. So, they did all the plays. I made my way up to stage manager, and I just stayed there for many years. Then I met Nina Simone.

So, you asked me if I knew anybody. In those days, you did everything. You were working two or three theaters and did hair. "Can you braid?" "Yes!" That's what you did back in the day. You always said, "Yes." You never said, "No." A girl named Irene Gandy called and asked me if I did hair. I said, "Yes!" I don't remember who I called, but I figured out it's for Stevie Wonder. That's what started that little part of my life. I did his hair. It was quite an experience. I'm still a young girl. I don't even think I was twenty yet. Judy Dearing, who was the love of everybody's life, was a costume designer—she passed away several years ago—and was very close to Miriam Makeba. Stokely Carmichael married Miriam Makeba. Through Judy, I did—she called her Zenzi—Miriam Makeba's hair. Her hair was that long [*gestures with thumb and index finger*]. What you see is extensions. We were doing that back then. Still working at NEC, sometimes working at the New Federal Theatre.

What did you do at the New Federal Theatre?

I was also the stage manager. I stage-managed the first play that Woodie King Jr. ever did there. It was called *Why Charlie Can't Win No Wars on the Ground & Misjudgement* [ca. 1970–71]. I remember we got the set and all our things off the street from people who had thrown away stuff. I used to live in Brooklyn and I was still doing hair. I'm trying to figure out who introduced me to Nina, but it was to do her hair.

You did Nina Simone's hair!

Well, I was her personal assistant. I was initially hired to do hair, but I became her personal assistant. The same thing happened with Aretha Franklin. Nina would come to my house to get her hair done, and one day Stokely and Miriam came with Nina to my house in Brooklyn, and we would all just talk. Those were the times. Nobody was like "celebrity" to us.

Was this before or after her song "Mississippi Goddam" [1964]?

Long after. But then Melvin Van Peebles had some plays on Broadway: *Ain't Supposed to Die a Natural Death* [1971] and *Don't Play Us Cheap* [1972]. I worked on *Don't Play Us Cheap* doing hair, not stage-managing. We had a little tryst, but he had one with everybody. It didn't matter in those days. Aretha Franklin was always my idol. When I was a little girl in Kansas they used to play her music. I loved Aretha Franklin. I told Melvin, "I'm going to work for her." He said, "You're always talking that spiritual shit." Those were his words. Didn't she come to see the play and didn't he have to introduce me to her? I said to her, "Ms. Franklin, I do hair. I do braids." She said, "I've been looking for someone to do my hair." "Well, you found me." I remember that conversation. So she gave me an address to come, and because I know Melvin she knew it was okay. I wasn't a serial killer. I wasn't a person who was going to embarrass her or him or anything. She was at the Essex House here on Central Park South, and I remember walking in and my heart was beating like this [*pounds her chest*]. She was playing "Bridge Over Troubled Water" on a keyboard. We sat down and we talked. I braided her hair once, but I became her personal assistant. She needed that more, she said. I stayed with her for about four years, so I was no longer in the theater for those four years. I think it ended in 1974 because I went to interview for the *Bubbling Brown Sugar* [1976] tour. They didn't hire me, and I cried because I wanted to go on the show *so* bad. Then the phone rang. They had fired the stage manager—see, I told you I like to surprise you—and sent for me. Life was magic back then. I went on that tour for nine months. Sometimes the Broadway stage manager and I would change. I would come to Broadway and they would go out on the road. I went to Europe with that show.

Bubbling Brown Sugar *was Rosetta LeNoire's concept, but the musical was written by Loften Mitchell. Did you interact with her at all?*

Yes, she had a theater and it used to be at Eighty-Sixth Street. The first show she had at AMAS was called *Bayou Legend* [1948] by Owen Dodson. Debbie Allen was the director, and I was stage manager.

Rosetta LeNoire made amazing contributions to black theater, and yet there is very little academic writing about her achievements. What can you tell me about her?

Rosetta was a very, very strong black lady who was able to get things moving. I think that a lot of us even today feel looked over. But a lot of white people are still doing things in her name. So, she is still being recognized but not so much by us.

Why do you think that is?

I don't know. She was nice and had the most pleasant smile. Maybe the disconnect was when she went to do that sitcom *Family Matters* out in Los Angeles? Reginald VelJohnson was one of the NEC people at one point. I think maybe the disconnect was her being there. She wasn't here in the city anymore, and she never came back. Not as far as I know. I liked her a lot. She was stern. She knew what she wanted and she was able to

`Fémi Sarah Heggie with Martin Luther King Jr., 1967. Photo by Jim Peppler. Courtesy of `Fémi Sarah Heggie.

get folks to move. Now, she could make white folk move a lot better than she could make us move.

I was wondering if her ideas of a more integrated theater during the time of Black Arts Movement contributed to her erasure?

It could be.

Also, being a black woman. What were some of the challenges of being a black woman artist during the sixties and seventies?

I think it is the same. I think that Ava DuVernay, Oprah Winfrey, and all these people are fortunate because they have each other. We didn't have anybody who broke through and made it big. Madam C. J. Walker existed before my time. I did meet Oprah, but it was in the eighties. We didn't know we could be strong and rich and on television. At least I didn't. I never thought of it as possible. I thought it was possible to meet Aretha. I thought it was possible to meet Nina and all of that because that was your life. You see these people all the time at functions and different things.

Again, the movement did not include us black women. Even Dr. King didn't. I have a picture of me standing right next to him. I was covering the story where he was preaching at Dexter Avenue Baptist Church. You got me talking; there's a lot of stuff to remember.

Tell me more about your experiences as a stage manager. Let's start with NEC.

Negro Ensemble Company was probably the most artistic place I felt I ever worked at. Everybody was so ensconced in their craft. We weren't playing. It wasn't like a community theater. These were professional people and they worked hard to present these plays. We always had a sold-out season. We did four plays a year. We usually had summers off. When you come to a theater and you work with the same people every day and you get to know each other, there is just something very special about that that I really miss. When this new group comes up and calls themselves the Negro Ensemble Company, that's not the Negro Ensemble Company. Charlie Weldon did work at the Negro Ensemble Company as an actor. I stage-managed a show for him, designed the sound, and asked to direct a show. He will not call me back to direct a show because he knows what's up here [*pointing to her head*] is what Doug taught me. Douglas Turner Ward, who was the head of NEC. He just seems to be one of those guys who is afraid of what I might be able to bring into that situation. It really hurt, but now I'm over it. We recently had this whole company coming together with the new company. I thought, "No. I'm not doing that, because just like the movement, they are going to ignore who I am and the years I put in." There's no question. One of the actors told me they did one of Samm-Art Williams's plays. They always stage productions in these little places about as big as my living room. I went to see it and I was just so discouraged that they were using the Negro Ensemble Company name because the production values were none. Because they don't know it! Then they won't consult you or talk to you. We learned. We did everything. Everybody who worked at NEC did everything—except acting—in terms of lights, sound, box office, and costumes.

Any other memorable experiences at the NEC?

Besides *Song of the Lusitanian Bogey*? Well, that one certainly was. *Home* [1979] was my favorite. Sam Jackson played Cephus. Elain Graham and S. Epatha Merkerson [also performed in the production]. This show was written by Samm-Art Williams and designed by Felix Cochran. It was so easy. I took it to the Philippines, Bangkok, and Kuala Lumpur. It went to Broadway. I didn't do it on Broadway. I directed a reading of it about a year ago in Brooklyn. Do you know the story at all? Well, Cephus is down on his farm by Kansas City somewhere and he likes Pattie Mae and he gets drafted. He says, "Vietnam? I don't know nobody in Vietnam." Anyway, he gets drafted, goes to jail as opposed to going to Vietnam, gets out, and comes to New York, and there's fast women. This is done with three actors. He didn't tell anybody he went to jail and gets fired from his job. As soon as his money runs out the lady he was seeing says, "I'm gonna find me somebody with some money. It's been nice knowing you. Bye." And she leaves. It had rhythm. It had what happens to people—especially our people—when we go against what they are trying to do to us. Like Muhammad Ali. It's not going to end well. If you go to Vietnam and don't come back crazy or dead, you're going to jail. All during the play, he's saying, "Where is God?" It's only ninety minutes. There is no intermission. At the very end, he goes back to North Carolina and he meets Pattie Mae, who in the interim had gotten married and divorced. Elain Graham played that so well. At the very end, he looks up and he says, "Welcome home" to God. His grandmother was always telling him about God. *Home* is a simple piece but is so dynamic.

CHAPTER 3

"Traveling with Ears to the Ground"

Black Arts Movement Drama, Ritual, Teleplays, and Musicals

> Black writers—most of them poets plus—have always been barometers, even when America kept bell jars on them. Have always been/still are/will be. Always traveling with ears to the ground; attuned to the drumbeats of the age.
>
> —Sarah Webster Fabio, "Tripping with Black Writing"

The dynamic playwright, poet, critic, and mother of black studies Sarah Webster Fabio (1928–79) lived in an era wherein the cultural achievements of black writers were often marginalized or simply ignored in academia and society at large. Her poetic essay "Tripping with Black Writing" confronts racist discourse that would deny the black writer's existence and celebrates black writers' tradition of attending to the "drumbeat" or concerns of the times.[1] First published in Addison Gayle Jr.'s seminal Black Arts Movement collection *The Black Aesthetic* (1971), "Tripping with Black Writing" represents one of only two writings composed by black women intellectuals.[2] *Does this mean that black women were not producing vast amounts of writing during the Black Arts*

Movement? Certainly not. With the advantage of hindsight, "Tripping with Black Writing" serves as a metaphor for black women's positionality in Black Arts Movement discourse and ultimate erasure in Black Arts Movement theater scholarship today. The placement of Fabio's essay, nestled among the writings of figures such as Langston Hughes, Dudley Randall, and Don L. Lee (later Haki Madhubuti), mirrors the reality that while black women writers were often outnumbered, they were still visible and did express their worldview from major Black Arts Movement publications. The inclusion of Fabio's essay also reaffirms that, while forgotten today, her works were highly regarded by her comrades.

The irony that Fabio publicly celebrates the existence of black writers only to have her works and those of other black women playwrights forgotten deserves further attention. More specifically, what barriers prevented more black women playwrights from publishing and having their works produced during the Black Arts Movement? Why have the accomplishments of black women playwrights of the era been obscured in theater history? Aware of the tenuous position of black women playwrights, Barbara Molette addressed similar questions in her article "Black Women Playwrights: They Speak, Who Listens?" (1976). Published in the final issue of *Black World*, "Black Women Playwrights" identifies *why* and *how* black women playwrights are systematically silenced. She begins by stating that "playwrights are at the mercy of media brokers," the majority of whom are white men who have financial interest in maintaining the status quo.[3] Molette understood that from the early antilynching plays of Georgia Douglas Johnson to the revolutionary drama of her time, black women playwrights have always resisted the reinforcement of the status quo, engaging in antiracist praxis for the betterment of the entire black community. Molette writes,

> Black women have traditionally written positive images of Black motherhood and tried to promote mores that were humanistic. But these works go against stereotypes of Black women that have been perpetuated by white America. To show a Black woman more concerned about her own child than her white mistress' child is heresy. To show a Black woman who treats her husband like a man is tantamount to revolution.[4]

Despite the purposeful suppression of their works, black women playwrights of the era continued the tradition of using their voice to transmit black history and culture for future generations.

Interviews with black women playwrights of the era confirm that they used the pen as a weapon of choice to simultaneously articulate black women's distinctive worldview and resist oppressive forces impacting black America. Their writings address a variety of concerns, including the black family, the complexities of black womanhood, the black liberation struggle, the feminist movement, police brutality, institutional white racism, the failing public education system, poverty, mental health, and much more. The narrators provide details about the challenges of seeing their works produced, demonstrating through their first- and second-person accounts how black women's dramas, ritual dramas, and even more commercial works on television and Broadway stages provided space to articulate the intersections of their identity.

While many of the black women playwrights utilized the Western convention of realism, some experimented with African modes of artistic expression, creating their own vision of ritual drama. Indeed, perhaps one of the greatest achievements of the Black Arts Movement was the experimentation with African American ritual drama. Carlton Molette describes this theatrical form as follows:

> In Afro-American drama in the ritual form, the dramatic event is not expected to create an illusion of time and place other than its own; just as a narrative storyteller or a preacher is not. Within the context of real and present time and place, the audience members are much freer to participate in the dramatic event according to their feelings. In Afro-American religious ritual drama, the structure does not hinge on the plot; it hinges instead upon the form—the patterned arrangement of actions.[5]

Of course, their level of engagement with African American ritual drama varied according to the artistic preferences of individual black women playwrights. For example, J.e. Franklin occasionally incorporated ritualistic structure to reinforce a more traditional dramatic premise. P. J. Gibson, Ntozake Shange, and Sonia Sanchez included rituals of childbirth and loss in their poetic works.

Barbara Ann Teer discusses *The Ritual* (1970) with Ellis Haizlip on New York's Channel 13 *Soul!* program. Still image. Courtesy of the author.

However, Barbara Ann Teer proposed a radical departure from realism and commercial theater more broadly, creating her own "ritualistic revivals" for the purpose of bringing about a cultural revolution.[6] Teer writes,

> [Black artists] should be concerned with the truth of our lives. After seeing the truth, we can begin to grow stronger and more positive as a body of people. That is why it is necessary to feed strong political and social messages into the minds of these black audiences. When we begin thinking and using our energies in this direction, we will be on the right road toward rehabilitation of black America and our ultimate survival as a people.[7]

Borrowing from Yoruba ritual, black women's cultural traditions, and Holiness, Baptist, and Pentecostal church worship practices, Teer crafted ritualistic revivals to actualize her goal of cultivating community, black consciousness, and emotional cleansing for both liberators and participants (i.e., performers and audience).[8]

Teer, Franklin, and Lee Hunkins also wrote and adapted black empowerment–themed works for public television. The broadcast of

Hunkins's *Hollow Image* (1979) on ABC television, Teer's *The Ritual* (1970) on New York's Channel 13 *Soul!* program, and Franklin's teleplay *Black Girl* (1969) on Boston's WGBH were produced during a broader shift in U.S. television programming. Political disputes about the Vietnam War; urban rebellions in major cities such as Los Angeles (Watts, 1965), Newark (1967), and Detroit (1967); and the assassination of black leaders such as Martin Luther King Jr. created a demand for black public affairs television.[9] New programs such as *For Blacks Only* and *Soul!* (1968–73) were created by predominately (if not exclusively) black staff for black audiences with the purpose of uncovering systemic racism and documenting black culture and politics.[10] The media studies scholar Devorah Heitner writes that Ellis Haizlip's *Soul!*, in particular, "occupied its own encompassing position in this spectrum of approaches to gender, questioning the marginalization of women, celebrating different aesthetics of masculinity and femininity, and offering an extraordinarily open space for the discussion of sexuality, particularly homosexuality."[11] Emboldened by Black Power discourse of the time, this daring new programming offered black women playwrights unprecedented opportunities to see their works realized on television. Interviews with Franklin and Hunkins offer insights into how they navigated a space for their works within this larger shift in television programming.

Finally, studies on Black Arts Movement theater rarely, if ever, discuss how new black musicals of the era—written for both adults and young audiences—contributed to the dissemination of Black Arts Movement and Black Power discourse. The scholar of African American musical theater Allen Woll acknowledges the revolutionary possibilities of these black-created musicals, writing that black artists "repudiated the sunny optimism of the white-created black musical, creating instead works that sought to understand the dynamic of Afro-American life in the United States."[12] Unfortunately, Woll's study focuses almost entirely on Broadway musicals and as a consequence does not attend to the relationship between black women's musical experimentation on Black Arts and Broadway stages. Jacqui Scott-Papke's article "Aduke Aremu's Harlem Children's Theatre Company" and my first book, *In Search of Our Warrior Mothers: Women Dramatists of the Black Arts Movement*, are the most rigorous studies to explore musical experimentation in Black Arts Movement theater. Both studies purport that black artists valued musicals for adults and young audiences and used them as vehicles to promote the black aesthetic and Black Power ideologies.[13] Interviews with book writers, composers, and lyricists such as Aduke Aremu and Micki Grant further these recuperative efforts.

For example, Micki Grant's narrative provides insights into her struggles of realizing her provocative musicals on experimental and commercial stages. Despite these challenges, she was able to see her works performed in a variety of spaces, from Broadway to New York's Henry Street Settlement community. While Grant continues to resist any dogma that would limit her artistry, she nonetheless collaborated with artists who espoused Black Arts rhetoric and crafted musicals that engage with Black Power milieu. Indeed, eradicating social inequality and stereotypical representations of black men, women, and children from the stage was her primary concern. Yet Grant's works are often excluded from Black Arts Movement theater narratives today, owing, in part, to her commercial success. Producing black art on the "Great White Way" was perceived as antithetical to the Black Arts ethos of creating black art for the black masses. This does not, of course, mean that blacks did not attend Broadway productions. In fact, Broadway saw a dramatic growth in black audiences during the seventies.[14] Nonetheless, the vast majority of Broadway audiences remained predominantly white, and the integrity of black artists who did receive critical acclaim within the confines of commercial theater were often viewed as suspect by Black Arts Movement compatriots. The poet and playwright P. J. Gibson, for example, theorizes that black women playwrights will not often be "catapulted" or find commercial success unless they "adhere to the stereotypical belief system of what outsiders believe is happening inside." While there is certainly historical precedent to support Gibson's argument, Grant's narrative also provides an example of the careful negotiations black women playwrights have had to make to maintain their own artistic integrity while navigating white and male-dominated power structures.

The following narratives demonstrate that although their individual approach to playwriting varied, collectively their writings engage with *what was*, *what is*, and *what will be* the future of black America with careful attention to black women's concerns. Indeed, long before Kimberlé Crenshaw would coin the term "intersectionality" as a legal concept, their works demonstrated how the interconnectedness of race, class, gender, and sexuality were used to create overlapping systems of discrimination that harmed black women.[15] In other words, these pioneers spent a lifetime traveling with their ears to the ground, writing for the cause of black liberation. Now, in keeping with Barbara Molette's entreaty, the following narratives allow black women playwrights the opportunity to speak. It is my hope that future generations will listen.

Sonia Sanchez

Sonia Sanchez grew to appreciate the power of theater through her experiences performing poetry at the National Black Theatre (NBT). Similar to Teer's ritualistic revivals, Sanchez's dramatic works incorporate poetry, dance, and ritual and are marked by a keen awareness of the audience.

Are you familiar with Teer's Five Cycles of Evolution? She theorizes ways to change the minds and hearts of performers and then participants from the Nigger, the Negro, the Militant, the Nationalist, and then the Revolutionary. She describes these five levels of black consciousness in a 1973 Essence *magazine interview. She states,* "The Nigger, . . . *he has strong materialistic and individualistic values;* The Negro, *he is also individualistic and materialistic, accepts white cultural standards . . . ;* The Militant, *an aware* Nigger . . . *not for real change, and is only angry and frustrated because the system won't let him in;* The Nationalist, *being non-materialistic, he is intellectually for the collective. This is the first step into true blackness, where you develop a consciousness and a love for your people;* The Revolutionary, . . . *deal[s] with the spirituality of blackness. You know who you are, what you have to do, and you simply go about doing it.*"[16]

Yes. I remember when all that came about, and I remember the controversy also too. Controversy in terms of some people seeing themselves in the cycle. There were certain kinds of people. If you were a Nigger, you saw a certain kind of person onstage. It's hard sometimes for people to see themselves onstage and have a certain kind of connotation that's you onstage. You see yourself onstage, and that's frightening sometimes. I think Sister Barbara was very much involved also with, as she said, changing the minds and the eyes and the hearts and the hands and the bodies of people who had been made Niggers and Negroes in a place called America. But I never just leave it with the terminology, my dear sister. Because, you see, at the time W. E. B. Du Bois lived, he was called a Negro with the capital *N.* In this day and age Du Bois would have been called a revolutionary. Later on, he was known as a communist. I think that we tag people at an early age. When the age changes, you then leave out people who in their time were very much revolutionaries, who were progressives, who were changers of the world and who wrote books and were in organizations that changed the way people thought, period. I think that as a process, to present the Five Cycles of Evolution to an audience so audiences can see themselves at a given point and want to aspire to be at this other point is very interesting. It's very informative. It's very much a teacher's tool and a part of that whole ritualistic thing that they did there at the NBT. From Nigger to Revolutionary is a ritualistic passage. When I was in their presence at a performance, she never called them plays.

They were called liberators, not actors.

Yes. These liberators would go out into the audience and engage an audience member with ideas. Liberators would bring an audience member onstage, which would then make that person a liberator too. You see, it's very brilliant how her ideas of the world were also very brilliant ideas for the theater. It was not just: here's the play, here are the words, here's the audience who are listening to the plays and what the actors are telling them. It was participation. *American Theatre* asked me to write something about Barbara on the occasion of her death.[17] I talk about Barbara: her birth, then her birth again as this person at NBT, and her actors/liberators who liberated a room to progressive ideas in the world. There was no division between the stage and the audience. The audience became the liberators and the liberators became what I consider "revolutionaries" because they presented something, saw change. Therefore, the participants had themselves evolved while they were onstage. That's important. The point of not tagging people is that you're saying that you have the capacity to change. So, you write the poems and you write the plays that will allow room for people to change.

Thank you. Now let's talk about your dramas. What was it like growing up in Alabama and how did this influence your drama?

One of the most important dramas that I saw in the South was the black church and the sisters who worked in the black church. My grandmother, "Momma," was a deaconess at the A.M.E. Zion Church. If you read the piece that I gave to my grandmother called "Dear Momma"—that is all drama in there. The drama of sisters coming in on Saturdays to cook the food for the Sunday service. But within that milieu of cooking food, snapping beans and stuff, would be conversations about dear Sister Ruth. "Her husband's beating her again," and there would be this sigh of "Hmm." My Momma would say, "Sister Louise: I want you to take the little boy because you have a little boy and they can play together. Sister Betty: I want you to take the baby because you're still nursing your baby so she can nurse at your breast." That's drama, my dear sister, but it's also life. As life as drama and drama as life.

I'm sitting there. I've come in from playing outside. I have slipped behind a couch and I'm listening to these women talk about life, and for some reason Momma let me stay, because she knew I was there. As long as I didn't make noise she let me stay there. I listened to that drama, and then there was this silence and you would hear the snapping of beans. Then one of them said, "I guess we have to go talk to Sister Betty or Sister Beulah, because we have to tell her what she has to do." There'd be this light laughter. What they told her is, "The next time your husband is sleeping put some hot grits or some hot water on the stove. Wake him up and say, 'The next time you hit me, right? The next time you go to sleep, you gonna wake up with these hot grits on you or this hot water on you.'" I actually heard that, my dear sister, and I remember laughing. Momma shot her eyes around the counter and said, "Girl, either you keep quiet or you get out of here." I'd never heard anything like that in my life. But I remember that when I wrote that piece about Momma. What they were saying is that you let somebody hit you once, if someone hits you twice, but if someone hit you that third time: it's on you. It's on you and nobody else because you can't let that happen a third time around. They were doing psychology and social work right there when they were doing the cooking for the church. It was a psychology of black women staying alive. The psychology of black women helping each other get by in marriages where a man decided to beat his woman. They were figuring it out how to do this without a psychologist, without a psychiatrist. Isn't that amazing? That's what that was all about. So that's drama.

What playwrights have influenced your own work?

I'd always read Langston Hughes. I read what you would call the classics coming out of Europe. Bertolt Brecht: I use him as almost a bible sometimes because I like his larger way of looking at the world and I like his politics. I like his very human face that he gives to his plays. I also read the plays that were in the anthologies *The Negro Caravan: Writings by American Negroes* [1941] and *Cavalcade: Negro American Writing from 1760 to the Present* [1971]. I also read Frederick Locker-Lampson in the Eighth Street bookstore. I went in the plays section and I picked up the plays of Locker-Lampson, who was also a poet. Every time I picked up some of the plays I recognized the fact that the people were poets and playwrights and so I connected right away.

I began to go to the theater—Off-Broadway—and I saw Genet's *The Blacks* [1959] and I became a participant. I went to see plays just to listen to the words. I didn't care who was saying it. I would close my eyes and listen to that. I would take notes. I would write down words that just stirred my heart. That's how I began to write these plays and become involved with words that moved onstage. Words that left the actor's mouths and went to the brains and ears and noses and hands and hearts of an audience, and then the audience gave it right back to the actor.

Would you consider your work an expression of feminism or perhaps womanism?

I've never called myself a feminist, but I love the idea that Alice Walker came up with, the term "womanist." I believe that I'm a womanist also too. I think as a consequence we include everybody in that then. As Alice says, simply you appreciate and prefer . . .

A womanist "appreciates and prefers women's culture."[18]

Right. My point is that we were committed to the liberation of men and women and children. There was not just one way of looking. I was not out there just saying, "Women are going to be freed." We were about the liberation of women, men, and children. Feminism began to surface at the end of the sixties, and it basically blossoms in the seventies. I was involved with a number of women's organizations, MADRE [est. 1983] for one. MADRE is an [international women's human rights] organization that had people like Alice Walker, June Jordan, and Kathy Engel. Latino, white, and black women [came together and] dealt with a lot of issues in Nicaragua, Cuba, and places where we would contribute hospital supplies and drugs for children.

I gave Toni Morrison and Buchi Emecheta posters at the time I was publicizing *Sister Son/ji* [1969], and they framed it. I don't have mine framed. What I like is that they were all innovative and at the time that I was doing it. I was doing it in the spirit of the Black Arts. That is, to move away from a very staid way of looking at the stage. The second play I did was *Sister Son/ji.* The first production I saw done was innovative. To have no furniture, just a woman on the stage going from one scene to another by just movement and the change of music. A certain part of the stage was a different scene. She starts out center stage in a rocking chair. There's only that rocking chair and a coat rack where she had a change of clothes. That's all we had on that stage.

Is this the New York production starring Gloria Foster as Son/ji?

Yes. Gloria Foster. She was amazing, my sister. If you had seen her. At first, she said, "I can't do it because I'm not a militant." I said, "You're an actor. If you're an actor you can do anything." I'll never forget that. You know who directed it? She's an actor herself: Novella Nelson. I attended a couple of rehearsals, but the thing about *Son/ji* is that it was done around the country and on college campuses. I'd walk in to do a reading and someone would perform it. It was short enough, you know. We were moving on the level of Brecht. At least I was in terms of engaging an audience with theater to make them do something or think something or act or move. That's what that play was about. I decided to write in the midst of all the crap that was happening to black women on college campuses, in their personal lives, in this movement. I don't care if you're a revolutionary or not revolutionary: black women were getting crap at some point. So, you can see that this woman who then at the end of the play puts on that gray wig and sits back down and challenges the audience. I love that play even till this day. It was just done at Riverside Church in New York. They did *Son/ji* and *The Bronx Is Next* [1968].

My first play was *The Bronx Is Next*. *The Bronx Is Next* had a lot to do with our discussions about the various cities in America. Harlem: it was just massive degradation. Either you live well in Harlem—some people still did—or you didn't live well in Harlem. Some of the brownstones were cut up into apartment buildings, and they just placed people in those apartment buildings left and right. A conversation some people had was that the best thing to happen to some of these so-called ghettos is to burn them down like they did in Europe (but for another reason than Europe). Burn them down and take the people South, where they were human beings. That was to be the first of a trilogy.

The revolutionaries in the play intend to leave Harlem and take on the Bronx.

The Bronx, yes. All they were saying was, "We'll move them out of here." What's the next thing they say? "The Bronx is next." They were going to burn that down. Then the second play was not going to be the Bronx. The second part was about the trek South, after the Bronx, and the opposition they get. It's not an easy trek South. People along the way throw things at them and shoot at them saying, "How dare you do this!" They take people back South, where they had come from, where they can live like human beings again. This was part of the whole [conversation that was happening]. The Nation of Islam [est. 1930] had bought land in the South. The Republic of New Afrika was talking about buying land in the South. The whole point was to say to black folk, "We need to get out of the urban centers and go. If you have good jobs in the North, stay." A lot of people didn't, and so they were suffering in these tenements. So, take them South, where there's land and farms. People have been farming forever. So, there's a place to live and to build within America. That's what *The Bronx Is Next* was about.

So, kind of like a reverse Great Migration?

Yes. Most of them blacks came up North at the turn of the twentieth century. They were coming up North and people were killing them. That happened in the midst of middle-class black people staying there who had jobs, who had funeral parlors and whatever, but the majority of the people didn't. So, it's on that premise of going back and that's important. That's the context of *The Bronx Is Next*. Last August or September Riverside Church produced it as a retrospective of the Black Arts Movement. It was really done quite well. I stayed afterwards and answered questions. One young man said to me, "At first I had great difficulty identifying with mostly the men in *The Bronx Is Next* because I had never been a part of that kind of a movement. But then I realized why I had difficulty. It was because I had never seen people take charge of their own lives. I realized that I have a job where I'm not in control of anything, but I saw people who decided to take control of their lives and do what they needed to do." That's what you see in the play. The point was to put men and women on stages where they were obviously in control of their own lives and they make decisions (right or wrong) about how they would live in this place called America.

Would you say that's even true for the character Black Bitch? Is she in control of her own life?

Well, yes. You notice I didn't give her a name? I didn't say Ruby, Jane, or Mary. She was a prototype and the men were also too. That was happening in many of the communities: be it a black man or a white man. Some of these women weren't making enough money to live anyplace. They had someone supplementing their income. She had White Cop supplementing her income. Of course, of all the times for him to be there, that was that time. What I liked about that whole section was that it was very surreal and tells you how these men thought. These men were thinkers, but they also understood some things. You know how in plays you get drama that is, like [*makes guttural noises*]? In the middle of this drama that's saying [*guttural noises*], Charles says, "Well, why don't you be me?" White Cop says, "I don't want to be you." Charles says, "You don't want to be me?" I like that whole section there because White Cop runs down [a street in Harlem], and then all of a sudden he becomes this black guy, and he realizes that if you run down the streets of Harlem at two o'clock in the morning, you're dead. That's what they were saying, and they wanted him to understand that. Just because he had that black woman didn't mean that he understood what was going on in Harlem. That kind of reality.

When I was up for tenure at Temple University there were three committees: there was a committee for my plays, a committee for my poetry, and a committee for my prose. One of the guys on the plays committee stopped me in the hallway and said, "Well, you know Sonia, we don't think you'll have any trouble getting tenure. But you know the plays, particularly *The Bronx Is Next*? I don't believe that a black boy running through Harlem would be killed." I said, "At three o'clock in the morning?" He said, "That's unbelievable to me." The next day I'm drinking my tea in the morning. I'm opening my *Times*, and on the front page was a young black man who had been killed running through the streets of Harlem. Two cops had killed him because they told him to stop and he didn't stop. I went to his office and I knocked on his door, and I held it up and said, "Look." He didn't say another word.

The thing about these plays: they were reflecting what was going on in the world, but at the same time we were also making a statement about it too. It's still happening today. Young blacks get killed constantly if they're out at a certain time of night. If you're a black person—especially a male—you cannot be out on the streets of any major city not knowing where you're going to. If you do, you die. You're dead. Even if you're in a car at two and three o'clock. You have got to know how to maneuver in the country and the world if you're out there as a young man someplace. It becomes impossible to stay alive even if you look respectable, you got a suit on, whatever. If a cop tags you, they're going to pull you over and ask you some questions. Does it happen all the time? But it does happen, because as Malcolm X said, "You might have a Ph.D., but to some people you still a nigga." That's very real to some people.

What motivated you to write plays?

My dear sister, sometimes I was writing a poem and the poem needed words spoken by someone. There were some poems I've done along the way that I would put in the margins, "To be sung, clap, stamp your feet, whatever." Then at some point, some of the poems I wanted the person speaking out loud, and I realized that this is very dramatic. Ed Bullins asked me for a play for the *Tulane Drama Review* [now known as *TDR: The Drama Review*]. It was *The Bronx Is Next*. Ed asked me, "Do you write plays, Sonia?" I said, "Yes." Let me tell you, my dear sister, if someone who is somebody ever asks you, "Do you write plays? Do you write poetry? Do you write short stories?" Always say, "Yes." Then proceed home and start reading every short story you can read, every play you can read, and then sit down and write. That's what I did [*laughs*].

The point of the Black Bitch in *The Bronx Is Next* is that she says something very relevant. She says to the guys, "Don't you go and say somethin' about what's going on here." She also says, "Well, what am I gonna talk about? Ain't nothin' important goin' on here. You people ain't doin' nothin' that I haven't seen before." Whoa. Now, that's interesting, and a lot of people don't pick up on that. Black Bitch is put there on purpose with that name because she was saying, "It seems what you're doing is this, but you ain't doin' nothin' that I'm gonna participate in. When you do that, I will participate and be a part of it." Now that's a heavy statement, because she was what I call the lumpen. She's *the people*, and what happens in our community is that black folks have survived and they will not join something until they can see a win. She wasn't seeing a win there with them so she said, "Hey, you don't have to worry about me saying anything at all because until . . ." I forget the language, but something to that effect is what basically black America says. That we will not participate until we see a win. It's not that they didn't come along, because she evidently is going to come along also too. They're going to make her come along. There were people on that migration South who were going to come who didn't know what was going on. She's not killed.

I thought she was actually going to die in that building along with Old Sister.

The old woman dies. Only one person dies in there. Now Dr. Arthur P. Davis, who was a professor at Howard University, is the person who initially said we were militants and we were hate-something. Then he changed. I went down to do a talk at Howard University, and he was in the audience. I shall never forget it. He stood up and said, "I'm Dr. Arthur P. Davis. I teach at Howard University. Blah, blah, blah." I said, "Oh, Lord, Lord, Lord! This man is going to blast me." He turned towards the stage and said, "Professor Sanchez is right. Everything she said here is right." He said, "The reasons why I wrote that article—that some of us wrote at some point looking at these young people—is that they scared us half to death. Here we were with our places—we knew our places along the way—and then they came around and said, 'There's no place that's safe.' That's frightening."

What he was saying at that particular point was what we had said with all that so-called militancy, with all that fervor, with all that passion. It had to be said at some point for people to look up and see the change that was coming. To see the impasse they were traveling, the lethargy that they were in. People were like, "I can't do anything." But you can effect some change. We became dear friends. I spoke at his funeral. I went down to visit and read to him a lot when he was ill. Dr. Davis used to tell me he told his student that, "The best black play that was ever written was *The Bronx Is Next.*" He said the students would say, "But what happened to the old woman?" He would say to them, "What do you think?" Some of them would say, "She wouldn't have killed her, right?" Dr. Davis would say, "Well, I think she did. Now what was that black old woman without a name?" She was part of the past. She had to die for our future to live.

Black Bitch was the future because she's saying things like, "When this gets to be firmer than it is, I'm gonna be in there 'cause I have these two sons that I want to grow up to be men. I'm giving them this and that. I know I'm just surviving now. I know I got this man who comes in once a week. I don't give a damn about him. I could care less about him, but he leaves money there. That means I can feed my children with that little old beat-up job that I have: I can survive. I'm a survivor. I'm gonna survive. I wanna survive like most of us survive when we came out of slavery and it's something that you don't even know about me. You men up here on this stage talkin' all this talk: you don't even have to take me into consideration at all. But I'm here and I am intruding on your thoughts and on your work 'cause you gonna have to deal with me for a revolution to happen."

You participated in the New Lafayette Theatre's Black Theatre Workshop [1968–71] led by Ed Bullins. How did you get involved in this workshop, and what did you do during the workshop?

Ed Bullins was the first person who published one of my plays. My participation with him was that of a playwright, as a person discussing the whole motion and movement of plays. I had come home to New York in 1969. I wrote some plays in that workshop, listened to some of the work people were doing, and did some scenes for myself. I'm always writing, and so from there I put some plays together for Ed for anthologies. I looked at Ed as a fine playwright. He was a playwright of *what is* and *what is now*. Those other playwrights who wrote are what we called revolutionary plays of *what could be* or *what is coming*. Sometimes people wanted to argue about which was more relevant, and I used to say, "They're both relevant because we are where we are now and we also want to be someplace in the future, so you can't get to the future unless you understand where you are now and what's going on now." I love Ed's plays, especially *You Gonna Let Me Take You Out Tonight, Baby?* [1969] and the one about the young gal Clara who flirts with Big Girl and brings Jack home—*Clara's Ole Man* [1973].

Why did you love Clara's Ole Man*?*

I like *Clara* because it's well written and it shows how the so-called black middle class, who really feel superior to everybody there, are educated but didn't have a clue about what was going on from the very beginning. As a reader, if you're hip, you got it from the very beginning. You read it to see what was going to happen along the way. Also, Ed was brave enough to write a play about a lesbian at a time when nobody would touch that. Nobody touched that unless it was a snide remark, and there was no snide remark about that. [He showed that] this is what's happening. Read it, agree with it, or disagree, but know that this is a reality. I love that play because it is well written. You hear the people living in Philadelphia. There's one place at the beginning of the play where Stoogie is talking about Philadelphia. He says, "We were the young men in Philadelphia, we walk these streets" and names the streets. This was the unpublished prologue. I told Ed that years later, when I came to Philadelphia, I went to that area and walked those same streets.

What was your experience like being a black woman playwright in New York during the sixties and seventies?

In the sixties, I ended up in San Francisco starting black studies. People did my plays in New York, but I was not in New York at the time. I came back into New York in 1969 and was seeing my plays done downtown.

Most of these productions were done in the East Village. But *Malcolm/Man Don't Live Here No Mo'* [1972] was first performed in Pittsburgh, Pennsylvania, when I was teaching at the University of Pittsburgh. It was performed by some children that we were teaching.

Do you believe that you faced any particular challenges as a woman playwright during the Black Arts Movement?

Well, no. I think most of the challenges that we experienced, at least I experienced as a woman, was the whole idea of having to keep alive—financially, workwise, familywise, raising children; making the time to write, teach, and grade papers; and do all the things that had to be done. I think I was blessed to have come through with Bullins and Baraka. I was blessed to have been part of a movement where people looked up at some point and said, "Are there any women who are writing?" Ed did that, by the way. Ed and the New Lafayette Theatre did that. No one gives them enough credit for that. Also, the brother Ron Milner who's a playwright in Detroit. He died a couple years ago and did a lot of work with Woodie King Jr.

What do you feel are the overarching themes within your plays?

Sometimes you ask a playwright what it is they are doing and it's a quick disaster.

I think your plays challenge audiences to engage with difficult issues that are important to the black community in order to inspire people to actualize change in their lives. For example, you don't shy away from talking about drug abuse and the need for strong black leadership.

Which play was that?

Uh, Uh; But How Do It Free Us? *[1974] instantly comes to mind.*

Exactly. Let me just begin by saying that some of the plays I wrote out of necessity. Being out in our community, I realized that there were some things that were not being written about. *Malcolm/Man Don't Live Here*

No Mo' meant that people were quoting Malcolm X so many years after his death. They hadn't moved beyond Malcolm and he was dead. Malcolm could no longer lead us. We can read him, we can understand him, we could internalize some of the things he said, but we need a live person leading us. *Uh, Uh; But How Do It Free Us?* meant a lot of people were talking in Pittsburgh about how they were going to make money off drugs to finance the so-called revolution. A number of men had two relationships: one with a black woman because it was necessary to be seen and one with a white woman because sometimes she was financing him at the same time. The other vignette was the whole idea of polygamy. Polygamy had entered into the conversation of our movement. Some people felt that polygamy was important to it.

The abuse of black women by black and white men also reoccurs in your plays.

It starts with *The Bronx Is Next.* It continues in *Uh, Uh; But How Do It Free Us?* and most especially in the vignette about the drugs. I had the set use three hobby horses because they used to say that people doing drugs were riding a white horse, so they were painted white. Heroin was called a lady, a white horse. The point about that was that motion and movement and how someone said the thing about drugs. Integration [happened] because you had white people with black folks doing drugs together. I have that in there. At the core of that world—what we call the whores within that culture—were these women. You have to pay particular attention, because if I don't give them names: watch out! The white guy [had to] decide who was the most beautiful queen of all, and that was that march around. The white guy trips Black Whore and says, "I win! I'm the queen!!" Yes, he hurts her, and those black men let that happen because they're so high. They're amused by the whores and they don't like the whores, which means there was a core of perhaps not liking black women at all, period. This black woman stands up and she gives that speech. She says, "Don't help me."

Then the last vignette was the thing that happened a lot in the movement that people didn't talk about: black men with white women and black women. They couldn't make a choice between the two of them. Someone questioned me and I said, "It's not an anti–white woman statement. It was something that was happening." It was basically a study on black men at that time: that they couldn't make up their mind which woman they wanted. It had nothing to do with me hating white women or white women hating black women. It was very much not being able to figure out who is the person that I'm really going to do this with. I'm in the movement and I need a black woman for show, but I need a white woman to love. A lot of black men were confused by that, which made for real confusion in relationships for a period of time.

Your plays also celebrate black motherhood.

Oh, yes. Not all of the women have children in my plays. The whores don't. Black Bitch does at the beginning and Sister Son/ji had children and took care of them, but the war killed them. She was a good mother. There's no real children in *Uh, Uh; But How Do It Free Us?*

Both Waleesha and Nefertia are pregnant by Malik.

But that's important. There's a play with no children. It's a play of pregnancy. Think on that. There's not one crying child in that play. But all are going to give birth, and there's the possibility it will all be aborted because of what's going on in each one of those lives. There are no children at all because what I'm saying is that children cannot live in that atmosphere. They will die outright, so don't even think about having children in the atmosphere of drugs. Even in the midst of duality of black woman/white woman and in the midst of polygamy, children were born. In my play, they weren't born. They were pregnant with birth. Maybe this will happen, but if something else doesn't happen, birth won't happen. They will always be at the point of giving birth, but never give birth. Life will not come out of these three vignettes that I'm giving you. No birth is really going to come out of that.

Would you say that your plays contradict, complicate, or critique Black Arts Movement rhetoric?

I think my play does all. I think all the women who were writing did that. Not all of the men necessarily, but all the women, because I think we came at it with a woman's point of view. Motherhood causes that to happen, being in love causes that to happen, and also being a woman that worked causes that to happen. We black women worked before a whole lot of women in America worked. Black women have always worked, but what we did is that we elevated work. We took it to a university, whereas our mothers were domestics. That was a huge jump.

Let's talk more about The Bronx Is Next. *Why did you choose the names Charles, Larry, Roland, and Jimmy for the black revolutionaries?*

Because they were what I call common names given. Every place I went there was a Charles, a Jimmy, a Larry.

So, the names don't necessarily connect to actual people? In other words, you're not actually talking about Larry Neal?

No.

I've always struggled to understand what these black men are doing. I understand their motivation, but their tactics . . . I'm a little confused.

Of the burning down the city?

Yes, burning down the city. Charles is the leader, and he seems to blindly follow the orders he's given over the phone even though a couple of his comrades question the efficacy of their policies.

Right. In any organization, there are some things you will follow and you disagree with. That's the only way that it functions. It will only function if you see it in everything. Have you ever been in an organization that someone just decided to go with this policy and you didn't believe in it, but because you were a part of the organization you went along with it?

Yes.

Right. They might have thought for a moment, "Maybe this isn't a great idea. We're just the workers. We lived in the buildings with the people for a year."

It's very easy to interpret these revolutionaries as sexist and abusive towards black women. They emotionally and physically abuse Black Bitch. What is the purpose? What is the symbolism?

Well, I think that at the very beginning of any movement there are very stringent ways of looking at people. If she didn't have a natural you'd say, "Well, she's not really a black woman." If you didn't wear a dashiki or if you didn't wear a long dress, you're not this. Lucky enough, people evolve and change and realize that people can straighten their hair and be just as [committed]. People change. I don't think this Black Bitch was a person that was put in there to show how much black men hated black women. No, she was a person put in to remind them of their humanity. To remind them that whatever you do, if you don't bring the family into it, it's not going to work. She was a single black woman with children. She was a family. Whether you like the idea that she was single or not. Unless you remind yourself as to how you deal with family, then you're doomed for failure. Whatever you're doing is going to fail because the impetus for any kind of change has got to be the betterment of your community, the betterment of women and children, the betterment of people, period.

Now I know that might sound as if it contradicts the whole idea of *The Bronx Is Next* if you have people who will take this old woman, give her a sleeping potion, and she'll go to sleep [and die in the fire]. But one: she couldn't make the trek. She would have never made the trek all the way, and they were moving. Also, she was symbolic of the old way of looking at things that had to die out. She came with this old way, "Oh, well. This is what I brought with me from Alabama." Even the young man said, "What do you mean, Charles? We're gonna leave her?" [Charles responds,] "Did you hear what I said? Give her something to put her to sleep. We got too much to do." So, even in a motion and movement towards change sometimes people die, some people get hurt, and some people don't make it.

Some people were not in the trilogy. The more I talk about this, the more I should continue it and finish. In the trilogy going South, people die on that trek. Only the strong survive that trip, my dear sister. We have a migration South already by black people. They're going by planes and trains and cars. They're retiring and going South again. They're buying houses in the South. They're doing it differently, at this particular time. In the trilogy, people are leaving the urban North. What they were going to do is take their children out of these places—because they're dying and ending up in jail—and just rescue them. What I call rescue means take them South and let them have a different kind of life, a place for them to *live.*

I notice that there aren't any women leaders within The Bronx Is Next. *I know that you are very thoughtful with symbolism within your plays—*

At that time, that's what we saw. What was surfacing in terms of the whole idea of this motion. Jeez, you make me really want to go back to that play! The person who had that idea about making the trek South was a woman! A woman leader. It never said in the play, but the person who said, "We have got to get our people out of here" was a woman. She had to persuade the leadership that the South is the best place. She says, "The North will not maintain us and keep us human because it's a man. But the South is a black woman and it will nurture us and keep us alive." The second part of the migration South is people arriving at five different states. They were the five states that the Republic of New Afrika had purchased and designated as the homeland of black folks.

Was the character Son/ji inspired by any particular person? For example, the name is very similar to the spelling of your own name.

I think I made myself and a lot of women I knew in the movement that woman. All of the things that happened to Son/ji didn't happen to me, but some of the things happened to a group of women. At some point every black woman I knew at the time had experienced everything that this young woman experienced, and so I wanted her to be like a woman for all seasons. I think that's what that man said in the *New York Times.* He said, "She's a woman of all seasons." It could be any woman up there on that stage talking.

When Son/ji later discusses the loves in her life, she doesn't name any man.

Exactly. At the end, she calls Mume husband. That was important. She does give one of them a name along the way. The whole point quite often was to just say "husband, child, et cetera." But you notice in that litany of people who die she gives names? That's important for the audience listening to hear a Westernized name and an African name at the same time. We did a lot of research on African names. People would say things like, "I'm having a baby. Professor Sanchez, do you know an African name?" So, we began to do research on names, and then we'd say, "Here's some names here! It means the following." The point of being a writer was that you were more than just a writer. You were a guardian of the culture, a bringer of new culture, a keeper of the culture, and an originator of the culture. You originated new words and you kept old ones that worked.

Let's move on to Dirty Hearts *[1973]. You have black characters and white characters in your plays, but this is your first play that includes an additional race in it.*

You mean Shigeko. She was a Hiroshima maiden.

This play also doesn't feature a black female character onstage.

The play is called *Dirty Hearts* and it's a game. If you get the queen of spades, it's the worst thing you can get. You get thirteen points. Thirteen points is unlucky. Someone explained to me many years ago, "Girl, you playin' dirty hearts. You do know what dirty hearts means?" I said, "What?" She said, "That's the black woman." The black woman had to be the queen of spades. Spades sometimes means a black person. She wrote down the genesis of that game, which was very racial. So, the point of that play was basically the nonappearance of a black woman other than the queen of spades in a game called dirty hearts. Her absence (I hope) was very pronounced in this world that we had come to know. Where this kind of malaise, this kind of nonmovement during the day was in response to the nuclear bomb. What people did is they left work and they gathered to talk to each other and to play at their lunch hours, because at some point they had begun to give up hope. In a sense, the black woman became the Japanese woman. Scarred. Who wore a hat to hide her face, her color, the scars, and everything else.

Can you explain the character Second Man and the Poet? For example, you mention that the First Man and Second Man are white, but it's unclear whether or not Poet is white.

That's a white man, right. Second Man appears as a white liberal. First Man is not liberal. I was trying to show you the types of white people who existed during the time of the nuclear bomb being dropped. At that particular time, the largesse was extended to the Hiroshima maiden. They had just dropped a bomb on Japan. I met Shigeko when she came here. I was part of a committee that hosted her.

She's based after a real person?

Well, many people. Many of the maidens who came over were scarred. She did wear a white hat with a veil. The largesse and the kind of attention that these the liberals paid her . . . Instead of saying, "We'll never drop another bomb again," liberals were like, "We're here to help you." This woman was probably scarred for life, because she already had an operation. This is the kind of thing that happened. A country that had dropped bombs on another country, then looked up and said, "After we dropped the bomb, now we're going to try to cure you." The subtext is, well, why the hell did you drop the bomb in the first place? History and herstory has shown us that you didn't have to drop the bomb. The war was over. The Japanese were making appeals and trying to negotiate. You and I know the scientists wanted to try that bomb out to see if it worked and how much damage it would do. So, that was very much a play about that. Shigeko is a person who, because she is being helped, cannot say what she really thinks. She said, "No, I don't blame you, it's not your fault." You know it is, but she's not going to say anything. She never really says, "I forgive you." She just says, "It's not your fault." Then there's the black man in there, Carl. Now you notice I gave him a name.

Yes, Carl and Shigeko are the only two with specific names.

Exactly. Well, I gave them an identity on purpose, because it didn't matter what the Poet, First Man, or Second Man names were. A lot of them were a lot alike at that particular time, so I didn't have to give them a name.

First of all, they already knew their identity by the very fact of their words. They knew who the hell they were. They knew they ran the world. One was a big-time businessman: he ran the world. The Poet, although he was having trouble writing, he knew that the only people considered poets were white male poets.

Carl screams when he goes outside. What is happening outside? Is Carl killed?

No. Carl lives, and the very fact that he screams saves the whole society. Because you see, one day they're going to come in there and they're not going to leave. The very fact that they thought that they could drop the queen of spades on Carl again. He says, "Why me? Why not Shigeko? Why not the Poet? Why me again?" What they're saying is, "Because it is so easy to drop stuff on you, Carl. You're the easiest target we have here. You're the likely one for us to mess up, to fuck over, and usually you don't do anything." But that day, everyone kept saying what a strange day it is. That's how the play starts. Nothing's moving, but when he goes out he says, "I'm leavin' out of here." He jump-starts the day again or in a sense he jump-starts life again. He jump-starts humanity again. If he could just get out of there and stay out of there, he would be okay. But the very fact that he gets all his energy from this group means he hasn't quite found himself as yet. He hasn't hit the sixties as yet. I mean the *real* sixties. The Black Arts Movement, Malcolm X, and all them people. He might hit them and he might not even do anything about it.

Why did you write Malcolm/Man Don't Live Here No Mo' *for children to perform? Why not adults?*

I had seen adults perform it for children, but I did it for children because there were not a lot of plays written for children to perform. That was done at the University of Pittsburgh by an organization that taught children. I saw adults here in Philadelphia perform it for children for a Kwanzaa celebration. The children [who performed the play] were not little tiny children. These were teenagers who had studied Malcolm in the Freedom Schools. They knew Malcolm, so they very much approached it in that way. I've seen people do plays about Harriet Tubman, and the children come and say [*high-pitched voice*], "My name is

Harriet Tubman. I am going to free the slaves. Come get on my freedom trains. Thank you." Well, Harriet Tubman was a very complex woman. She says, "Get on my train. If you can't keep quiet I'm gonna kill you. You gonna die." So, if you got on her freedom train you better bring some sugar for those babies to suckle, because it would be deep trouble. She'll get one of her spells and she might stop. The whole freedom train gets derailed until she comes out of that spell. All I'm saying is that I've seen some simplistic productions about Harriet Tubman, and it bothers me.

People don't ever talk about the complexities of women. What I try to say from the Black Whore in *Uh, Uh; But How Do It Free Us?* to the Black Bitch in *The Bronx Is Next* to *Sister Son/ji* is that these are complex women. The Black Bitch says, "If you don't include me in this revolution, you ain't got no revolution." That's real. That's not make-believe stuff right there. *Uh, Uh; But How Do It Free Us?* you get those two women who've said, "Yes, I believe in polygamy" and they don't. So, you get the subtext of women; what they say sometimes to get a man and keep a man. Also, they're going to end up hating each other because of some man. It's still happening today. Black Whore is knocked down by the white man in *Uh, Uh; But How Do It Free Us?* The black men stand there and watch her and laugh at her. She says, "I know I can do this. I can get up from here. I've been knocked down by better black men than you, but I can get up from here." The man in a relationship with the white woman and black woman . . .

The black woman named Sister describes herself as "the new black woman."

Yes. Finally, she says, "Let me outta here. I'm not gonna stay here and be a part of this." It's important for us to understand that out of all that madness of polygamy and drugs came a new black woman that had jobs, took care, had kids, maneuvered around crazy people, and helped change the world. That's what I'm talking about. In *I'm Black When I'm Singing, I'm Blue When I Ain't* [1982], Reena has the multiple personalities. That's how we see Mama B (who is Bessie Smith), Toni (who is Billie Holiday), and Malika (who takes the baton from Nina Simone). The hospital—the insane asylum, really—is fascinated by her because she has these three personalities and she has to let them see only one. Then she lets them see the second one, and the doctor is just going crazy. She holds back on the third one because the third one has proved to be the strongest one. We know that third one would take over.

In Uh, Uh; But How Do It Free Us? *Sister says that she's the new black woman, but towards the end of the play Brother actually strikes her. He then kisses her, and she agrees to continue to be with him. Do you see how that might complicate the idea of the new black woman?*

Does she leave? Doesn't she say she's leaving at the end?

She says she's going to, but she doesn't actually do it.

I think she does. I'm not sure. I don't remember [*laughs*]. Oh, I might be rewriting my play right now. Maybe she didn't leave.

Sister gets on her knees and she prays and then she "goes over to her two bags and starts out. Sits down and begins to unpack. Slowly. [She] begins to rock back and forth . . . Begins to sing a tune as she continues to rock."[19]

But it doesn't say that he's there.

No. He exits.

That is the point. Why should she leave her space where she's going to have a child? But that's over. When he leaves she stays there and that's going to be her home. She's going to take care of that child and that home. I didn't think I had them together.

How has your drama changed throughout the years?

My drama has changed and not changed, like my poetry has changed and not changed. The central theme of my plays and my poetry has always been: what does it mean to be human? Then I show you sometimes some very inhumane people populating those plays. But at the core of it all is that we have got to, as African Americans and as people on this earth, try to figure out how can we act in a more humane fashion towards each other. I show you characters either doing that or attempting to do that. Doing it well and not doing it well.

The last play that I wrote, *2x2* [2009], is in the new book *I'm Black When I'm Singing, I'm Blue When I Ain't and Other Plays* [2010]. *2x2* is a play about a mother and a daughter. It's just the two of them, and it's very much an avant-garde kind of play because all you have are two chairs. Just these two people and stairs that lead up to nowhere on either side. It uses footage from the daughter's house in North Philadelphia. The daughter's strung out on drugs. It's a conversation between the two of them, and you find out this daughter was the light of this woman's . . . It's very complex because initially you see this older black woman and you say, "Oh, yeah. Look at her. She goes to church and all that stuff." Then you learn that she left her husband once and took that same daughter and left her with an aunt in Baltimore and came back to Philadelphia. Just because her husband cheated on her and became a player. When her daughter wanted to remind her of something she begins to sing the same cry that she sang when the mother left her with her sister in Baltimore. "Mommy, mommy, mommy." Every time the mother would then give her money for the drugs and take her back in. That was the subtext along the way. But the central theme of that is a mother-daughter relationship, which I have never really explored in any of my plays before. This mother-daughter relationship is a very important one. We're dealing—in a very real sense—with what has gone on in some of the communities, how grandmothers are now raising our daughter's children. Some of these daughters have been strung up on drugs for a long period of time. This is what we see right now.

There are about three subtexts in this play: the mother-daughter relationship, the grandmother as prime caretaker, and the young black woman. No one really writes about the young black woman as a druggie. They do it on a large scale but not on a human scale. In this play, you see her through her eyes as a young girl. What does she do? On the screen, this brother fights Mayor Frank Rizzo to get black studies put in the high schools. That's her history, but that's the history of a lot of druggies you see out there. This mother who is a grandmother now said to her, "Girl, you betta stop that stuff." She explains to her mother later on, "When I stopped [my activism], I had no protection from the men in my neighborhood. You left me out there for them. I was a victim of theirs. That means they really noticed my big legs. They really noticed my big butt.

When I was fighting out there, all they said was, "Girl, go on. Keep up the good work." Activism can save you from people who have one idea about a woman. She says something like, "Stars were shining in my eyes and I would say, 'How you doin', brothuh.' They respected me and said, 'Sistuh.' Momma, when you took that from me I had nothing. I was naked before them and they saw my nakedness and attacked."

Ntozake Shange

While Ntozake Shange was not aware of Sanchez's dramatic works during the Black Arts Movement, she appreciated her poetic voice and shared a commitment to privileging the unique concerns of everyday black women while also attending to the broader concerns of black America.

Do you feel that your work contradicts, complicates, or critiques the ethos of the Black Arts Movement?

I think to a certain extent my work reflects the female-centered or woman-centered possibilities that existed in the Black Arts Movement that were ignored.

Where did you see the woman-centered aspects that were ignored?

I saw it in the work of the men who were writing it. There were very few female characters who were black who were of any merit or any inspiration or substance in the work of the men I mentioned before. There were no images of black women. There were no references to female metaphor. There was no lyricism to speak of that reflected a feminine possibility. The strength of the female as a character or as an aesthetic tool was not present in the Black Arts Movement. I found it to be very masculine, very phallic.

Do you see your work as a departure from the Black Arts Movement or taking the Black Arts Movement in a new direction?

I think that's very hard for me to answer because I was very much a part of the feminist writing movement. I was at the beginning of a woman-centered sense of writing in terms of journaling, self-examination, attention to the personal, and believing that the personal is political without unashamedly believing that. I think that flies in the face of a lot of the politics of the Black Arts Movement, because I remember being made fun of because the personal was political for me. One of the people who did that was Amiri Baraka. I remember at one point he said, "People who pay attention to something like the hairs on your navel or something are of no consequence." Later, in one of my lines of poetry or in one of my novels, somebody paid attention to the hairs on her navel! So I said, "Well, so much for that" [*laughs*].

You were definitely identifying issues that later black feminists would address. What challenges did you encounter as a black woman artist at this time?

Being taken seriously was the first one. The second one was not to be seen as a knockoff of one of the guys. Developing an arena where my work and the aesthetic of my work could take hold on its own. That was a great challenge. That required making sure I got through a lot of readings. I continued to read all the time and I stayed true to my own voice.

What did you do to get others to take you seriously?

Show up.

So, being visible was a part of it. Were you in any way influenced by the National Black Theatre's use of ritual in your own work?

Yes. I believe in ritual. In the first version of *for colored girls* in Oakland and the first version of *for colored girls* at the New Federal Theatre as well, there were ritual dances at the beginning of the productions through movement and sound. Not words but through sound and movement and breath. Sounds of breath and movement tracing life from the womb to womanhood before you heard somebody sing a black girl's song.

Wow. That's powerful.

Well, that got cut.

A scene from *for colored girls who have considered suicide/when the rainbow is enuf*, 1976. Photograph by Martha Swope. Copyright © The New York Public Library for the Performing Arts. 1696713.

Who cut it?!

Woodie.

Why did he cut it? Do you know?

God, you'd have to ask him.

What was it like working with Woodie King Jr.?

It's always been very good working with Woodie. The problem is I had to recognize that he is working on a very limited budget and time constraints that are really humanly impossible to live up to. For him to produce as many shows as he has on limited budgets has been absolutely meteoric and amazing and quite commendable. He's a supportive producer. He's not intrusive. He contributes ideas that sometimes you throw out and other ones are very good. You have to take him with a grain of salt because one time he said to somebody that "the best thing about *for colored girls* was it was really wonderful looking at all those legs."

He said that?!

Yes [*laughs*].

Is there anything we have not discussed that you would like to comment on?

Black music and dance have been the grounding of the impulse for my work. I dance as I type. My body moves in the chair. I write novels and poems to Cecil Taylor and Willie Colón. The music's rhythm and the sweat of the dancer's body are associated with my writing in a way that I hope is reflected in the energy in it.

I'm going to be interviewing Halifu Osumare about dance's place within the Black Arts Movement.

She was one of my teachers. My first dance company was with her.

That's where you learned about African American dance history?

Yes.

Halifu Osumare

Shange and Halifu Osumare collaborated early in their careers, with Osumare performing improvised dances during Shange's poetry readings and Shange performing in Osumare's theatrical dance piece *Four Women: Images of the Black Woman in Monologue, Poetry, Song and Dance* [1973].[20]

I'd like to hear about some of the works you conceived, directed, and choreographed during the Black Arts Movement. We spoke about The Evolution of

Black Dance *[1974]. Could you tell me about* Four Women: Images of the Black Woman in Monologue, Poetry, Song and Dance*?*

During that time I was experimenting with writing, I saw myself as not only a dancer but also a playwright. *Four Women: Images of the Black Woman in Monologue, Poetry, Song and Dance* was my one-and-only theatrical play that I put together. Ironically, Ntozake Shange was in it. She was one of the four women. I would say Nina Simone was an inspiration for that, but I also used the term "four women" [because I had] four females play many different characters.

I did talk about some of the actual characters that I wrote about in *Dancing in Blackness: A Memoir*. It was my foray into playwriting that really never developed but it did begin to put me on the Bay Area stage again after I had been away for about five years. The other part of *Four Women*—now that I am looking at it—was my statement about bringing together my black consciousness and feminine consciousness. It was my first stage production that really focused on the black woman, in particular, and the friends that we have in black culture. I did not think of it as a feminist statement at the time. Now, Ntozake: she definitely was a part of a women's movement in the Bay Area as well as the Black Arts Movement at the time. She was very much conscious as a feminist activist. I was just doing what came natural to me. I have always felt that the black woman was very strong and needed to be highlighted. In hindsight, I am looking at that as a part of my feminine statement which I did not consciously say at that time. Another piece, an actual dance choreography that I did in about 1981, is called *Feminine Trinity*. [The dance piece has] the image of three different kinds of archetype women: the mother, the power woman, and the coquette. I juxtapose those three kinds of iconic archetypes of women throughout that particular choreographic work. I danced in the first incarnation of *Feminine Trinity*, and after that I got other dancers to take my part. You know the part I played? The power woman! *Four Women* definitely brought together my black and feminist statement.

You mentioned that you didn't develop your talent for writing plays. Why didn't you continue developing your playwriting skills?

I just felt that dance was taking more and more of my time. In fact, if I was going to develop playwriting, I was going to have to take more time away from dance to really develop that particular skill. I felt I had it, but, like any art form, it takes time to develop it. I felt my time was better spent with dance, and at that point I knew I was better at dance than playwriting. I decided to spend more of the time that I had developing my technique and my choreography.

Have you thought about publishing your theatrical pieces?

That's interesting! No, I haven't! I did copyright it, but I have never published it. It was a major force back in 1973 when I first came back, and we performed it at a place that is now defunct called the Rainbow Sign. It had four actors and live musicians that I pulled into that production. Again, it was one of my ambitious productions that made a statement but didn't last.

J.e. Franklin

J.e. Franklin was also inspired by Nina Simone's "Four Women" (1966), using the song as a source for her own play, *Four Women* (1973).

You were telling me an interesting story earlier about your first experience watching a professional theater production. Could you tell me more about that?

It was at Judson Poets' Theater down in the Village. I was living in the Judson Stewart House, which was around the corner and upstairs from the theater. I went to see a production of *Home Movies* [1964] by Rosalyn Drexler. Barbara Ann Teer and James Anderson were in the play. They were the first black actors that I had ever seen on the professional stage. Of course, I'd seen black actors in the films. I'd seen Lena Horne, Cab Calloway. I'd seen all those black performers, but not on the live stage. It was the first time that I started getting a passion, a spark that made me want to write for the stage. I remember just seeing Barbara, James Anderson, and George Bartenieff on the stage and being so happy doing what they were doing. What they were doing made me want to write something for people to be on the stage and be that happy doing what they were doing. That's really what lured me into wanting to be a playwright.

Who were your dramatic influences?

Alice Childress. Definitely Langston Hughes. I read Ed Bullins. Among the Irish playwrights: Eugene O'Neill. Louis Gregory. I really, really like Anton Chekhov.

What about the Mau Mau Room? *How did you come up with that idea? What's the title's meaning?*

Well, the Mau Mau was an organization in East Africa in the fifties and sixties. The name means "death to the whites."

That is a strong title.

Right. Growing up in the system at that time, we had some pieces of history about what was going on in Africa, what nations were trying to gain their independence, and what nations were leading the resistance on the white colonists. We admired Jomo Kenyatta and how he aspired for his freedom. So of course Jomo Kenyatta's name came up. The term "Mau Mau" was associated with moving out of the past over to the civil rights movement in America. In the *Mau Mau Room*, these young children (which is what they were) at this recently desegregated college were trying to find the answer to a question they had, which was, "How do you deal with the oppressive forces that are upon you? How do you liberate yourself from white oppression?" That's a question that's still being batted around today, because people [have] not really found the answer to dealing with the systemic forces that devastate. How do you respond to oppression? What methods do you come up with? We tried them all. Martin Luther King said, "Love will fix it." Malcolm X basically said, "Eye for eye, tooth for tooth. Kill your oppressor." W. E. B. Du Bois said, "Get your education." Booker T. Washington said, "Set down your buckets where you are."

There've been a number of our leaders who had different takes on how to deal with this white man. To be honest, they were all wrong.

So where does that leave us, then? Because in the Mau Mau Room *they have all these different ideas and what happens at the end—*

Well, at the end the idea that they came up with is the same thing in our daily lives. That is, we come up with all these ideas about how to fix the problem and the problem doesn't get fixed, and the only ones who get messed over is us. The only ones who're really the victims of these solutions is us. Look at how many warriors have just died from stress. Trying to deal with institutional white racism, which is over there in the white community. People who have stretched themselves out, and we turn on each other, we go around in circles. We fight one generation thinking that, "Oh, our children won't have to go through this." Then our children get grown, and then we see them go and do the same thing. Then it keeps going on, and on and on. We just keep dying, so obviously we haven't really put our finger on what the problem is. Those of us who have put our finger over what the problem is . . . Well, is anybody listening?

At the end of that play the young black students end up leaving, and the play doesn't end with a nice, neat resolution. Were you commenting on the debates about how to fight oppression?

Well, the question didn't get answered. Because it hasn't gotten answered yet in our society. It's a question we still have. It's why they were searching for the answer. These are the things that came back on them. Because they were young. They were children. They were naive. They hadn't read anything that could lead them to the answer. They were on this white campus, in this disembodied world, in this nonsensory disembodied world, and their professors weren't dealing with that question. They were isolated. And what happens in isolation is that you only get a piece of the picture.

Have you found a path that we should take?

Well, we first have to define the problem. The Kerner Commission identified and named it. They said that the basic system driving the American culture, one of the most fundamental causes of the unrest, is institutional white racism. The Kerner Commission says that. That was the first time I'd ever heard the term.

Institutional racism?

Institutional *white* racism. They didn't say "institutional racism." They said institutional white racism. They were very specific about that. They didn't say racism. They didn't say institutional racism. They said *institutional white racism*. Now, once they said that, they didn't tell anybody what that meant. Not a single person did they tell. Even when we went to Durban in 2001 for the World Conference Against Racism with people from all over the planet, they didn't define it. They came out of the Durban conference talking about slavery and reparations. They didn't even talk about institutional white racism. Racism in the world is white racism and there is no other brand. But they didn't define it. And it's not anything that has to do with skin color.

Did you ever have any interaction with other black women playwrights at this time?

What do you mean by interaction?

Did you attend any workshops with them? You mentioned you attended a production with Barbara Ann Teer as an actress. Did you ever go to the National Black Theatre and watch her productions?

Yes, I did. I saw a few things there. Since I was learning how to be a playwright, everything I saw influenced my writing. But I'd never been impressed by any particular one form because I was just gathering impressions and energies and really trying to create my own form at that time. I was basically a spectator and learner. I wasn't really that involved in any of those workshops. I was a member of the Harlem Writers Guild [est. 1950], [and they] really didn't have any playwrights. Alice Childress wasn't really a focused writer connected with the Harlem Writers Guild. She was not one of the members in the sense that other people were members. They were more into the short-story writing and essay writing.

Maya Angelou was a part of the Harlem Writers Guild at the time, but Maya wasn't writing plays: she was writing poetry. Rosa Guy wasn't writing plays: she was writing novels. Those were the more prominent members of the Harlem Writers Guild at the time, and so those were my early interactions with black women who eventually started writing plays. [Lynn Ahrens and Stephen Flaherty] did a piece called *Once on This Island* [1990]. It was a musical that was based upon Rosa Guy's novel *My Love, My Love; or, The Peasant Girl* [1985].

Are there any particular plays by Alice Childress that inspired you?

I like *Wine in the Wilderness* [1969] very much. *Wine in the Wilderness* was a part of this On Being Black series that George Houston Bass and Luther James put together out of WGBH in Boston. I was at a Harlem Writers Guild meeting when a representative from WGBH came looking for black writers to write something for the series that they were in the process of putting together. It was right after Dr. King's assassination that door kind of cracked open. White America was wondering, "What's wrong with us? What did we do to them? Have we been good to them?" So, this white man came to the Harlem Writers Guild and said that they were looking for people to write something for the series, and quite a few of us turned in treatments. Mine was the only one that was selected. My treatment turned out to be *Black Girl*. Based upon maybe three pages of dialogue and a little narration of what I said I was going to do they bought it and hired me to write it for WGBH. It was a video production. So that very first production and presentation of *Black Girl* was a video production that was broadcast on NET. Based upon that presentation, it was picked up a couple of years later by the New Federal Theatre [in 1971].

What do you feel is the purpose of your own plays? What did you want audiences to take away?

I don't write that way. I don't write with the consciousness of "I want you to take this away." It doesn't work like that. It doesn't.

I was wondering if you felt your drama worked to help people become connected with their own humanity?

Well, I'm not even starting out with that kind of consciousness. I have to be conscious of my own humanity, and I feel that if I do that . . . Well, you were there last night [for the production of *Coming to the Mercy Seat: J.e. Franklin's Ten-Minute Folk Dramas*]. I saw people crying. I don't know if you did, but I saw people crying [during] some of the other plays too. Just different plays hit people in different ways. Every play did not touch the same person. I say that's the beauty of the ten-minute play. You can put seven different crises up on the stage and somebody's going to get touched by one of them, and then when he's touched, tears are so liberating. Tears are. It's the sign that we're human. Because as far as I know, we're the only form of life on the planet that has tear ducts. We're the only ones that can cry. The other animals can whine, but not shed tears. Human beings are the only ones who shed tears. We're the only ones who have tear ducts. There's something cleansing and there's something very liberating about tears. They only come when you are connected, when you have touched down inside yourself. You've got to touch down. You can't be unhooked, soul from flesh. You can't be double bodied. You have to be at one with yourself. Then once you are at one, once there's this interflow, then you're gonna touch down. Once you get touched down like that, you're gonna cry. You've hit the most human part of yourself. It'll happen.

Those plays were very powerful. I also appreciate your comments about how audiences bring their own life experiences into the theater and are able to connect to that humanity.

They bring their pain here. They bring their wounds. I invited them to at the beginning of the play. I said, "Bring your wounded hearts."

Do you feel that as a female playwright in New York during the midsixties to midseventies, that you faced any particular challenges because of your race and gender?

Well, I cannot separate this challenge. I felt that I was an ethnic woman challenge, ethnic challenge. Specific race challenge. I wish I could break them all apart and say, "Okay, that happened to me because of this or that." I wish I could categorize that stuff. I'd probably be a millionaire right now because then I could help everybody else categorize it too. But I can't. I'm one human being.

I didn't mean to suggest that. The idea of race and gender are not something that can be separated, because one identity category often informs another. Here's an example: there's plenty of scholarship that suggests that black theater during the Black Arts Movement was very sexist. I'm wondering, was your own experience like that? Your plays were produced, and from what I've read in reviews they were well received. So I'm wondering, did you in any way feel marginalized?

Well, the thing was . . . let's not kid ourselves. Marginalization is a fact in American society. There's white society and then everything else is on the margins. Human society is on the margin of the white body politic. The white—

The disembodiment that you were talking about?

Yes, they're disembodied. They know that. They know that going in the white world is a disembodied world. And everything else is marginalized. Not simply black people. Anything that ain't white is marginalized. And it's designed that way to prevent contamination. I'm not over here by myself as a black woman feeling marginalized.

It's not just you.

It's not just me over here. My agent was a white agent, and he sent my work out originally under my whole name, my given name, the name my mother gave me, and theaters . . . Those weren't black theaters that he was sending those to [because] there were no black theaters. We were sending those [plays] to theaters all across the country. Those were white theaters [but] there were no women.

Is that why you use the J *with the little* e *instead of Jennie Elizabeth Franklin?*

My agent told me to use my initials. I changed it, sent the same play out, and then . . .

It was accepted.

Yes! So it wasn't about me being black. They didn't know I was black. My name, Jennie, is not a black name. They didn't want women. If you talked to white women and Asian women who are playwrights, they'll tell you the same thing. They didn't want them neither. So, there was a gender thing, but that wasn't a color thing, it wasn't an ethnic thing. They didn't want them either. They'll tell you the same thing. They have the same kinds of problems.

There was an article that came out in *The Dramatist* magazine recently in which some women had done research on the name you use and the possibility of being produced or not produced. If your name is Tanika you're not going to get produced. Even black producers are not going to produce your work. If your name is Maria you might get produced. Because it's all about what your audience thinks the play is about. Someone whose name is Tanika or Monika or whatever, they figure, "Oh, she's writing about black-white relationships. Maria. Oh, she might be writing about something that we can relate to." Because these theater groups that go to the theater, they look at things like that. You have to sell these groups on something that's going to happen. You've got to sell them on the story, whatever it is that you're offering. What the researchers found—because they were only researching women playwrights—is that there is something in a name. People bring that something to it when they're looking at your name. So when they see my initials, they don't know what I am. They don't know if I'm a male. They don't know whether I'm black. They don't know whether I'm white. They don't know.

Why the little e*?*

Because if I put a big *E*, then they'd figure, "Okay, this is a man." If I put the little *e*, there's, "Hmm, I wonder." Good. Keep wondering. I like that. Let them wonder.

Let's move on to Miss Honey's Young'uns *[1984]. Could you discuss the character of Miss Honey? Is she merely an Aunt Jemima stereotype, as one of the college girls describes her, or is Miss Honey something more? What does she symbolize or represent?*

I think Miss Honey symbolizes a character who just knows what she knows. She's just about seen it all, but what she's really trying to tell these young children is that, "You just think you know what the problem is. You just think you can fix this stuff that you're doing. But you cannot fix the problem with what you're doing." Basically, they [the students] needed her wisdom in order to keep them balanced. They came there to learn. They came to school to be scholars. She was very proud of them.

I don't know anything about Aunt Jemima. Just because they used the term "Aunt Jemima" doesn't mean they really understood what they were saying. They don't know what they're saying when they say "Uncle Tom." They think they know what they're saying. If you ask them to give the history of Uncle Tom and to really define where does the name come from? [The students would answer,] "I had an uncle, his name was Tom. Yeah, I called him Uncle Tom." But what's the difference between Uncle Tom and an Uncle Tom?

Mavis, the den mother and law student, appears the most aggressive. She seems to represent this new black woman, meaning she's an independent, strong, takes-what-she-wants type of woman. She also values black beauty and encourages the younger girls to grow their hair out natural instead of putting chemicals in to straighten their hair. Did any particular person inspire Mavis? Say, Angela Davis or anyone you knew at the time?

You know all my characters are really composites of people. They're not based upon any one person that I've seen in my lifetime. You take a character trait here and a character trait there and someone reminds you of something, and the next thing you know you've got a whole new character. You have someone that you have seen before and yet you haven't seen before, because all those parts did not exist all in one person. You just drew upon everything that you'd experienced, and next thing you know you've got a character. A lot of writers don't know the difference between an individual and a character. They'll see an individual, and they think that's a character. The character is a created persona from several individuals.

The role of religion in black life appears in several of your plays. Does Miss Honey's Young'uns *posit religion as a tool of pacification? Because when the girls and young men are trying to think of solutions to institutional white racism, Miss Honey often will say, "Let the Lord take care of that." She'll use that kind of biblical wisdom. Did you intend to make a social commentary about religion?*

No. I was not trying to make any kind of a social commentary. I was letting the character speak, and that's what she was saying. You have to let all your characters speak. I can't have her coming out and saying, "Child, don't you believe in Jesus, because Jesus ain't gonna help you." She ain't gonna say that. Nobody's gonna. She's not going to say that.

I noticed something interesting about this play. Unlike some of your other plays, Miss Honey's Young'uns *isn't divided into scenes or acts. You call them rituals. Could you talk about why you chose ritual and what this means to you in this play?*

Well, I would say that just the word "ritual" signifies something that [is] really a common occurrence and a practiced way of doing a thing, that eventually it's transformative. Ritual is transformative. It's known by the group. It's a practice. It's a known by the group. We know it. We don't even have to be taught it. It's almost automatic. It's almost an institutional part of your life. They are rituals because you know they're gonna occur again. You're familiar with it. You're very familiar with it. For example, when you go to church, you know that you're gonna take your seat and first the announcements are going to happen. Then the minister's gonna get up and he's going to preach and choir's going to sing their song. All of these pieces of action are part of something that has happened in the past, has happened now, and it's going to continue to happen in the future unless someone comes in and breaks the ribbon of what that is. Someone has to move one action out of the way and replace it with another action. If that doesn't happen, then you've got a ritual.

Peggy Pettit as Billie Jean in *Black Girl*, 1972. Still image. Courtesy of the author.

Can you explain what you mean by "transformative"?

Well, the word "trans," crossing over, and "form," you're going from one form over to another. You're transforming. You're crossing forms. You're moving from where you are over to another place even. Traveling.

Let's move on and talk a bit more about Black Girl. *Could you discuss the title of that play? Why did you choose it?*

Well, what about the title? It was about a black girl.

The title Black Girl *holds a lot of weight. We're not seeing at this time, maybe not today either, a lot of plays that focus on the experiences of young black girls. One of the things that I really love about the play is that Billie Jean wants to become a dancer. That's particularly important because historically black bodies, and black female bodies in particular, have been controlled and dehumanized. I'm thinking of Sara Baartman, for instance. So, the fact that she wants to become a dancer really dismantles ideas of what the black female body is capable of. I was wondering if Mama Rosie's discouragement of Billie Jean's desire to become a dancer is because of social or religious pressures? Why is she so opposed to that idea of Billie Jean becoming a dancer?*

I think that all mothers, in general, want their children to be able to be self-sufficient. So they don't come back home and ask them for money, for one thing. So, if you see your child choosing to do something that you don't think is gonna make them self-sufficient, make them any money, parents just unintentionally try to steer them (sometimes it's intentional too) away from poverty. Steer them away from what they think is not going to bring them anything. I don't think that they necessarily meant any harm.

I don't think Mama Rosie meant any harm. I think that she just . . . growing up in a culture and in a time when—well, even now the arts are not that valuable—the American nation and Western society in general never really valued art in the same way that Eastern societies did. The American nation certainly don't value the artists, and certainly don't value the black artists in many ways. That's why a lot of black artists went to Europe. Let's remember: musicians went there, dancers went there. It's a whole list of black artists who went to Europe because they were not valued here in this country. Let's remember that this play was written during the time when I recognized that black artists weren't valued. What is Mama Rosie going to say to Billie Jean, "Oh yeah, you're going to be valued." Josephine Baker wasn't valued, that's why she left the country. Richard Wright wasn't valued, and that's why he left the country. No. They were not valued, that's why they left the country. So, she's telling her child the same thing that the society was telling all these other black artists: "You're not valued here. You're not doing anything of value. You're not white, so obviously you're not a real dancer, you're not a real singer, you're not a real writer, you're not a real poet or a real novelist, or a real anything. Because you're not white."

What else is Mama Rosie supposed to say to her child? "Yeah, kick your legs on up." No. She's not going to tell her that. Based upon her own experience, that child is about to let herself in for a whole lot of heartache. A whole lot of pain. As the parent, it's your natural tendency to protect your child from that even if you have to get harsh. It's a credit to Billie Jean's resilience, her strength, her passion, and her determination to be who she is, to forge a way for her own self . . . in spite of her mother's

Black Girl, 1972 tour. Photograph by Friedman-Abeles. Copyright © The New York Public Library for the Performing Arts. 5030975.

negative comments. Her mother wasn't the only one making them. She got her sisters: they were making them. She got a stepfather: he was making those negative comments. Even at school: her teachers were making those negative comments. So that's the tenor of the time. Your teachers don't even want to see their children wasting their time on something that they think ain't going to make them money. I loved to draw when I was in third, fourth, and fifth grade. I was just drawing and drawing. I was a good artist. I felt I was. One day, my teacher said, "Can't do that all your life." Because they know what the society has in store for you. So, on the one hand they're being truthful, but on the other hand they're crushing dreams.

Where does Billie Jean draw her strength?

Well, she's living in a house with two strong women. These are not weak women. Rosie's not weak. Look at how she handles Earl. "What you driving? You got me any money? Don't come in here not bring my mama no Mother's Day present. You better come in here and you better bring a present for me and her." You see these two women [Mama Rosie and Mu'Dear] and how they deal. They're keeping the family together. They bring food in the house and they bring money in. They're self-sufficient, they survive, and they work. These are strong women and they're not begging anybody for anything. They're right there in the house with her. Then Billy Jean sees her teachers. That's what I was saying, that black women had role models in the community. We didn't need no women's lib. We were already liberated. We needed economic resources in the black communities that we lived in, but other than that we were free people, and we were already liberated. We were free. Freedom is an interior spiritual quality, anyhow. We were free.

Let's talk about your play Four Women. *I assume you had to have been somehow inspired by the Nina Simone song "Four Women." Could you talk about the black women characters and what they represent? For example, you describe Sarah as "slightly heavy, not too weighty, but heavy enough to feel a little self-conscious about being in a bathing suit"; Peaches as "a regular-looking sister, brown complexion, medium build, attractive, subtly assertive, mischievous and bitter-sweet"; Sweet Thing as "a tall sister with a pampered look. Her hair and clothes are well-kept, as if great care were taken to acquire 'that look.'"[21] Could you talk to me about those three characters and what they represent?*

Those four women represent those four characters who are mentioned in the song. I wrote it when I was teaching a course at Lehman College in the education department. I had some students who wanted to do some plays and they couldn't find any material that they liked. I wrote *Four Women* based upon the Nina Simone song, and the young women performed it there at Lehman College. They played the record and they performed their play.

You added the character Mae and describe her as "a hippy-looking Afro-wigged white girl . . . dashiki, beads, the whole bit."[22] *In the song, there's no reference to a "Mae." At one point in the play the black female students refer to her as Mae West. Why this Hollywood connection with Mae West?*

Probably the play was also drawing upon some dialogue that I heard [from] some of the black women students, some interchange between them, and some of the white girls on the campus. That character of Mae was probably based upon something that they said, that it gave me a visual picture of who she was and then I took that . . .

One of the moments in The Prodigal Sister *[1974] that I really enjoyed was Reverend Wynn's pronouncement of "better unwed than dead," and this shocks Ms. Johnson. Could you explain what appears to be an unusual response to an unwed-teen pregnancy?*

That was unusual? I don't think it was unusual. I think that, as I said, the black church has always been very liberated. We just generally have a value system within the black community. Although it's not written down, it's very oral. We say, "Live and let live. To each his own." That's something that's just . . . even the black church doesn't try to stop that, because you can't. And like I said, we don't have a systematized interference with our personal growth. What you have is a systematized attempt to bring out the best in us, to give us, to carry on with our lives that we have to live in from day to day, but there's no racism. There's no racism in the black church. There's no racism in the black community. We don't have that. We don't have procedural tools for unhooking anything inside of us, and if the culture's not engaged in that, they're not engaged in no racism. We don't have that. We've always been about liberation. So if a girl came out pregnant, well what are you gonna do? You better not get rid of no baby, that's it. You bring that baby into the world and you bring it up. As much as these black ministers are always going around muckin' with everybody in the choir, they can't . . . it's just like in *Hot Methuselah* when Bonnie the wife says, "What sister here tells me about him. He better not preach no sermon to me!" And so really—

"Even a monkey don't see his own ass!"

"Even a monkey don't never see his own ass." You can't preach no sermon to us. He can open the Bible and he can read it, but after that, he gotta close it and then everybody go home and do what they wanna do. He doesn't come after anybody. He can't. It's like coming after his own self. He's doing it too.

Micki Grant

The Prodigal Sister resulted from Franklin's collaboration with Micki Grant, who had already achieved critical success with the musical *Don't Bother Me, I Can't Cope* (1972).

Don't Bother Me, I Can't Cope *was conceived by Vinnette Carroll. What did that mean?*

She had heard a lot of my material, and she decided that people needed to hear it, but it had to be done in some form. I wasn't just a singer standing in front of a mic. That's not the kind of person I was. I was an actress. So she had to devise a form in which she said, "People have to hear your work!" She devised a structure and surrounded me with a cast and the choreography. In other words: put it in the musical form.

What is your writing process like? Does it change depending on the project?

Well, I sort of hear whole things in my head. I walk around with it a long time before I start writing. I'm like what you hear about: I do very little rewriting. By the time I start writing, I pretty much have thought of it. Or, maybe I should do more rewriting?

Your work is brilliant. Please don't. I just want a window into how your brain works.

I wish I could tell you. Like I said: if I hear a line, that line will come to me melodically, which is probably why I haven't done a lot of collaboration when it comes to writing music.

The Prodigal Sister *was a collaboration with J.e. Franklin. She told me that the original production grew out of an early straight play called* The Prodigal Daughter, *which was performed in the streets. Then Woodie King Jr. wanted to produce the play as a musical and invited you to work with J.e. How did you contribute?*

I did the music for the lyrics. But at the same time, I did my own lyrics for the songs that I contributed. So, there are lyrics in the piece by both of us and all the music is by me.

I noticed that all the projects you've worked on are meaningful and address issues that are actually impacting the black community.

Oh, absolutely! I wanted everything I did to have a message, a reason for doing it. Sometimes the message was contrary to what other messages were like during the sixties and seventies when people were [*shakes her fist*]. Everybody was angry! I came in just the opposite, trying to talk about how people could get along. There was a song, "Time Brings About Change," in *Don't Bother Me, I Can't Cope*, where we said, "Time brings about a change / Time will bring a change about," and then we went *boom* [*raises fist in Black Power salute and slowly changes fist into a peace sign*]. That was the way it ended. Look at the fist. And it came down like that. It means that we could learn to live together. As Martin Luther King said, "We will do that or we'll perish as fools." White people said they were so stunned and that they had gotten so used to the angry that they didn't want to go to the black theater anymore. The show ended with people actually holding hands.

Did the audience actually hold hands at the end of the song "Good Vibrations"?

They actually did, and that's what I wanted. That's what the song "It Takes a Whole Lot of Human Feeling" was about. By the end of that show, I wanted that same man who wouldn't shake my hand in "Human Feeling" to be ready and anxious to shake my hand!

You also include a song in Don't Bother Me, I Can't Cope *called "Questions." The characters talk about the different ways to pursue black liberation. You tease out a lot of questions but don't offer an answer. At the very end of the musical,*

Original cast of *Don't Bother Me, I Can't Cope*, 1972. Photograph by Friedman-Abeles. Copyright © The New York Public Library for the Performing Arts. 5116268.

I get the sense that perhaps loving one another and seeing each other's humanity is one of the answers.

Yes. At that time, I'm saying, "I'm still trying to find answers." In the show, I'm still looking for answers.

So the musical is meant to be ambiguous?

Yes. I'm trying to find some answers of my own. At the same time, I wanted you to know where I'm coming from with "My Name Is Man." I'm a man and I'm not a boy anymore!

"My Name Is Man" affirms the importance of black masculinity.

Yes. At the same time: *yes*, I'm offering my hand to you, but I'm offering not as a boy. I'm offering my hand to you man-to-man.

At the same time, you also have the black women in the musical expressing their desire to not be confined to just cleaning the home. They want to pursue their dreams. Was the song considered controversial? The women sing, "Show me that special gene—"[23]

"—that says I was born to make the bed"? No, our audiences liked it. It's amazing. By the time that show closed, it was almost half-and-half white, or mostly white (the whites started to dominate toward the end of the run). The show ran two and a half years. By that time, you could walk out and see more whites in the audience. I think they wanted to see this show that's been running for so long. By that time the album had been out too.

Don't Bother Me, I Can't Cope *includes a song called "Billie Holiday Blues." Did Billie Holiday influence your own musical career?*

No. I just always thought she was a fascinating personality because of what I read and saw about her life. She was just an interesting character to me. She had a sound that was very unique. It was totally her sound.

One of my favorite lines of the song is "It takes a lot more than just tryin' / It takes a whole lot more to win / It takes a lot more than just tryin' / It takes a whole lot more to win / When the world can't see beyond / The dark brown wrapper that you're in."[24]

Yes. A pretty good line, right?

You also discuss stereotypes about black women in "Time Brings About a Change." Don't Bother Me, I Can't Cope *is a musical that engages with heavy topics! When people think of musicals, that's not necessarily what comes to mind. I see your work as revolutionizing what we think of as the American musical.*

Yes. That's what a couple of the critics said. I don't know if he used those words, but they said it wasn't the usual fare.

For example, you have this up-tempo beat as characters talk about rats. A character says, "I hardly slept at all 'cause the rats were having a party in the hall."[25]

You're talking about tenements in Harlem and these major issues going on and using the musical form to reach both black and white audiences.

Yes.

Who influenced your work?

I can't say anybody. I think I've been more influential than they have been on me. Vinnette Carroll may have been giving me a direction in which way to go, because she was always ready for the next project! She never stopped. She was never ready to take a break. Yes, so that kept you on your toes! After that I was mostly just my own influence. People were coming to me with projects, but they didn't really all pan out. But *Working* [1978] was one of the big successes. Stephen Schwartz came to me and asked me to write one song for *Working*. I ended up writing three, and one of them became the theme song of the show: "If I Could've Been What I Could've Been." In fact, it was just done in England.

Nora Cole

To learn more about Grant and Carroll's collaborative efforts, as well as Carroll's artistic philosophies and dramatic works, I turned to "Corps Kid" Nora Cole for answers.

Carroll made history by directing Don't Bother Me, I Can't Cope, *forever marking her as the first black woman to direct a musical on Broadway. What kind of art did she want to create?*

You know she was West Indian? I think it was Alvin Ailey who took her to a Baptist church in Brooklyn, and that clicked everything for her with the gospel music and the pageantry.

So, not necessarily the teachings of, say, Malcolm X? It was the church.

Yes. But being black and conscious encompasses all of that. As a theater artist, Vinnette was about relationships between men and women. *Alice*—her take on Lewis Carroll's *Alice's Adventures in Wonderland* [1865]—was about a black girl navigating life and her experiences as she meets all these characters down the rabbit hole, but as it pertains to a black girl. There was a big dance at the top of the show. It's the chessboard of life, and the set was a turntable that lit up like a chessboard—[*singing*] "Remember how you started out." All the songs were about a young black girl growing up and navigating life.

Did the characters represent some of the issues black girls were encountering in their everyday life? How far did she take her adaptation?

She did not change a lot of the Lewis Carroll text, but the songs said different things.

That's where you probably get the church coming in.

Right. Yes.

You also write in your article "Vinnette Carroll: The First Black Woman Broadway Director" that she "could always create a brilliant first act, but she always struggled with the second acts."[26] Why do you think Carroll struggled with the second act?

I don't know, but she always struggled with the second act. Vinnette was not a writer.

Yes, I've read that she considered herself an adapter, not a playwright.[27]

Yes. But she was the one that would come up with the idea, and she was the one that could say, "No, that's not right. No, I need this."

So, she conceived ideas.

Yes. That's why all the shows used to be billed . . . there's a lot of legalese. Not with the adaptations but legalese with the other things that she did, because her name was always above the title: "Vinnette Carroll's *Your Arms Too Short to Box with God*" and "Vinnette Carroll's *Don't Bother Me, I Can't Cope.*" The shows were conceived and directed by her.

Micki Grant often wrote part or all of the book, music and lyrics, but these were her conceptions.

Well, it's her conception. It was like, "Micki, I need a song for this" or "I need something for that." Vinnette would put it together, and she would either throw this out and put this in or whatever. Like in *Your Arms Too Short to Box with God*: Micki wrote the two sermons for a preacher and the Mary songs, but it was also Alex Bradford's gospel music. There's also the book of Matthew from the Bible [incorporated into the musical]. *The Ups and Downs of Theophilus Maitland* [1976]: I don't know about that script, but it is a West Indian folk tale. *Alice* she adapted straight from Lewis Carroll. And then there's James Cleveland. James Cleveland was Vinnette's musical director for many years, and his only interaction with theater was with Vinnette. He would do anything for Vinnette, and he wrote a lot of the music for *Alice* along with Micki and H. B. Barnum.

Aduke Aremu

Much like Carroll, Aduke Aremu was also inspired to create theatrical works that celebrated her cultural heritage through music, song, and dance.

You were saying that you participated in the Frank Silvera Writers' Workshop [est. 1973]?

Yes, I met Garland Lee Thompson when I was very young. He did an [early workshop of] *Sisyphus and the Blue-Eyed Cyclops* [1975], a play which was esoterically interesting. *Cyclops* is about somebody who has a nervous breakdown and uses Greek mythology and African ritual. At the time, I was at Hunter College studying theater and was the only African American theater major. I went backstage, and I said to Garland, "I like your writing and this is the direction I'm going to go with my writing because I'm very political." I had just come back from West Africa studying art, music, and theater. I met with some of the West African writers. I met Fela Kuti, who was a famous musician, and I went to his temple. I met Barbara Ann Teer roaming around West Africa. I said, "I want my writing to be reflective of who I am as an individual, which is a cross-section

Aduke Aremu at the Billie Holiday Theatre in Brooklyn celebration following a production of *The Liberation of Mother Goose*, directed by Abdel Salaam, 2014. Courtesy of Aduke Aremu.

of being African, African American, growing up in Brooklyn, having Native American ancestry, and being Geechee." My family came out of Savannah and South Carolina, so there was a lot of Gullah traditions in there. "I'm going to put all of this together in one writing form, and I'm also musical. I'm going to intertwine all of my plays with a lot of music, a lot of dance, and a lot of costuming." Color is very important to me. Each scene in my plays will be color coded to represent different emotions or different philosophical point of views. I studied all of that when I was in Africa. I was also a classically trained violinist. So I knew music and I could hear different forms of music.

I do not decide to write a play. I sit down and all of a sudden it comes out and I write very quickly. I could write a play in two weeks. I could write a poem overnight. It would speak to me, and I had so much training going to these high school clubs and studying. I could pull from genres because I had studied. I had studied Greek literature in high school, so I could pull metaphors and illusions. I call myself a studied playwright. I really studied the world.

I wrote *The Liberation of Mother Goose* [1973] right out of college. I looked at European fairy tales and said, "Okay, these fairy tales are all political. Little Red Riding Hood was not running around the woods looking for grandma with a wolf running after her. Humpty Dumpty represented a king. Why don't I write the black version of this? Why don't I write the multicultural version of the Mother Goose story? Let's do it from our perspective. It was a hit. It was presented at Lincoln Center Street Festival. I tell you: it's my ancestors in heaven who must be very good negotiators with God, because the *New York Times* wrote an article about me. They said, "*The Liberation of Mother Goose* is incredible. There are a hundred kids on this stage, in full costume, dancing and singing. They did fifteen songs." We had real music coming out. Robert Williams, who was prolific, was my music director. I wrote all the lyrics, I wrote all the plays, and he wrote all the music. He brought in other musical composers like Marcus Miller, who was a jazz musician. I had a choreographer, Gwen Jackson, who was a fabulous dancer. I had Michelle Fields, who was my music director. Then I brought in Dawn Alli.

I believed in music, dance, and theater together as a combination piece. So, every play I've ever written (except for two of them) were musicals. What happens is that anybody of any age could enjoy it because it wasn't children's theater as they knew. The dialogue was always on two levels. In other words, you had the children's spectacle part, which is the singing, the dancing, and all of that. But then there's a dialogue running through that has double entendre. So when they say, "Little Bo Peep has lost her sheep. Little Jack Horner sat on the corner, put in her thumb and out come . . ." All of it had implications that were adult themed. The rabbits were really deep. They could be prostitutes. All the rabbits come out and they're dancing and singing with Alice, but their dialogue is very frustrating for her because they're speaking on many levels. "Fly me. Come on down. This is the Pepsi generation." Then another rabbit says, "We really know what kind of Pepsi generation you're in, girl." So the rabbits were talking all this stuff.

I made a correlation between the African civilizations and modern times; how they fell from grace. Why does Humpty Dumpty have a problem? What's with this black man? Why is he so shattered? He sings a song about being a king and losing his kingdom. Little Red Riding Hood lives in the woods, but she is really a little voodoo girl. She carries major herbs around her waist, and her grandmother is really one of those old healers who taught her how to survive. Little Red can't find Grandma because when colonization came in, the grandmas disappeared. So people no longer knew how to heal themselves with herbs. They didn't know the old tradition, and that's what Little Red is really looking for: her grandma. Little Red says, "Grandma talks about the kings and the queens, but Grandma is dead now, so I am now on my own and I'm trying to piece together . . ." Little Red's costume has kente on it and all these different rags, but she's really a collection of a civilization that woke up in another world. Little Red was trying to put together her culture. Alice is the new urban black kid who doesn't know nothing about nothing. She's the new technological girl and doesn't know culture, so these other characters are bringing her into her own. It's like a rite of passage. Little Red is the deep one. Little Red travels throughout the whole play with Alice. In most of my plays Little Red was eight years old. She was played by brilliant actresses and fabulous singers and dancers. Little Red is the hot one. She's the realistic girl and the one who knows everything. She has a group with her called Gremlins. They all dance in the woods. Little Red becomes Alice's best friend and exposes her to a whole different culture.

Tell me more about how you learned your craft.

I took a playwriting course at Hunter College. I read every play I could get my hands on. I read all of Ed Bullins, Joseph Walker, Edgar White, and Shakespeare. I read Arthur Machen's *The White People* [1904]. I wrote *Bum Sonata* [1991] like a Greek trilogy with African style. Same technique with the choruses. When you study and then visit cultures in Africa and the Caribbean you pick up [ideas]. I tell people, "My plays are not city plays. They're universal." So you might have a reference to a Greek myth or you might have a reference to African tradition.

I like to keep my environment very cultured and rich so that it gives me stimulation. I set every room in my house up as a gallery, so I might write a play in a different room. I go in a room, sit down, and that's the energy I'm trying to pick up. A lot of times I'll play music when I'm writing. If I'm looking for a different thought, I'll play the music which brings me into the continuity of that energy that I want. Plus, I think as a female writer our journey is different than men. I don't think we're really in control of this universe as much as we might think we are. A lot of men are in control in the arts, so you have to create a female platform. When you come into my environment, you know you're in a female platform. I'm not trying to be like you. I don't want to be like Woodie King Jr., who I love. I strongly believe in women being who they are. I have a book called *The Princess Chronicles* [2010], where I write, "You have to be a princess. *Be yourself!*" I'm not trying to be like any other male playwright. I'm trying to be Aduke, so I'm not writing like anybody else, because I don't think you need to. Write like yourself.

The most important thing if you're going to be an independent female writer: You need to have some money. You need to make sure you do make money, because nobody is helping you. You're black and you're a woman, so get a grip. Nobody is coming to give you gold nuggets. The men are going to get it first, and so you're second. Nobody's coming to you with a charity bowl, so you better make your own money. That was my first priority: make enough money with my day job to support my theater career. I was a high-level teacher with the Board of Education. They paid me a lot of money, because I was also a drama specialist. I came out of Hunter College and was mentored by Dr. Feldman and Dr. Elaine Block, who was one of the forerunners of children's arts. They sent me out as a warrior on arts education. There weren't that many of us in the public-school system, so I rose quick and was able to carve out my own agenda and my own schedule. I became an assistant principal and then I was a principal of a high school, and Bill Gates gave me millions of dollars. So I was able to create an empire where I had money. Let's say the production failed and the box office wasn't good because I gave away the seats. Sometimes I take hits. You have to be able to take the hits. Legacy is about taking the hits.

Barbara and Carlton Molette

Whereas Aremu focused on building an empire to produce her own works and ensure her theatrical legacy, Barbara and Carlton Molette focused their energies on expressing truth onstage.

What kind of art did you want to create?

BARBARA: I read that [on the list of interview] question[s] and the words that I wrote down by the question were, "Truth. Truth." The first play that I wrote as an adult was called *Telling the Truth*. Getting out what I felt was the truth. Do you think so, Carlton?

CARLTON: Yes. I think that one of the things that we talked about a lot in the late sixties is that we were not really interested in "commercial success" as playwrights. We wrote what we wanted to write and didn't worry about who would or would not produce it.

BARBARA: We really didn't care.

CARLTON: Yes. The connection with the Negro Ensemble Company just sort of happened. It wasn't something that we had aimed at or predicted. I was shocked when we got a phone call from Fred Garrett saying, "We want to do your play." It was like, "You do?" [*laughs*].

What led to that happening?

CARLTON: Baldwin Burroughs, who was the head of the theater department at Spelman College, had some Ford Foundation funding available internally to bring in important guest artists. Seeing as how the theater program for both Morehouse College and Spelman College was located on Spelman's campus, there was a leaning in the direction as much as possible to bring in outstanding female guest artists. The year before, Baldwin had gotten Efua Sutherland, who was the founder of what eventually became the National Theatre of Ghana. Barbara had written the first draft of *Rosalee Pritchett* while she was in grad school. The first draft was only about the women, and so all of the white male characters in the play did not exist in that version. After it was no longer a grad-school project—we both tried to maintain a level of intellectual honesty and not participate in each other's homework as grad students—and she had her M.F.A., my participation was no longer an issue. We had moved from Tallahassee, Florida, to Atlanta, Georgia, and I said, "You know, this play needs to have the rape scene in the play, and we need to meet these guys who commit the rape. They need to become real people in the play." At that point, I was

Barbara Molette, mid-1970s. Courtesy of Carlton Molette.

fresh out of the U.S. Army Reserve. This is in the days of the draft and the eight-year-obligation phenomenon. I had just completed my eight-year military obligation, having served most of that time in the reserves and having spent at least four years of it in Tallahassee in a predominantly white reserve unit. So I said, "I can write about these guys. I know these guys." That's how it became a coauthored play.

BARBARA: Right. The other thing is we saw a play here in Atlanta that was done by a local black group. I can't think of the name of it.

CARLTON: It was called the Black Image Theatre, and it was founded by Andrea Frye and Young Hughley.

BARBARA: Right. Well, we went to see a play that they did, and while watching the play it dawned on me that we needed to elevate the characters.

CARLTON: I had forgotten. Yes. The play you wrote in grad school—this woman was a waitress.

BARBARA: I actually leaned over to Carlton and said, "You know what? I've got an idea. She needs to be not a waitress but a middle-class woman." I could hardly wait to get out of the theater to come home and start writing. Which I did, and that was the thing that I think turned it around.

CARLTON: Yes. At the same time, you were saying these needed to be middle-class women and dealing with their middle-class aspirations. Within the mix of that same thing, I said, "Yes, and the Army Reserve guys need to actually be in the play."

BARBARA: Right. Somehow or another, it just came together.

CARLTON: I think one of the things that probably struck a chord with Douglas Turner Ward was that we actually said in the script that we wanted the soldiers to be played by African American men in white-faced makeup. I have periodically revisited that thought, and for the most part I am still very much happy that we did that. There have been a couple of times since then when I worked with a white actor . . . like I think when we did *Prudence* [2007] and also when we did *Fortunes of the Moor* [1995]. We did those two plays in Connecticut. We were able to work with white actors, but we're talking now about a whole different generation of white actors who were willing to play a character who is motivated by racism. At the time of *Rosalee Pritchett*, there were really three guys in the program—two were in the Ph.D. program, one in the M.F.A. program—who later became successful professional actors. They were my example for why we shouldn't use white actors in the role. [*Barbara laughs.*] One of them considered me to be a really close friend of his. He and his girlfriend used to come over to our house and hang out on Sunday afternoons. When they got married, he had the unpleasant responsibility of telling us that we couldn't come to the wedding because the wedding was going to be in First Baptist Church in Tallahassee and they didn't allow black folks. I think there have been close to a dozen productions of *Fortunes of the Moor*, and the most enthusiastic advocates for productions of that play at white universities have been people who had sometime in their career played Othello. They were faced with the chore of answering, "What is my motivation for murdering my wife?" The reality is there is none.

BARBARA: Right.

CARLTON: The only motivation that Othello has for murdering his wife is that he is a beast to begin with. Unless you can accept the notion that this black man is a beast, then there is absolutely no reason for him to murder his wife. I'd say the strongest advocate for a production of *Fortunes of the Moor* was a former student named Reggie Montgomery. He is now deceased but played Othello several times as an actor. Eventually, Reggie became a director and wanted to direct *Fortunes of the Moor*. He went to several artistic directors at places that had hired him and asked to direct. I know he advocated at Hartford Stage and Long Wharf Theatre in Connecticut—"Why don't you do a production of this play?" I think he also went to the Public Theater [est. 1967] when George C. Wolfe was there. Reggie was in the original production of *The Colored Museum* [1986]. He plays Walter-Lee-Beau-Willie-Jones in the takeoff on the Sidney Poitier role in the "The Last Mama on the Couch Play" scene. He also plays the aging gay guy. Reggie tried diligently to get somebody to produce the play. He's a former student and all that, but the real thing [that motivated him] was having done Othello several times and having been faced with the question, "What are some of my motivations?" It's obvious that the only motivation is fundamentally based in racism. The only way to deal with that is to face that fact. We keep running into people who want to do *Fortunes of the Moor* because they've been put in a position of asking, "As an actor, how do I motivate myself to murder my wife?"

What was your experience like working with the Negro Ensemble Company and the Free Southern Theater [FST]?

BARBARA: I'm going to go first. I'll make mine real short. I loved working with Shauneille Perry and working with the women and the men who I have come to adore at Negro Ensemble Company. But it was like, "We have this play out there and they're going to do it." I just sat and I just absorbed everything that I could because I had never been in that situation before and it was exhilarating! John O'Neal at the Free Southern Theater was a different kind of experience. Now, I never met Doris Derby, neither did I meet Gilbert Moses or Denise Nicholas.

Carlton Molette, 1974. Courtesy of Carlton Molette.

CARLTON: Our involvement with FST was after a lot of the folks had gone out to Hollywood and made a lot of money.

BARBARA: Yes, but working with John was truly a learning experience for me. During the seventies and eighties and early nineties, I had two little girls who were growing up. I was more concerned about our family and everything outside of our family was like an add-on. So the Black Arts Movement and the politics that revolve around it was sort of secondary to me. I was really never that involved in the politics of it. So when I was reading these [interview] questions, it was like, "Have I missed something?"

No, not at all. Part of what I do as a theater historian is recover the works of black women playwrights. I am curious to know which women you feel made the greatest contributions to the Black Arts Movement.

CARLTON: There have been a number of occasions recently when I have felt like one of the things that Barbara has been penalized for over the years is being married to me [*Barbara laughs*].

Really? Are you difficult? Is that why?

CARLTON: No. I think that when people start talking about black women playwrights, she is often defined out of the conversation. There's this very interesting phenomenon that happens. I think it makes me angrier than it makes her, or at least she has learned to cope with it. It may make her angry, but she's just learned to pretend that it doesn't. For example, we have donated our papers to the Emory University Library. We get stuff from Emory Library that labels things as "Carlton Molette." Apparently, the library is stuck with a nomenclature system that dates back to a time when male chauvinism was "appropriate." But it happens a lot. We'll send something to somebody as "coauthored," and the response is to me. It happens too often for it to be a coincidence. So it's something that I understand and appreciate; the concern of a feminist perspective. Then the irony is that the feminists also define Barbara out because of me. There was something that we got recently. It was probably in a Dramatists Guild publication, or it was HowlRound. I don't know which one it was, but it actually overtly stated, "So-and-so is the first woman to do such and such." Then as sort of an aside to that, it grudgingly pointed out that she really wasn't the first woman but she was the first woman to do it who wasn't attached to a man.

BARBARA: You're right, and I can't think of what it was.

CARLTON: I can't think of what it was either, and I said I was going to save it because it was such a classic response. It's like, "Well, this is a female writer. She writes. She gets stuff done. And you are going to discredit her?" If there were two females collaborating on a play, then you would be willing to give both of them credit. But if one is male and one is female, then you get attacks on both sides.

Exactly. How has that impacted you, Dr. Barbara Molette? Do you feel that you faced challenges as a black woman playwright writing during this time period?

BARBARA: Actually, I don't, because we started off writing together and we have continued. And now I guess I have forgiven myself for any thoughts I had about it, and I have forgiven others and I go on. I don't worry about it anymore.

CARLTON: But periodically it aggravates you. [*Barbara laughs.*]

P. J. Gibson

Similar to Barbara and Carlton Molette, P. J. Gibson has made profound contributions to the growth of black drama in the United States. Yet Gibson has not received the broader recognition she deserves. Keenly aware of her position, Gibson understands that she is writing for the ages.

How did you get involved in theater?

I started writing poetry when I was in junior high, and then when I got to high school one of the clubs I joined was the drama club. I remember doing the play *Spoon River Anthology* [1963], which helped me write *The Black Woman* [1971]. I made all these monologues working with every black and Puerto Rican girl on our campus. We toured it. We were just too through with [the problems on the Keuka College campus]. I would go into the cafeteria and you would hear things like, "It's true! It's true! It's true!" So I go over to one of my white friends and say, "What's true?" There was a white sociology professor who had told the students in the class that it was true that black men's penises were larger than white. I hit the ceiling. I went to the professor and said, "Okay, what were your statistical testing factors here? Did you line six white men and six black men up, get erections, and pull out a ruler?" The ramifications of it was deeper. Remember I told you that the Hobart College guys would not date us? Well, a lot of that was because these white girls believed it and they zeroed in on these black guys who already historically were drawn to the white women. So we had a whole college that just didn't date us.

We had to go to Cornell University, Colgate University, and Hamilton College! That's where we dated.

Did The Black Woman *address the fact that there was a lack of dating opportunities?*

No. *The Black Woman* came about because the John Birch Society [est. 1958] was out there doing horrible things. *The Black Woman* dealt with people touching your skin thinking you were a whore. They had Loretta Devine playing prostitutes and whores and she would cry. The last laugh is on them, because you know where Loretta Devine is now. History is what it is. She is in the original *Dreamgirls* [1981]. Anyway, I made a decision that she and no other black actor would ever have to play those roles. I was going to create complicated, layered characters so that when they had to do scenes, they didn't have to go to Tennessee Williams to get a good monologue. Again, I am not equating myself to Tennessee Williams. I am always honored when I get a call from a college asking for permission to do a scene. What I have been doing is trying to leave a legacy of work for companies, actors, and classes to draw upon. Characters who are representative of their world in roles that are void of all the stereotypical negatives. I made a decision in the late seventies that I would not create any negative black characters unless it was part of a commission that was based on history. Enough people have written about pimps. I do not need to write about a pimp. We don't need another pimp. That is not to say we don't have pimps, but we need to balance it off. When Adrienne Kennedy became the surrealist, people asked, "Why?" I said, "Black drama is not black drama unless *all* of the drama is representative: the ritual, the surrealism . . ." To be stuck in naturalism and realism is not . . . When I first started teaching black drama it was all realistic and naturalistic. I like to break that fourth wall.

You do that particularly well with The Taking Circle, *the first play in the* Ancestors Series: A Trilogy *[1998]. When you mentioned not creating stereotypes, it made me think of* Weeding *[1998]. The character Candace is a young mother and drug addict, but you show her humanity.*

I wrote that because I was literally walking down Forty-Second Street between Ninth and Eighth Street and it was raining. I could see this streetwalker with this white man from Westchester or a New York suburb with his attaché case. As I was walking towards the corner, a red light came, and we stood close. I could now hear their conversation. She started at ten dollars. "Okay, eight dollars." But when she got to "Two fifty"—that was it. I had to write that because it was real. He took that two dollars and fifty cents' worth of whatever it was and then he went to suburbia with his child's little tricycle sitting in the driveway. So, that is why. Also, I was down in Houston, Texas, and I met an older woman whose grandson became the source for the brother character. He was stealing from the neighborhood, and these were churchgoing people who owned their property. Everybody in the family always owned homes, pay their taxes, and go to church. Not all of them were college educated, but they were all career working people. They didn't know where he came from. I saw the pain in this woman, who was in her seventies—a well-kept woman—and I went, "I have to write this." My whole thing was: kill him. As you noticed, I kill a lot of characters. But historically, that happens. So I had to look at that moment.

In The Taking Circle *the enslaved women perform a ritual that includes infanticide. It's heartbreaking that they have to perform the ritual to begin with, but they do so out of a love. The shame the women feel was not caused by the new mother's actions. Their shame was caused by living in an environment in which black women were considered property or subhuman. As such, they could not be "raped."*

Which makes today so painful what we are doing now. The way black women are presenting themselves. I just know that people are turning over. So, going back to George Houston Bass and responsibility: I can't be from the fabric of "art for art's sake." The history of our people, the dilemmas and the complexities of who we are, where we have been, and Lord knows where we are going is for a person like me. It is my responsibility to create responsible work that addresses something. I'm not trying to preach. I'm just saying: this is what it is. I'm not going to whitewash it. Lena Larsen Salvinoni from *Brown Silk and Magenta Sunsets* [1986] came out of what I heard when I first moved to the city. There was a black woman who lived on Second or Third Avenue in the sixties. She lived in a penthouse, was filthy rich, and she was a recluse. That just grabbed my attention. If you had that kind of money, why are you a recluse?

A great number of these plays were written once I came into New York in 1978. In those early days when I was reading everything that black women were writing, there is a short story (I think by Alice Childress) where the character says that she cannot go crazy. She wants to go crazy, but she can't because she has children. So, with Lena Larsen Salvinoni I give her the luxury of going crazy. She doesn't have to be worried about being put out on the street. I met a famous black singer who came into a lot of money and, unfortunately, got caught up in the drug world. I was at her house before the mighty fall when she was selling grand pianos and wall-to-wall carpeting. It was very sad. I was sitting there and she had a delivery from a high-end restaurant that I didn't know delivered. But they do deliver if you have enough money. That is what I learned. That is when I looked at Lena. So you can be a recluse and have everything brought to you. Now, this is before the internet. That is what that play is: to have the luxury of going crazy. Most of us can't afford to be put in a mental institution. I couldn't go crazy. Who would take care of [my dog] Cookie? I don't have that luxury.

Can I ask you about Lena and her relationship with Abel, the young artist and delivery worker? I know you probably have been asked before, but is he actually her son? Or is this something you want to leave to our imagination?

I leave it to your imagination. The thing that I want you to walk away with is: with everything that I write I want you to think about the next day. How does the next day affect everyone? Look at *Long Time Since Yesterday* [1986]. Which of those women are going to contact one another and remain friends or need six months before they can talk about what happened? In *Brown Silk*, when Abel comes to do his work and he is told she is dead, that she shot herself after he has had sex with her: how is this going to affect him the rest of his life? So, it becomes even more than, "Is he really her son?" This older woman has destroyed two young people: her own daughter and Abel. She is also a very selfish woman.

Lena treats her daughter, the poor man she married, and her own friend terribly.

Everybody.

She pursues her own pleasures. The one thing I will give her credit for is that she embraces her own sexuality. You don't often get to read plays where black women experience their sexuality and are not somehow destroyed.

My plays have been used as audition pieces by actors who have gotten into companies and theaters that my works have never been done in. Sometimes I'll be on the bus and I will run into an actor, and they'll name a regional house they got into. The purpose of what I set out to do started from graduate school with Loretta Devine. I was the first black and first black woman student in the history of Brandeis University's master of fine arts program in playwriting.

As you said earlier, you are many times "the first." Is it sometimes lonely being the first?

Well, I had a weird life, so I was alone a lot at things. What happens is that you have to deal with all the stereotypes, the clichés, the isolation. In my graduate work, it started off that we were all writing a two-character ping-pong for our thesis play. That is one of the hardest plays to write. Eventually, I did do well with that play, *Konvergence* [1978]. So I was writing really well, but I was the only one who was black doing really well, and so things were changed midstream. It went from a two-character to a three-character, and that play ended up being my "prostitution play" called *Swing/Slide* [1975]. It was the worst play ever. As a playwright, I did not know how to introduce a white character and then not deal with that issue of whiteness. I also allowed my professor to talk me out of using my initials and use "Pat," so it is the only play I have written under Pat Gibson. It was a big learning experience for me and it was horrid. *But* I was very fortunate. Sometimes the universe is very kind to you. The angels walk with you. After I graduated from Brandeis, I started teaching as a graduate student. I went to Brown University to work with George Houston Bass at the Rites and Reason Theatre [est. 1970] in Rhode Island. George became my mentor. He helped me find my voice. I graduated from Brandeis with no voice as a playwright. I could write well. I had been writing all my life, but I had no specific voice or philosophical belief system in what I was writing and why.

He's done the same with J.e. Franklin and other playwrights.

I am the one he started with. The Rites and Reason's Research-to-Performance Method: that's me and George.

Tell me more about those early plays.

One of my plays, *Shameful in Your Eyes* [1971] . . . guess where that one came from? It was originally entitled *The Forgiving Room*. In the play, I use a college as opposed to being tied in the basement. Your first plays are often autobiographical in some way. I got away from that quickly because the history of our people is so broad. There are so many stories. I can't live long enough to do them all. I wish I could.

Is that therapeutic in some way? To give voice to the childhood trauma of being tied up in a basement for hours?

It is not therapeutic for me. It is exposure. That is one of the things that George said to me as I found my voice. I think he would be very pained by a lot of what is going on now, because people have talent and there is no responsibility rooted in the foundation of their talent. George was a genius. I am honored to have known him. I used to run around the country when I was giving talks and speak about George. Then one day I realized I had never told George that. It was a Monday. I called George and told him that I needed to say this to his ears so that he could hear what he had done for me. That Wednesday he was dead. George hired me as the project administrator of Rites and Reasons Theatre, which was a joke.

When did he hire you?

I was the project administrator in 1975. Karen Baxter does that now, and she is a real project administrator. I had already taught at Brandeis and Boston College. That was a fluke. I was working in the theater department in the office, and I got a phone call from the black studies department. Did I want to teach a course on black theater? I went, "Yes!" Never took a course, but I was an avid reader. Then I got a call from Boston College:

same course. I had that behind me and I had been writing. I had about four or five plays under my belt, lots of short stories, and lots of poetry. So, George hired me to be project administrator. The first thing I did was I painted this big ol' red arrow up the stairs to the Rites and Reason Theatre office.

George understood I had a clear marriage of academe and the arts. That was our bond. He created the Research-to-Performance Method, and I'm the first playwright he commissioned to write. The process began with George selecting the scholars, and they would write monographs from their field on a particular topic. The monographs were then given to the playwright to digest and regurgitate as a play. Then George would bring the playwrights, the scholars, and the directors—New York directors or he would direct—together for a roundtable to make sure you were on top of it. *My Mark, My Name* was the first play done. It was produced for the bicentennial of the Revolutionary War, so we had historian scholars, including Rowena Stewart, the director or chair of the Rhode Island Black Historical Society.

If you look at the U.S. Constitution, this whole thing about the "right to bear arms" has to do with militia. It has nothing to do with having guns in your house so you can have two thousand guns and rounds of ammunition. They didn't even have bullets in those days. Rhode Island did not have enough men to protect Rhode Island, so George Washington and the generals came up with this idea for the slaves to become part of the first black regiment of Rhode Island. At the conclusion of the war, they would get their freedom and some money. There were some of them—as in the character of Nuba—who were free black men who believed in the philosophical premise of the war and joined alongside slaves. At the conclusion of the war, they were released and disbanded at Saratoga to get to Rhode Island any way they could. Many of them ended up being caught and put back into slavery. There were a few who got down to Philadelphia and they got their money back, but most did not get their money. That is the heart of the research.

Rowena took me to underground railroads, and I learned the funny stories of churches being moved because of the political belief system. This one minister was just not doing what the people wanted. They picked the church up, put it on a wagon, and moved the church. So he went to preach, and the church wasn't there! They took it over a bridge.

It was hilarious. I looked at those boulder walls that were made by slaves. I saw the dairy farms where Tiver's character comes from. The historical Newport Gardner was a phenomenal person. He was a black seaman who voluntarily walked on a slave ship. He was a seaman, saw this beautiful ship, and didn't know until halfway across the Atlantic that they made him a slave. A lot of people don't know that in triangle trade, there were ports that they would go into. Newport was one of the ports. People who needed workers who were craftspeople would take what they considered the "best of the slaves" or the one with skills. So, Newport Gardner was bought by the governor of the state of Rhode Island, and he became the manservant for the governor. He had champagne parties on the governor's lawn. He and several free black men and women boarded the boat because he knew how to work the seas, went back to Africa, and established what we now know as Liberia. Talk to any Liberian and they will tell you that the heart of the problem that is going on are these people who went back with all this colonial American bullshit. I don't think they went back with the superiority kind of thing, but they had already been . . .

Socialized . . .

Exactly. So, the heart of that clash started in Rhode Island with this man who was able to get them back. *My Mark, My Name* talks about the cobblestone street the slaves and the free men are putting down. I went to the cemetery where they were buried. I was under twenty-five years old when this was happening. I didn't know the logistics of getting the permission of the descendants of the original people to use their real names. I had their real names, but I needed to write the play. I made up the stories so Newport Gardner is not in the play. Cefar's character is based on Newport Gardner in terms of his knowledge of Africa. The other slaves are second and third generation. Cefar came right from the water to Newport. Cefar's monologue about the well? There is a well in Newport much like you see in many of the slave narratives with the ships where one would jump over, and because they were chained together fifty would go in the water. That happened in Newport, where one of the slaves jumped in the well and they all went down. That's real. That is why that scene is there.

So, we get to the cemetery and I knew that to make the play as historically accurate as I possibly could, I would need to go and look at the dates on the tombstones. I made a list of female names, a list of male names, and a list of last names, and I just wrote down what I saw. Rowena and I were walking through the cemetery and then I stop because I see a funeral procession back in the 1700s coming. I'm standing there. She's watching me watch them because she knew some people could see these things. I watch the procession and I watch them go over to Siliah, so I write Siliah's name down. So I have all these names of all these characters and then I come back here to write it. When I am writing the piece, I have this list. Their names kind of raised up and got bold, so I just circled them, and those are the characters' names. That is how they were chosen.

I was the first playwright [to use George's Research-to-Performance Method]. Many playwrights went through, but I am the only one who was commissioned to write four. I wrote *Void Passage* [1977], *My Mark, My Name* [1978], *Konvergence* [1978], and *Clean Sheets Can't Soil* [1983]. Dr. Joyce Ladner, who I wrote *Konvergence* with, was one of the leading black sociologists in the country. She used to be president of Howard University. I've worked with Houston A. Baker Jr., basically as a writer. I'm a good storyteller. That's my gift. Studying characters. Why should I go to the library and do the research that scholars do when they know how to do it? So this was a perfect marriage for me: to have the scholars give me research and then I ingest it and create these worlds. They are there to let you know if you're going off.

Has the Research-to-Performance Method continued to influence your writing?

That is how I found my voice. It is rooted in philosophical, sociological, and historical fact.

How did your experiences as a Black Power activist impact your writing?

I have always understood our history and our contribution to the history of the world. I had an uncle and my cousin that I could sit and talk with. Africa was never a bad thing to me. Egypt was always black. Egypt is not an island. They will say, "Africa and Egypt." I'm going, "No." It has two countries on two sides of it. Egypt is *not* an island. I've been to Egypt.

I've seen the indigenous people, the Nubians. They're black. Africa has always been very important to me. I have been blessed with having visited and stayed. The first time I got a National Endowment for the Arts Playwriting Grant [1978], I paid my rent up for a year and went to Europe and Africa. I was always in search of some of the visions that I had [as a child]. That was why I went into Africa: looking for what I saw with my Granny. I have had spiritual experiences in almost every country that I have gone to. From the perspective of a lot of people I was weird in that I embraced Africa. But I was real clear that civilization started there, so get over it.

How did that connect with your idea of art? What kind of art did you want to create?

I never sat down and said, "This is what I am going to do as an artist." No.

You weren't necessarily reading Amiri Baraka's manifesto about revolutionary theater.

No. I am more interested in the psychological and sociological ramifications of who we are, if that makes any sense. I take a moment in time and I dissect it psychologically and sociologically. I made a choice in the late seventies that I was going to write about middle-class black people who either inherited the position, were educated into the position, or economically thrust into that position. Now, the definition of middle-class is altered since then. I thought it was and still think it is important.

That's my responsibility—to tell all of our stories. I am just able to listen to *your* story and be able to tell your story in a way that will emotionally affect you. People ask me what I am and I say, "I am a descendant of slaves." In this city, particularly taxi drivers, go crazy. They say, "Oh, don't say that!" I say, "What do you mean? I am! I am a descendant of slaves. I can't get more truthful than that. You have to get over it. I don't have a problem with it." I come from a line of people who survived the forts, the Middle Passage, the plantations, Jim Crow. That's my lineage. That's some badass blood. When you asked the question on slavery, my people were smart enough to outsmart the killers. I don't know how they did it. I deal with different ways of how they did it with *The Taking Circle*.

I love that play because you get to see these women sharing their stories. While they appear as if they don't have power, they use their intelligence and their knowledge of spiritual forces to survive the institution of slavery.

And calling upon your ancestors. My thing as a writer is if I touch one person, I've done a really good job. I remember I got the key to the city of Indianapolis for *My Mark, My Name*. After the production, World War II and Vietnam War veterans came up to me and thanked me for the play. Who would have thought? If for nothing more than those four guys, the production did its job. That is how I see it. I'm really blessed if I can get a great many.

In the foreword to Destiny's Daughters: Nine Voices of P. J. Gibson, *Joan Hepburn writes, "I fully expected that a woman of her vision and voice would be a household name by now. With her new anthology, I feel strongly that Gibson's time has come . . . There is so much food for thought, and her characters are so fully drawn that actors will find in this volume much material from which to draw for their readings. Poets will hear her unmistakably poetic voice in the language of many of the characters."*[28] *From what I have read, you should be a household name. Your work is there with Ntozake Shange, August Wilson, and Suzan-Lori Parks. Why aren't you a household name?*

I don't know why. You don't become one, I guess, until you get something like a MacArthur "Genius Grant" or something like that, and they are such a secret group. I don't even know how that happens. Sometimes I look at it like maybe my path is Vincent van Gogh's path?

How so?

They figure it out after I'm gone [*laughs*].

Woodie King Jr. describes you as "a major voice in black theatre in particular and American theatre in general."[29] *You've worked with King on several different productions. Can you describe what your experiences were like working with him?*

Woodie is my third producer in New York. Woodie catapulted me. *Long Time Since Yesterday* is a classic in black theater, and Woodie produced it twice within a six-month period, two different casts. *Miss Ann Don't Cry No More* [1980] was produced by Fred Hudson at the Frederick Douglass Creative Arts Center in New York. That show closed to a hundred and twenty people standing outside trying to get in. *Miss Ann* was successful. At the time *Long Time* was produced, it gave middle-class black educated Americans a visual representation of their lives. These women in the play are educated and professionals. That idea came out of my years at Keuka College. This play is popular and is done in scenes at colleges and competitions and the like. There are great monologues in there for actresses. The set was pretty, the costumes were pretty, and the women are complicated and enunciate their *k*'s and *g*'s and *t*'s. I also deal with subject matter that many people hadn't looked at. There are three different kinds of circumstances that happened in the lives of these women that weren't primarily looked at until then. So, Woodie is responsible for that. I owe Woodie for *Long Time*. He always tells me not to say it, but it was a fluke, a joke. I figured if a one-act play can be done in thirty minutes, you should be able to write a one-act in one weekend. I write fast. But I realized that it was bigger than a one-act, and so it took me a month. Woodie said, "Stop telling people that!" [*laughs*]. But this is the truth! Here's the other thing: I don't believe in writer's block. I don't sit down to an empty page. I don't try to conjure up something. I write the whole thing in my head before I sit down. Now, I give room for things to change and develop, but I don't go in not knowing the end.

My first book was the result of my search for black women writers of the sixties and seventies. Part of the reason no one had done the work was because very few people had thought to ask, "What were women writing in between the Broadway productions of Lorraine Hansberry's A Raisin in the Sun *[1959] and Ntozake Shange's* for colored girls who have considered suicide/when the rainbow is enuf *[1976]?"*

Lorraine Hansberry is why I am a playwright. When I went to Keuka College, I was going to be a fiction writer or a poet. It was one of those spiritual moments. There was Sherry (a Native American dancer), Denise (a Puerto Rican visual artist), and myself. We went to Rochester to see *To Be Young, Gifted and Black: Lorraine Hansberry in Her Own Words* [1968]. They had this giant photo of Lorraine on an easel on the side of the stage. We watched the play, and at the end of the play the three of us were sitting there crying. The theater's empty and we had decided to dedicate ourselves to our art. There we were as young, gifted . . . the black was the umbrella. Each of us continued to pursue those areas. I became a playwright because of Lorraine.

What about Lorraine Hansberry's work inspired you?

Well, she looked into the souls of individuals, and maybe they weren't saying the things that people wanted to hear, but she went after what was driving her characters. That's how I began looking at the psychological and sociological aspects. What makes people tick? Why do they make these decisions? Why do you have to be the man of the house? Why are you going to lose all the money? That was just one story. For me, that became the problem: that for a long time *A Raisin in the Sun* was the *only* story of us.

There are a ton of really good women playwrights out here—and the keyword is "commercial." Who deems what is commercial? I have a theory that in many instances if you denigrate, you are catapulted. Just look very carefully at a number of the works. If you don't adhere to the stereotypical belief system of what outsiders believe is happening inside, you are relegated. Those are very broad statements because they encompass many stereotypical images. What is the container of the play? Where is it taking place? Is it in a living room? Is it in a kitchen? Is it on a front porch? When I teach playwriting, I tell my students, "Do not write a piece that is in a living room or a kitchen. Think outside the box." White writers have the luxury of doing that because they have been able to be "in the box" for a long time, so they can think about outside the box. If a white playwright can center a play on the top of a grain silo in the middle of America, why can't a black playwright—who knows land and has black people in their history who own land—write plays that take place out in the vastness of the land? For instance: *Unveilings* [1982]. *Unveilings* is a piece that takes place on the property of this family. These are some crazy women in there. Abigail is the one who has cancer. She is outside painting, so there is an easel and picnic stuff. She's out there trying to mind her business, to do her thing, and everybody is coming down from the big house. Now, I'm not saying that everybody should write *that* scene. But black folks fish. Why aren't people out there on the dock somewhere or on a river's edge with a fishing pole?

Why do you think emerging playwrights are not thinking outside the box?

I think that many young writers are not taught to think originally. I remember when MP3 players came out and I got one, and I went, "Oh, hell no." I need to eavesdrop. I wouldn't have got "two fifty" if I wasn't eavesdropping. You can't be listening to music and walking down the street and not seeing. Well, you *can*, but you're not going to come up with an original idea, so then everybody is reinventing the wheel. Look at Broadway. Therein lies the rub: commercial. People wanting to make the money have to have a name. Sometimes they sacrifice a good production for an actor who ought not be in the role.

All I can do is be ready. I went to see Glynn Turman give a talk at City College of New York to actors, and I thought, "Why am I up here listening to an actor talking to actors?" Glynn said, "You must be ready in order not to get ready." It felt like a spotlight came on me. That was what I was there to hear: be ready in order not to have to get ready. Fast-forward. I put together a biographical packet and I have my nice little binder folders. One morning, the late Matt Robinson—I met Holly Robinson's father on a train coming from Trenton when he was doing *Sesame Street*—called me up and said, "P. J., do you want to write for Bill Cosby?" I went, "Yes." He said, "Can you be at Astoria Studio at five o'clock today?" I went, "Yes." The packet was ready, my hair was done, my clothes were ready, and I was out there at four fifteen. Cosby hired Kasi Lemmons, who wrote and directed *Eve's Bayou* [1997], Lee Hunkins, and I to write a film. We were written up in *Essence*, but then the writers' strike happened and we couldn't write. When it was over, Cosby took it from Columbia Pictures and gave it to Paramount Pictures, who said, "We want our own writers." So the screenplay is written, sitting on a shelf, and it will never be done. Ever.

You may have been spared knowing what we now know about Bill Cosby.

I actually went, "I don't know what was wrong with me because he didn't try to hit on me." But he gave us a chance. He put computers in our homes. He sent us to school to learn how to use the computer. I won't tell you all the rest of it. I'll leave it there.

Lee Hunkins

In contrast to Gibson, Lee Hunkins was not actively involved in theater as a youth. Rather, she discovered the world of playwriting and theater production as an adult while holding a full-time job in the Social Security Administration.

I went to a party in Boston and [Maxwell] "Maxie" Glanville was there. I didn't know him, but I came across him while wandering through the rooms getting bored with everybody. He had a whole group of people sitting around on the floor just listening to him. I said, "Who's that guru that everybody's looking at?" So I went and stood in the doorway, and he was telling them about theater and what it takes to be a playwright and what it takes to be an actor. He was going on and it was just fascinating listening. He must have seen how I was just staring and listening because when it was over, I got ready to walk away, and he says, "Excuse me. Do you write?" I said, "No, I don't know anything about writing." He said, "Have you tried?" I said, "No, I haven't tried. I don't know how." He said to me, "All you need is a beginning, a middle, and an end." I said, "That's it?" He said, "Yes." So I went home and I wrote a play. The first page: this couple fell in love. The second page: they had an argument and broke up. Third page: they fell in love again and got back together. The End. They would say, "Hi, my name is so-and-so." Then, "My name is so-and-so."

Did you take the play to Maxie Glanville?

I remember I met him at a bar, of all places. He looked at what I wrote. I had even double-spaced it, but it wasn't a lot. When I say that the couple met, I think I wrote down, "Two people meet. They like each other." That was all that was on page 1. Page 2 says, "They met again and went to dinner and fell in love and got married." Third page is, "They had an argument but they made up. The end." So he looked at it. If he had laughed, I don't think I'd be where I am today. But he didn't laugh. He said, "Honey, it takes a little more than this to write a play." I was insulted. I said, "You told me a beginning, a middle, and an end! I gave you a beginning, a middle, and an end." He said, "You know what? You ought to join my theater and learn from the ground up." It was called the American Community

Theatre [ACT] in Harlem. He said, "I hope you're a hard worker, because we don't fool around." I said, "Okay."

In the meantime, the only other thing I had done was enter a short-story contest with the *Pittsburgh Courier* [1907–66]. Again, I didn't know anything about short stories, but I knew that is what they wanted. So I wrote a story called "The Testimonial of Henry Bannister." It was about a black man who was having a dinner dedicated to him, and everybody else in the room was white and they thought he was too. They were honoring him for twenty years of service in this company. When he got up to make a speech, he said, "As a black man, I thank you so much for this honor." The room got still and the people were shocked because he was very fair and they didn't know he was black. After the dead silence, one of the men at his table started clapping, and they all started clapping and they all stood up. In other words, they didn't care about the color at that point. The story won the *Pittsburgh Courier*'s Countee Cullen Award in 1958. I got this telegram about this fifty-dollar award. Of course, we went crazy in the house. Everybody was so happy. We even gave a party on the weekend. All for this fifty-dollar check.

Maxie Glanville invites you to join the American Community Theatre in Harlem to help you learn the fundamentals of theater so you could write plays. What did you do there?

Everything. I painted sets. I collected tickets at the door. Most of the time, we were in a church basement, but the church basement was always leaking. My job was to walk with the buckets and catch the water. So, I had the bucket brigade. Maxie—his name was Maxwell but we called him Maxie—was so funny and was a good actor. He was in a lot of movies, like *Cotton Comes to Harlem* [1970]. We learned everything. There was one actress who was very good but was a little tipsy when she got to the theater because she would always stop at the bar on the corner. Maxie got tired of her. So one night he put her understudy on, so by the time she got there the play had started and the people were loving it. She was so angry. He called us together at the end and said, "I have a lesson for you all when you leave here. Have you been to the circus?" We said, "Yes, sure." He said, "Have you ever noticed the monkeys at the circus? Have you ever gone anywhere like that where you only saw one monkey come out?" We said,

"No." He said, "You know why you don't see one? Because it takes more than one monkey to run a show!" I never forgot that.

So many artists (who are now well known onstage and in the movies) went through Maxie. Actors, directors, playwrights, et cetera, who at some point passed through ACT doors include Steve Carter, Arthur French, Clebert Ford, Leah Scott, Clarence Williams III, Helen Martin, Juanita Torrence, Nick Latour, and David Downing. There were more, but these are enough names. Maxie taught us how to be very humble. If I go to a play of another friend and something's not right or they don't have anyone to give out the programs, I give out the programs. I had a certain humility by coming from the ground up like that. For me, humility meant that you had to know that you could help anybody that needed it in theater no matter what you were doing. You weren't too good. Maxie taught us to just watch and listen. I watched the plays and how they put them together. I was at rehearsals. I was on the stage doing the props. I was everywhere.

After about one and a half or two years I said to him, "I think I'm ready to write." He said, "Fine. It's about time." He watched me watching everybody, and after the play was over he would ask, "What did you think?" I would say, "Well, I liked it, but I don't know why she started crying like that." I wouldn't know, and every time he would just smile and say, "Good, good." He never told me if what I said was right or not, but I could tell that I was on the right track. So I wrote my first play, *The Square Peg*, in 1960. All my plays have a theme; they have something to say. In that play, it was: you can't put a person who is a certain way and try to make them somebody else. Because you can't put a square peg into a round hole; it doesn't fit. My main character was the type where he wanted to be something else, and he really couldn't be. Sidney Poitier came to my play. He was a good friend of Maxie's, and I thought I was going to collapse. And the people went crazy. We didn't tell the actors he was there, but they were just buzzing. I was thrilled. I meant to bring a picture because I have a photo of me accepting flowers and Sidney Poitier and everybody is on the stage for *The Square Peg*.

Sidney Poitier visits the cast of *The Square Peg* at the American Community Theatre in Harlem, 1960. Courtesy of Lee Hunkins.

Lee Hunkins with Sidney Poitier after an American Community Theatre production of *The Square Peg* in Harlem, 1960. Courtesy of Lee Hunkins.

Was The Square Peg *a successful production?*

Very much so. From there, I just took off with Maxie doing one-acts, doing monologues, doing everything. *Another Side of Tomorrow* was the second full-length play.

Meanwhile, you're holding down a job too?

I was working from 1948 to 1985. I worked five days a week, and Saturday and Sunday I was at the theater. I was able to leave a theater in Brooklyn, the Bronx, or wherever we were at two in the morning and jump on the train. I might get home at about six or seven, shower, change, and go to work. I had to do it.

How did you balance your involvement with American Community Theatre and work a full-time job?

Balance? I never thought that I was even balancing anything. It was just that you worked five days, and on the weekends you worked on the plays or you go to the theater. If you didn't have a play running, you were helping do something else in the theater. But if it was my play running, then I had to stay for all the performances on the weekends or whenever it was. A lot of times I just had time to shower and change. It's a thing where if you love what you're doing, it's not like work. There is excitement with it. So even if you're tired, when you hit the theater door the adrenaline starts pumping and then you go.

What sparked your passion for playwriting?

I don't really know. I don't have an answer for you. It's just there. Now with television—I didn't know anything about writing for television.

How did you begin writing for television?

All the way through the sixties I was writing and at the same time learning, but mostly with Maxie. After about ten years with Max, I was with Ed Bullins's playwrights workshop down at the Public Theater. That experience was good. He had us writers bring in assignments of scenes, and he would tell us whether the scene worked or didn't work. So it was more helping us with structure and things like that. He helped us in a very laid-back kind of way. A lot of time you would say, "What is he trying to tell me?" Then you would figure it out because he would push you or guide you. He wouldn't write the scene for you. He would ask you questions about something, and if you came up with the answers you knew that he was trying to tell you what you didn't yet do in the script.

So he taught with questions.

He was very good at it. It was a good workshop, and I was with that one for a while. I didn't know anything about TV, but I heard about the Eugene O'Neill Center in Connecticut, and I said, "Let me see what that is." They wanted you to submit either a play for television or a play for the stage. At that time, they were taking sixteen playwrights and only four for television. Well, I decided I didn't have a play that I thought might work, so I said, "Maybe I can write something for television." Then I said, "How do you write for television?" So, I go to Barnes and Noble and I get a book on how to write for television. That was in 1977–1978. After I read the book—how to set it up, fade in, fade out, do this, do that—I said, "Well, what do I want to write about?" I went to Harlem to where I used to live to either visit somebody or do something. For some reason, I wanted to get a feeling for the place that was my home for so long. I ran into people I knew, but it was so different. Everything had changed so much. I felt different when I went there, [as if] this isn't where I belong anymore or something. You get a little bit snobby and you get a little too caught up with yourself. When I was leaving, there was a big crowd and a fight going on between these two guys. I couldn't see them good, but people were screaming. I panicked and I said, "Oh my God, they are fighting and carrying on!" I ran to catch a bus on Eighth Avenue to get back home to where I thought I belonged.

Half my life—from the time I was three years old until I was thirty-something—was in that block. Now there was nothing. The tears started coming down, and my brother said, "Well, you know you should write about it." I said, "Write what?! I can't write about this!" And that is when

S. Pearl Sharp as Harriet Gittens and Dick Anthony Williams as Danny York in *Hollow Image*, 1979. Still image. Courtesy of the author.

Hollow Image [1979] first came to mind. I had to write about a black woman who lives in Harlem, leaves, becomes successful, and then discovers that old saying, "You can't go home again." My whole idea was that a black woman would become successful and then go back home and almost fall in love with her old boyfriend but finds out you can't do it from where you've been. You've got to do it from where you are. I didn't know what I was doing, but I sent the script in anyway, and suddenly I get a letter saying, "You have been accepted for the O'Neill."

We stayed in Connecticut and had our own rooms at the college. They rehearse your play, and we were all assigned to a professional writer. They were supposed to keep reading whatever you were writing and instruct you that maybe this character should do this or that. I had Richard Wesley as my instructor. I was really lucky because Richard never found much to criticize me about. Every time I said, "Is this okay, Richard?" he would say, "It's fine." Every now and then he would ask me a question about something in the script that would trigger and improve a scene. He never criticized. Other people were saying, "Oh, boy, he's giving it to me." They were fussing about their mentor, but not me. It was always like he was saying to me, "You just write it. Write what you think." Then we viewed it up there. My brother came. We invited people to the showing and had black and white audiences.

After they broadcast mine and the other films on ABC, I started finding letters in my mailbox from all these different agents saying, "When you come back to New York, we would like to see you." Everybody is saying, "You must have won!" They gave away one ten-thousand-dollar prize every summer. I said, "Nobody told me anything." They said, "Lee, it must be." Every time I opened the mailbox there was another letter from an agent: William Morris and all the big ones. I said, "Wow! I wonder what's going on." As it turned out, Lloyd Richards, who lived in a brownstone right down my block, was at the O'Neill dealing with plays. I remember I saw August Wilson go by. So, the fact is I really had won this award. I was shocked. I was in Las Vegas playing slot machines and I was lucky there. I was amazed. My friends kept saying, "You can't lose!" When I came back to the John F. Kennedy International Airport, there were about half a dozen friends with a champagne bottle and glasses and everything. They knew before I did that I had won this award. So then I had to decide about an agent. I don't believe that you make a wrong move, because I believe in destiny. But I went with Flora Roberts, who at that time was big. I thought it was better to go with somebody . . . she was an older woman, an agent by herself, and had been in the business a long time, but I think I made a mistake.

You won a big award. This signals that you are on the cusp of becoming a household name. How did she manage your career?

She didn't. I was so thrilled and excited about the whole thing that I wasn't looking at the big picture. That was the time when I should have been going around to the different networks meeting people. She didn't do anything. After about eight months to a year, I had to finally send her a telegram and tell her I don't think this is going to work. I didn't even know what it was to have an agent or what they did or didn't do, but I knew that this wasn't right. I wasn't getting any work. She understood my decision, but by then it was too late. I was cold. I could have been going around to agents right after and everybody knew it. ABC got more telegrams—because they didn't have emails—that night than they had gotten in the whole month or whatever. Telegrams poured in from all over New York, Chicago, the South and everywhere with people saying, "We want to see more drama like this. Where is it?"

What did you do after this major success?

I went back to working my stage plays.

This experience is heartbreaking.

I know, because there was no way for me to get in. *That* was my in. So I think about it now. P. J. [Gibson] and I were talking about it too. I said, "I guess maybe it wasn't meant to work that way for me." But then I said, "Jeez, just think if I had really had enough . . ." I was so happy and then later just having this experience. When my name came up on the television screen that night, I said, "I wish my mom and dad were here to see this."

Your play The Dolls *was produced by Hazel Bryant at the Afro-American Total Theatre in 1969. Hazel Bryant is someone who passed away very young. What can you tell me about her?*

She was a nice person, very serious about theater, and did a lot of good things. She tried very hard, but at that time most of the producers like her—their hands were tied. First of all, they didn't have money. It wasn't like now, where you could go on GoFundMe. If you didn't have a connection with money, you just didn't do the production. But she was out there. She would fight to get productions and get things done. She was good like that. She wasn't the first one to do *The Dolls.*

She wasn't? I thought the play was first produced in 1969 at International House.

No. *The Dolls* was first done at Speedy's Bar and Grill down in the East Village. I remember when I was standing in the bar waiting, I saw my brother—who was totally unlike me, the conservative type—peering through the glass in the window. I'm saying, "Come in." When he came in, he stepped over a collie and said, "Now what?" I said, "The play is in the back room." He looked back there as if to say, "Oh, God." But he went wherever I was doing something. He was always there and so was my sister-in-law, Marilyn, and my niece, Lynette. *The Dolls* was about a man, a puppeteer. My casts never have a "color thing," but they are what I want them to be. I used to say, "Mary Smith: black, forty years old." Now I don't. *The Dolls* could have been anybody. A lot of times in my scripts it could be done by anybody.

Some scripts, like *The Best of Strangers* [1985], have to be done by blacks. When *The Best of Strangers* was done here in New York City it was fine. When it was done in Buffalo at a conference . . . it's only P. J. that stopped me from being in jail now. Because I was going to kill the director. *The Best of Strangers* is set in a hospital with two women: one black, one white. They could never become the best of friends, but they became the best of strangers. That is why it is named that. She was from Nigeria and we had talked on the phone back and forth, but when it got to Buffalo, suddenly she decided to switch the parts. The woman that was black was now white and the one that was white was black. So when they came out and started talking, and the one that was black says, "My parents were so upset when they heard I was going to marry a black man"—the audience is like, "What's up?" She was black, so they are wondering, "Why are they so upset?" I looked up at P. J. and my hair must have been standing on end, because P. J. had my shoulders where I could not get off the seat. I was going to go find the director. She was standing way over on the side. So now everything was mixed up and the play made no sense. Since then, I watch my work being done like a hawk watching her children.

That casting choice totally changes the meaning of play. However, The Dolls *can be performed by anyone and the dolls actually come to life.*

Yes. *The Dolls* was about control and the fact that when you think you have it, you would be surprised that you don't. Mr. Rinaldo didn't have it. He was going to get rid of the dolls because he was going on a world tour or something and he didn't need them. He had made enough money and he did not need them anymore. The dolls come to life and tell him at the very end the fact is he can't get rid of them, because one of them has his heart, one has his mind, and one has his emotions. They find this out when he is not in the room. They suddenly come to life, and one of them says, "Why am I crying?" The other one is saying, "And I can dance." Then they tell him, "You can't without us." The female puppet was in love with him, so she had his heart. At the very end, the cleaning lady comes in and she says, "Mr. Rinaldo, I put the puppets back in the trunk for you." He comes out of the room and he is angry and screaming at her, "No, open it up! They have to have air!" Now he knows. So at the very end, he has to admit he can't ever get rid of them. That was *The Dolls*. It was just about people trying to do something mean and by themselves and realizing that life is not going to let you do that.

Now the only time I did not like a production of *The Dolls* was up at City College of New York or someplace. My friend Steve Carter, who was at Negro Ensemble Company for quite a while, was there. So, before the curtains opened, the dolls were supposed to be playing a little flute music, but they decided the play had a whole different idea. The curtains were closed but African drums were playing. I looked up at Steve, and he turned my head back. I said, "What drums?! There are no drums in the play. What are these drums?!" They had taken it into a whole different direction . . . like an African something or other.

So they placed an Afrocentric idea on top of the original concept.

And took off with it. I was so angry. I don't remember who did that production, but I remember telling them, "You will never do my work again. I'll be dead before you do my work again."

It sounds like one of the challenges you encountered was not having an agent to properly represent you. Another is people putting their own spin on your work in a way that disregards your concept. What other challenges did you encounter as a black woman navigating the television and theater industries at this time?

Now of course I have more strikes because of age. Most of the theaters don't want to say, "We only want young playwrights." So they say "emerging." Well, I haven't emerged. I'm out there, but I haven't emerged. If I have emerged, it means I am doing regular work all the time and my plays are getting done everywhere.

Why do you think that isn't happening?

There is something going on in the whole industry. Now every time older people are depicted, they are either senile or silly or something. They don't see women.

After you left Maxie Glanville and the American Community Theatre, who mentored you?

Nobody. So a lot of ways that I went . . . I could have maybe gone a shorter way or different way. I had to just depend on my instincts to say, "Do it this way" or "Do it that way." But I didn't have any mentoring, no. I often wished I had a person that could just be there for me or advise me. I didn't have it.

You mentioned that about six months after you received the ABC Theatre Award, you ran into Lloyd Richards at the supermarket, and he asked you how things were going. How did you respond?

I told him, "Well, it's not going good. I got Flora Roberts." He said, "Oh, I've heard of her. I know her." I said, "Yes, but she is not sending me out. She's not doing anything with me, and it has been six months and there is nothing happening." He said, "Hmm. That shouldn't be. That shouldn't be at all." It was as if to say, "Well, that's the way it goes." But he didn't say, "Why don't you see about another agent?" Or, "Let me make a phone call." Or, "Let me do something." He didn't do it and I wasn't going to ask [just] because he lived down the street.

CHAPTER 4

Performative Embodiment on Black Arts and Alternative Stages

> If we want to reach our people, we have to educate them. The job of education is long and hard . . . To reach an audience, we must understand something about how people listen and how they see in order to know when and where to put those potent statements that we feel will help to advance people's understanding in terms of what we want to show them.
>
> —Martie Evans Charles, "The Dramatic Crisis . . ."

Sonia Sanchez remains one of the most dynamic performers I have ever met. I first witnessed Sanchez perform her poetry at a Black Arts Movement event in Chicago on February 24, 2010. Although well into her seventies, Sanchez moved with grace as she walked to the podium. Surrounded in darkness with only a single spotlight on her, she delivered an unforgettable performance. Poised with a solemn expression on her face, she stared directly into the eyes of the audience and used her poetic voice to conjure the spirits of our ancestors. Complete silence descended upon the large auditorium as we listened to her punctuate the name of each ancestor with the click of her tongue and a well-placed pause.

Sara Baartman. Harriet Jacobs. Betty Shabazz. Shirley Chisholm. Abbey Lincoln. Nina Simone. Malcolm. Assata Shakur. While I cannot recall every ancestor Sanchez summoned, I certainly remember feeling almost as if I were being transported back in time through her skillful use of rhythm. I understood, even as a twenty-something-year-old with limited life experience, that she was using the performance of poetry as a vehicle to disseminate black history and culture. Performance allowed her to breathe life into what might otherwise have been a long list of names lying dormant on the page. She later told me that she always wrote poetry with an audience—not a reader—in mind. She remembers Barbara Ann Teer "engineering" or providing opportunities for her to apply her newfound skill of eliminating traditional barriers between performer and audience.

Sanchez, along with many of the other black women intellectuals I interviewed, conceptualized performance as a powerful means of attending to the mind, body, and spirit of black Americans. At times, this took the form of dancers, playwrights, and poets embedding didactic sociopolitical statements in their works. Other times, this meant performers, designers, administrators, stage managers, and directors simply working together to create performances that reflected the complex and multidimensional lives of black women, men, and children. At the heart of both approaches—which often coexisted—was a concern for the collective well-being of black America and a belief in their fundamental right to exist.

While their modes of performance varied, nearly all the black women intellectuals in this study identified performance as a liberatory experience that could be enjoyed by the performer, production team, and audience. For example, Halifu Osumare remembers that when she began researching black experiences in the United States and on the African continent, she discovered that dance had always served as an important tool of survival. She then translated this historical narrative into bodily movement. As Osumare performed this fundamental truth to audiences at Black Panther Party headquarters, she remembers feeling empowered though her embodiment of this ancestral legacy. Former National Black Theatre liberator Shirley Faison also describes the process of creating ritualistic revivals as "empowering" and the actual events as "life changing" for all involved, including participants.

While the narrators reveal that performance helped promulgate the black aesthetic and empower those who created and witnessed such events, there were also moments of strife among artistic communities. There was no single approach to creating black art, and as such friction did occur through policing the boundaries of blackness. For example, stage manager `Fémi Sarah Heggie remembers witnessing Roscoe Orman and members of the New Lafayette Theatre leave during the middle of a Negro Ensemble Company (NEC) production in protest. According to Heggie, the New Lafayette Theatre was "*real* black" and considered NEC members "downtown Negroes" because of their interactions with white patrons. However, Barbara and Carlton Molette also remember the New Lafayette Theatre and NEC members supporting one another's work. In fact, the Molettes argue that critics *created* an image of contention where none actually existed. However, neither narrative takes into account that these theaters were in operation for *years*. Perhaps it is unduly harsh to define any institution by a singular event or perspective.

The interviews that follow explore how black women intellectuals used their talents to embody the Black Arts ethos. The narrators share their most vivid memories creating performances as actors, dancers, poets, lighting designers, and stage managers. At times, they also share their more painful experiences navigating discrimination within artistic communities because of their race, gender, and sexuality. When taken as a whole, the narratives provide a rich production history, incorporating performance modes that range from Osumare's dance concert *The Evolution of Black Dance* (1974) to the Broadway tour of Loften Mitchell and Rosetta LeNoire's Tony-nominated musical review *Bubbling Brown Sugar* (1976).

Halifu Osumare

What kinds of opportunities were available for black women dancers during the Black Arts Movement?

I write about two major thrusts that I think happened in the Black Arts Movement during the sixties in my book *Dancing in Blackness: A Memoir* [2018]. The first thrust was art as a social-political tool. That

Halifu Osumare dancing at Everybody's Creative Arts Center in Oakland, California, 1974. From the personal archives of Halifu Osumare.

was a revelation to me that I could actually use dance to make social and political statements about who I was as a person. I was beginning to be conscious of my collective identity as a black person. The other thrust was the sense of dance as an ancestral legacy and that was a part of black people's survival. That took on a new meaning with the Black Arts Movement. I began to want to look at black history and discovered that dance was a part of every era of black history and was a survival tool. I began to develop my production that had many different iterations called *The Evolution of Black Dance*. That production was the beginning of my research into black history through a dance lens. I began researching Africa and what dance meant among the various cultures of Central and West Africa. I researched dance on the slave plantation. I began to put together shows that were a cross between my research and pushing demonstration narrative through dance that told that history. As I did that, I began to internalize how much dance was a part of our survival. I felt that I was illuminated by that and began using dance as a social-political tool and performing at the Black Panthers headquarters, their Sunday showcases, et cetera. I began to see that dance really was a part of ancestral legacy and I saw what I was doing in the sixties as a part of that continuing legacy.

You describe Ntozake Shange as a major artistic influence throughout your life. Can you tell me a little bit more about that?

We met within the growing early-seventies Black Arts Movement in the Bay Area, where poets, musicians, and dancers were all collaborating. I first heard of her through the kinds of music she played on her radio show and the poetry she read. We did a reading together in New York during my book tour for *Dancing in Blackness*. She reminded me that the Bay Area was really not the first time that we met, that we first met in New York. I think it was the Village Vanguard, a jazz club in New York, back in 1972 when I was dancing with Rod Rodgers. She went to the jazz club and saw me jump up—like I said I was known to do—and start improvising to the music. She was totally fascinated. When she found out I was in the Bay Area the following year in 1973, she looked me up and started taking my dance classes. We developed a strong artistic relationship and a strong friendship that has lasted for decades. She learned a lot from me about dance and relationship between movement and the word. I learned a lot about how to *interpret* language and imagery through my body through improvising to her poetry. I think we really influenced each other with that whole choreopoem format that she is noted for. I know that she gained a lot from performing in *Four Women: Images of the Black Woman in Monologue, Poetry, Song and Dance* [1973], because she was very shy as a performer and it took me a lot as a director to bring her out. By 1976 when *for colored girls who have considered suicide/when the rainbow is enuf* went on Broadway, she had overcome that and she was one of the characters.

Janet League and Ntozake Shange in a scene from the Broadway production of the choreopoem *for colored girls who have considered suicide/when the rainbow is enuf*, 1977. Photograph by Martha Swope. Copyright © The New York Public Library for the Performing Arts. Swope_209554.

Could you share a memorable lesson that you learned from your mentor, Katherine Dunham?

I started a lot of my formal dance training with the Dunham technique in Afro-Haitian dance with Ruth Beckford here in the Bay Area. I didn't really go deep into that study with her until about 1986. That was a revelation because Dunham was—as she has been called—a renaissance woman of the twentieth century. Her aura and her consciousness really blew me away. I had never met a black dancer/choreographer who was just so naturally engaging. When she walked into a room, the whole atmosphere changed. She taught me that dance was way beyond just its expression of culture. That it was a coming together of mind, body, and spirit in a way that was deeply ingrained in the human consciousness. She taught from that kind of understanding and level, and so I felt I had come full circle back to the technique that I had started as a young dancer with Ruth Beckford in the Bay Area. Now I had the founder of that technique giving me the underlying philosophy of it. Studying with Katherine Dunham made the Dunham technique a revelatory, life-changing, and consciousness-changing way of life for me. The experience really brought me to a level I was trying to get to all my dance career: an understanding of the integration of mind, body, and spirit. Katherine Dunham gave it to me. Now I feel like I have to be one of the proponents of her legacy. I will do anything to promote her legacy and understanding about life, death, and the arts. She brought the understanding of dance as a social-political tool (which she definitely used), as well as that sense of ancestral legacy that she showed in her choreography and the Katherine Dunham Dance Company. I felt like meeting Katherine Dunham and gaining the sense that I wanted to promote her legacy for the rest of my life was the culminating aspect of my dance career.

Shirley Faison

Similar to Osumare, Shirley Faison conceptualized performance as a means of empowerment.

I participated in black theater when I was in college, Rutgers University. We talked about a lot of the theaters that were around at the time. Avery Brooks was a teaching assistant [in one of my courses] when I was an undergraduate. He was affiliated with NBT [National Black Theatre] through Adeyemi [i.e., Michael Lythcott], and he brought us to NBT. There were a lot of black theaters around at that time, but NBT appealed to me more so than any of the other theaters. NBT appealed to me inside, as opposed to just being a performer. It was more than just being on the stage. It appealed to my personal growth. That's why I chose NBT, and everyone said, "Oh, but you're not gonna get in there because it's hard to get in there." And I did [*laughs*].

Was there an audition process?

Barbara invited me to be a part of the theater. When I started, I worked in the office. I probably did every job there was to do at the theater. After

I had been around for a while, she said, "Why don't you be a part of this?" The first production that I ever did was *Soul Journey into Truth* [1974].

I was able to read Soul Journey into Truth, *but I imagine the script is just a fragment of what actually happened. How did you perform the ritualistic revival? For example, what did those testimonial portions within the script look like during rehearsals and productions?*

The rehearsal process was pretty amazing, actually. The production was always changing, so the first time we performed it was totally different from the last time we performed it. The "decrudding" happened during the process. There are a lot of mantras in the production. Which, even to this day, something will come up, and I will say one of them or I will say it to an actor that comes into this office. There's, "Nothing happens to you unless it first happens through you." So, nothing can happen to me unless it passes through my mind.

You felt that these ritualistic revivals were more than a performance, that they were meant to change lives.

They actually did. They did during the rehearsal process, while thinking about it as a performer, and then once we started performing it they did it for the audience. Because you had to be authentic when you were saying those lines. One of the challenges was to not say no. That's really challenging, because growing up as a child I know my parents didn't mean to be damaging, but they would tell me no. "No" can stifle your growth if you're a child and you have aspirations to be or do something. You want to experience. You want to touch the bowl, for example, but are told, "Don't touch that bowl! You might break it!" Let the child touch the bowl and also let them know that there's consequences if the bowl drops, without saying no.

That example is in a monologue that one of the liberators gives.

Kabu.

Did Teer incorporate the experiences of liberators, or draw from her own experiences and incorporate them into the script?

Some of it was collaboration, and then there were certain things that were told by her.

How long was the rehearsal process, and what did a full rehearsal look like?

It seems like it was about six months. That's what it feels like. Actually, what we did was we liberators met all day long for two days a week. It was like a workshop experience and the production grew out of the workshop experience. So for me to say "collaboration" means that the collaboration probably happened in that workshop experience. The actual words that were on the paper grew out of that workshop experience that we had.

Could you tell me more about some of the exercises that happened during your workshops? You mentioned the "decrudding" process. How does this relate to the Five Cycles of Evolution?[30]

That was a very interesting experience for me because I am from Massachusetts. I was not aware of the Five Cycles of Evolution. I was out of college. I approached it from a very academic point of view, which didn't really work. So when I was doing the "Nigger" cycle and I went to the bar, I had a notebook with me. Everybody in the bar noticed me, and they were like, "Are you a social worker?" Then somebody said, "No, she's the police" [*laughs*]. That was a very liberating experience for me, so I began to approach the cycles differently. More internally, as opposed to more externally with the notebook.

I can say that going through those experiences at NBT changed my life. It changed the way that I viewed the world. It was very empowering to me. Even now, I feel that I can be in a room with anybody and know that I make a difference. I'm not less than. Someone can say something very negative to me, and it's like, "You know what? That's their conversation, not mine." Even as a talent agent, people walk in and they see two desks and assume I'm the secretary. "No, I'm an agent as well." I'm able to communicate with that person. If they want to think that I'm the secretary, that's fine. I know who I am.

And that's part of what you were all doing: finding out who you were, what you wanted to do, and not take "no."

Exactly.

You also mentioned that the productions changed in that the first one was not the same as the last one.

I'd say that they grew. In the beginning it was always an experience to empower. It was always an *experience*, and you would get something from the journey. By the end it was elaborate costumes, so that it was great to look at as well as experience.

I've watched a recording of The Ritual, *and I remember the costumes being very vibrant and rich looking. Was that typical?*

Yes. Now, with *Soul Journey into Truth* there was a part when we were flight attendants and taking the participants on a journey. In the beginning of the production, before we actually journey, our costumes were white skirts and tops. Then we go on this journey and we change costumes into these beautiful African costumes, but they're modern costumes, so they're sparkling. Larry LeGaspi—who did the costumes for Patti LaBelle and them when they used to wear those big costumes—designed the costumes for *Soul Journey into Truth*. So that although we were flight attendants, we had these beautiful costumes. I *loved* the costumes.

Was it difficult for you to be that emotionally invested in what you're doing while also encouraging the passengers [i.e., participants] to take the journey with you each night?

No. I think it had to do with the training. I loved doing it. It was almost like it *never* failed.

Did audiences ever resist?

Some people resisted, but overall?—no. You may have one or two people who are like, "Oh, no." But if you had twenty-five that were like that, by the end they were open. I remember one time when somebody from the Eli Lilly Foundation came to see the show. I remember him saying, "I came, I saw, I concur," and we got this big grant after that.

Sonia Sanchez

In contrast to Teer, Sonia Sanchez published her early works before they were ever produced. Although Sanchez offered specific details about how her plays should be staged, she was less directly involved in the production of her works.

I've been asked to act. I think it was Ed Bullins who wanted me to act in *Sister Son/ji* [1969], but I told him that I can't memorize lines. I did a walk-on during a ritual with the New Lafayette Theatre. Bob Macbeth was directing. I used to hang around there all the time. I do believe that many of us who perform our poetry believe that it is theater. It is theater. I think that's why it's not by chance that a lot of poets also write plays, because their poetry is drama, as it were. You notice a lot of my plays are in poetry form on purpose. I maintain that we speak poetry most of the time—especially people of color and Irish people. When you listen to Irish people speak, it is the most amazing language. You just sink down and just listen to the lilt and the singing and the lyricism and the beauty that's in there also too. I know there are connections. It's not by chance that during the Harlem Renaissance [ca. 1918–mid-1930s] there were connections between many of the poets and playwrights.

I did many a program for Barbara Ann Teer onstage at workshops as what I would call an "actress" telling a story. When I read some of the stories I had written, I became an actor on the stage. I did not realize I could become an actor, but I became an actor on the stage, and Barbara engineered that. She knew exactly what she was doing, period. So I was a regular at NBT, seeing what they were doing and how they engaged an audience with their work. There was sometimes no division between the audience and the actors. So what I tried to do as a poet and a playwright and an actor was make for no division between any of us at all. I think that is very important.

How did you go about getting your plays produced? You mentioned earlier that you weren't even in New York but your plays were being done there.

Yes. I got cards from people who wrote, "I did your play." I would go to universities and the plays were being done by students. That's what kept a lot of our plays alive: the student population. When Joe Papp asked to produce my play *Sister Son/ji* with Gloria Foster at the Public Theater, I did go because the sister who directed it was Novella Nelson. I did go and sit in on a couple of rehearsals. I'm a mother, so I had to be home after I taught, and then I would go there for rehearsal. I was there for opening night. People gave Gloria Foster a standing ovation and stamped their feet because she was brilliant. Gloria Foster was a brilliant actor. Novella and Gloria would ask me questions like, "What did you really mean at this point? What is your reference point? What are you trying to say?" I remember once a particular question was about the sex scene at the very beginning of the play when Son/ji's a young girl. I thought it important for that to be simulated. No obvious kind of thing. Just the movement from lighting and her saying, "Do you think each succeeding love is just like the first?" Which is to give you clues to this woman. That her life will be alike sometimes and maybe she will love more than one person in her life. As a very young woman she might love this college guy, but as she moves throughout life perhaps she's going to love more than one person along the way. Maybe there will be, because of deaths, no permanencies along the way.

You've talked about Gloria Foster's performance as Son/ji. Are there any other productions of your plays that are particularly memorable to you?

I saw a sister at the University of Buffalo do *Sister Son/ji*, but I can't remember her name. She was a brilliant Sister Son/ji, my dear sister. I saw Jomandi Productions do *I'm Black When I'm Singing, I'm Blue When I Ain't* in Atlanta [in 1982]. I did the lyrics and they had a brother do the music. That's a musical per se. It's a play with music. There are choruses, and it's done in poetry form also too.

Some of your plays deal with controversial topics. Do you feel that your plays were well received within Black Arts Movement institutions?

You have to posit it in the times, my sister. You had students on campuses who believed what you were writing: that's why they were being performed. They were not being performed as just "Let us do a play because it's interesting." No. They came to see plays that reflected what was going on in their own lives, in the country, and in the world. So they were always well received. I gave Jomandi Productions *I'm Black When I'm Singing, I'm Blue When I Ain't* because they were floundering. Jomandi Productions needed money, and that play ran for months. [The coartistic directors] Tom Jones and Marsha Jackson-Randolph said that the play saved them from going under. They made that much money with that play, and the point was to give it to them. I never have tried to make money off my plays, but what I have tried to do is to do the writing, to get it out so people can see themselves on stages and change. They can see other people out on stages and know that they don't want to be like them or they want to be like them. They can see ideas onstage and begin conversations. They can see things happen onstage and know that they could be that person or those persons and walk with a different kind of walk when they left the theater. That's what that was really about.

So, you've always been about the audience.

Always about the audience; not just pen on paper. Well that was what we were all about. It was like writing a poem: you always wanted it to be heard. Louise Bogan, who was a poet and my professor at NYU, was also the poetry editor at the *New Yorker*. She used to say to the class, "You must read your poetry out loud to train your ear so therefore you'll know whether it works or not." That was very real what she said. That's what we did. We learned how to do it with this woman who insisted that you read your poetry out loud and let your ear tell you what was working and what was not working.

What I did in *Uh, Uh; But How Do It Free Us?* was divide the stage up into three parts. I thought that was very creative stage directions. I hadn't seen that done except in old Greek and African plays. We had dancers around at the foot of the stage, and at the conclusion of each section the dancers danced and told the story better than even the words.

Did you choreograph these dances?

I did. I gave the directions on how it should be staged. Some of the choreographers added to it, of course. I wasn't a choreographer, but I can certainly tell you what I thought it should be. The woman in Pittsburgh did a brilliant choreography, and it was so funny that the audience broke down each time the dance happened. I remember when they finished dancing—especially the first part with Malik, who was in college and had two women—the dancer was walking like a cock, and the two women were coming behind him like they were robots.

This is sounding humorous!

Yes! Of course it was! Something serious has got to have humor attached to it. But, as they followed him, the first woman tripped the other one, so the other one fell. Waleesha really didn't want [a polygamous marriage]. She would say to Malik, "Oh yes, dear. Bring anotha woman in." But she really didn't mean it. I had to remind people it was a major discussion in the movement about polygamy. It was major. It was not minor, okay. That play was somewhat controversial because a lot of people didn't want to be laughed at with the idea of being a polygamist. It's an amazing thing having seen how Reena's [multiple personality was] acted out onstage.

Did the same actress play Reena, Mama B, Toni, and Malika in Jomandi's production of I'm Black When I'm Singing, I'm Blue When I Ain't*?*

Yes! She puts her soul in a handkerchief and then she puts her handkerchief in her pocket and says, "I'll always hold you close to my heart. You'll be alive, but you gotta rest now because you've been out here so long. You need to rest now." That's that "new woman" we're talking about: the one who did not curse her, the one who did not beat her up, the one who didn't call her a bitch, the one that didn't call her stupid motherfucker. The "new woman" is the one that simply waited very patiently. She says, "No, I understand what you've been through. I understand the pain. I understand all of that. Now I'm gonna continue your dream, your life." That's what we see. So that's that new woman I'm talking about.

Judy Juanita

Sanchez's mentorship and writings influenced a generation of artists, including Judy Juanita.

You asked what role did Sonia Sanchez play in my development as a poet. She had an enormous impact on me as a mentoring figure. I met her at San Francisco State. I read her first book of poetry, *Home Coming* [1969], in manuscript form and performed it with the Black Student Union's [BSU] Black Arts and Culture Troupe at San Francisco State, and from there I began to write my own poetry. She was a direct, *strong* influence on me. I performed her work. She wasn't a big name [then], but the person who introduced me to her work is named James Garrett. He was the first head of the BSU and the model for the character called Chandro-Imi in my book *Virgin Soul* [2013]. At the time, we called him Jimmy Garrett. Jimmy Garrett said, "You're going to read these poems tomorrow at the Student Union." Her poetry was a revelation to me. I had liked poetry before, but I had never written it except as a class assignment.

Performing poetry is so different than reading it.

Yes, I performed poetry. I had a lot of experience with performance. In church, I was always called upon—because I had good recitation powers—to recite at holiday events. I was always a member of the choir, so I was always singing. So much of Sanchez's work I sung because it is so lyrical [*sings "What Can the Matter Be" (ca. 1970s)*]. She uses a lot of lyricism, and that has influenced me to use a lot of nursery rhymes, chants, and songs in my writing.

You also participated in BSU's Black Arts and Culture Troupe, which was headed by LeRoi Jones [Amiri Baraka]. You describe him as "a gentle man" offstage and his onstage persona as "ferocious, shrill, harsh, demanding killer, scary."[1] *Could you share any memorable experiences working with him or performing poetry?*

As a poet, I fell in with the Black Arts Movement and fought for the student body funds to bring LeRoi Jones, Sonia Sanchez, Gwendolyn

Brooks, and Don L. Lee [Haki Madhubuti] to campus. The cities were enflamed, the nation was at war, and there I was smack-dab on the front line of revolution and resistance. As a black activist, I advocated for change in the black communities in Oakland and San Francisco. When I first saw LeRoi Jones in the flesh, he had changed from beat nihilism to black nationalism. Moved uptown from Greenwich Village. He was with us at San Francisco State. We brought him on—Jimmy Garrett was primarily responsible for that. The white students who controlled the student body budget wanted to pick a fight with the BSU over our altogether legitimate and defensible hiring of LeRoi. We packed the classroom for the meeting with students—black, white, Latino, Asian, and community people. See that: here is the blend. The community people were all black and formidable. They just went in there and said, "Hey, what's going on?" So, academicians, cherubs, goodbye! We drowned them. Every time they tried business as usual we up against the wall motherfuckered them. The white boys got tired real quick of beating their heads against a united front, and they had grudgingly agreed to give it up. LeRoi immediately set the BSU to rehearsing and performing his play *A Black Mass* [1966]. We were the Black Arts and Culture Troupe. We got a van and sewed costumes. My other friend sewed and we made up costumes at our house. We put on shows within a matter of days, and that taught me a lot about theater. I was the warm-up act.

How did you warm audiences up?

I would be in the back behind a scrim or out at the podium and just read a poem.

Your poem or someone else's?

It didn't matter. Sometimes I read mine if I had written one. Sometimes I would read one of Sonia's. Sometimes I would read all over the place: Langston Hughes or what have you. So, LeRoi was the engine. We had an array of talent in the BSU right there. We had actors, singers, and modern dancers to supply motor force or the cars, if you will. I, as usual, was the caboose. I was bringing it up. We took the show to college centers and anyplace they would have us: East Palo Alto (which is the black community), West Oakland (black community), Western Addition (black), South Berkeley (black), Marin City, Seaside, and Hunter's Point. It was a wonderful opportunity. This mirrored for me what happened to me when I was in the seventh grade. The Oakland Public School District used to be an outstanding school district and had an instrumental music program. I learned to play both the violin and the string bass. My instructor wanted the bass to be played in both the band and the orchestra. That meant I got to travel in the seventh, eighth, and ninth grades throughout Northern and Central California in bands and orchestra competitions. It was just wonderful, so Black Arts Cultural Troupe was an echo of that experience. I always remember that because that was motivating. Music motivates me, politics motivates me, and writing motivates me. If it is not those things, I am not so interested.

You mentioned that participating in the Black Arts and Culture Troupe taught you a lot about theater. What lessons did you learn?

I learned that whatever you need done, just do it. You have to do everything. Do your best and maybe it's not going to turn out all right. I knew how to sew from my mother. I knew how to sew at least two pieces of material together and make a fabric dress if we wanted to look African. Whatever you learned how to do—ten years ago, five years ago, fifteen years ago—somehow it is going to come in handy in the theater, in writing, in teaching.

I'm a journal keeper. I know the value of keeping journals. I tell students: keep a journal. I don't care if you write in it one sentence per time. People who are used to putting their thoughts down on paper in some form are going to be able to write essays better. So, it goes back to that old James Brown lyric, "You got to use what you got to get what you want."[2] I liked that about theater. I think my hiatus from theater, though, happened because I got a lot of learning on the spot in college and I didn't get as much formal learning with writing as I might have had if I had majored in English or drama. So I had to go back and do the autodidact thing and teach myself writing. I also got into writing workshops, which I was in for a good thirty years and loved. I made *huge* friendships through workshops and learned my craft.

You helped with costumes and you performed poetry with the Black Arts and Culture Troupe. Did you act in any of their plays?

No, I didn't act at that time.

You have the personality and a dynamic presence that would translate very well onstage.

Yes. I had other friends who were doing it, but I am more the "stir the troops up" or "keep the spirit of the troops up," because I'm a joker. I think I use my personality more in that way. I enliven things or keep things lively to keep people up. I had a roommate who was kind of moody. She was also the best dancer on the whole campus. A teacher used to say that she had the most natural dancer's body and movements of anybody she had seen, but she didn't have a personality to be a dancer. When she performed—she was so statuesque and beautiful—she would break out in hives. So everybody is not for everything, and I think I am far too much an observer to be an actor. I did act in my one-woman play *Counter Terrorism* [2004], but I was so happy when it became a two-character play and the San Francisco Playwright Foundation said, "Don't act in it. We want you to keep writing." So, being a teacher, you're onstage all the time.

I very much enjoyed the collaboration within theater because it is challenging and self-revealing. I see parts of myself that surprise me that I didn't know that I had in me. I get a lot of confidence when I do theater. It is just that theater takes a lot of time. And it takes money. Every theatrical production I have been in or put on of my own has cost me money. I believe actors should be paid. So I generally pay the actors twenty-five or fifty dollars, depending on how involved it is going to be. Theater costs money.

J.e. Franklin

Rather than self-produce her works, J.e. Franklin relied on black producers to see her works realized.

You spoke to me earlier about how playwriting was a calling for you. How did you go from accepting that calling to seeing your work actually produced? For example, did you have connections with Woodie King Jr.?

No, I didn't know Woodie. The Federal Theatre goes back to the Federal Theatre Project of the thirties. Then when Woodie came along, he just took the idea of the Federal Theatre and added the "New," and it became the New Federal Theatre. The first play that he produced when he brought the theater into being was *Black Girl* [in 1971]. I really don't know how he got the play, but I know that his wife, Willie Mae King, saw *Black Girl* on WGBH. His wife was a script reader. She picked *Black Girl*. That's probably why they did it, because as far as I know Woodie doesn't just pick up scripts and read them. Someone recommends.

Are there any productions of your plays written during the midsixties to midseventies that are particularly memorable for you?

Midsixties? No. The only one that I wrote in the midsixties was in 1964, and that was the very first play that I wrote: *A First Step to Freedom*. Yes, that's memorable.

There's also The In-Crowd: A Rock Opera in One Act *[1967]. Could you discuss the genre of "rock opera"? Why did you choose that form?*

There were a number of names that were kind of titles that got bandied around at the time. To be honest, it was just my attempt to write something for some children who didn't have any material to get up on the stage and act. I wrote it for some children at the New Federal Theatre or somewhere on the Lower East Side. Woodie was involved. One of those funded programs for youth. They added some music to it and some dance movements and took it to Montreal for the International Youth Festival Mobilization for Youth. The production was selected to go to Canada.

Were you able to attend that production, or just hear about it?

Yes, I attended.

What was the experience like?

Well, that was my first trip to Canada and all expenses paid. I thought it was lovely. I got on very well. It was very nice.

The Negro Ensemble Company Workshop performed Mau Mau Room—

It was a workshop and it gave Richard Roundtree his beginning in the theater. That was his first play. Someone saw him in the role of Jimmy, and the next thing I know he's Shaft.

What did you like about this production?

Shauneille Perry's direction. Really excellent. I remembered it because she has a kind of kinetic energy that makes the play move. It moves. It's not static. Some directors have a static touch where everything just sort of freezes. But something about the way she has the actors moving on the stage is almost like a film.

The Prodigal Sister, *which you wrote around 1973, deals with teen pregnancy. What inspired you?*

I wanted to write a play that was in rhymed couplets. It was just coming natural to me at that time because I had written a play called *MacPilate* [1974]. I wrote *MacPilate* and I liked it and next thing I know I'm writing *The Prodigal Sister.* I think originally it was *The Prodigal Daughter*, and I'd written it because I was working with an organization that was doing street plays. We were trying to find plays that could be performed in the street or street corners. *The Prodigal Daughter* was one of the ones that I felt could be performed on the corner. I was working with a Jesuit priest named Brother Jonathan. Might have been Franciscan, but I think he was Jesuit. He liked the play very much. It was very short at the time; I hadn't really expanded it into like a full-length musical. It was just something for the neighborhood youth. Might've been about ten pages long. It worked so well on the street that I expanded it, sent it to my agent, my agent sent it to Woodie, and the next thing I know I've got a production.

You wrote the book, Micki Grant wrote the music, and you both cowrote the lyrics to The Prodigal Sister. *How were you introduced to Micki Grant, and what was the process like working with her?*

Well, Woodie King produced *The Prodigal Sister*. As the producer, he has to find all the parts to cull. He has to find the person who can do the music since it was a musical. I wrote it with the intent that it would be a musical, and so he probably contacted Micki because at that time she had a play that was on Broadway called *Don't Bother Me, I Can't Cope* [1971]. He was just reaching out to someone he knew and felt would work well with the project, and it turned out okay. I liked some of the music but felt that some of the lyrics that I had written, the way I had envisioned them, got stretched a little bit too long. But these things happen. If you collaborate with someone, they're going to bring their stuff to you, and it really changes. It does change the fabric of the piece. Sometimes it changes the intent even, but that's the way it goes. Same thing happens with film. Same thing happens in the theater with just straight plays. I had to trust my director.

This was your third time working with Shauneille Perry. What was that experience like?

I liked working with Shauneille because Shauneille delivers.

Have you ever participated in the theater in a capacity other than that of a playwright?

Not that I can think of really. I did direct *Mau Mau Room* [1969] at Skidmore College. We had changed the title by that time. I say "we" because

I had an agent (who's now dead), and we were talking about the title of the play. I don't know how it evolved into *Throw Thunder at This House*, but one day that was the title. Sometimes your plays go through a number of titles until you've found . . .

The one?

Yes.

Micki Grant

In contrast to the other playwrights in this study, Franklin's musical collaborator Micki Grant initially envisioned a career as a film actress. While she never achieved her dream of performing in a film, she did find opportunities to combine her musical and acting talents by starring in her own musical productions.

How did you get your start in theater?

My cousin Jeni LeGon was one of the few stars who had roles that you could be proud of. She wasn't really a star, but she was always featured in major films. She was one of few people to ever dance with Bill "Bojangles" Robinson. In fact, he always danced by himself. She was a fantastic tap dancer and actress. She was living in California; I was living in Chicago. I decided that this was what I was going to do: I was going to be an actress. My grandmother lived in San Diego, I had an aunt in Los Angeles, and I also had three aunts in San Diego. They were all my mother's sisters, and most of them had migrated to California. That's where the movie industry was and that's where I headed after having an unsuccessful marriage that lasted about two years. I went to Los Angeles first.

How did you get your first acting role?

I met Nick Stewart. Nick was one of the people that had to play one of those stereotypical roles on *Amos 'n' Andy*. He played Lightnin', but he also had a theater. You just never know. You see people in these stereotypical roles, but he's a brilliant and bright man. He was a playwright and founded the Ebony Showcase Theatre so we could get roles and experiment with playwriting. So I met him and worked at the theater there. I came to know Juanita Moore. We were doing a play that Nick had written. She had started a theater too and went along actually to be nominated for an Oscar.

Jim Hatch and Bernard Jackson, who were both working at the University of California, Los Angeles, started a show at the university called *Fly Blackbird* [1961]. Then they were going to produce it commercially, which would be considered here in New York as Off-Off-Broadway. Los Angeles was not a great place for theater. It's a film town. So that was a major step. I got the role of the ingenue, Camille. It was the first time I got to act with Rosetta LeNoire (who played my mom) and Theresa Merritt (who went on to have her own TV show, *That's My Mama* [1974–75]). Producers came to see it and decided to bring it to New York, but they wanted to cast all New York actors. I decided that I was going to follow and come on my own and audition. I couldn't believe they didn't want me. Here I was: I had gotten these great notices playing the lead. I thought that was going to be my ticket to New York. I just couldn't let it go that way, so I bought my own ticket. I had to audition, and I was cast as the understudy. Yes, for my role. Of course, had I been a New York actor I would have wanted to be cast too. I would have said, "Why are you bringing someone in here from California?" I can say that now!

Where does college fit into your career trajectory? Are you cast in Fly Blackbird *and then you go to Lehman College?*

I thought when I left the University of Illinois that I was going to continue and get my degree in Los Angeles, which I didn't. So I still hadn't gotten my degree when I got to New York. Lehman College had a big theater program there. I met one of the women professors at Lehman College. She's African American and was involved in theater.

She encouraged you?

Yes. I think that's where I started to deal more with writing (with the professor there) and studying plays.

Do you feel that you faced any particular challenges as a woman playwright navigating Broadway and black theaters at this time?

Well, yes. There weren't that many of us in the black theater. Woodie King Jr. was the one who was pushing and giving us, [including] Shauneille Perry, the opportunity.

Do you remember observing Shauneille Perry's directing process?

Well, it's much lower-key than Vinnette [Carroll's], that's for sure. She got very involved into the process.

Would Vinnette get up on the stage?

Yes! I think Vinnette had her own style, and it was a combination.

Of all the musicals you have created, do you have a particular favorite?

The one musical that I did that failed and shouldn't have: *It's So Nice to Be Civilized* [1980]. It's a wonderful musical, and I hope one day it will be done. The script is my script, but *that* script was not done. I wasn't allowed in the theater. They took the play away from me. I saw the preview the same time the audience saw it.

How did that happen?

I have no idea. I guess it should not have happened because the Dramatists Guild of America protects you from that. I was a new member of the guild at the time. I should have gone to them immediately, and they actually could have closed the show or just taken my name off the show because it was not my show. They wrote the show around the star—I love her and she's a great performer—Vivian Reed. She had just come out of *Bubbling Brown Sugar*, which my show had actually nothing to do with. The lead character, Gus, was a man, and he didn't even appear in the show at all! It was done Off-Broadway and was a big hit, which is why it went to Broadway. They only had maybe two backer auditions. Everybody wanted to put money in the show. Even the actors wanted to put money in the production because they were so sure it was going to be amazing! Can you believe it? If they had simply taken the show that I wrote! They did not take the show that I wrote.

Do you feel that you've been able to assert your authority as a playwright, or is this one of the few times that—

Oh, no. That was it! That was the one time. I saw that you can be destroyed if you don't . . . I didn't know that I could . . . The very fact that you could keep a playwright out of a rehearsal and not see what they're doing to your play. One of the cardinal rules of a drama is that you don't change anything.

You can't change a word.

Not a word! Not a comma!

Who mentored you?

I didn't really have any mentors. My agent at that point was . . .

An agent is different than a mentor because there's a financial incentive. A mentor, on the other hand, is someone who's really helping you.

Yes. Right.

So you didn't have a mentor who could guide you through that Broadway experience?

No.

Nora Cole

Despite this setback, Grant should be remembered for providing opportunities for actresses such as Nora Cole. Cole performed in the 1982 Broadway production of Vinnette Carroll's *Your Arms Too Short to Box with God*, with music and lyrics by Grant and Alex Bradford.

Why did you decide to move to New York? Is that where you saw opportunity for black actresses?

There was no point in me going back to Louisville. I'd had so many racial incidents in Chicago and I could not bear another winter there. It was also my last semester at the Goodman School of Drama and I was still suffering from my engagement being broken off. I was really in a state of depression. I had picked out a dress. The whole nine yards. I proposed to do this solo show for myself and I was not making any headway. I borrowed money from the school and I said, "On my spring break I'm going to New York." So I came to New York City. I stayed with my friend Joseph ["Joe"] Bigelow (who had been kicked out of school), and I went to see *The Wiz* [1975]. I saw about three or four Broadway shows. I looked around and said, "I can do this." I actually met Vinny Liff, the casting director for *The Wiz*. He was a friend of Joe's and asked, "Can you sing?" I said, "Yeah." He said, "Well, do you wanna audition?" I went back to Chicago, got myself together, and flew back to New York just to audition for *The Wiz*. This is my first professional audition. I'm wearing my Sunday best. I started singing and completely forgot the lyrics. But I didn't freak out or anything. I just carried on.

What song did you sing?

[*Sings "Soon as I Get Home"*] "There's a feeling here inside / That I cannot hide / And I know I've tried."[3] I couldn't sing Dorothy's role. I wasn't right for anything else in the show. I was still very green. I still carried a little bit more weight, so I was still going to get characterish kind of roles as opposed to an ingenue. I was never going to really be an ingenue anyway. So that gave me some inspiration to come back and start working on that show at the Goodman. I got that show up and then I moved to New York.

As far as opportunities: black theater was thriving but everybody was kind of in their own camps. You couldn't get an audition at NEC [Negro Ensemble Company] because they had their own company. NEC really was about playwrights. There was a core company that developed around the works of those playwrights.

What about New Lafayette Theatre?

I didn't know about New Lafayette Theatre.

Barbara Ann Teer's National Black Theatre is also very close-knit as well.

I don't even remember her theater even being there yet. When I first came to New York in 1976, almost everything—all the auditions, rehearsal halls, agents, casting directors, and offices were in Midtown except for, say, Vinnette's theater. There was no reason for me to go above Seventy-Second Street. I didn't go above Seventy-Second Street except maybe once or twice. I did do *Women of Troy* for Glenda Dickerson.[4] She's out of the Howard University community. I replaced somebody playing Cassandra. Glenda had me come up to her place to put me through some paces, because everybody else had been doing the show before. But I did not come up to Harlem. Vinnette was down on Twentieth Street in the Chelsea neighborhood. At that time, Chelsea was deserted at night. Chelsea was not what it is right now. Rosetta LeNoire had her theater, AMAS. I did the last show for the last season that she had when she was using a space on Eighty-Sixth Street. Then she moved to a theater space on the Upper East Side. Actors have a lot more information now because of technology. There was nobody to tell you how to approach the business. You were just looking for shows or a showcase to be in. For about the first two years I only did shows with Vinnette, and she kept me very busy.

How did Vinnette Carroll help you develop as an actress?

To me it was just the rehearsal process.

The rehearsal process sounds strenuous.

[*Nods*] Strenuous. Coming out of school, you have been given all these different techniques that you really get a chance to apply. Directors look for actors to bring a lot to the table. There's a saying, "Ninety percent of directing is casting." And the environment that she created. If she ever asked you to do anything, she would ask somebody else to do the same thing right there. So, it's like you're auditioning again. You put your best forward. You go for it.

In your article "Vinnette Carroll: The First Black Woman Broadway Director"[2012], you write that "Vinnette constantly challenged you to be daring and jump off a cliff. But she could be merciless when you crashed."[5] *It sounds like one of her methods was getting performers to take a risk. Were there others?*

Yes. You were just put on the spot. You were in that atmosphere and everybody is [talented]. Vinnette could assemble triple threats: you have to sing, act, dance, and be able to move. I got to do *Your Arms Too Short to Box with God* because she wanted an actor in the role. Salome Bey was the original Singing Mary in *Box with God*. She's an amazing singer. I didn't have a gospel voice. Vinnette liked heightened drama. She liked Greek drama, and that's how she saw that role of Singing Mary. Micki Grant wrote the Mary songs. There's only two sermons in *Box with God*; the rest of it is all song. The first act is the story of the book of Matthew and then the second half was basically a concert. Delores Hall, Jennifer Holliday, Sheila Ellis, and Patti LaBelle end up singing songs in the second act that really feature [their vocal talent]. It was Vinnette's rehearsal process and creating an environment that made you just go for it. And if it wasn't the best choice, she would see whether you could take direction to change the choice. Some people could and some people couldn't. Some people didn't have the instrument to do that. But when she recognized that you did, then she could do that with you.

Aduke Aremu

Aduke Aremu began her theater career where Cole rarely ventured: above Seventy-Second Street in New York City. Despite some criticism from her peers, Aremu decided to move her theater company from the heart of Harlem to the new redevelopment project known as Theatre Row.

Harlem Children's Theatre Company was thriving. My first year at Theatre Row I said to everybody, "This is how I operate. We're an ensemble company. I'm just the Pied Piper. I am a little dictator. If it looks crazy, I can be a little off. But this is your field. I'm going to deliver the goodies. I never tell you what to do musically." I'd look at the music and I might say, "This is where I want to go with this." But I allow them *total freedom*! They were loyal. You could say nothing about Aduke. Nothing. They got paid August 1st for the whole year. I'd ask, "Listen, how much do you want for the year?" They would say, "Well, I need around eight thousand." It was a lot of money, but I'd say, "You got it." I would tell my accountant, "Give everybody their checks." I don't want to be paying people like they're working for McDonald's. That's not Aduke. You're paid for the year. Let's go do art. I did it for my whole career. I gave everybody a lot of credit. Everybody got props on all my flyers. If we had a press release, all my people were interviewed. I wasn't like a demigod, even though some people say we are. I let everybody share in the fame, because I believed, as an ensemble, everybody got the goodies.

How long were your rehearsal periods?

Usually I need around six weeks. Depending on how talented the young people are. You can turn a production around pretty fast if you have the right artistic team and the right staff that knows how to work with kids.

I want the audience to feel good. Even to this day, I don't really enjoy seeing pieces that make me feel bad at the end of a production. I think that hope and love—all of that—is important for you to survive as a human being. You don't want to have to go to the nearest bar and get a drink when you finish seeing a play because it's so depressing. Audiences should be inspired. I always closed with a big dance number. *The Liberation of Mother Goose* [1973] always had "Celebration" as the last number.

Every play had a closing kick-butt number with everybody onstage. It was phenomenal, fifty kids dancing. Sometimes I would ask my choreographer to choreograph that number first. The audience has to be standing up and cheering. For *JuJu Man* [ca. 1973], we had stilt walkers come down the aisles at the end. To me, the end number is the most important one! Sometimes the cast would spend weeks working on the last song. I would say, "It has to be a showstopper."

Dawn Alli

Dawn Alli contributed not only her business skills to the Harlem Children's Theatre Company but also her artistry by directing and supporting Aremu's celebratory musical productions.

Throughout my career, I've done a lot of public speaking at libraries and designing many programs. For the life of me, other than college and university, I've never been able to act. I've directed one of the Harlem Children's Theatre Company's productions of *The Liberation of Mother Goose* [1973] at the John F. Kennedy Center for the Performing Arts [in 1979]. I worked in the lighting booth.

Wait. You directed it and you called the lights?!

Yes. Something happened. Someone didn't show up.

What was your experience like directing a cast of fifty children?

Well, a lot of it is dance moves. The choreographer decides your exits and your entrances. Then you work around the choreography with your cast. At least we do, because it's a visual production. At that time, we were innovative. We had cast members come from the audience. We had cast members come down from the sky, from backstage, and left stage. Anything we could think of. We weren't using a lot of set: we wanted to paint the floor, do lots of lighting, and hang material from the back. We wanted to do all of those things because we didn't bring big sets. We were moving little things around the stage: blocks, trees, and things that were movable.

Aduke described the set as "colorful." Can you tell me what kind of palette was used?

It depended. With *The Liberation of Mother Goose*, every character had a color scheme. When the character came out, a fabric would come down and the color scheme would come out. And the language was beautiful. You have to read the script. Some of it rhymed, but it was almost like rapping. Let me give you one of the songs. [*Sings*] "I am black and comely, some say / Some say because I'm black, I'm homely / Step back they say, you're not blessed like me / I am black and comely / Da da, da da, da da, da da." That's just the first stanza. It's beautiful. Now, the melodies and rhythms change to suit the time the play's produced to stay relevant. But some of them don't have to change because they stay relevant. They just do. The last production was done in 2014 at [Restoration Youth Arts Academy's Drama Department in] Bedford-Stuyvesant. Children came out and were looking for the rabbit [*laughs*].

Shirley Prendergast

Movement and color were also a source of inspiration for Shirley Prendergast. She used the knowledge gained from her earlier experiences as a dancer and photographer to design lights for theatrical productions.

What kind of art did you want to create and why?

Well, because of photography I think color helped me a lot. I decided that you could use color for so many things, but it also depended on the choreographer, the music, and the dancers.

You are the first African American woman to hold a United Scenic Artists of America card in lighting design. What opportunities were available to black women designers during the 1960s and 1970s?

The opportunities were there, if you went out and really searched for them.

What would searching for these opportunities look like?

Well, to me it wasn't very obvious. By that time, I was working with the Alvin Ailey American Dance Theater. I used to travel with them. Tom Skelton was doing Broadway, and I assisted him in a lot of things. Let me put it this way: I didn't know really what was going on. I knew what I wanted to do. I don't care what color you were or anything like that. For instance, the first time I went on the road with the Alvin Ailey American Dance Theater was when we went down to Atlanta. When I walked into the theater, the doorman decided that he was going to send me to a costume designer, and I said, "No. I do light." He looked at me funny and then he called over the electrician and the electrician knew my name or something like that . . . and that was it. It was no big deal. It was no big deal *for me.*

Did you hear of other people having different experiences than you, specifically other black women designers?

Not really. I decided that if you go into the theater and you know what you're doing, you're fine. You don't try to tell electricians what to do or anything like that, because he knows his theater. You just ask him about the theater and he will tell you. They like to tell you things and they really like to help you.

I don't disagree with you, but I also notice that there's a disproportionate number of black women who are able to achieve the kind of success that you did. I'm curious to know your thoughts on why that was happening during that time?

Actually, there weren't that many black women going into lighting design—let me put it that way—when I was coming along. There were a lot of men. But that was about it. As I say: no matter where you went, if they looked at your light plot and they really knew that they could read it and you could tell them exactly why you did it and all that, you will be fine.

Did you face any particular challenges as a lighting designer?

Not really. The only thing I can remember is the first time I did a play at the Negro Ensemble Company in New York. I think it was Douglas Turner Ward. When I spoke to him, I had to tell him I had done a lot of dance but I hadn't done a play. Doug says, "Well, if you can do that, you can do a play." And that was it!

Can you tell me about your design process? More specifically, how does knowledge of photography and dance inform your designs?

Well, Peggy Clark was one of my teachers. Peggy used to say, "When you read a play and after you've seen the set, what you have to do is decide what it's going to look like." If you can sit down and decide that? All right, this moment I want to look like this and from this moment we'll go to this moment. I want it to flow to the second part . . . you're straight. It's all a matter of how you feel about what you're doing.

It sounds like moment to moment and feeling *informs your choices?*

Precisely.

Could you tell me more about designing your first professional production? I know you worked with Negro Ensemble Company on their production of Summer of the Seventeenth Doll *in 1967.*

Well, it was fine. The actors were marvelous and the set designer, Ed Burbage, was great. There was a staircase coming down from a twelve-foot ceiling. I told Ed, "I want to put a light up there." He said, "You're going to burn something?" I said, "No, I just want to put a light up there." So we went out and got a small lamp that wouldn't burn the wood that he had up there, and it worked.

Do you have any other memorable experiences working with Douglas Turner Ward? I know you worked with him on a 1973 Broadway production of River Niger.

No. I also worked with him with *Ceremonies in Dark Old Men* [1969]. He acted in it, but he was also the director. Every time I wanted to do something, I would go to him and make sure that it was all right with him because he was also acting. We just sat down and talked and that was it.

You also designed for the Billie Holiday Theatre. Did you ever get the opportunity to work with Marjorie Moon?

Marjorie Moon? It was fine. I mean, we just . . . I talk a lot sometimes. As long as I can tell them how I feel about it and what I want to do with it, and they either say yes or no. If I can talk them into doing it my way, fine. If they can talk me into doing it their way, we can do it. Depending on how it works, we'll be all right.

Can you tell me more about your approach to helping someone see things your way?

It's not that my way is right; it's the way I think about this particular thing. Melvin Van Peebles would want to do something that was out of the way for *Waltz of the Stork* [1982]! I mean, there's no two ways about it. I said, "No, it's not gonna work." We did it his way and one of the reviewers panned it. He then came over to me and said, "Maybe you were right." And that was about it.

I also read that you worked with Hazel Bryant at the Richard Allen Center for Culture and Art.

Oh, working with Hazel was fine. Hazel would say, "What you gonna do?" I would tell her, and she would say, "Yeah, that's okay. Okay, now what else you gonna do?" Hazel always knew what she wanted. There's no two ways about that.

Any memorable stories working with her?

I remember the set designer and I had a meeting or something like that, and Hazel came in. Hazel said, "Okay, what are you doing?" We tried to explain to Hazel what we were doing. She said, "Well, as long as you get it straight, that's fine."

Do you have any memorable experiences working with Woodie King Jr.?

As long as Woodie King laughs, you're in business. I didn't work with him as a director as much as say, Tee. You know Tee, right?

Antoinette Tynes, the lighting designer.

I worked with Woodie as a producer more than as a director, and Tee really worked with him a lot as a director.

Are there any other important women designers whose names come to mind?

Well, besides Tee, there was Melody Beal. She's a lighting designer. Judy Dearing used to do costumes. Gertha Block. Most of the costume designers went out to California.

Kathy A. Perkins

Prendergast's legacy lives on through the work of Kathy A. Perkins and the countless number of designers she mentored throughout her career.

Why did you decide to pursue a career in lighting design?

This was a life-changing experience. Your freshman year in most theater programs you have to take a practicum class. You have to do costumes, sets, lights, and so on. So I was working on a show at Howard University: Alice Childress's *Wine in the Wilderness* [1969]. I had never heard of Alice Childress in my life. I was working backstage with props and was hang crew. My friend, Doug Farnham, was lighting the show or maybe master electrician. He was a sophomore. We were sitting backstage one day and he said, "What are you going to do with a bachelor of fine arts in acting?" I said, "I'm going to New York. I'm going to Broadway. What do you think?!" He just started laughing. He said, "This is 1973. There are no jobs out there for black women. The roles that are out there are very stereotypical. Because you're dark-skinned you'd be playing either the mammy or the prostitute. I saw you hanging lights and working with me. Have you ever thought about lighting?" I said, "No." He said, "Why don't you try? We don't have enough black people behind the scenes. Everybody can't act; we need lighting people." Howard University has a huge touring house called Cramton. During this period, every entertainer who was anybody was coming through Howard and performing in this theater because it was one of the biggest theaters in town for performing concerts. Doug worked over there. Students who were tech majors had an opportunity to work in the touring house and they got paid very well. He said, "Why don't you come and work? You can get paid and we need people. Why don't you think about it?" And so I did. I started working over there with him and I said, "Oh, this is interesting." Then I switched over from acting to lighting and technical theater.

You describe lighting and technical theater as "interesting." Was this a passion?

No. I think part of it was originally my ego was deflated when he said I couldn't act. He didn't say, "You can't act." He said, "Oh, I have seen you do some scene work. Mmm."

So, Doug said there's limited roles you could perform onstage. Did you believe that?

I did because I'd heard them talk about there not being a whole lot of work for black women. Being at Howard, they told us what goes on. But the idea was because you were at Howard—we had this networking [system]—you would work. Doug said, "There are greater opportunities if you're in technical theater. You'll never be a waiter or waitress." That is what people did then; now they do Uber. So I started working next door at the theater with him and was like, "This is pretty good. Oh, I'm getting paid for this! Oh, I'm meeting these stars! Oh, this is fun!" Then I just switched over. My faculty were very supportive because there were other women who were doing technical theater and it was something that they really did encourage. So, it wasn't like I was the only woman doing tech theater. There were two other women doing lighting and working in the roadhouse.

Did you have other opportunities throughout the years to perform onstage?

No. Actually, I really didn't want to. After that, it was like, "No. This is it."

When did you develop a passion for lighting design?

When I started looking at my weekly paycheck [*laughs*]. "Whoa! This is what I make?! Oh, this is how much I can make? Are you kidding!"

Who has mentored you throughout the years?

I've had so many different mentors. I have had my mentors for lighting, in education, and so on. I would say my friend Doug was my first big mentor. Like I said: this was a life-changing moment for me. He was a communications major and he stayed in lighting. He ended up going into TV and worked for NBC News. Then my professors. When I decided I wanted to go to graduate school, my professors were very supportive of me. Then the guy who was head of the touring house on campus—we called him Daddy Dines. His name was Ralph Dines. I would say he was one of my greatest mentors. He really taught me the business end. This was my sophomore year when I started working there, so by my senior year I'm in charge working crew chief at this theater. I'm still going to school full-time. Luckily, the theaters were back-to-back. You can go from one theater to the department's theater. So I was running back and forth. The crew chief (usually a lighting person) lit all the concerts coming in unless an act brought their lighting person. I was also sort of like the stage manager as well, so I was in charge of backstage. I determined who could come in and out of that back door.

The year I was the crew chief, I was informed that I was the highest-paid student on campus because it was such a demanding job. Not only did we get paid hourly but also [earned additional pay] if a concert group came in [late]. I will never forget George Clinton and the Funkadelics. We were at a university so they had to be off the stage at eleven o'clock. They went on until about one o'clock in the morning. So the policy was: every ten minutes or fifteen minutes overtime, that's a hundred dollars. That hundred dollars gets divided between the crew people. So, if there were five of us working the show that night and there's six hundred dollars in fines, we split that. That happened *a lot*, because there would be an early show and the early show would run over. Then the late show: usually entertainers were so high and boozed out, they would come on late and then the show would go late. Chaka Khan, Isaac Hayes, Stevie Wonder, and Kool & the Gang came through. I'm sure I'm really dating myself. I will never forget the Funkadelics. These guys came in wearing diapers. I said, "Whoa. What is this?!"

Patti LaBelle: Well, they were called Patti LaBelle and the Bluebells at the time. I think she admits now that she was difficult to work with; she really was. One of the things that Mr. Dines always told me was, "This is going to be a very hard job for a woman when you go out, particularly if you do concert lighting. It's really a white man's world. Whatever you do, don't ever let anyone make you cry." When I did the Patti LaBelle show, this woman almost had me in tears. What happens is you set up the lights for the artist; the artist never comes in to rehearse. They send their backup people. You make sure the mics are right. This is 1976. We are talking about the days before wireless microphones. So, we have mic cable running all over the place. We've got the mic here and it's taped where the microphone is going to go. Her backup people came out and tried the microphone and say, "This is where Ms. LaBelle is going to go." All right. So, twenty minutes before the show, she comes onstage and she says, "I don't want the mic here. Let's move all the mics downstage." We're thinking, "We got to pull this tape up." I say, "I have special lights focused on these microphones." She says, "Who the hell are you?" I just wanted to burst out in tears. I say, "Well, I'm the lighting designer." She says, "Well, I don't give a whatever." Then Nona Hendryx says, "It's okay. Don't worry about it." So the house had to open almost an hour late because we had to redo the lights for this woman. Then Daddy Dines was ticked off. They ran over time and he charged them extra. He said, "We're going to make sure this was worth your while."

Could you tell me more about why you felt concert design was a "white man's world"?

Well, lighting in general. Definitely concert lighting. Concert is still definitely a white man's world. During this period—we're talking about the seventies—I'm in Washington, D.C., and D.C. is "Chocolate City." During that time, you didn't have what they call production companies. If somebody wanted a lighting person, they would just say, "Oh, I know so-and-so, she's a lighting person." Also, a lot of these groups really didn't carry a lighting person with them. Some of them did, but if they were going to a big university venue, they would just use whatever was available. They would tell us in advance. That was the other thing: I got free records if a group was coming. "Earth, Wind & Fire's coming: here's their five albums, so know the songs." I had so many albums. That was just an amazing experience for me.

How did you navigate the white male–dominated world of lighting design? Or did you just do the work, as Shirley Prendergast said?

I did. But at Howard: everybody was black.

What were your experiences like after graduating from Howard?

It was difficult, but I was prepared. I remember when I told Daddy Dines and my professors in the department, "I think I'm going to go to grad school." Originally, I wasn't going to go. I almost dropped out of school several times because a lot of times there were groups who said, "You're great! Do you want to go on the road with us? We're going on a world tour." I would call my sister Linda, who was a big influence in my life. I said, "Linda, I think I'm going to take some time off from school. Earth, Wind & Fire wants me to go on a tour with them." She said, "No. These groups will always be there. Just finish your education."

Did you go directly from Howard University's bachelor in fine arts program to a master of fine arts at the University of Michigan?

I didn't even take the summer off. I went straight from undergraduate school. I did work with the Smithsonian Folklife Festival [est. 1967]. Normally, I would tell my students, "Don't go straight to grad school. Take some time off and get some work experience." But I had work experience. I knew what was out there and I knew exactly what I wanted to do. At the time, there were M.F.A. programs where you could get the degree in two years, but it was still a three-year degree. You just went all year-round. So the University of Michigan had that program.

What was it like entering the world of professional lighting design?

It was difficult trying to find work because, again, this is before computers. I remember writing tons and tons of letters just before I was graduating. You had to use a typewriter. The one job I got was from a friend of mine who knew somebody who worked with Dianne McIntyre. I was prepared, because Daddy Dines sat me down and said, "This is what is going to happen. You're going to have to be expecting this. People are always going to challenge everything you do, so you need to be prepared. You got to have a tough skin. Don't let anybody make you cry!"

Some people would challenge you because you were a black woman?

Because I was a black woman. Even my professors at the University of Michigan said, "You're a black woman." As far as I know, I'm the first black woman to get an M.F.A. in lighting at Michigan. They said, "We don't know that many black women who have gone on to get an advanced degree, so be prepared to be challenged, to be questioned." Of course, that happened even when I was in graduate school. My adviser created this nickname for me, "Perky." Then everybody else started calling me Perky. I hated that! I would never forget, my adviser would say, "My little token." Yes, he thought that was funny. He swears he doesn't remember saying this when I see him at conferences. I said, "No, that's not amusing." He said, "Well, we've had very few women come into the program, and they always drop out by their first semester." I said, "What's your point?" Then he said, "You're the first black person we've ever had." I just said, "What's your point?" But he has no recollection of that. My classmates would say, "Perky, do you think somebody's going to hire you when you get out of here?!"

How did you remain focused and confident in what you were doing?

Well, I think after the first semester they saw that I was serious about what I was doing and I knew what I was doing. In fact, I was better in what I was doing than a lot of them. One: I had so much practical experience. I didn't have the theoretical experience. My drafting was not great. My professor [at Howard] said, "We don't have the resources to do all the detailed drafting work like they have at these big white schools. So you will probably be lacking in those areas." And I was. It took me longer to draft.

Michigan used to bring in a lot of famous lighting designers. I was assigned—I guess because it was *Othello*—to be the lighting assistant for this guy named Lee Watson, who was a very famous Broadway designer. I was his lighting assistant, and I was also the board operator. Michigan is one of the first schools to have a computerized lighting board. I worked on one when I was in the D.C. area so I knew how to use one. So they said, "Perky, why don't you work with Lee." I did, and Lee Watson was very impressed with my work. There was another designer who came through while I was there. They were all like, "We're really impressed with you." So when I got out of graduate school, I called each of them. I said, "This is Kathy A. Perkins. I was the black woman who worked with you. I remember you saying you were very impressed with my work. Can you bring me in as an assistant in New York?" They all told me no. One guy was very upfront and he just said, "You realize when you are working with a lighting designer you are in rehearsals all day, running with them. You all go out to lunch and dinner. How am I supposed to explain this young black woman following me around all day long? Do you think anybody is going to seriously think you're my assistant?" He just said, "The time's not right." Everybody kept saying, "You need to meet Shirley." Even when Woodie King Jr. came to Howard he said, "Oh, you got to meet Shirley."

Kathy Perkins and Woodie King Jr. at the University of Illinois at Urbana-Champaign, 2002. Courtesy of Kathy Perkins.

How did you first meet Shirley Prendergast?

I ended up calling her and just said, "Everybody told me I need to meet you." She said, "Oh, yes. Woodie told me all about you, too." She was just amazing. I've done four hundred shows. I assisted her on Melvin Van Peebles's Broadway show *Waltz of the Stork* [1982]. That was my first Broadway show, only one with her.

How did Shirley Prendergast mentor you?

Well, one: just from watching her work. She also helped me when I took the United Scenic Artists of America union exam. I didn't pass it the first time.

She didn't either.

Yes. During that time, it was very difficult, because you had a take-home exam and then you had two days where you were there doing exams.

When I didn't pass it, I wanted to find out from her why I didn't pass, and she explained to me why. So I worked with her on the Paul Robeson piece and something else. Then when I would do my shows, I would invite her to come in and say, "Can you give me advice? What's working? What's not working?" I will never forget—I didn't even learn this in graduate school—she came in to see the Booker T. Washington show. I said, "Shirley, something doesn't look right with this picture. I don't know what's wrong." She said, "Well, you don't have any lights coming through your window, and the set looks dead. You have to treat the set like it's a person. Bring that set to life." That has always stuck with me. So when I have windows, there's always light shafts coming through the window. There is something through the outside, or I use gobos on the set just to give it texture. It's very subtle, so you don't know if this is the lighting or paint. Sandra Adell just saw [my lighting design for Lydia R. Diamond's] *Smart People* [2008]. She said, "Oh my God, it was great! I couldn't tell: was that your lighting, or was that the projection we looked at?" I said, "It was a combination of both, so that's good you couldn't tell." *Waltz of the Stork* was my first time working in a Broadway show. That was a real experience, and I think that made me realize I had no interest in working on Broadway.

What about the experience made you realize that?

Shirley had done the lighting plot and she sent me in early. She said, "Why don't you go in first and start focusing the back light and I'll be in later." I walked in (this is in 1981), and the crew, of course, was all white. One guy looked at me, says, "I ain't working with her," and walked away. Now, if you know anything about union rules—at that time and even now—you have to have four people on an A-frame ladder. One person on each side of the ladder. That's four people plus the person that goes up. So, you have to have five people to focus the light. He left, so we have four people. I said, "Well, can we focus this?" They said, "This is a union hall. You got to have five people." I said, "Well, what are we going to do? This guy just left." It's the union. It's a brotherhood, so they're going to look out for each other. So he said, "Well, I got to call somebody and see if we can get somebody to come over." He had to call some guy from New Jersey. I said, "New Jersey? How long is it going to take for him to get here?"

Shirley Prendergast and Kathy Perkins, Black Theatre Network awards ceremony, 1996. Courtesy of Kathy Perkins.

"Well, with traffic it will probably be about an hour or so. Guys, go and have some coffee." So I wasted an hour, because on Broadway people get paid by the hour. I just wanted to cry.

But you didn't because you were taught not to.

I didn't want to cry because he said, "I ain't working with her." I wanted to cry because this is my first time doing this and I'm wasting an hour. So I had to explain that to Shirley, and she understood. Anyway, it was a great experience working with her on the show and working with Melvin Van Peebles and his son and his daughter. He had his whole family in the show. Shirley is such a giving person. She didn't like to travel. She's a real homebody. So, if somebody would call her to do a show [she'd refer them to me]. You ever heard of Lena Horne? Shirley was asked to light a Delta Sigma Theta sorority conference featuring Lena Horne. So they called me and said, "Shirley said she can't do it but you would probably be interested." I said, "Yes!" It was amazing. The conference was down in New Orleans and lasted a whole week. I did the whole convention. New Orleans was close to Mobile, so my father came. My father had been in World War II, and at the time Lena Horne was the person for the black soldiers.

How did you become interested in museum lighting?

Oh, that came much later. That was after I left Smith College in 1985 and worked in Los Angeles. There was a job that opened at this brand-new complex called the Los Angeles Theatre Center. So, I was at this theater; I was hired to be one of the resident designers. The artistic director who was there was really crazy. One of the things I have always believed in is: I'm not working anyplace without a contract. Out of all the people that worked there, there may have been about 5 percent of people with contracts. Not only did I ask them for a contract, I said, "After six months, I want an evaluation to know that I'm coming back." I think he forgot he had given it to me. I lit everything. It was an amazing theater. He brought in directors from all over the world. I worked with some amazing actresses, because a lot of film actresses liked to be onstage from time to time. So, there were all these stars that I had a chance to work with in Los Angeles. Then I did dance concerts. One day there's this gospel show that was going on, and I'm lighting it. The artistic director comes in and says, "I want flashing lights and all this stuff." I said, "This isn't that type of concert. You wouldn't ask me to light the Mormon Tabernacle Choir [that way]. This is religious music." He got upset, but he was the type of guy that if you ticked him off, the next day he would say, "Get out of my theater." All right, so he got ticked off about that. The guy who was head of design said, "Let's go have a cup of coffee." He says, "The artistic director wants you to leave at the end of the season." He didn't see my contract. I said, "That's really interesting. We just had an evaluation of my work less than a week ago and all the other resident designers were sitting at the table when you gave me my evaluation. I also have a contract. My contract says after the six-month evaluation I'm here for another year. If he's going to terminate me, then we have a legal problem." He said, "Oh, you have a contract?" I said, "Yes."

While I was at Smith College, I met this black woman, Sandra, who ended up going to law school at the University of Michigan while I was there. We stayed in touch. Come to find out she became one of the top entertainment lawyers at NBC, so I called her. I said, "I have a legal issue. I don't have any money. I'll give you some free tickets." She said, "I'm going to do something even better. I have a friend who has a law firm in Hollywood. People really look at addresses. I'm going to write the letter, and I'm just going to have him sign it and send it." He sends my boss a letter, and the guy says, "How can you afford a Hollywood lawyer?!" The letter basically says, "You cannot terminate Ms. Perkins. If you don't want her to do any work, that's fine. But you still have to pay her salary." So that's what he decided to do. He gave me fewer shows, but I still got my full-time salary.

It was a blessing for me because he thought he was going to blackball me from working. He used to do that to people but I'm not going to lose any sleep over what he said. By then I was working with the Japanese American Cultural and Community Center [est. 1971] doing lighting. I was involved in all the communities, and by then I was at the University of California, Los Angeles. I had gotten this grant to be at UCLA for two or three years. So, during my free time, I said, "Oh, there's this wonderful Los Angeles museum: the California African American Museum [est. 1977]. I should learn a different lighting skill. I love museums. Maybe I can just volunteer my time so I can learn about lighting displays, because that's a whole different world." Next to the Charles H. Wright Museum of African American History [est. 1965] in Detroit, the California African American Museum was one of the biggest museums in the country at the time. So, I was working with the woman who was a visual curator. By this time, I had started my book project, *Black Female Playwrights: An Anthology of Plays Before 1950* [1990]. This was in 1986 or 1987. The visual arts curator and I got to be friends. She knew that I was working on this book on early black women and I was doing this work at UCLA. One day, she comes to me and says, "We've got this new guy coming in named Lonnie Bunch. He spent some time working at the Smithsonian, so he's going to be the history curator. He's looking for somebody who can help him do research, and I told him you knew all about research, museums, and research centers, and he'd like to know if you would be interested in talking to him." So I went by to talk to him, and it was just like a dream job. He said, "We're doing this whole series called Black California." He was going to start out with a town called Allensworth and do a big exhibit on that. He said, "Part of your job will be to go out and interview people. We want to start collecting artifacts and stuff like that. Is that something you'd be interested in?" I said, "Sure." He said, "It's a contract job." I said, "I work in a theater. There may be some weeks I may have a show." He said, "It doesn't matter. This is your assignment, and you can get it done within x number of weeks, and I'm fine with that." I was with him for three years at the museum, and it was a wonderful experience. Who knew thirty years later he would be the director of the Smithsonian Institution's National Museum of American History?

How did you get involved with the National Museum of African American History and Culture? Did Lonnie Bunch call you?

Well, no. We always stayed in touch. He left the California African American Museum, the Smithsonian hired him back, and he asked me if I wanted to come to D.C. I just said, "Lonnie, I'm not a nine-to-five person. I don't want anybody's full-time job, but if you have special projects . . ." Then he ended up coming to Chicago. He was the first black person to run the Chicago Historical Society [from 2001 to 2005], which is a big deal. So, I would see him in Chicago. He would come to one of my shows, and then the next thing I knew he said, "I'm going to D.C., to open a museum." I said, "Where?" He said, "We don't have it yet. It's not built and we don't have anything. I'm starting from scratch." We stayed in touch and maybe four or five years ago I get this call that said, "Lonnie Bunch said you might be interested in working with us as a theater consultant for the exhibit." I said, "Sure."

What is your lighting design process, and how does your research inform your work?

It's been evolving over the years. Every show is different. It just really depends on the show, because I work with so many different cultural groups. It changes. If I'm doing a Pearl Cleage show, of course, I'm going to read the play. I like plays based in realism . . . although that's not true. I enjoyed working on *Smart People*. Now I'm more interested in doing plays that I wouldn't normally do. I did a production of *1984* that was done in a futuristic way. Lighting-wise it was a real challenge. I'm beginning to do more plays like that.

I've been traveling so much. As I look at different cultures, that also informs my work and how I use color. Because I've traveled so much in Africa, I'm sensitive to the sky and colors. I enjoy using color in my plays if it lends itself to it. I enjoy working with saturated colors. I love working on plays where I have a backdrop to light. That was one of the things I loved about doing *Flyin' West* [1995]: I could have this beautiful backdrop. Anyplace I go in the world, I take pictures of skies. I use that as my research, because the director may say, "Oh, I'm thinking about this for a show." The director [for a show I was working on] said, "Oh, have you ever been to Africa and seen . . ." I said, "Do you want to be a little bit more specific about where in Africa?" He says, "Have you ever been to Ghana?" I said, "I have photos from different parts of Africa. Let me bring in some pictures." He was like, "Oh my God, I love this! Can you make our sky look like this?" So I usually start that way and say, "These are the colors I have in mind for the background. I'm not going to put these on the set." Most directors cannot visualize anything. It's really important for a director to try and communicate. I don't want anybody dictating to me: "I want this color and that color."

You worked with producer Hazel Bryant on Paper Dolls *at the Richard Allen Center for Culture and Art in 1983.*

I think Susan Watson was directing the production. Yes, it was Hazel Bryant producing the play. She was very gracious. At the time I was doing *Paper Dolls*, I think Hazel was sick and a lot of people didn't know about it.

Her life was cut out too short.

Yes, just really short.

I know you worked with director and playwright Glenda Dickerson.

Actually, I did my first New York show with Glenda.

Is that The Glorious Monster in the Bell of the Horn *in 1979?*

Yes [*laughing*].

Woodie King Jr. also produced the play at the New Federal Theatre. Could you tell me about that experience?

The Glorious Monster in the Bell of the Horn was written by Larry Neal, who was very famous during the Black Arts Movement. Larry Neal was wonderful to work with. He and Max Roach died young, too. I was just flattered to be working with Max Roach. He was a famous jazz musician. He did the music. The music was absolutely wonderful, but nobody knew what the show was about. I went to Glenda and said, "I'm not sure what do to with this." She said, "Just put some light on the stage!"

The production was meant to be more of an emotional experience? An artistic creation?

Yes. It was this guy's journey. To be quite honest, I can't even tell you what the play was about. I said, "What's going on here? Glenda, I need some guidance on this one." She said, "I don't know. You've got the M.F.A." She was so funny. That's the only show I have ever worked on with her. I was working with some amazing people. To be in the room with Larry Neal and Max Roach. Then my next New York show was *Lagrima del Diablo* [*The Devil's Tear*, 1980] at NEC [Negro Ensemble Company]. This was another experimental play. It's like, "What is this play about?"

Do you think that there are fewer designers of color working in theater today than, say, back in the 1970s when you first started working professionally?

I don't know. I think there might be fewer people in theater in general. I think kids are being told to go into the science, technology, engineering, and mathematics areas. I think they are being told to go out and get jobs where they can make a living.

But clearly, you made quite a living in theater, right?

Well, I consider myself very fortunate. I always had teaching, which I love. Although I never started out to teach. That was something that was not even on my radar.

`Fémi Sarah Heggie

`Fémi Sarah Heggie also worked behind the scenes during the Black Arts Movement, refining her craft as a stage manager.

I wanted to create something, and a stage manager is a very important job. Douglas Turner Ward used to say, "If there's five characters in a play, the sixth is the stage manager." When you're calling a show, you have to call the lights and the sound—whatever it is the director has chosen. You do it correctly, then there is a voice in doing that. It's like you're there. You're making the audience see what the director wants them to see. The lights go out for a reason. They don't just arbitrarily go out. So, I loved it. I'm getting chills thinking about it. Just being behind stage, calling the cues for a show was exciting. It's sort of like being in a band; the drummer keeps the beat. For me, the stage manager keeps the beat. Because all the parts of that production have to come through that person. I did a lot of writing back then. I wrote a lot of poems. I have a letter from Toni Morrison that said I "have the gift; don't give it away." It's hanging on the wall in my office. I love Toni Morrison. Simply love her.

Why do you love Toni Morrison?

First of all, she's the first black woman at Random House, and that was when I was at Sarah Lawrence College. And she was kind. But her writing is no less than fantastic. I can't find words for it. *The Bluest Eye* [1970]. I cried. I think it should be required reading for *everybody*. She was probably the first black woman to my knowledge to incorporate what was happening here and how it was affecting people, characters, children in stories. You could put yourself in them, so to speak. I wrote a piece of prose called "The Lady of Grand Central Station." It is about a black woman in Grand Central Station who was homeless. I would see her all the time on my way from Manhattan to Bronxville to Sarah Lawrence College. She would be shuffling around. I said, "Who is this woman at Grand Central Station? She's somebody's daughter, somebody's sister. Certainly, somebody's child." I sent Toni Morrison a copy, and that is when she wrote me that letter.

[*Reads from framed letter*] "You really ought to concentrate on the prose. Write some fiction. You have the gift. Don't throw it away. Regards, Toni. *November 3, 1975.*"

If I ever get this book written, this will be in the front of it.

Oh, you need to! "You have the gift. Don't throw it away."

I feel like I have. There have been so many distractions in life.

You've had so many opportunities in life. I understand why you've done some of everything. Do you consider yourself an artist?

I consider myself a writer.

Do you also consider yourself a stage manager?

Yes. Stage management is what I know in terms of a skill to survive, make money.

What advice would you give to those who want to pursue a career in stage management?

Get a mentor on Broadway. That may sound counterproductive in terms of black people, but you know what? When you're doing community theater, you're not going to get any opportunities. We don't help each other in that way. No one helped me.

Even back then, you don't feel like anyone helped you?

No. No one said, "Here. Come work on this show on Broadway." I was just one of those people who was out there. I was one of the first black women to get an Equity card.

Earlier you talked about the importance of images. Did you have images of black women stage managers, or did you carve out that space for yourself?

Yes, for myself. I didn't know any other ones.

Did you ever encounter other black women stage managers?

When I went to Europe with *Porgy and Bess*, the production stage manager was Helaine Head, and she was a black woman. There was a friend of mine, Beverly Jenkins, who went to Howard University and right to this day is probably the only black woman stage manager on Broadway. She is always working, but she has never called me for a gig and I have let her know that.

What are some of your memorable experiences while on tour as a stage manager?

When I was young, I used to be able call shows in whatever language in the country I was in while in Europe. I would always learn how to call cues in their language. I couldn't do that now if you paid me, but that was incredible. Germany, Switzerland, France, all these different places. *Porgy and Bess* was my favorite of all. My company . . . when I say "my company," there are many companies of *Porgy and Bess* and they do not all have the same set or the same direction. What they did on Broadway was not *Porgy and Bess*. That was just a musical. I sat there and was like, "This is not *Porgy and Bess.*" It's not the opera. So that was my favorite show to stage-manage. Because you had so many cues to do. You were doing it from a score and there's fifty people in the company. You're the fifty-first character. On that tour, I was also doing lighting cues with my hands, having buildings turn around, and just all kinds of wonderful things. The music—you've heard the music—is fantastic. I was in heaven. The *Bubbling Brown Sugar* tour was before *Porgy and Bess*. *Bubbling* was wonderful. I worked with Charles "Honi" Coles, Avon Long, and Vivian Reed. Honi Coles was one of the tap dancers. His partner, Cholly Atkins, was the one who taught the Temptations all those moves back in the day. Atkins and Coles did things at the Apollo Theater [est. 1913] back before I was even here.

You were never really mentored throughout this process except for . . .

Honi Coles. When I met him, we were doing *Bubbling*. I remember I was doing *The Wiz* in Japan, someone was trying to get me to sleep with them, and I had to call Honi all the way back in New York. I'm crying because I thought this person was just a friend. So he was the one who kind of led me. He said, "You're so stupid." I'm like, "What?" He said, "She wants you." And I'm like, "What?" That's who I was. That is who I still am. Because I'm never there with you.

Why did you choose to work with Negro Ensemble Company rather than, say, the New Lafayette Theatre?

Well, that's interesting, because the New Lafayette was *real* black. I don't think they would have accepted my lifestyle or who I was. I don't feel they would. In those days, the black movement was about black men finding *themselves* and running whatever they could run. That's what it was. But they would come to NEC. Roscoe Orman and I are friends to this day, but back in those days those guys got up in the middle of a show and walked out as a protest because they considered us "downtown Negroes." I didn't have that kind of prejudice. I still don't.

So that's the lifestyle you are talking about? They wouldn't have been open to the fact that you were working with—

We interacted with white folks. We didn't have a problem with white people.

That was the problem they had with you?

That's a good question, because a lot of people have a lot of problems with me, but they don't tell me. They used to say, " `Fémi is rough and tough and you can't do this and that and the other." Then a lot of people . . . I never have my personal life in my work life. They are separate. A lot of people tried to cross them, but I always reneged. No.

You're protective of that separation.

Absolutely! People think they know who I am and what my preferences are. I never say anything because it's not your business. I don't think your personal life belongs out there. What else do you have that's yours, that you don't have to share? I'm not one of these persons who is going to be at the Gay Day Parade. I'm not going to be there. I don't care about that. I care about black people. I'll be at *that* parade.

When you said your "lifestyle" was something that wouldn't be accepted, I was wondering if that intersection of your identity came into play? Did anyone know you had relationships with women?

They probably did.

But you are about black people.

I am *always* about black people and civil rights and equal rights. I don't care who you sleep with. What does that have to do with anything? I really don't understand that now, and I'm seventy years old. When it comes to making decisions for groups, civil rights and all of that . . . "Oh she's good but she's gay." I would hate that. What does that have to do with us being able to sit at the lunch counter? I eat. You eat. Come on now. Let's get real here. But a lot of our men, too, are intimidated by strong black women whether they are gay or not. If they can't have you, then there's something wrong with you. And that still goes on. Until a black man is secure . . . I don't know why black women are more secure in ourselves sooner.

CONCLUSION

Legacy

> For women, then, poetry is not a luxury. It is a vital necessity of our existence. It forms the quality of the light within which we predicate our hopes and dreams toward survival and change, first made into language, then into idea, then into more tangible action. Poetry is the way we help give name to the nameless so it can be thought. The farthest horizons of our hopes and fears are cobbled by our poems, carved from the rock experiences of our daily lives.
>
> —Audre Lorde, "Poetry Is Not a Luxury"

I was invited to present a portion of this study to graduate students enrolled at a private research university. As we discussed the process of reclamation, I was a bit taken aback by the instructor's interjection that my recovery efforts were part of a "trend" in theater studies. I felt ill at ease to correct the instructor's disparaging tone and cavalier attitude in front of their students, so I remained silent. Besides, as a black woman academic who must constantly negotiate her interests from within historically white colleges and universities, I had heard and experienced far worse. Yet I could not forget the comment. A couple of months later, as I reexamined Audre Lorde's "Poetry Is Not a Luxury" (1977), I came to an understanding of why I could not dismiss this offhanded remark. The word "trend" implies a fleeting interest or fad, not a genuine and long-term investment. Just as poetry is not a luxury for black women, so too are our recovery efforts. Simply put, history has not been kind to black women. The expressive arts have provided a powerful means for black women intellectuals to articulate their experiential knowledge and galvanize the black community into action.

Remembering black women intellectuals' struggles and honoring their legacy constitute a vital component to our survival as a people. Black women intellectuals—from the abolitionist Sojourner Truth to the Black Lives Matter movement cofounder Patrisse Khan-Cullors—have a longstanding tradition of using their voices to address issues impacting the black community. Khan-Cullors and journalist Asha Bandele acknowledge how the broader tradition of black intellectual thought and black women's activism has inspired the Black Lives Matter movement in the memoir *When They Call You a Terrorist: A Black Lives Matter Memoir*. "We do this work today because on another day work was done by Assata Shakur, Angela Davis, Miss Major, the Black Panther Party, the members of the Black Arts Movement, SNCC, the RNA, Malcolm X, Martin Luther King, Ella Baker, and so many others. We owe you and the world a debt of gratitude," write Khan-Cullors and Bandele.[1] The stakes have always been high as black women such as Ida B. Wells-Barnett risked their very lives under the threat of Jim Crow laws and lynch mobs so that black women, men, and children could flourish. Black women intellectuals of the Black Arts Movement continued this tradition, creating daring new works that addressed the importance of black families in combating systemic racism, the multidimensional lives of black women, the black liberation struggle, police brutality, the failing education system, poverty, black sexuality, healing from trauma and oppression, and much more. Their artistry and activism continue to offer important insights for building strong black communities and cultural institutions.

Black women intellectuals of today and their anti-racist allies are charged with the solemn task of preserving this important legacy. P. J. Gibson perhaps best articulates the labor involved in reclaiming black women's intellectual tradition in her poem "Rolling Cinquain" (2018). Gibson writes,

> Few . . . few
> Reach into the dark
> Corridors of history
> Fingering through *past's* damp soil

Searching
Nestling
In dusty books
Memorabilia's wings
Old programs, posters, photos . . . things
History
Voices
She elicits
Sing, sing yesterday's songs
Ponder footprints . . . left in soil
Our paths
Conjure . . .
She summons . . . calls
Gathers a . . . *Speak* . . . circle
Living anchors—echoing winds . . .
Journeys
She finds
Cloaked in wisdom . . .
Tempest's waves . . . *documents*
A gathering of pen's writing
Drama.[2]

Gibson presented this poem, along with a copy of *Long Time Since Yesterday* (1984), as a gift to me upon our first meeting in a New York City café. Inscribed in the play script is a note that reads, "Thank you for your work you are doing as you document the voices of black playwrights, theater, and history. Much needs your investigation and care." I know that I am not alone in this endeavor. Yet Gibson's poem, coupled with the inscription, serves as a powerful reminder that we must continue to conjure the voices of the past and reclaim our ancestral legacy.

As such, I close by providing space for black women intellectuals of the Black Arts Movement to articulate their legacy. *What do they want us to know and remember about their life's work? What do they think the future has in store for the development of African American theater and performance?* I received a variety of answers to these questions, including Ntozake Shange's reflection that she wants future generations to know not just of our oppression but also of our celebrations and triumphs, a spectrum of life experiences outside the purview of dominant society. Judy Juanita imparts powerful advice, admonishing black artists/activists to battle within their own communities and archive their labor for future generations. In terms of the future of black theater, Kathy A. Perkins is optimistic and believes that new black theaters and regional festivals might continue to afford opportunities for emerging black theater artists. Ultimately, it is my hope that by conjuring the voices of our foremothers, we might gain a better sense of the past and a purpose for the future.

Ntozake Shange

I want people to know I tried to leave memories of the hopes and the joy and laughter of people of color—especially Black English speakers in the Western Hemisphere—for future generations to share so that our history will be more than dates and places and what white people did to us. I want our struggles to be understood as not only a historical phenomenon but as personal trials and triumphs because the masses cannot move without the individual taking a step.

Shirley Faison

I want people to know that Barbara Ann Teer used her life to support people to have creative freedom, to support people to experience their personal power, to support people to empower their communities, and to support people to share their voice. It's very important that we share her legacy with the world so it doesn't become just like a grain of sand.

Jackie Taylor

I want people to know that there are no colors except black. The human race began in Africa. Therefore, we all are of African descent. All of us, period. We have to stop defining ourselves as white, as black, as brown, because we are all African. We are all from the same tribe and we need to start understanding and realizing that. We divide ourselves because we want to feel we're either oppressed or we're the oppressor. That's how our society operates: there has to be the oppressed and there has to be the oppressor. The way that we have found to do that is to separate ourselves by colors. Black Ensemble Theater is called black ensemble because it means we are all one. Once we accept that and understand that, we can recognize the stupidity of how we operate as human beings. When are we going to stop being so stupid?

In terms of legacy, the important thing is that the mission and philosophies that I have created continue way beyond my lifetime. We're not going to achieve eradicating racism in my lifetime or in my grandson's lifetime or, good Lord, maybe [not even] in his grandchildren's lifetime. I would like for my legacy to be that two hundred years from now, there is no need for a Black Ensemble Theater. Society has transformed itself and I have become obsolete. This is something that I did. I want to be remembered like the Wright brothers are remembered. The Wright brothers flew a flying machine. Well, it's a gazillion-dollar industry now, and we don't even think about it, but we know that the Wright brothers started it. I want that same kind of thing. A little name [on a plaque] that says, "When there was racism in the arts, Jackie Taylor had a theater dedicated to eliminating it."

Micki Grant

I don't know what others should know and remember. I always like it when people tell me that they remember something about my work, especially if it's a line or a thought . . . then it's worthwhile.

J.e. Franklin

I think that if you perform the word, you feel the word, you know the word, you have learned the word. Because maybe it's true [that] in the beginning there was the word, and the word made flesh. The word was made flesh, and so if you perform the word, you probably will not forget it in the same way that you will if you are introduced to the word in some nonsensory form, just through a textbook. I think that that's the one thing that we are up against and that we have to confront. That is this nonsensory disembodied way of learning, that static mode of learning. I want people to see my work as dynamic, rooted in the human feelings, and liberated.

Shirley Prendergast

I know what I want to do. Now, if you like what I want to do, fine. If you don't like what I want to do, fine. Tell me about it and maybe I can change. But otherwise . . . All I can do is give advice and tell people, "Think about it."

Nora Cole

Vinnette Carroll was the most passionate and the most visceral and just creative from her groin. Whatever she worked on. She liked large canvases. I got to do *Medea* with her, and she liked the big dramatic. She never got to do a lot of the straight plays that she wanted to work on. She also liked music and dance so much that there would always be an element of it [in her productions]. One of the pieces that she did over and over again was *Desire Under the Elms* [1924]. That's a piece that she worked on quite a bit. But there was no mistaking her passion. She almost exorcised that passion out of her actors by making you do the most incredible moment-to-moment work in a piece. Vinnette used to get a cold sore on her lip the week before a show opened. That was nerves. Her passion cannot be matched. Coming from an actor point of view, too, and wanting to get that performance out of you. She was able to do that and make it reach to the back row of an audience. Her productions were like celebrations.

By the time I performed in *Your Arms Too Short to Box with God*, the musical had already been on Broadway twice. Then we went on tour. Even after we had finished rehearsing and were going from city to city, Vinnette would rehearse and rehearse and rehearse. Even before I started working with Vinnette, I heard stories about how people used to go hide so that she couldn't find them to make them rehearse during a show. I learned that too when we performed *When Hell Freezes Over I'll Skate* in 1983–84 at the Coconut Grove Playhouse in Miami. We had already started the second act and Tommy Hallis had the first lines but wasn't onstage. She was giving Tommy notes backstage. For me to now run into young actors that have never heard Vinnette Carroll's name is like, "Well, I know I've been in the business a long time now . . . but, wow! You've never heard of her?! You've never . . ."

Dawn Alli

I would be satisfied if people just remembered that I did something other than just live for myself. That would be nice.

Aduke Aremu

I want people to know that Aduke Aremu, as a woman of color, was one of the pioneers and progressive warriors for theater for young people. I added a different type of theater for young people because I went into the music, poetry, and dance venue, whereas some of the earlier children's pieces were just plain dramatic plays. I did full-fledged musicals and I still do. I believe that we need to captivate the total child. Children are visual. I wanted to captivate their auditory and kinesthetic senses, so I tried to bring in different aspects of theater so that a child who was watching it would almost be transformed to another world. I'm trying to train them, but I'm doing it in a nonacademic manner. I'm not beating them over the head with, "You have to do this. You need to stay in school. You need to be good." What I do through my type of work is try to show the audience a lesson or moral imperative through the theater form so that they come out feeling good about themselves.

Doris Derby

I want people to know that the black family is my core and our community and the African diaspora is my frame of reference. I didn't stop when I was in graduate school and was part of the minority graduate student alliance, the African Student Association. When I came to Georgia State University, as founding director of Office of African-American Student Services and Programs, I established a foundation for a partnership between the Ivory Coast and Georgia State. I continued to expand my networks and projects related to Africa and the Caribbean. I have a few African students that I mentored and adopted as godchildren. My third phase right here in Atlanta is just a continuation of embracing black family, history, and culture, and combining it with the arts, expression, and activism.

Judy Juanita

People are going to form their own [opinion]. That's why I try to write. I love writing in different mediums. I try to make my point over and over again. I told my grandson it will be his grandchildren who will uncover it. That's why I made a point of leaving all of my stuff at Duke University in the archives with the other student activists from the Student Nonviolent Coordinating Committee. Yes, it's there for future generations. Just like the ex-slaves left their accounts for us. If we didn't have their accounts, we wouldn't have known how terrible slavery was. Their accounts are what got the abolitionists in London to trumpet it to the world: "This is what is going on in America!" It was the abolitionists, including Frederick Douglass and many whites—who were probably racist and sexist and didn't give a damn—who trumpeted these writings to the world. My writings? They're there for the world. The world will figure out what to do with them. I am just an observer. Or as I like to call myself, an observational ironist.

`Fémi Sarah Heggie

I want people to remember my sincerity across the board with any job I've ever had. I've never been late. In all my career, I missed one show in California for a person's wedding. And then she got divorced [*laughs*]. My eagerness for perfection, which may not even be possible. Any on-Broadway or Off-Broadway production I've ever worked on—*Jelly's Last*

Jam [1993], *Song of Jacob Zulu* [1993]—I gave it my all. That's what my grandmother talked about, too. Any job worth doing is worth doing well. I guess my grandmother was my first mentor. It's interesting to learn things in retrospect now that she's gone. I hear her voice and think, "Ah, this is what she meant!" She prepared me for life.

Barbara Molette

I want people to know that Carlton and I told the truth back then and to think, "Wow, they said that?!"

P. J. Gibson

I'm interested in putting a spotlight on the lives of thinking black people. Not whitewashing their flaws—let them have their warts—but also show that many of them are offering something and have a concern for the next generations. I believe in ancestors because ancestors and angels believed in me. I want to make sure that people don't get so crazy as to think that they have gained all the things they have gained on their own. That's just not true. You can think it, but the reality is a lot of blood has been shed for people to get where they are. The whole adage of, "If you don't know your history, you're damned to repeat it." Well, I think it goes a step further. If you don't know your history, you can't know what to do. There's absolutely no way you're going to see me doing some of the things that our women are doing to their bodies. Do some of these women really understand what horror Sara Baartman had to go through, and now you're sucking out fat from your waist and putting into your [butt]? Do they understand what that was? We are lacking a historical perspective on why we are and where we are today. I think it is incumbent upon me to leave an arsenal of information that gives a glimpse into the black presence in America during the twentieth and twenty-first centuries. That's my job.

I think I was given the ability to write for a reason. I've been given the ability to think for a reason. All the things that happened to me as a child and young adult—being tied in a basement, being left alone, being an outsider in my own family, and an outsider in the economic world—prepared me for this. I'm not saying that it's hunky-dory; it's painful. But on the other hand, if not me, who? Someone has to do it. Someone has to go through it. It is painful to not be a household name. I'd be lying if I say it didn't. It's just so important that we document this. I made a conscientious choice to try to get as much published as possible so it's here. It's not just one or two plays. That's what I set out to do, but there's a price when you do that. It hurts when the major theater houses don't do your work. It hurts if you have a production that is sometimes lacking in talent or production quality. All I can do is keep writing.

Lee Hunkins

I want people to remember that I was honest and I tried to get not only to the audience's mind but also their heart. I tried to not only give them something to think about or compare their own life to but also something dealing with the emotions and feelings from the heart. A message to make people think more positive about their life.

Kathy A. Perkins

I want people to know that I tried to be a good mentor. My students have always said I've been a good mentor. I've always tried to encourage people to go into this field. I'm in touch with students from thirty years ago. A lot of them are hiring me now, which is really interesting. Hopefully, my work speaks for itself.

I think black theater is going to get better. Maybe not so much. I don't know. So many companies are having a difficult time financially and in general. What I'm very excited about are all these festivals that are happening. I think maybe it is going to be the festivals that make the difference. There's a young woman named JaMeeka Holloway-Burrell who just started her festival in Durham, called the Bull City Black Theatre Festival [est. 2018]. It's a festival of black people in the triangle: Durham, Raleigh, and Chapel Hill. I understand it was very successful and she wants to do it next year. So, there are all these festivals cropping up. You've got the National Black Theatre Festival [est. 1989] that happens every other year in Winston-Salem. Then you've got the Atlanta Black Theatre Festival [est. 2012] and the DC Black Theatre and Arts Festival [est. 1986]. That is one way that a lot of artists are getting their works out. At least playwrights. They rely on the festivals to get their works done. I see a lot of hope in festivals, and there are some new theaters that are taking off. I think a lot of the so-called mainstream theaters are feeling pressure to hire more people of color. I'm very hopeful regarding the future of black theater.

APPENDIX A

Notes from the Field: Establishing Ethics and Rapport

My ethical standards require me to acknowledge my own motivations for resurrecting the past. I began this study out of a personal desire to learn more about the generation of black women intellectuals who preceded me. As a black woman, activist, and theater historian, I find resonance with the struggles our foremothers encountered during the sixties and seventies. I knew that I wanted to recover their efforts and provide a space for them to voice their experiential knowledge, but I wasn't sure how to do so until I read E. Patrick Johnson's *Sweet Tea: Black Gay Men of the South; An Oral History* (2008). Utilizing more than seventy interviews with everyday black gay men throughout the southern United States, Johnson beautifully weaves together their experiential knowledge into the very fabric of both black and southern identities. *This was the model I had been searching for!* While ten years have passed since the inception of this project, my intention remains the same: I want to use my position of privilege to give voice to the most vulnerable in our society. Reclaiming and celebrating black women's intellectual tradition is at the heart of everything I do. To feign objectivity is to deny the core of who I am. My black female subjectivity inspires my labor as an agent of change.

When I began calling potential narrators, I did not fully understand the importance of building rapport upon initial contact. The anthropologist Christine Obbo notes that a "collector of oral narratives must attempt to familiarize him- or herself with three things: *rapport*, *listening*, and *writing*."[1] Obbo defines rapport as a "friendly relationship" that grants access into the informant's life.[2] Unfortunately, in my initial quest to situate myself as a seasoned "scholar," I did not present myself as *human* and consequently failed to capture their interest. *Why was I failing?* After a series of rejections, I discussed my concerns with my partner, explaining how I always introduced myself, my institutional affiliation, and provided an overview of the study in a professional manner. My partner pointed out, however, that I failed to communicate my *intentions* during these telephone introductions. I later discovered that some potential narrators—especially those who felt marginalized in Black Arts institutions, mainstream theaters, and greater society—were protective of their work and wanted to know *why* I was interested in their life story. Eventually my partner helped me realize that my racial identity might also be a factor in my inability to gain a potential narrator's trust. While I was cognizant that some informants felt a deep-seated distrust of white academics, it never occurred to me that my Pacific Northwest dialect and academic affiliation might lead them to misidentify me as white. So I chose to test the waters. I decided that I would call a potential informant and share a part of myself: who I am and my personal interest in the topic. Within the first two minutes of our conversation, I would say, "as a black woman theater artist." To which the first informant responded, "Oh. I didn't know you were a sister. Sure, let's talk." I felt elated to discover this important aspect of building rapport yet incredibly crushed as I realized my earlier failure to perform my blackness.

Critical performance ethnography requires the ethical treatment of narrators throughout each stage of collaboration. My ethical standard includes transparency about the process. *Where and when would the interview take place? How long will the process take? What am I asking of narrators during our interview? Can they withdraw from the study? How will I use their words after completion of the interview? Can they edit their words after completion of the interview? Will they receive monetary compensation for their participation?* Foremost in my process is following a set of procedures that included informed consent on the part of narrators. I invited potential narrators to meet with me for no more than two hours at a location and time of their choosing. A few narrators requested phone interviews, but the majority preferred to meet in person at a variety of locations, including their homes, hair salons, hotel lobbies, restaurants, public parks, and even the banks of the Hudson River. This meant that for several years I had to be willing to drop everything and fly across the United States, anywhere from Oakland, to Atlanta, to New York to conduct interviews. As a mother of four and tenure-track assistant professor, this was not an easy feat. Also, several narrators insisted that two hours was not sufficient time to recount their life stories with me. Luckily, the countless hours my mother spent socializing me to uphold black cultural norms paid off. I was aware that as a youthful-appearing black woman collaborating with mostly elderly black women, I must demonstrate deference and patience. As a consequence, I remained respectful of their wishes and stayed with some narrators in their homes for as long as eight hours as they shared their memorabilia and recollections. However, if a narrator appeared tired or in need of rest, I carefully vocalized my observations and offered to return at a time of their choosing or follow up with them by phone.

My ethical standards included specific protocol before and immediately following an interview. I provided interview questions in advance to give narrators enough time to reflect upon the past and recall major events, people, and influences in their lives. I used a small digital recorder for all interviews and took notes about a narrator's vocal tones and body language during in-person interviews. I informed narrators before each interview that they could choose not to answer any question and still remain in the study, request the recorder be turned off at any point during the interview, stop the interview at any time, or withdraw from the study at any time. Thankfully, most narrators enthusiastically took part in the study, many were candid in their responses, and none chose to withdraw from the study.

At times, this high level of transparency conflicted with my inner desire to maintain a sense of intimacy and togetherness as I witnessed narrators perform their vision of the past. For example, I found that the sight of my digital recorder immediately put a barrier up between narrators and myself. With some trial and error, I learned to place the recorder near, but not exactly in, the sight lines of narrators. I found that as I told narrators what I was doing and why, they responded with vocal agreement, mitigating any ethical concerns I had. For the most part, interviews proceeded in a much more organic, conversational manner without the constant reminder that we were being recorded. There were still a few instances when a narrator picked up the digital recorder, spoke directly into as if it were a microphone, avoided eye contact with me, and proceeded to tell their life story as if they were performing for the history books. These moments served as important reminders that (1) I was clearly not the "authority" of the Black Arts Movement, (2) they alone were the masters of their own narratives, and (3) they had perhaps been waiting for an opportunity to share their experiential knowledge and understood that their legacy was at stake.

It was equally important for me to provide the means to empower narrators immediately following our interview. Within thirty days of the interview, narrators could request a compact-disc recording of the interview for review. After receipt of the interview, they were given an additional thirty days to edit content from the interview. If narrators requested a transcribed copy of the interview, I mailed these to their home and gave them ample time to return them. Several narrators made these requests, and I complied with their wishes. Only one interviewee requested major changes to their narrative, and these alterations included omitting their comments on unrelated events. While I did not have the funds to compensate narrators for their time and for furthering our understanding of Black Arts Movement theater and performance, I always recognized their labor by providing a small token of appreciation (i.e., a box of chocolates and thank-you note). Whenever possible, I invited narrators to lunch or dinner, because, as Judy Juanita reflects, good food often serves as payment black women give to one another.

My ethical standards included demonstrating a genuine interest in each narrator's life stories. I did so by researching as much as I could about the narrator's life *before* the interview and listening to them during our conversations. However, my best-laid plans sometimes went awry. For example, I did extensive research on Aduke Aremu, founder of the Harlem Children's Theatre Company, prior to our interview in Atlanta. Unbeknownst to me, Aremu's former administrator Dawn Alli had also arrived in Atlanta on the day of our scheduled interview. After meeting Alli at Aremu's office and telling her about the project, she agreed to an unanticipated on-the-spot interview. Thankfully, our conversation went very well. While I clearly lacked background information about her life prior to and immediately following her work with the Harlem Children's Theatre Company, I suspect that my genuine excitement to meet her and strong listening skills cancelled out my lack of preparation.

When I first began these interviews, I tried to demonstrate my listening skills by remaining completely silent while narrators spoke. However, my silence was not appreciated. After all, I was not only a witness to the event but also a *coperformer*. I learned to validate while not distracting from their narratives by employing black-church practices. With some trial and error, I found that I could encourage narrators and (when appropriate) demonstrate empathy by vocalizing sounds of affirmation. A simple and well-placed "mm-hmm" could propel a story forward. Of course, there were times when I did not personally agree with a narrator's ideology. In such cases, I did not feign agreement but neither did I vocalize my dissent. I had to discover my own careful balance of validation and neutrality to complete each interview. I learned that while I do not have to agree with everything a narrator says, I do have to present their narrative as accurately as possible.

Ultimately, I held the responsibility of transcribing and editing each interview. More than a hundred hours spent with black women intellectuals of the Black Arts Movement, their children, and their colleagues resulted in a few thousand pages of transcribed audio. After I spent weeks completing a transcription for just one audio interview, I knew that I could not manage this process on my own. A medical-transcription company was then utilized to complete the first round of transcriptions. I then listened to each interview and edited the original transcription for accuracy. There were times when a recording of a narrator did not sound intelligible. In such cases, I contacted the narrator for additional help in discerning their words. All but one narrator responded to such a query, demonstrating to me that most were invested in the project. Those that did respond also expressed appreciation for the careful way I dealt with their narrative.

I did not anticipate that building rapport would elicit a depth of emotion from both narrators and myself. On one end of the spectrum was laughter—at one point or another I laughed with every narrator as they relived their antics as children or career-minded adults. However, it was activist-playwright Judy Juanita, actress and Tony Award–winning playwright Micki Grant, and screenwriter and playwright Lee Hunkins with whom I laughed the most. They share my appreciation for the absurd and are quick to find humor in almost any situation. For example, during one particularly memorable trip to visit Juanita in Oakland, my flight was cancelled and my luggage was lost. When I finally met her, I was exhausted from just a few hours of sleep and sporting a travel-worn Kenny Rogers T-shirt and pink skinny jeans. Fortunately, she also performed stand-up comedy, so we were able to connect by finding humor in the situation. On the opposite side of the emotional spectrum was fear. Fortunately, in all my travels I only once felt actual concern for my safety. As I sat with George Lee Miles, former director and actor of the New Lafayette Theatre, on a New York City park bench discussing the legacy of playwright Martie Evans-Charles, what looked to me like a drug exchange occurred. Thankfully, once the transaction was completed, the group of men quickly left and we resumed our discussion. From this experience, I learned to always meet narrators in reputable establishments.

Finally, the most unexpected outward display of emotion—and that which I believe produced the greatest feeling of togetherness—was tears. Any shred of "emotional detachment" that I may have felt obligated to profess evaporated when P. J. Gibson and `Fémi Sarah Heggie shared their stories of survival with me. Both allegedly endured years of physical, sexual, or emotional abuse at the hands of the very people who should have protected them. I did not know of these experiences prior to our meeting, nor did I ask such personal questions during the interviews. These strong black women took it upon themselves to share their deeply personal and devastating experiences with me so that we could continue to break the black community's silence surrounding the sexual assault and abuse of black women. After they told their stories, I asked both women if they would prefer that I omit their tales. I do not want to sensationalize their trauma. Yet both Gibson and Heggie insisted that I include their references to abuses because they want others to understand that they are not alone. Their struggles and efforts to break silences about the abuse of black women and girls brought me to tears and emboldened me to share my story.

While I have never personally experienced sexual assault, as a child I was groomed by a sexual predator and witnessed sexual violence firsthand. When I was nine years old, my mother asked me to go upstairs and tell my preadolescent sister that dinner was ready. A simple chore that

I had repeated countless times. However, on this particular evening her bedroom door was shut. I opened the door and saw my maternal uncle, who had been living with us for a few months, on top of my sister as if he were doing push-ups. But something seemed wrong. I tried to leave but he forced the door closed. He insisted that he was simply wrestling with her. Apparently I looked unconvinced because he then proceeded to make me repeat after him and swear to God that I would never tell a soul about what I had seen. I remember quite vividly him making me spread each finger and toe so I could not cross them (i.e., make a false promise). He then threatened me, promising that he would kill me if I ever told. I believed him. For what felt like an eternity but was actually only a matter of days, all I could think about was my certain death. I knew I could not keep this a secret. Another sibling could tell something was wrong and pestered me until I told them. Eventually this sibling convinced me to tell our mother what had happened. Unfortunately, he was a master manipulator, and my uncle remained in our home. I held my breath, feeling certain that any moment would be my last. A few days later my uncle kidnapped my sister. He later impregnated her and orchestrated vile acts upon her body that eventually resulted in his *very* brief incarceration. It was not until I received a formal notice of his death a couple of years ago that I felt I could breathe again. Unfortunately, my sister has never fully recovered.

For quite some time I thought my family unique in this regard, not understanding until much later that one of the greatest threats to black women is violence perpetuated by those within their own community. Patricia Hill Collins writes,

> Much of this violence occurs within the context of Black heterosexual love relationships, Black family life, and within African American social institutions. Such violence takes many forms, including verbally berating Black women, hitting them, ridiculing their appearance, grabbing their body parts, pressuring them to have sex, beating them, and murdering them . . . Black girls are especially vulnerable to childhood sexual assault.[3]

This does not imply that black men and women *do not* or *cannot* have loving relationships with one another. Neither do I want stories of abuse misconstrued to reinforce the racist belief that black male bodies are inherently a threat. Simply put: black women—especially poor black girls—are often not afforded any measure of protection in the U.S. legal system or from within our very own communities. The need to protect black men and the fear of providing more ammunition to discredit our communities remain a pressing concern. It is my hope that by reorienting our stories of survival from the margins of history to its center, we might continue to break these silences and inspire the next generation of black women intellectuals and their allies to eradicate all forms of oppression.

APPENDIX B

About the Narrators

Dawn Alli

Dawn C. Alli was born in Somerville, New Jersey, to an upper middle-class family. She remembers being a rather shy child and having a love of reading. She did not discover her passion for theater until she became friends with Aduke Aremu, founder of the Harlem Children's Theatre Company (1971–90). Alli spent approximately ten years working for the Harlem Children's Theatre Company, eventually becoming the company's administrator while also pursuing her master of arts degree in theater from New York University. In addition to her administrative duties, Alli fulfilled a variety of roles when needed. For example, she taught acting courses, directed the Harlem Children's Theatre Company's 1979 production of *The Liberation of Mother Goose* at the John F. Kennedy Center for the Performing Arts in New York, and even replaced a lighting-board operator when called upon. After leaving the Harlem Children's Theatre Company, Alli taught theater courses at the University of Ibadan (Nigeria) until her retirement.

Aduke Aremu

Aduke Aremu was born Gwendolyn Holmes in Brooklyn, New York. She graduated from Wingate High School in Brooklyn, which she describes as "a Mecca of cultural awareness." Aremu continued her education at Hunter College, where she received bachelor of arts and master of arts degrees in education and speech communication. Immediately following college graduation, she traveled to Nigeria, where she received the name "Aduke Aremu," meaning "someone who is loved by everyone." This life-changing experience reaffirmed her commitment to celebrate African history and culture and also led to her chance encounter with costume designer and painter Myrna Belgrave Simmons (later Omodele Folayani). With the help of Simmons, Aremu founded the Harlem Children's Theatre Company in 1971. Aremu's early efforts resulted in numerous awards, including a 1974 AUDELCO producer of the year award for staging her work *Babylon: The Musical.*

As an award-winning producer, theater founder, director, playwright, poet, composer, lyricist, and self-identified "revolutionary," Aremu is best known for her children's musical *The Liberation of Mother Goose* (1973). She has since written a dozen musicals and produced her works across the United States, Nigeria, Ghana, Bermuda, Jamaica, Barbados, Tanzania, and throughout Europe. In addition to her creative work, Aremu had a twenty-seven-year career in education, becoming a public school principal after earning a Ph.D. in education administration and supervision from New York University. After the closing of the Harlem Children's Theatre Company in 1990, she produced the national talk radio show *The Princess Chronicles* and founded the Atlanta-based production company Dove LLC. As CEO of Dove LLC, Aremu is working to adapt *The Liberation of Mother Goose*, now retitled *Goose*, into a television series or a film. In 2010, her lifetime of achievement received commendation from the U.S. House of Representatives.

Nora Cole

Nora Marie Cole was born September 10, 1953, to Lattimore Wallis and Mary Lou Cole in Louisville, Kentucky. Her first major acting credit was the role of the Duchess in the Louisville Children's Theatre 1965 production of *Alice in Wonderland.* She later studied acting at Beloit College in Wisconsin and the Goodman School of Drama in Chicago. Upon graduation, Cole performed in numerous Urban Arts Corps (1967–83) productions, including Vinnette Carroll's *The Ups and Downs of Theophilus Maitland* (1976; Obiah Woman) and *Your Arms Too Short to Box with God* (1982; Singing Mary). Cole has performed on Broadway, Off-Broadway, and at Off-Off-Broadway venues such as the New York Shakespeare Festival, Alvin Theatre, Studio Arena Theatre, Eugene O'Neill Memorial Theater Center, Hartford Stage Company, and Vinnette Carroll Repertory Theatre. Her television credits include performances in the movie *The Cosby Mysteries* (1994) and the series *H.E.L.P.* (1990) and *We Are New York* (2009).

Doris Derby

Doris Adelaide Derby was born into a close-knit and politically active family in the Bronx, New York, in 1939. She was been involved in civil rights activism since her early teens, joining organizations such as the National Association for the Advancement of Colored People, youth chapter. As an adult, she taught at the Child Development Group of Mississippi (1965–68) and worked as a field secretary for the Student Nonviolent Coordinating Committee (SNCC) from 1963 to 1972. Her involvement with the SNCC led to her participation in a literacy project in Tougaloo, Mississippi, where she met John O'Neal and Gilbert Moses. The trio cofounded the Free Southern Theater (FST) in 1963. Derby remembers that the original intention was to make the FST an "arm" of the SNCC. She and John oversaw public relations for the theater while they continued their literacy advocacy. She remembers that about a year later she was outvoted, and the FST moved from Tougaloo to New Orleans. However brief her participation, forming the FST allowed Derby to combine her interest in disseminating black politics, educating the black community, and archiving black history and cultural achievements within one mode. After the FST departed, Derby continued her civil rights activism with the Poor People's Corporation and traveled across the country from 1965 to 1972 providing public relations interviews for the handcraft cooperatives. Throughout all these experiences, Derby kept several cameras about her neck so she could document this history.

Derby left Mississippi in 1972 to pursue her education, earning a master of arts degree in African American studies and a doctor of philosophy degree in social anthropology from the University of Illinois at Urbana-Champaign. She became the founding director of the Office of African-American Student Services and Programs and an adjunct associate professor of anthropology at Georgia State University in 1990, where she remained until her retirement in 2012. Derby supported black student organizations on campus, creating programming such as the Black Student Film Festival and Performing and Visual Arts Council. Derby remains active since retirement, producing films and displaying her collection of civil-rights-era photographs in public exhibits across the United States.

Shirley Faison

Shirley Faison was born Shirley Clemons in 1953 and raised in Massachusetts. She majored in African American studies at Douglass Residential College, Rutgers University. She began performing as a "liberator" at Barbara Ann Teer's National Black Theatre (NBT; est. 1968) of Harlem in 1973. She married fellow liberator Nabii Faison in 1974 and continued to work at the NBT until 2014, receiving a 1989 Audience Development Committee Producers Award for her artistic achievement. The actress, director, and award-winning producer currently works as a talent agent in New York City.

J.e. Franklin

Jennie Elizabeth Franklin was born August 10, 1937, in Houston, Texas, to domestic worker Mathie (née Randle) and small-business owner Robert Franklin. After receiving her bachelor of arts degree from the University of Texas at Austin in 1964, she moved to New York and developed a passion for theater after witnessing Barbara Ann Teer and James Anderson perform in *Home Movies*. Franklin then worked with the Mississippi Freedom Democratic Party and taught at the Freedom School

(Carthage, Miss.) during the summer of 1964. During this time, she discovered that performance was an effective tool to teach children how to read. Using the actual life stories of the children she taught as her foundation, Franklin wrote and directed her first play, *A First Step to Freedom*.

Franklin wrote eleven plays and musicals during the Black Arts Movement, including *The In-Crowd: A Rock Opera* (1965), *Mau-Mau Room* (1969; later retitled *Miss Honey's Young'uns*), and *The Prodigal Sister* (with Micki Grant), and her best-known play, *Black Girl* (1969). Initially a teleplay, Franklin later revised *Black Girl* into a feature film and Off-Broadway play directed by Shauneille Perry at Woodie King Jr.'s New Federal Theatre (est. 1970). Franklin has received numerous awards and honors for her work, including a Drama Desk Award for *Black Girl*, a National Endowment for the Arts Creative Writing Fellowship, and a Rockefeller Fellowship. Franklin has also taught and held residencies at several universities, including Skidmore College, Brown University, and the University of Iowa. She continues to write plays and serves as producing artistic director of her organization, Blackgirl Ensemble Theatre.

P. J. Gibson

P. J. Gibson was born Patricia JoAnn Gibson on October 14, 1951, in Pittsburgh, Pennsylvania. She was raised by her affectionate grandmother in Trenton, New Jersey, with infrequent visits from her birth mother. Gibson developed a love of storytelling and metaphysics from her grandmother, who also practiced astral travel. Upon her grandmother's death, Gibson was placed with her mother in Washington, D.C. Despite being raised in poverty, Gibson displayed a keen intelligence at an early age and was able to secure academic scholarships to attend college. She received a bachelor of arts degree in English, drama, and religion from Keuka College in 1973. Gibson then pursued a graduate education at Brandeis University, earning a master of fine arts in playwriting in 1975. She has received numerous awards and honors for her playwriting, including a 1978 National Endowment for the Arts playwriting grant and 1985 AUDELCO Best Dramatic Play of the Year award for *Long Time Since Yesterday*. In addition to playwriting, Gibson has written poetry and screenplays and has taught at several U.S. colleges, including Boston College; University of California,

Berkeley; and Douglass Residential College, Rutgers University. She currently teaches at John Jay College of Criminal Justice in New York.

Micki Grant

Micki Grant was born Minnie Perkins in Chicago, Illinois, to Oscar and Gussie Perkins on June 30, 1941. Grant's parents cultivated her love of music, writing, and acting, skills she would refine while pursuing a degree in English and theater at Lehman College, City University of New York. As an actress, she appeared Off-Broadway in Jean Genet's *The Blacks* (1959) and Marc Blitzstein's *The Cradle Will Rock* (1937), before landing a role as secretary Peggy Harris Nolan on the daytime soap opera *Another World* in 1965. As a lyricist and composer, Grant often collaborated with actress, playwright, director, and Urban Arts Corps (1967–83) founder Vinnette Carroll. Their collaborations resulted in musicals such as *Croesus and the Witch* (1971); *Step Lively, Boy* (1973); *The Ups and Downs of Theophilus Maitland* (1976); and the Tony Award–nominated Broadway production *Don't Bother Me, I Can't Cope* (1973). Grant's other Broadway credits include *Your Arms Too Short to Box with God* (with Carroll; 1976) and *Working* (with Stephen Schwartz, Craig Carnelia, James Taylor, Mary Rodgers, and Susan Birkenhead; 1978). Grant also cowrote the music and lyrics to J.e Franklin's *The Prodigal Sister* (1974), wrote the music and lyrics to *Phillis* (1986), and wrote the lyrics for *Eubie!* (1978) and *It's So Nice to Be Civilized* (1980). She has received numerous awards and honors for her work, including a 1972 Drama Desk Award for outstanding performance, 1972 Drama Desk Award for most promising lyricist, and 1973 Grammy Award for best musical theater album for *Don't Bother Me, I Can't Cope*. She more recently received a 1997 Helen Hayes Award for outstanding lead actress (nonresident production) for *Having Our Say*. Grant is currently writing her memoir.

`Fémi Sarah Heggie

Olufemi " `Fémi" was born Sarah Heggie in Kansas City, Kansas, to Mattie Scott and James Heggie Sr. on March 6, 1948. She was left orphaned at an early age: her father passed before she was born, and her mother died when she was an infant. As a result, she was sent to live with her grandmother, whom she called Momma, a kind and highly intelligent Mississippi-born woman with little formal education. As the daughter of a slave, Momma valued learning and encouraged Heggie to ask questions about the world around her. Momma died when Heggie was twelve years old, and Heggie was placed in the care of family members who allegedly abused her. "So, when I was eighteen and the day after I graduated from high school, I was gone," recalls Heggie. She secured a scholarship to Sarah Lawrence College and never returned to her abusive home. She remembers that she later took the name Olufemi, meaning "God loves me," as a reminder that, despite her trials, she has always been loved. Heggie majored in journalism at Sarah Lawrence College and spent her summers working at Alabama's *Southern Courier* (1965–68) newspaper, where she witnessed the struggle of the civil rights movement firsthand.

Heggie was inspired to pursue a career in theater after attending the Negro Ensemble Company's (NEC; est. 1967) production of *Song of the Lusitanian Bogey* in 1968. After graduating college in 1971, she moved to New York and began working at the NEC. While initially unskilled, she acquired the necessary skills to hold the position of stage manager at the NEC. She also served as stage manager for productions on and Off-Broadway, including performances at Woodie King Jr.'s New Federal Theatre (est. 1970) and the 1977 national tour of Rosetta LeNoire and Loften Mitchell's *Bubbling Brown Sugar*. When Heggie was not busy stage-managing, she worked as a hair stylist for singers Stevie Wonder and Miriam Makeba. She later worked as a personal assistant for performers Nina Simone, Aretha Franklin, and Lena Horne. Heggie continues to write, stage-manage productions, and teach theater courses at universities across the United States. She is completing her memoir.

Lee Hunkins

Leecynth "Lee" Hunkins was born January 1, 1930, in New York's Harlem community. Hunkins remembers that her mother initially performed "days work," or domestic work, until her father, a former dock loader, insisted that he would be sole provider for their family. Raised with just one sibling, Hunkins describes her childhood as "exceptionally good." While her family was certainly not wealthy, there was a spirit of togetherness and love in her home. Although Hunkins discovered a passion for poetry at a young age, she decided to pursue a more practical career and joined the Social Security Administration in New York in 1948. A few years later, she happened to attend a party and heard the actor and American Community Theatre (1958–late 1980s) founder Maxwell "Maxie" Glanville discuss theater. This chance encounter led to her working with sound, lights, props, and sets at the American Community Theatre in Harlem. These production experiences inspired Hunkins to begin writing her own dramas. Her early plays include *The Square Peg* (1960), *The Cage* (1961), *Another Side of Tomorrow* (1964), *Fading Hours* (1965), *Revival* (1967), *The Dolls* (1967), *26501* (1968), and *Maggie* (1976), many of which were produced at the American Community Theatre. Writing for the theater led to her successful career writing for television. In fact, she is perhaps best known today for her work with the Public Broadcasting Service's *Reading Rainbow* (1983–2006) and her teleplay *Hollow Image* (1979), winner of ABC's 1978 Theater Award. Hunkins has received numerous awards and honors for her television work, including two Emmy nominations. Now a retiree, Hunkins spends her time writing, mentoring teens enrolled in the New York Theatre Workshop's Mind the Gap, and taking DJ lessons.

Judy Juanita

Judy Juanita was born Judith Hart on July 19, 1946, in Berkeley, California, but spent her formative years in Oakland, California. She attended Oakland City College at the age of sixteen and transferred to San Francisco State College her junior year; there she joined the Black Student Union (BSU; est. 1966) and Black Panther Party (1966–82). Juanita used her creative talent to further her activism by participating in the BSU's Black Arts Cultural Troupe, headed by Amiri Baraka/LeRoi Jones. She helped mount productions and performed her poetry at Black Arts Cultural Troupe events. Joining the Black Panther Party allowed her to participate in activities at Black House, a political and cultural center in San Francisco formed by the party's minister of information, Eldridge Cleaver. She worked alongside Eldridge and Kathleen Cleaver at the *Black Panther* newspaper (later known as the *Intercommunal News Service*).

In 1968, Juanita assumed the role of editor in chief of the newspaper after Eldridge Cleaver fled to Cuba to avoid charges of attempted murder.

A talented poet, novelist, and playwright, Juanita continues to publish a variety of works, including the semiautobiographical novel *Virgin Soul* (2013) and *De Facto Feminism: Essays Straight Outta Oakland* (2016), a collection of critical essays. Her more recent plays have been produced by the San Francisco Mime Troupe. She continues her activism at Laney College—where she also teaches English courses—because she believes that "you don't have to fight all of society. Your battle is where you are. Fight where you are."

Barbara and Carlton Molette

Barbara Jean Molette was born January 31, 1940, in Los Angeles, California, to Baxter R. Roseburr and Lora L. Johnson. Barbara earned a bachelor of arts degree from Florida A&M University, master of fine arts degree from Florida State University, and doctor of philosophy degree from the University of Missouri. She married Carlton Woodard Molette in 1960. Carlton was born August 23, 1939, in Pine Bluff, Arkansas, to Carlton and Evelyn Molette. He received a bachelor of arts degree from Morehouse College, master of arts degree from the University of Iowa, and doctor of philosophy degree from Florida State University. Early in their careers, Barbara worked as a costume designer, model, artist, and actress while Carlton pursued a career in set design. By the late sixties, the two began a lifelong writing partnership that did not cease until Barbara passed away in her Atlanta home on March 9, 2017.

Together the Molettes have written more than twenty plays and dozens of critical writings about black theater. Their most notable works include the musical *Doctor B.S. Black* (1969); the one-act play *Rosalee Pritchett*; *Fortunes of the Moor* (1995), an Afrocentric sequel to William Shakespeare's *Othello*; and *Prudence* (2007), a play about the education of black girls during the 1830s. Their scholarly works include two major book publications: *Black Theatre: Premise and Presentation* (1986) and *Afrocentric Theatre* (2013). The Molettes have received numerous awards and honors for their creative and scholarly endeavors, including lifetime achievement awards from the Black Theatre Network, National Black Theatre Festival, and Atlanta Black Theatre Festival.

Halifu Osumare

Halifu Osumare was born Janis Miller on November 27, 1946, in Galveston, Texas. She received the name Halifu—meaning "the independent, rebellious one in the family" in Swahili—from playwright, poet, and dancer Ntozake Shange during the early seventies. Osumare's career as a dancer, choreographer, and black popular culture scholar spans more than forty years. She received a bachelor of arts degree in dance and theater arts from the University Without Walls, Berkeley, California in 1975; a master of arts degree in the ethnology of dance from the departments of anthropology and dance and the School of Ethnic Studies at San Francisco State University in 1993; and a doctor of philosophy degree in American studies from the University of Hawai`i at Mānoa in 1999. She has taught at a number of universities, including the University of California, Berkeley and Riverside campuses; the University of Ghana, Legon; Bowling Green State University; and Stanford University. She is professor emerita at the University of California, Davis. She published her memoir, *Dancing in Blackness: A Memoir*, in 2018.

Kathy A. Perkins

Kathy Anne Perkins was born in Mobile, Alabama, on August 27, 1954. She originally envisioned a career as an actress and enrolled in Howard University's drama department in 1973. However, Perkins quickly discovered that there were greater opportunities afforded black women offstage than on and began to study lighting design. By the time she graduated with a bachelor of fine arts degree in drama in 1976, she had acquired professional concert-lighting skills through her experiences working for Ralph "Daddy" Dines at Howard University's touring house. After graduation, she continued her educational path, earning a master of fine arts degree in lighting design from the University of Michigan in 1978.

Perkins's award-winning lighting designs have appeared on Broadway, Off-Broadway, on regional and international stages, and at the Smithsonian National Museum of African American History and Culture in Washington, D.C. As a scholar, she has authored and edited numerous books and collections and served as an assistant to curator Lonnie Bunch at the California African American Museum in Los Angeles. As a teacher, she has held several professional titles, including professor of theater at the University of North Carolina and professor emerita at the University of Illinois at Urbana-Champaign. Now officially retired from academic teaching, she works as a freelance lighting designer for professional theaters across the United States.

Shirley Prendergast

Shirley Prendergast was born Merris Shirley Prendergast on June 15, 1932, to Wilford and Dorita Prendergast in Boston, Massachusetts. She attended Brooklyn College and graduated as a premed student in 1954. She then enrolled at Columbia University to pursue a master's degree in microbiology but left the program to take care of her ailing mother. Afterward, Prendergast found employment as a bacteriologist for the New York City Health Department. She did not discover her passion for lighting until she took a course in photography. This experience, coupled with dance lessons at the New Dance Group (1932–2009) and participation in a dance company, inspired her to pursue her creative passions. She decided to take a lighting-design class at her local YWCA and realized she could combine her interests through lighting theater and dance performances.

Prendergast broke racial barriers throughout her nearly fifty-year career in lighting design. In 1969, she became the first African American woman lighting designer to earn a United Scenic Artists of America union card. She later became the first African American woman to design lighting on Broadway with the Negro Ensemble Company's 1973 production of *The River Niger*. She designed lighting for dance and theater throughout her illustrious career, receiving four AUDELCO awards, an Obie Award for Sustained Excellence in Lighting Design (1997), Black Theatre Network's Winona Lee Fletcher Award (1998), and National Black Theatre Festival's Outstanding Achievement Award in Lighting Design (2009) for her efforts. She mentored a generation of artists, including lighting designer Kathy A. Perkins.

Sonia Sanchez

Wilsonia "Sonia" Driver was born September 9, 1934, to Wilson L. and Lena Jones Driver in Birmingham, Alabama. After her mother's death, Sanchez lived with her paternal grandmother, who provided her first understanding of drama. Upon her grandmother's death, Sanchez was sent to live with her father in Harlem. Sanchez demonstrated a thirst for knowledge at an early age and was eventually admitted into Hunter College in New York. She excelled in her studies, earning a bachelor of arts in political science in 1955. She continued her education at New York University, taking graduate courses in poetry with poet laureate Louise Bogan in 1956 before publishing her own poetry in literary magazines.

Sanchez actively participated in social change. Between 1963 and 1965 she taught at the Downtown Community School in New York and joined the Congress of Racial Equality's (est. 1942) New York branch. In 1965, she answered Amiri Baraka/LeRoi Jones's call to join him in establishing the Black Arts Repertory Theatre/School (BART/S) in Harlem. After the closure of BART/S, she joined Baraka, Ed Bullins, Sarah Webster Fabio, Marvin X, and many other artists and activists at San Francisco State College to found the first black studies program in the United States. She later joined the Nation of Islam (est. 1930) for the educational opportunities afforded her children but eventually left the organization once the conflict between her own womanist sensibilities and the practices of the Nation became too severe.

A prolific writer, Sanchez published five plays, six books of poetry, an anthology, a book of fiction, a children's book, and performed audio recordings of poetry during the Black Arts Movement alone. She has taught at universities across the United States, including Temple University, where she is professor emerita. She has received many awards and honors for her efforts as a poet, playwright, teacher, and activist, including the prestigious Robert Frost Medal in 2001.

Ntozake Shange

Ntozake Shange was born Paulette Linda Williams on October 18, 1948, in Trenton, New Jersey, to educator and psychiatric social worker Eloise

Williams and Air Force surgeon Paul T. Williams. The Williams family moved to the racially segregated city of St. Louis, Missouri, in 1956. She and other black students were bused to white schools following the groundbreaking 1954 *Brown v. Board of Education* U.S. Supreme Court decision. She remembers her experience of integrated public schools as "abysmal" and "humiliating." She later moved to New York City and enrolled at Barnard College, Columbia University, where she met fellow poet Thulani Davis. Shange graduated cum laude with an undergraduate degree in American studies. She then earned a master of art's degree in American studies from the University of Southern California in 1973. After suffering from depression, she found her internal strength and changed her name to Ntozake Shange, meaning, respectively, "she who has her own things" and "s/he who walks/lives with lions" in Xhosa.

Shange is most known for her choreopoem *for colored girls who have considered suicide/when the rainbow is enuf* (1976), winner of an Obie, Outer Critics Circle, and AUDELCO awards. As only the second straight play written by a black woman to appear on Broadway, this groundbreaking work utilizes poetry, dance, song, and music to express the intersectional concerns of black women in the United States. Shange followed up this critically acclaimed play with *A Photograph: Lover-in-Motion* (1977), *Where the Mississippi Meets the Amazon* (1977), *A Photograph: A Study of Cruelty* (1977), *Boogie Woogie Landscapes* (1979), *Spell #7* (1979), *Black and White Two-Dimensional Planes* (1979), *Mother Courage and Her Children* (1980), *Three for a Full Moon* (1982), *Bocas* (1982), *From Okra to Greens/A Different Kinda Love Story* (1983), *Three Views of Mt. Fuji* (1987), *Daddy Says* (1989), and *Whitewash* (1994). In addition to writing plays, Shange published nearly twenty books of poetry; half a dozen novels, including *Sassafrass, Cypress & Indigo* (1982); and half a dozen children's books. Shange passed away at the age of seventy on October 28, 2018.

Jackie Taylor

Jacqueline "Jackie" Elizabeth Taylor is the embodiment of a modern-day renaissance woman. She wears multiple hats as an actress, director, playwright, singer/songwriter, producer, artistic director, and theater founder. The Illinois native was born August 10, 1951, and raised in Chicago's

Cabrini Green housing project. She earned a bachelor of arts degree in theater at Loyola University, master of arts degree in education from the American College of Education, and an honorary doctorate degree from DePaul University.

Taylor has been involved in the theater and film industries for nearly fifty years. She performed in Chicago's Free Street Theater for two years before receiving a five-thousand-dollar loan to found the Black Ensemble Theater in 1976. Her major film credits include performances in *Cooley High* (1975), *Losing Isaiah* (1995), *Hoodlum* (1997), *Barbershop 2: Back in Business* (2001), and *Chi-Raq* (2015). A prolific playwright, Taylor has written more than a hundred theatrical works, including her most popular musical, *The Other Cinderella* (1976). She has received many awards and honors for her efforts, including the declaration of Jackie Taylor Day by former Illinois governor Pat Quinn in 2009.

NOTES

Introduction

Epigraph: bell hooks, *Talking Back: Thinking Feminist, Thinking Black* (Boston: South End Press, 1989), 8.

1. Interview with Raushanna Majeed Pauley, October 6, 2018.

2. Salena Zito, "The Day That Destroyed the Working Class and Sowed the Seeds of Trump," *New York Post*, September 16, 2017, nypost.com/2017/09/16/the-day-that-destroyed-the-working-class-and-sowed-the-seeds-for-trump/ (accessed December 21, 2017).

3. Patricia Hill Collins, *Black Feminist Thought: Knowledge, Consciousness, and the Politics of Empowerment* (Boston: Unwin Hyman, 1990), 15.

4. Collins, *Black Feminist Thought*, 97.

5. DoVeanna S. Fulton finds black feminist orality rooted in black women's slave narratives but also notes that it "is found in multiple incarnations of oral discourse," including "conversational speech" (*Speaking Power: Black Feminist Orality in Women's Narratives of Slavery* [New York: State University of New York Press, 2006], 124).

6. Fulton, *Speaking Power*, 2.

7. Sue Armitage, Patricia Hart, and Karen Weathermon, eds., *The Frontiers Reader: Women's Oral History* (Lincoln: University of Nebraska Press, 2002), ix.

8. Sherna Berger Gluck, "Has Feminist Oral History Lost Its Radical/Subversive Edge?," *Oral History* 39, no. 2 (2011): 64.

9. The feminist psychologist Kim Marie Vaz's edited collection *Oral Narrative Research with Black Women: Collecting Treasures* (Thousand Oaks, Calif.: Sage Publications, 1997), is one of the first book-length studies to examine black women's oral narrative methodologies. Vaz's interdisciplinary collection privileges the process of black women investigators conducting oral narrative research with black women participants.

10. Larry Neal, "The Black Arts Movement," *Drama Review* 12, no. 4 (1968): 29; emphasis added.

11. Margo Natalie Crawford, "Natural Black Beauty and Black Drag," in *New Thoughts on the Black Arts Movement*, ed. Lisa Gail Collins and Margo Natalie Crawford (New Brunswick, N.J.: Rutgers University Press, 2006), 160.

12. More recent book-length studies that explore the contributions of women poets of the Black Arts Movement include Carmen L. Phelps, *Visionary Women Writers of Chicago's Black Arts Movement* (Jackson: University Press of Mississippi, 2012); Robert L. Douglas, *Resistance, Insurgence and Identity: The Art of Marti Evans, Nelson Stevens and the Black Arts Movement* (Trenton, N.J.: Africa World Press, 2008); and Cheryl Clarke, *After Mecca: Women Poets of the Black Arts Movement* (New Brunswick, N.J.: Rutgers University Press, 2004).

13. Mike Sell, "The Black Arts Movement: Performance, Neo-Orality, and the Destruction of the White Thing," in *African American Performance and Theatre History*, ed. Harry J. Elam and David Krasner (Oxford: Oxford University Press, 2001), 65.

14. Mike Sell, *Avant-Garde Performance and the Limits of Criticism: Approaching the Living Theatre, Happenings/Fluxus, and the Black Arts Movement* (Ann Arbor: University of Michigan Press, 2008), 229.

15. Sell, *Avant-Garde Performance*, 229.

16. James Smethurst, *The Black Arts Movement: Literary Nationalism in the 1960s and 1970s* (Chapel Hill: University of North Carolina Press, 2005), 89, 92.

17. Smethurst, *The Black Arts Movement*, 99.

18. Dwight Conquergood, "Rethinking Ethnography: Toward a Critical Cultural Politics," in *The SAGE Handbook of Performance Studies*, ed. D. Soyini Madison and Judith Hamera (Thousand Oaks, Calif.: Sage Publications, 2006), 360.

19. E. Patrick Johnson, *Sweet Tea: Black Gay Men of the South* (Chapel Hill: University of North Carolina Press, 2008), 8.

20. D. Soyini Madison, *Critical Ethnography: Method, Ethics, and Performance* (Thousand Oaks, Calif.: Sage Publications, 2005), 7.

21. Barbara Christian, "The Race for Theory," *Feminist Studies* 14, no. 1 (1988): 68.

22. La Donna L. Forsgren, *In Search of Our Warrior Mothers: Women Dramatists of the Black Arts Movement* (Evanston, Ill.: Northwestern University Press, 2018), 9.

Chapter 1

Epigraph: Toni Cade Bambara, "Salvation Is the Issue," in *Black Women Writers (1950–1980): A Critical Evaluation*, ed. Mari Evans (New York: Anchor Press, 1984), 41.

1. For secondary scholarship on Panther women's lives and legacy, see Angela D. LeBlanc-Ernest, "'The Most Qualified Person to Handle the Job': Black Panther Party Women, 1966–1982," in *The Black Panther Party (Reconsidered)*, ed. Charles Jones (Baltimore: Black Classic Press, 1998), 305–34; Ericka Huggins and Angela D. LeBlanc-Ernest, "Revolutionary Women, Revolutionary Education: The Black Panther Party's Oakland Community School," in *Want to Start a Revolution? Radical Women in the Black Freedom Struggle*, ed. Dayo F. Gore, Jeanne Theoharis, and

Komozi Woodard (New York: New York University Press, 2009), 161–84; Tracye A. Matthews, "'No One Ever Asks What a Man's Role in the Revolution Is': Gender Politics and Leadership in the Black Panther Party," in *Sisters in the Struggle: African American Women in the Civil Rights–Black Panther Movement*, ed. Bettye Collier-Thomas and V. P. Franklin (New York: New York University Press, 2001), 230–56; Mary Phillips, "The Power of the First-Person Narrative: Ericka Huggins and the Black Panther Party," *WSQ: Women's Studies Quarterly* 43, nos. 3, 4 (Fall/Winter 2015): 33–51; Mary Phillips, "The Feminist Leadership of Ericka Huggins in the Black Panther Party," *Black Diaspora Review* 4, no. 1 (2014): 187–218; Jane Rhodes, "Black Radicalism in 1960s California: Women in the Black Panther Party," in *African American Women Confront the West, 1600–2000*, ed. Quintard Taylor and Shirley Ann Wilson Moore (Norman: University of Oklahoma Press, 2003), 346–62; Robyn C. Spencer, "Engendering the Black Freedom Struggle: Revolutionary Black Womanhood and the Black Panther Party in the Bay Area, California," *Journal of Women's History* 20, no. 1 (2008): 90–113; Rhonda Y. Williams, "Revolution, Struggle, and Resilience: Women in the Black Panther Party," in *The Black Panthers: Portraits from an Unfinished Revolution*, ed. Bryan Shih and Yohuru Williams (New York: Nation Books, 2016), 102–10.

2. Ed Bullins briefly served as the Black Panther Party's minister of culture in 1967.

3. La Donna L. Forsgren, "From the Black Arts Movement to the Contemporary Chitlin' Circuit: An Interview with Woodie King Jr.," *Journal of Dramatic Theory and Criticism* 33, no. 2 (2019): 68.

4. Woodie King Jr.'s New Federal Theatre produced J.e. Franklin's *Black Girl* in 1971 and Ntozake Shange's *for colored girls who have considered suicide/when the rainbow is enuf* in 1975.

5. Mike Sell, "The Black Arts Movement: Performance, Neo-Orality, and the Destruction of the White Thing," in *African American Performance and Theatre History*, ed. Harry J. Elam and David Krasner (Oxford: Oxford University Press, 2001), 59.

6. Sell, "The Black Arts Movement," 66.

7. *BaddDDD Sonia Sanchez: The Life of a Renowned Poet and Activist*, dir. Barbara Attie, Janet Goldwater, and Sabrina Schmidt Gordon, California Newsreel, 2015, https://www.kanopy.com/product/baddddd-sonia-sanchez (accessed November 5, 2019).

8. W. E. B. Du Bois Papers (MS 312), "Krigwa Players Little Negro Theater" (1926), Special Collections and University Archives, University of Massachusetts Amherst Libraries.

9. Kellie Jones, "Black West: Thoughts on Art in Los Angeles," in *New Thoughts on the Black Arts Movement*, ed. Lisa Gail Collins and Margo Crawford (New Brunswick, N.J.: Rutgers University Press, 2006), 65.

10. Judy Juanita, "Meeting LeRoi Jones and Other Reflections," *Black History Bulletin* 80, no. 1 (2017): 10.

11. Judy Juanita, "Five Comrades in the Black Panther Party, 1967–1970," in *De Facto Feminism: Essays Straight Outta Oakland* (Oakland, Calif.: EquiDistance Press, 2016), 40.

12. Judy Juanita, "Black Womanhood #1," in *De Facto Feminism: Essays Straight Outta Oakland* (Oakland, Calif.: EquiDistance Press, 2016), 45.

13. Judy Juanita, "De Facto Feminism," in *De Facto Feminism: Essays Straight Outta Oakland* (Oakland, Calif.: EquiDistance Press, 2016), 161.

14. Interview with Haki Madhubuti, January 11, 2017.

15. Ntozake Shange, untitled author's note in *for colored girls who have considered suicide/when the rainbow is enuf* (New York: Macmillan, 1977), xi.

16. Halifu Osumare, *Dancing in Blackness: A Memoir* (Gainesville: University Press of Florida, 2018), 1.

17. Osumare, *Dancing in Blackness*, 27.

18. Osumare, *Dancing in Blackness*, 33.

19. Osumare, *Dancing in Blackness*, 1.

20. Osumare, *Dancing in Blackness*, 1.

21. Osumare, *Dancing in Blackness*, 147.

22. Jackie Earley, "The Gospel Truth," African American Registry, 1972, https://aaregistry.org/poem/the-gospel-truth-1-and-2-by-jackie-earley/ (accessed August 2, 2018).

23. Doris Derby's photograph of Alice Walker appears on the cover of Alice Walker, *The World Has Changed: Conversations with Alice Walker*, ed. by Rudolph P. Byrd (New York: New Press, 2011).

24. For more information about the Child Development Group of Mississippi (1965–68), see Crystal R. Sanders, *A Chance for Change: Head Start and Mississippi's Black Freedom Struggle* (Chapel Hill: University of North Carolina Press, 2016).

25. Katharine Capshaw, *Civil Rights Childhood: Picturing Liberation in African American Photobooks* (Minneapolis: University of Minnesota Press, 2014), 122.

26. Resurrection City began May 12, 1968. Three thousand people set up tents on the lawns of the National Mall in protest of poverty. The occupation lasted six weeks.

27. Ta-Nehisi Coates, *Between the World and Me* (New York: Random House, 2015).

28. George Napper, *Blacker Than Thou: The Struggle for Campus Unity* (Grand Rapids, Mich.: Eerdmans, 1973).

29. P. J. Gibson, *Destiny's Daughters: Nine Voices of P. J. Gibson* (Bloomington, Ind.: 1st Books Library, 2002), xv.

Chapter 2

Epigraph: Barbara Ann Teer, "We Can Be What We Were Born to Be," *New York Times*, July 7, 1968.

1. Teer, "We Can Be."

2. Gary Anderson, "Black Theatre Survey 2016–2017: A Report on the Health of Black Theatre in America," *Black Theatre Matters*, June 14, 2018, https://blacktheatrematters.org/2018/06/18/black-theatre-survey-2016-2017/ (accessed January 16, 2019).

3. Anderson, "Black Theatre Survey."

4. Anderson, "Black Theatre Survey."

5. Anderson, "Black Theatre Survey."

6. Anderson, "Black Theatre Survey."

7. Shirley Faison is referring to Diana Ross's single "Reach Out and Touch (Somebody's Hand)" (1970) and July 21, 1983, performance in Central Park.

8. The New York Showcase Code is a set of guidelines or rules that allows members of the Actors' Equity Association to perform without an Equity contract in New York City. While performers do not receive a minimum salary or protections of an Equity contract, they are afforded an opportunity to "showcase" their talent so that they might obtain future employment.

9. Nora Cole, "Vinnette Carroll: The First Black Woman Broadway Director," *Black Masks* 20, no. 3 (2012): 14.

10. Cole, "Vinnette Carroll," 14.

11. Barbara Ann Teer took the liberators on campus tours and international festivals during the 1960s and 1970s.

12. Nellie McCaslin, *Historical Guide to Children's Theatre in America* (Westport, Conn.: Greenwood Press, 1987), 155.

13. Errol G. Hill and James V. Hatch, *A History of African American Theatre* (Cambridge: Cambridge University Press, 2003), 397.

14. Hill and Hatch, *A History*, 398.

15. The video Doris Derby is referring to can be found at https://www.junebugproductions.org/our-founding (accessed November 5, 2019).

Chapter 3

Epigraph: Sarah Webster Fabio, "Tripping with Black Writing," in *The Black Aesthetic*, ed. Addison Gayle Jr. (New York: Doubleday, 1971), 191.

1. Fabio, "Tripping with Black Writing," 191.

2. Addison Gayle Jr.'s *The Black Aesthetic* includes critic Carolyn F. Gerald's essay "The Black Writer and His Role." Gerald and Sarah Webster Fabio represent the only black woman intellectual perspectives in this seminal Black Arts Movement collection.

3. Barbara Molette, "Black Women Playwrights: They Speak, Who Listens?," *Black World* 25, no. 6 (April 1976): 28–29.

4. Molette, "Black Women Playwrights," 30.

5. Carlton Molette, "The Way to Viable Theatre? Afro-American Ritual Drama," *Black World* 22, no. 6 (April 1973): 7.

6. La Donna L. Forsgren, *In Search of Our Warrior Mothers: Women Dramatists of the Black Arts Movement* (Evanston, Ill.: Northwestern University Press, 2018), 20.

7. Barbara Ann Teer, "We Can Be What We Were Born to Be," *New York Times*, July 7, 1968.

8. Forsgren, *In Search*, 20.

9. Devorah Heitner, *Black Power TV* (Durham, N.C.: Duke University Press, 2013), 1.

10. Heitner, *Black Power TV*, 4.

11. Heitner, *Black Power TV*, 126.

12. Allen Woll, *Black Musical Theatre: From Coontown to Dreamgirls* (Baton Rouge: Louisiana State University Press, 1989), 253.

13. Jacqui Scott-Papke, "Aduke Aremu's Harlem Children's Theatre Company," *Youth Theatre Journal* 31, no. 2 (2017): 129; Forsgren, *In Search*, 96.

14. Woll, *Black Musical Theatre*, 249.

15. The term "intersectionality" was coined by Kimberlé Crenshaw; see "Demarginalizing the Intersection of Race and Sex: A Black Feminist Critique of Antidiscrimination Doctrine, Feminist Theory and Antiracist Politics," *University of Chicago Legal Forum* 140 (1989): 139–67.

16. Charlie L. Russell, "Barbara Ann Teer: We Are Liberators, Not Actors," *Essence*, March 1971, 57; emphasis in original.

17. Sonia Sanchez is referring to her eulogy, "Barbara Ann Teer: 1937–2008," *American Theatre* 25, no. 8 (October 2008): 20.

18. Alice Walker, *In Search of Our Mothers' Gardens: Womanist Prose* (San Diego: Harcourt Brace Jovanovich, 1983), xi.

19. Sonia Sanchez, "Uh, Uh; But How Do It Free Us?," in *The New Lafayette Theatre Presents: Plays with Aesthetic Comments by Six Black Playwrights*, ed. Ed Bullins (Garden City, N. Y.: Anchor Books, 1974), 213.

20. Halifu Osumare, *Dancing in Blackness: A Memoir* (Gainesville: University Press of Florida, 2018), 147.

21. J.e Franklin, "Four Women: A Play in One Act" (unpublished MS, 1973), 2.

22. Franklin, "Four Women," 5.

23. Micki Grant, *Don't Bother Me, I Can't Cope* (Alexandria, Va.: Alexander Street Press, 2002), 22.

24. Grant, *Don't Bother Me*, 16.

25. Grant, *Don't Bother Me*, 9.

26. Nora Cole, "Vinnette Carroll: The First Black Woman Broadway Director," *Black Masks* 20, no. 3 (2012): 14.

27. Karen Lynn Smith, "Vinnette Carroll: Portrait of an Artist in Motion" (M.A. thesis, University of California, Los Angeles, 1975), 25.

28. Joan E. Hepburn, foreword to *Destiny's Daughters: Nine Voices of P. J. Gibson*, by P. J. Gibson (Bloomington, Ind.: 1st Books Library, 2002), ix.

29. Woodie King Jr., introduction to *Destiny's Daughters: Nine Voices of P. J. Gibson*, by P. J. Gibson (Bloomington, Ind.: 1st Books Library, 2002), xiii.

30. Barbara Ann Teer explains her Five Cycles of Evolution in her published interview with Charlie L. Russell, "Barbara Ann Teer," 57.

Chapter 4

Epigraph: Barbara Lewis, "The Dramatic Crisis . . . ," *New York Amsterdam News*, February 14, 1976.

1. Judy Juanita, *Homage to the Black Arts Movement: A Handbook* (Oakland, Calif.: EquiDistance Press, 2018), 12.

2. Juanita paraphrases James Brown's "Hot Pants (She Got to Use What She Got to Get What She Wants)," *Hot Pants* (People Records, 1971).

3. William F. Brown and Charlie Smalls, *The Wiz* (New York: Samuel French, 1979), 20.

4. Glenda Dickerson's *Women of Troy* was adapted several times and is also known as *The Trojan Women: A Tale of Devastation for Two Voices*.

5. Cole, "Vinnette Carroll," 9.

Conclusion

Epigraph: Audre Lorde, "Poetry Is Not a Luxury," in *Sister Outsider: Essays and Speeches by Audre Lorde* (Berkeley: Crossing Press, 2007), 37.

1. Patrisse Khan-Cullors and Asha Bandele, *When They Call You a Terrorist: A Black Lives Matter Memoir* (New York: St. Martin's Press, 2018), 257.

2. P. J. Gibson, "Rolling Cinquain" (unpublished poem, 2018).

Appendix A

1. Christine Obbo, "What Do Women Know? . . . As I was Saying!," in *Oral Narrative Research with Black Women: Collecting Treasures*, ed. Kim Marie Vaz (Thousand Oaks, Calif.: Sage Publications, 1997), 62.

2. Obbo, "What Do Women Know?," 62.

3. Patricia Hill Collins, *Black Sexual Politics: African Americans, Gender, and the New Racism* (New York: Routledge, 2005), 225.

BIBLIOGRAPHY

Anderson, Gary. "Black Theatre Survey 2016–2017: A Report on the Health of Black Theatre in America." *Black Theatre Matters*, June 14, 2018. https://blacktheatrematters.org/2018/06/18/black-theatre-survey-2016-2017/. Accessed January 16, 2019.

Aremu, Aduke. *The Princess Chronicles*. Atlanta: Dove LLC Publishing, 2010.

———. *Reaching Out with Love*. Atlanta: Urban Thought Books, 1982.

Armitage, Sue, Patricia Hart, and Karen Weathermon. Introduction to *The Frontiers Reader: Women's Oral History*, edited by Susan H. Armitage, with Patricia Hart and Karen Weathermon, ix–xii. Lincoln: University of Nebraska Press, 2002.

BaddDDD Sonia Sanchez: The Life of a Renowned Poet and Activist. Directed by Barbara Attie, Janet Goldwater, and Sabrina Schmidt Gordon. California Newsreel, 2015. https://www.kanopy.com/product/baddddd-sonia-sanchez. Accessed November 5, 2019.

Bambara, Toni Cade. "Salvation Is the Issue." In *Black Women Writers (1950–1980): A Critical Evaluation*, edited by Mari Evans, 41–47. New York: Anchor Press, 1984.

Brown, Sterling, Arthur P. Davis, and Ulysses Lee, eds. *The Negro Caravan: Writings by American Negroes*. New York: Citadel Press, 1941.

Brown, William F., and Charlie Smalls. *The Wiz*. New York: Samuel French, 1979.

Capshaw, Katharine. *Civil Rights Childhood: Picturing Liberation in African American Photobooks*. Minneapolis: University of Minnesota Press, 2014.

Christian, Barbara. "The Race for Theory." *Feminist Studies* 14, no. 1 (1988): 67–79.

Clarke, Cheryl. *After Mecca: Women Poets of the Black Arts Movement*. New Brunswick, N.J.: Rutgers University Press, 2004.

Coates, Ta-Nehisi. *Between the World and Me*. New York: Random House, 2015.

Cole, Nora. "Vinnette Carroll: The First Black Woman Broadway Director." *Black Masks* 20, no. 3 (2012): 9–14.

Collins, Patricia Hill. *Black Feminist Thought: Knowledge, Consciousness, and the Politics of Empowerment*. Boston: Unwin Hyman, 1990.

———. *Black Sexual Politics: African Americans, Gender, and the New Racism*. New York: Routledge, 2005.

Conquergood, Dwight. "Rethinking Ethnography: Toward a Critical Cultural Politics." In *The SAGE Handbook of Performance Studies*, edited by D. Soyini Madison and Judith Hamera, 351–65. Thousand Oaks, Calif.: Sage Publications, 2006.

Crawford, Margo Natalie. "Natural Black Beauty and Black Drag." In *New Thoughts on the Black Arts Movement*, edited by Lisa Gail Collins and Margo Natalie Crawford, 154–72. New Brunswick, N.J.: Rutgers University Press, 2006.

Crenshaw, Kimberle. "Demarginalizing the Intersection of Race and Sex: A Black Feminist Critique of Antidiscrimination Doctrine, Feminist Theory and Antiracist Politics." *University of Chicago Legal Forum* 140 (1989): 139–67.

Davis, Arthur P., and Saunders Redding, eds. *Cavalcade: Negro American Writing from 1760 to the Present*. Boston: Houghton Mifflin, 1971.

"Deputy Who Tossed a S.C. High School Student Won't Be Charged." *New York Times*, September 2, 2016. https://www.nytimes.com/2016/09/03/afternoonupdate/deputy-who-tossed-a-sc-high-school-student-wont-be-charged.html. Accessed August 2, 2018.

Derby, Doris. "My Involvement in an Era of Change—the Civil Rights Movement." In *The Nation's Longest Struggle: Looking Back on the Modern Civil Rights Movement*, edited by D. C. Everest Area Schools, 436–51. Weston, WI: D.C. Everest Area Schools Publication, 2013.

Douglas, Robert L. *Resistance, Insurgence and Identity: The Art of Marti Evans, Nelson Stevens and the Black Arts Movement*, Trenton, N.J.: Africa World Press, 2008.

Earley, Jackie. "The Gospel Truth." African American Registry, 1972. https://aaregistry.org/poem/the-gospel-truth-1-and-2-by-jackie-earley/. Accessed August 2, 2018.

Fabio, Sarah Webster. "Blowing the Whistle on Some Jive." *Black Scholar* 10, no. 8/9 (May/June 1979): 56–58.

———. "Tripping with Black Writing." In *The Black Aesthetic*, edited by Addison Gayle Jr., 182–91. New York: Doubleday, 1971.

Forsgren, La Donna L. "The Black Arts Movement (1965–1976): An Interview with Playwright J.e. Franklin." *Callaloo* 37, no. 5 (2014): 1139–57.

———. "From the Black Arts Movement to the Contemporary Chitlin' Circuit: An Interview with Woodie King Jr." *Journal of Dramatic Theory and Criticism* 33, no. 2 (2019): 61–80.

———. *In Search of Our Warrior Mothers: Women Dramatists of the Black Arts Movement*. Evanston, Ill.: Northwestern University Press, 2018.

Franklin, J.e. "How Methuselah." In *Coming to the Mercy Seat: J.e. Franklin's Ten-Minute Folk Dramas*, 25–42. New York: Blackgirl Ensemble Theatre, Inc., 2003.

Franklin, J.e., and Micki Grant. *The Prodigal Sister: A New Black Musical.* New York: Samuel French, 1974.

Fulton, DoVeanna S. *Speaking Power: Black Feminist Orality in Women's Narratives of Slavery*. New York: State University of New York Press, 2006.

Gerald, Carolyn F. "The Black Writer and His Role." In *The Black Aesthetic*, edited by Addison Gayle Jr., 349–56. New York: Doubleday, 1971.

Gibson, P. J. *Destiny's Daughters: Nine Voices of P. J. Gibson*. Bloomington, Ind.: 1st Books Library, 2002.

———. "Rolling Cinquain." Unpublished poem, 2018.

Gluck, Sherna Berger. "Has Feminist Oral History Lost Its Radical/Subversive Edge?" *Oral History* 39, no. 2 (2011): 63–72.

Grant, Micki. *Don't Bother Me, I Can't Cope*. Alexandria, Va.: Alexander Street Press, 2002. First published in 1972 by Fiddleback Music.

Greenberg, Polly. *The Devil Has Slippery Shoes: A Biased Biography of the Child Development Group of Mississippi (CDGM), a Story of Maximum Feasible Poor Parent Participation*. London: Macmillan, 1969.

Hall, Jacquelyn Dowd. "Broadening Our View of the Civil Rights Movement." *Chronicle of Higher Education*, July 27, 2001.

———. "The Long Civil Rights Movement and the Political Uses of the Past." *Journal of American History* 91, no. 4 (2005): 1233–163.

Halley, Catherine. "Sarah Webster Fabio: Mother of Black Studies." *JSTOR Daily*, March 26, 2016. https://daily.jstor.org/sarah-webster-fabio-the-mother-of-black-studies/. Accessed June 4, 2018.

Hansberry, Lorraine. *Lorraine Hansberry in Her Own Words: To Be Young, Gifted and Black*. New York: Vintage Books, 1995. First published in 1969 by Prentice Hall.

Heitner, Devorah. *Black Power TV*. Durham, N.C.: Duke University Press, 2013.

Hepburn, Joan E. Foreword to *Destiny's Daughters: Nine Voices of P. J. Gibson*, by P. J. Gibson, ix–xii. Bloomington, Ind.: 1st Books Library, 2002.

Hill, Errol G., and James V. Hatch. *A History of African American Theatre*. Cambridge: Cambridge University Press, 2003.

hooks, bell. *Talking Back: Thinking Feminist, Thinking Black*. Boston: South End Press, 1989.

Huggins, Ericka, and Angela D. LeBlanc-Ernest. "Revolutionary Women, Revolutionary Education: The Black Panther Party's Oakland Community School." In *Want to Start a Revolution? Radical Women in the Black Freedom Struggle*, edited by Dayo F. Gore, Jeanne Theoharis, and Komozi Woodard, 161–84. New York: New York University Press, 2009.

Johnson, E. Patrick. *Sweet Tea: Black Gay Men of the South*. Chapel Hill: University of North Carolina Press, 2008.

Jones, Kellie. "Black West: Thoughts on Art in Los Angeles." In *New Thoughts on the Black Arts Movement*, edited by Lisa Gail Collins and Margo Crawford, 43–74. New Brunswick, N.J.: Rutgers University Press, 2006.

Juanita, Judy. "Black Womanhood #1." In *De Facto Feminism: Essays Straight Outta Oakland*, 45–51. Oakland, Calif.: EquiDistance Press, 2016. First published in 1967 by the Black Panther Party *Intercommunal News Service*.

———. "De Facto Feminism." In *De Facto Feminism: Essays Straight Outta Oakland*, 145–64. Oakland, Calif.: EquiDistance Press, 2016.

———. "Five Comrades in the Black Panther Party, 1967–1970." In *De Facto Feminism: Essays Straight Outta Oakland*, 39–44. Oakland, Calif.: EquiDistance Press, 2016. First published in 2013 by *The Weeklings*.

———. "Meeting LeRoi Jones and Other Reflections." *Black History Bulletin* 80, no. 1 (2017): 10–14.

———. *Virgin Soul: A Novel*. New York: Penguin, 2013.

Khan-Cullors, Patrisse, and Asha Bandele. *When They Call You a Terrorist: A Black Lives Matter Memoir*. New York: St. Martin's Press, 2018.

King, Woodie, Jr. *The Impact of Race: Theater and Culture*. Milwaukee: Applause Theatre & Cinema Books, 2003.

———. Introduction to *Destiny's Daughters: Nine Voices of P. J. Gibson*, by P. J. Gibson, xiii–xiv. Bloomington, Ind.: 1st Books Library, 2002.

LeBlanc-Ernest, Angela D. "'The Most Qualified Person to Handle the Job': Black Panther Party Women, 1966–1982." In *The Black Panther Party (Reconsidered)*, edited by Charles Jones, 305–34. Baltimore: Black Classic Press, 1998.

Lee, Maureen. *Black Bangor: African Americans in a Maine Community, 1880–1950*. Lebanon: University of New Hampshire Press, 2005.

Lewis, Barbara. "The Dramatic Crisis . . ." *New York Amsterdam News*, February 14, 1976.

Lorde, Audre. "Poetry Is Not a Luxury." In *Sister Outsider: Essays and Speeches by Audre Lorde*, 36–39. Berkeley: Crossing Press, 2007. First published in 1977 by *Chrysalis: A Magazine of Female Culture*.

Madison, D. Soyini. *Critical Ethnography: Method, Ethics, and Performance*. Thousand Oaks, Calif.: Sage Publications, 2005.

Matthews, Tracye A. "'No One Ever Asks What a Man's Role in the Revolution Is': Gender Politics and Leadership in the Black Panther Party." In *Sisters in the Struggle: African American Women in the Civil Rights–Black Panther Movement*, edited by Bettye Collier-Thomas and V. P. Franklin, 230–56. New York: New York University Press, 2001.

McCaslin, Nellie. *Historical Guide to Children's Theatre in America*. Westport, Conn.: Greenwood Press, 1987.

Mitchell, Loften. *Black Drama: The Story of the American Negro in the Theatre*. New York: Hawthorn Books, 1967.

———. *Voices of the Black Theatre*. Clifton, N. J.: White, 1975.

Molette, Barbara. "Black Women Playwrights: They Speak, Who Listens?" *Black World* 25, no. 6 (April 1976): 28–34.

Molette, Carlton. "The Way to Viable Theatre? Afro-American Ritual Drama." *Black World* 22, no. 6 (April 1973): 4–12.

Napper, George. *Blacker Than Thou: The Struggle for Campus Unity*. Grand Rapids, Mich.: Eerdmans, 1973.

Neal, Larry. "The Black Arts Movement." *Drama Review* 12, no. 4 (1968): 28–39.

Obbo, Christine. "What Do Women Know? . . . As I was Saying!" In *Oral Narrative Research with Black Women: Collecting Treasures*, edited by Kim Marie Vaz, 41–63. Thousand Oaks, Calif.: Sage Publications, 1997.

Osumare, Halifu. *Dancing in Blackness: A Memoir*. Gainesville: University Press of Florida, 2018.

Perkins, Kathy A. *Black Female Playwrights: An Anthology of Plays before 1950*. Bloomington: Indiana University Press, 1990.

———. "The Remarkable Career of Shirley Prendergast." *Theatre Design & Technology* 50, no. 3 (Summer 2014): 30–39.

Perkins, Kathy A., Sandra L. Richards, Renée Alexander Craft, and Thomas F. DeFrantz, eds. *The Routledge Companion to African American Theatre and Performance*. New York: Routledge, 2018.

Phelps, Carmen L. *Visionary Women Writers of Chicago's Black Arts Movement*. Jackson: University Press of Mississippi, 2012.

Phillips, Mary. "The Feminist Leadership of Ericka Huggins in the Black Panther Party." *Black Diaspora Review* 4, no. 1 (2014): 187–218.

———. "The Power of the First-Person Narrative: Ericka Huggins and the Black Panther Party." *WSQ: Women's Studies Quarterly* 43, nos. 3, 4 (Fall/Winter 2015): 33–51.

Rhodes, Jane. "Black Radicalism in 1960s California: Women in the Black Panther Party." In *African American Women Confront the West, 1600–2000*, edited by Quintard Taylor and Shirley Ann Wilson Moore, 346–62. Norman: University of Oklahoma Press, 2003.

Russell, Charlie L. "Barbara Ann Teer: We Are Liberators, Not Actors." *Essence*, March 1971, 48–52.

Sanchez, Sonia. "Barbara Ann Teer: 1937–2008." *American Theatre* 25, no. 8 (October 2008): 20.

———. "Uh, Uh; But How Do It Free Us?" In *The New Lafayette Theatre Presents: Plays with Aesthetic Comments by Six Black Playwrights*, edited by Ed Bullins, 165–218. Garden City, N. Y.: Anchor Books, 1974.

Sanders, Crystal R. *A Chance for Change: Head Start and Mississippi's Black Freedom Struggle*. Chapel Hill: University of North Carolina Press, 2016.

Scott-Papke, Jacqui. "Aduke Aremu's Harlem Children's Theatre Company." *Youth Theatre Journal* 31, no. 2 (2017): 129–39.

Sell, Mike. *Avant-Garde Performance and the Limits of Criticism: Approaching the Living Theatre, Happenings/Fluxus, and the Black Arts Movement*. Ann Arbor: University of Michigan Press, 2008.

———. "The Black Arts Movement: Performance, Neo-Orality, and the Destruction of the White Thing." In *African American Performance and Theatre History*, edited by Harry J. Elam and David Krasner, 56–80. Oxford: Oxford University Press, 2001.

Smethurst, James. *The Black Arts Movement: Literary Nationalism in the 1960s and 1970s*. Chapel Hill: University of North Carolina Press, 2005.

Smith, Karen Lynn. "Vinnette Carroll: Portrait of an Artist in Motion." M.A. thesis, University of California, Los Angeles, 1975.

Spencer, Robyn C. "Engendering the Black Freedom Struggle: Revolutionary Black Womanhood and the Black Panther Party in the Bay Area, California." *Journal of Women's History* 20, no. 1 (2008): 90–113.

Teer, Barbara Ann. "We Can Be What We Were Born to Be." *New York Times*, July 7, 1968.

Thomas, Lundeana. *Barbara Ann Teer and the National Black Theatre: Transformational Forces in Harlem*. New York: Garland Publishing, Inc., 1997.

Walker, Alice. *In Search of Our Mothers' Gardens: Womanist Prose*. San Diego: Harcourt Brace Jovanovich, 1983.

———. *The World Has Changed: Conversations with Alice Walker*. Edited by Rudolph P. Byrd. New York: New Press, 2011.

Williams, Rhonda Y. "Revolution, Struggle, and Resilience: Women in the Black Panther Party." In *The Black Panthers: Portraits from an Unfinished Revolution*, edited by Bryan Shih and Yohuru Williams, 102–10. New York: Nation Books, 2016.

Woll, Allen. *Black Musical Theatre: From Coontown to Dreamgirls*. Baton Rouge: Louisiana State University Press, 1989.

Woodson, Carter Godwin. *The Mis-Education of the Negro*. Washington, D.C.: Associated Publishers, 1933.

Zito, Salena. "The Day That Destroyed the Working Class and Sowed the Seeds of Trump." *New York Post*, September 16, 2017. nypost.com/2017/09/16/the-day-that-destroyed-the-working-class-and-sowed-the-seeds-for-trump/. Accessed December 21, 2017.

INDEX

Page numbers in *italic* refer to images.